Julia Levitina grew up in Moscow with her Ukrainian Jewish mother and grandmother, who were both Holocaust survivors. She studied design and worked as a theatre designer before immigrating to Australia in 1991 with her family, two children and $200 to her name.

Julia completed a Masters of Theatre Design at the University of Technology Sydney. While teaching set and costume design, she wrote short stories, and her short story 'E-Love' was acquired by Radio National.

The Girl from Moscow is her first novel. It was shortlisted for the ASA/HQ Commercial Fiction Prize for unpublished manuscripts. Julia lives in Sydney's eastern suburbs with her husband and their toy poodle, Honey.

JULIA LEVITINA

The GIRL FROM MOSCOW

PANTERA
PRESS

PANTERA PRESS

This is a work of fiction. Names, characters, organisations, dialogue and incidents are either products of the author's imagination or are used fictitiously, and any resemblance to actual people, living or dead, firms, events or locales is coincidental.

First published in 2024 by Pantera Press Pty Limited.
www.PanteraPress.com

Text Copyright © Julia Levitina, 2024.
Julia Levitina has asserted her moral rights to be identified as the author of this work.

Design and Typography Copyright © Pantera Press Pty Limited, 2024.
Pantera Press, three-slashes colophon device, *sparking imagination, conversation & change* are registered trademarks of Pantera Press Pty Limited. Lost the Plot is a trademark of Pantera Press Pty Limited.

This book is copyright, and all rights are reserved.
We welcome your support of the author's rights, so please only buy authorised editions.

Without the publisher's prior written permission, and without limiting the rights reserved under copyright, none of this book may be scanned, reproduced, stored in, uploaded to or introduced into a retrieval or distribution system, including the internet, or transmitted, copied or made available in any form or by any means (including digital, electronic, mechanical, photocopying, sound or audio recording, and text-to-voice). This book is sold subject to the condition that it shall not, by way of trade or otherwise, be lent, re-sold, hired out, or otherwise circulated in any form of binding or cover other than that in which it is published and without a similar condition being imposed on the subsequent recipient.

Please send all permission queries to:
Pantera Press, P.O. Box 1989, Neutral Bay, NSW, Australia 2089 or info@PanteraPress.com

A Cataloguing-in-Publication entry for this book is available from the National Library of Australia.

ISBN 978-0-6457578-1-1 (Paperback)
ISBN 978-0-6458691-4-9 (eBook)

Cover Design: Christa Moffitt
Cover Images: © Baturina Yuliya/Shutterstock.com, Maja Topcagic/Stocksy
Publisher: Katherine Hassett
Project Editor: LinLi Wan
Copyeditor: Dianne Blacklock
Proofreader: Bronwyn Sweeney
Typesetting: Kirby Jones
Author Photo: Riccardo Riccio
Printed and bound in Australia by McPherson's Printing Group

MIX
Paper | Supporting responsible forestry
FSC® C001695

The paper this book is printed on is certified against the Forest Stewardship Council® Standards. McPherson's Printing Group holds FSC® chain of custody certification SA-COC-005379. FSC® promotes environmentally responsible, socially beneficial and economically viable management of the world's forests.

For my family

A Note on Russian Names

The publisher has chosen to keep the names as they are used in the Russian language for only the main characters to avoid confusion for English readers. Traditionally, Russian names can change from a formal full name to the very personal diminutive one used for a close friend, a child or a loved one. The change occurs by using a suffix or by a name being shortened.

Ella Ashkenazi: Ellochka, El, Elka, Ella Gregorievna
Vladimir Zacharov: Vlad, Vladik, Vladechka
Roman Abramov: Romochka, Roma
Ilya Bezsmertniy: Ilusha, Ilya Pavlovich
Olga Ashkenazi: Olushka
General Ivan Lubov: Ivan Petrovich, Vanya
Gregory Ashkenazi: Grisha, Gregory Natanovich
Leonid Ashkenazi: Leon

Prologue

Moscow, USSR
1976

Ella and Vlad huddled together underneath the plaid blanket. The darkness smelt of the cigarette they'd shared at Patriarch's Ponds before creeping upstairs into Vlad's apartment. They hoped that Daria, the Zacharovs' housekeeper, wouldn't force them back to school.

Vlad's shoulder pressed into Ella's. The transistor radio that Vlad's father had brought back from Japan splattered and hissed on her friend's lap like an untamed animal. Still, it was better for listening to the enemies' broadcast than the Soviet Spidola.

Ella pulled the hem of her brown school uniform over her knees, aware of Daria's steps outside Vlad's bedroom door. They'd skipped the last class, which was sport anyway, so Daria shouldn't mind them being home a little early. As long as she didn't know, or pretended not to know, what they were doing – trying to catch the *Voice of America* through the clatter of KGB interference on the shortwave radio.

They had managed to capture the frequency on more than one occasion. *Radio Liberty* too, and BBC, if they were lucky.

'Do you think she knows?' Ella whispered. The radio's racket finally became intelligible. The announcer spoke about Solzhenitsyn and his book, *The Gulag Archipelago*.

'I think she does,' Vlad replied. 'She thinks the neighbours might report us and my father will get in trouble. But he won't. He never does.'

Under the red and green woollen canopy their breaths mixed. The illicit voices united them in a secret club. Ella felt her muscles tense. Every time they listened, she was scared, but she didn't want Vlad to know.

'Could we get hold of the book?' Her whisper merged with the radio's hissing and Vlad didn't answer.

The transmission became muddled and she leaned closer to grasp the words. What Solzhenitsyn had written couldn't be real. It was too horrible to be true.

'Is this the kind of thing you talk about at your meetings?' Ella asked.

A knock at the door made Vlad's knee jolt and the radio lost the wavelength. Only the clunk of interference reached them and Daria's polite but persistent knocking.

'Ella. Vladik. The dinner is ready.'

Vlad sighed and climbed out from underneath their blanket-tent set on top of his bed. She could bet it was Daria who made it up every morning as well as cooked his breakfast. Ella scrambled off the bed too, her head full of Solzhenitsyn's words.

The early afternoon light seeped through the lofty windows, harsh after their self-inflicted darkness. At the overhang, the icicles melted and the water dripped onto the ledge.

Vlad switched off the radio. 'Don't tell Daria anything. She'll just worry.'

She held her index finger to her lips. The secret was safe with her. She only wished that Vlad would be more open with her and explain things.

What was the point of their conspiracies when nothing could be done to change the country they lived in? There wouldn't be another revolution. Not according to Marx, who they studied at school.

The kitchen in the Zacharovs' apartment was the size of the living room in her parents' flat. Daria wore an apron and placed dinner plates with meatballs on the table. Ella's brain switched from the revolution to the more peaceful activity of having dinner with her best friend.

'Thank you, Daria. It smells delicious.'

Vlad winked at her and stuffed a forkful of mashed potatoes into his mouth.

The room with the *Voice of America* under the blanket was all but a dream.

1

Ella
Moscow, USSR
November 1982

Ella Ashkenazi watched her boot slide on icy asphalt. Her arms flayed. If she fell, she could kill this baby and no one would be any the wiser. She ran a few more steps and stopped on the unlit corner of Arkhipov Lane. The side street was empty, but the sound of people chanting came from the direction of the old synagogue, where Vlad had arranged for them to meet. She squinted into the darkness and wondered if she should turn back.

Vlad would help her. He had studied medicine and worked as a nurse. He would know some doctors. She held the collar of her sheepskin coat tighter at her throat and started walking towards the chanting voices.

Around her were merchants' houses built in the last century, lined in a row, connected by gateways.

The voices grew louder.

Only two months ago, trucks had blocked off all traffic for Simchat Torah. Their headlights had lit the street, turning the narrow lane into a once-a-year matchmaking fair. Dozens of Jewish youth gathered by the synagogue to dance and sing. But no crowds would be allowed here tonight.

And then she saw them. Forty or fifty people stood in tight groups on the footpath in front of the synagogue and on the steps of the portico.

All she'd told Vlad was that it was urgent, but she hadn't counted on meeting him near a pack of his dissident friends. Her eyes refused to focus on the placards above their heads. She had no idea what this rally was about and no desire to find out.

Like them, she listened to the enemies' voices and read illegal, clandestine books, but she declined to stick her neck out to fight the Soviet regime. They didn't stand a chance.

Ella edged closer, wary of being singled out by the protestors or seen mixing with them. Still, she was unsure how else she could find Vlad. After all, these people were his kind, and he had always been there for her ever since they'd met on the first day of primary school thirteen years ago.

Hesitant, she half-nodded to a woman in a hand-knitted headscarf who stood apart from a nearby group. 'Excuse me, do you know Vladimir Zacharov?' She felt stupid for asking. The chances that all dissidents knew each other's names or were willing to disclose them were slim.

The woman narrowed her eyes. 'And who are you?' She peered above Ella's head and turned to check behind her.

Ella peeked over her own shoulder, but no one seemed to be watching them or taking photos.

'A friend. He told me to meet him here.'

The others in the group whispered among themselves and threw sidelong glances.

The woman's gloved hand waved in the direction of the stairs, where a group of people stood holding a banner. 'He's over there.' She grabbed Ella's wrist and dragged her along towards the synagogue. 'I'll take you.'

Freedom for Sharansky. Ella read the banner and stopped walking.

Like them, she hated the country of her birth, the Soviet empire, hated it deeply and with a passion. The submissive drunkenness and arrogant rudeness of its slaves. The cunning ways of those in power. She loathed the necessity to lie, to hide, to pretend, all to become one with the crowd, invisible but safe. But risking her life for the cause was another matter entirely.

'Elka!' Vlad called from the stairs.

A few people turned towards her. Ella didn't like the determination on their faces. Semite and gentile, they all had the same expression with shiny eyes and locked jaws. A man in a leather jacket held out his hand and helped her climb the stairs.

On the top step, Vlad smiled as if nothing out of the ordinary was happening. He pulled her closer to stand next to him. 'Friends, this is Ella.' He lowered his voice. 'Sorry. This wasn't planned.'

He didn't sound sorry at all. She wondered if it was a plot to get her involved.

From her vantage point, she could see the street below with terrifying clarity. Two *militzia* vans were parked at either end of the lane and a dozen or so uniformed guards lurked in the shadows, their faces half-hidden by walkie-talkies.

'I can't stay,' Ella blurted out and moved to get down the steps.

The crowd pushed towards the synagogue and, following some invisible signal, started chanting again.

'Freedom!' they repeated in unison. 'Freedom!'

She read the placards – *Follow the Helsinki Agreement*; *Freedom of Speech* – and felt her head spin. If she was seen at this protest, she would be marked a dissident like the others, like Vlad.

The protesters had caught the beat and, hypnotised by their own unity, chanted the one word, not loudly, but with persistence.

'Freedom! Freedom!'

It was not a plea but a demand. She looked beyond them for a way to escape. Vlad placed his hands on her shoulders. They were warm and reassuring. 'We'll have a drink later, when we are done. You can tell me what happened.'

Ella shrugged him off. Around her, people swayed and repeated the chant.

'Freedom! Freedom!'

She turned to Vlad and the flash of a camera blinded her. Then came another, and another. She ducked. People screamed and started running in all directions. The *militziamen* surrounded the group and pushed it towards the stairs. In their grey uniforms the guards pressed from the back through the middle and divided the crowd in two.

Militzia whistles and the thud of footsteps on the frozen ground kept her trapped. Below her, on the street, people dodged and scurried. It was too late to run. Then someone yanked at her hand. Vlad's iron grip led her stumbling down a set of steps to the side. He squeezed her fingers and led her into a narrow passage between two buildings.

'What do we do?' she asked.

'Just run! Towards the metro.'

*

Kropotkinskaya metro station looked clean and quiet and surprisingly empty. Rush hour was almost over. She stopped running and freed her numb fingers from Vlad's grip.

'Why the hell did you ask me to meet you there? I wanted to talk.'

Vlad collapsed onto a marble bench at the end of the platform. He smiled sheepishly and peered towards the tunnel.

'Sit.'

She surveyed the platform but could see no other protesters. Had they been arrested on the spot or didn't dare to hide in the metro? They were probably right to avoid it.

'You can sit. I'm going. First you lure me to the synagogue promising to talk, then you get me involved in some stupid protest.'

She turned away, and he grasped her hand. 'We have to protest. If we don't fight them every step there will be no democracy in Russia. You know what they say: "There is no such thing as a little bit of freedom."'

Ella glared at him. 'But why get me involved? And why did they photograph us?'

'I'm sorry.' The glint in his eyes betrayed him. He must have enjoyed it, the fight and the flight.

'What will they do with those photos?'

He shrugged. 'What did you want to tell me?'

A yellow and blue train slid out of the tunnel and came to a stop. Vlad trailed her into the carriage, which was full of dour-faced men and women dressed in grey and brown winter coats on their way home from work. Ella held on to the rail. Vlad's body was jammed against hers, and she peered at her reflection in the carriage window above the heads of seated passengers. With her spare hand she unbuttoned her coat and wiped her brow.

In the reflection she caught her friend watching her. 'I need your help,' she said. Vlad leaned closer, his cheek almost touching hers. Blood rushed to her face. 'Could you help me to find a doctor?' Her voice was almost a whisper, but having finally said it, she exhaled.

He blushed. 'Does your boyfriend know?'

'Roman is planning to leave. For the States, I think, via Israel. I can't have a baby now. I'm too young, and what about my acting career? I want to play Natasha Rostova.' Her throat tightened. She let go of the rail to wipe her sweaty palm on her coat and grabbed his arm for support.

Vlad kept staring at her in the glass. 'You'll have to find money. About three hundred roubles. You won't change your mind?'

She looked away from the carriage window and he turned to face her. His eyes were shiny and feverish and too close.

'Instead of wasting your life with Roman, you should join us. Amazing people. You know Andrei Dmitrievich Sakharov, don't you? He won the Nobel Peace Prize.' Vlad's pale face glowed pink. 'You saw how many of us were there tonight? We'll get what we want. Just wait.'

The train door opened and closed. The crowd shifted around them.

Ella stood on tiptoes and stretched her neck to his cheek. 'Russia is a colossus on clay legs.' She mimicked his favourite expression and felt immediately guilty. It didn't make her stop though. Her lips brushed his ear. 'You told me this before, and look what happened. Those who made most of the noise were deported before the Olympics. Then the gates closed for good.'

She glanced over her shoulder, but no one was paying them any attention. Vlad tilted his chin in disagreement, but he didn't argue. The train stopped again. A few people shuffled towards the exit and new passengers flooded the carriage.

He leaned closer. 'Have you really decided? Maybe you should keep it.'

'Are you mad? What would I do with the child when Roman leaves?'

She'd raised her voice without intending to, and an older woman with a fox pelt collar elbowed her.

'We could get married.' Vlad winked at the woman and squeezed to stand between her and Ella. His lips smiled but his eyes were sombre. 'Would you accept me as a father?' He spoke louder, without caution, and a couple of other passengers turned their heads.

Ella almost choked. 'What sort of a father would you be?' She had to whisper it. 'They could arrest you at any moment.' She checked if anyone was still watching them, but people didn't seem to be listening anymore.

Vlad waved his hand and looked disappointed. 'You're right,' he breathed. 'We can't have children in captivity.'

2

Perched on a stool in the middle of a sparse rehearsal hall, Ella tried to concentrate on her lines and forget the doctor's verdict. The former ballroom of a Belle Époque mansion, the room was centrally heated, but still she shivered. She struggled to imagine what Natasha Rostova would feel, sixteen and carefree, as Tolstoy had envisioned her.

'Start from the top, Ella.'

Podolski faced a group of young actors, her fellow students, who stood around him by the grand piano. With his straight actor's back and a lion's mane of white hair, he looked regal despite him being the same age as her grandmother.

She willed the words Tolstoy had written for Natasha to pervade her soul. 'Sonya! Sonya! Oh, how can you sleep? Only look how glorious it is. Ah, how glorious!' She tried to get the words to penetrate, but their joy eluded her. The doctor's question looped through her head: *Do you plan to have any children?*

Podolski gazed above her head at the arched windows of the Moscow Theatre Academy. 'Tolstoy wrote that the one thing that is necessary, in life as in art, is to tell the truth.' He lowered his eyes to peer at her furrowed brow, his famous expression full of distaste. Then he turned to his audience. 'Natasha Rostova is naive and dreams of love, like any girl her age. It's not directed at Prince Andrei yet, but at everything around her. She is in love with the world.'

The other actors' eyes crawled over her face and her body, attempting to figure out what she'd done wrong. Her throat tightened. Natasha's soul, pure and innocent, evaded her. Would Natasha Rostova keep the baby if she got pregnant that young? Ella cursed at herself for having such stupid thoughts.

'May I try again?' she asked her teacher.

Podolski wasn't looking at her. 'Raya, would you please read Natasha's part?'

Raya smiled and edged forward. The room grew darker. Outside, snow fell in chunky flakes that plastered the glass. Ella lifted her head up to prevent her tears from spilling. The damp patches on the ceiling mapped the mansion's past. Natasha Rostova could have danced in this hall in her empire-line dress and ballroom slippers.

Raya took a deep breath. 'Do just come and see what a moon ... Oh, how lovely! Come here ... Darling, sweetheart, come here.' She said it very simply. Her face was turned up, her neck exposed, vulnerable. She *was* Natasha.

Ella dug her nails into her palms. Until this moment she'd thought the role was hers. Podolski loved her as an actress, more than he'd ever loved Raya.

Raya sat on the floor. 'There, you see? I feel like sitting down on my heels, putting my arms around my knees like this, straining tight, as tight as possible, and flying away. Like this ...' She opened her arms as if she was going to take flight.

Podolski clapped. 'Bravo, girl. This is the Natasha I wanted.'

Ella stopped breathing. Her blind faith in providence had been misplaced. Why had she decided that her will not to fall pregnant was enough to protect her? She would have to tell Roman.

'Everyone is dismissed,' Podolski said. 'Ella and Raya, please stay behind.'

The students rushed to the doors, throwing side glances at her and Raya. They had all been there before. An actor needed thick skin.

'What's going on, Ella?' Podolski pursed his lips and clasped his hands. 'I'm giving you both two weeks to learn the parts, Natasha's and Sonya's. Whoever does better at the dress rehearsal will play Natasha on the opening night. Do you understand?'

Ella nodded a few times and pretended to take no notice of Raya, whose face had lit up like the Central Telegraph facade on May Day. The artistic directors of most Moscow theatres attended each other's premieres, especially if someone like Podolski was involved. The leading actress would be noticed and might be offered a job in a State theatre.

She strode out of the rehearsal hall. She couldn't let a baby cost her this chance.

*

On the edge of the snowfield, a tiny church topped with green-coloured onion domes appeared dwarfed by the towers of identical high-rises. Ella's heart twitched. It was as if anything spiritual or soul-searching was crushed by the State.

The seventh-floor balcony where she stood with her back to the stuffy room full of TV noise hung over the snow sludge. Fresh November fall turned into mud the moment it touched the ground. She rubbed her forehead, tingling from cold, and hunched her shoulders, warm and itchy under her coat.

Two hours had passed since she and Roman had arrived at this flat in Kolomenskoe, a newly built suburb where Ilya and Marina lived. Inside, Marina and two young women Ella had never met before lounged on the sofa, oblivious it seemed to the black and white movie on TV and tobacco fumes from the kitchen where their men played poker.

It was only the second time she'd met Ilya and his wife Marina, yet Roman had known them forever. The photograph in the living room of those three holding skis and smiling at the camera was the first thing she noticed after entering the handkerchief-sized bedsit. It stood on the bookshelf next to the few tomes Ella knew and loved: Pasternak, Bulgakov, Tsvetaeva. The same photo she'd seen in Roman's room in his parents' communal apartment. She wondered whose books those were – Ilya's or Marina's.

Her fingers squeezed the balcony's handrail. She tore her eyes off the forest that stretched out behind the church under a washed-out sky. They had to have this talk. And Roman had promised her a walk before she agreed to accompany him to his weekly poker game. Still, she stood there motionless, unable to force herself to join the girls or drag him away.

Both groups, the men in the kitchen and the women painting their nails on the sofa, talked politics – how Andropov's rule could turn out to be bloodier than Stalin's. The Butcher of Budapest, he'd been called, the KGB tzar. Since Brezhnev's death and Andropov's seizure of power, all news channels spat out the same pro-communist slogans or otherwise faded into Swan Lake ballet re-runs.

Ella pushed the balcony door open, pinched her nose against the stink of nail polish, and stormed towards the kitchen. Delaying her confession didn't make sense. To have a baby instead of playing Natasha Rostova under Podolski's direction was out of the question, but she had to at least let Roman know. Besides, she didn't have money for the anaesthetic needed for a safe and painless abortion.

In the kitchen, she met Ilya's eyes. He grinned and Ella forgot what she was about to say. She smiled at Ilya, at his black eyes, shiny under the kitchen lamp, with fine wrinkles in the corners. He was likely the same age as Roman. Twenty-eight. They were conscripted in the same year, she thought, before remembering her grievances.

'Roman, I have a rehearsal tonight. Do you think we still have time for a short walk?'

The other two men measured her up and down, their eyes grim. Boris and Sasha. She always forgot which one was which. Cards at their chests, cigarettes in hand, they stared at her, the invader.

Roman lifted his head and looked through her. 'Sorry, El, another hour or so.'

'I'll go then.'

Ilya got up. 'Let's have a break, guys. The girls must be bored.'

Ella nodded, grateful, but the three men at the table didn't budge.

'We need to finish.' Roman looked down at his cards, his fingers tapping on the formica table.

'Come on, El.' It was either Sasha or Boris. 'You can't stop the game.'

She turned to go and felt Ilya's fingers on her shoulder.

'I am sorry, Ella, just a few more minutes. I'll put on the kettle. We'll have tea.'

Ella stepped out and bumped into Marina, who screwed up her face. The tall blonde, older than her, perhaps the same age as Roman and Ilya, squeezed past her into the kitchen and closed the door.

Unsure, Ella sat on the sofa next to the girls. 'What are you watching?'

One of the girls shrugged and changed the channel. The Politburo news came on. 'They don't want us to think at all. We are like cattle for them. This man, Andropov, he is the one who sent tanks to Prague. That's what I hear. The KGB chief.'

Ella perked up. 'Sorry, I am Ella, and you are?'

'Lena,' the girl said. 'Boris invited me.'

'You know you can't speak like this,' said the other girl, who was younger, the same age as her, Ella thought.

Lena shrugged again. 'Who can hear us, ah, Tanya?'

Tanya examined her nails. 'Do you like the colour?' she asked.

Ella nodded. 'What do you do, Lena?'

'Study art, and you?'

'Acting.'

Both women sat up. 'Where do you act?'

'I am about to graduate from the Theatre Academy. Rehearsing Rostova.' This much was true, but it wasn't a fact that she would get to play the role.

Lena and Tanya looked impressed.

'El, we're going.' Roman stumbled out of the kitchen. He stuffed his wallet into the pocket of his sheepskin jacket, which hung on the hook in the hallway.

'Goodbye, girls. Ella has a rehearsal.' He chuckled as if he shared a joke. 'We have to go, no tea.'

Ella got up and joined him at the entrance door. Ilya came out too. They all crowded the hallway while Roman fussed with the lock.

Ilya's handshake lingered and she regretted they couldn't stay longer. 'Say goodbye to Marina,' she said and backed onto the landing.

3

Roman looked out of place on the futon in Ella's arty bedsit, with its chintz curtains and Vietnamese mat. Dressed in his beige poloneck and corduroy pants, he sat cross-legged and cradled a guitar. The quiet sounds of a ballad had started to lull Ella to sleep, but she sat up beside him and fought it.

'I asked Vlad to help with the doctor.'

Roman met her eyes, but he didn't stop plucking the guitar's strings. She pushed down her anger. The least he could do was offer to pay for painkillers.

'The doctor said I have three weeks to decide ... before the New Year.'

Her silly hope that he would beg her to reconsider dissolved when he averted his face to tune his guitar. The lamp lit a spot on the floor next to the futon, but it did not illuminate his expression. She moved to get up but Roman took hold of her upper arm. He put the guitar on the floor and lay on the futon.

She let him gently pull her onto the bed beside him. 'Do you want to have children at all?'

His body, warm and pliable only seconds ago, tensed. Ella propped herself up on her elbow to see his face.

Roman sighed. 'Maybe in a few years.' He leaned across her to pick up the guitar from the floor and fiddled with the strings. 'You know we're applying to emigrate. It could take us six months to a year to get an exit permit and it's not a fact we'll get one at all. It might get worse with Andropov.'

Ella nodded. 'We' meant him and his parents – the Abramovs. She was optional. It didn't change her predicament. It was Roman's feelings towards her that mattered. She put her hand on his to stop him strumming. The expression on Roman's face softened, he let go of the guitar and held her fingers. 'You *do* want to keep it?'

Soothed by the feel of his skin, she allowed herself to relax. She could be mistaken but perhaps Roman did love her in his own weird way. 'Only if we both want it. But if you are thinking of leaving, I'd better not.'

She faked a laugh, and an image of a young woman with a pram in some foreign city that looked like New York invaded her mind. Not that she ever saw New York on TV.

He pulled her closer and put his arm around her. His hip pressed into hers. The heat of his body was too much to bear and she shifted away slightly. For a moment having his baby didn't feel so foolish, but like something akin to fate.

'Would you come with me, if we apply?' Roman's voice wavered and his hand slipped underneath her top. He toyed with the hooks of her bra.

Ella tried to think fast, distracted by his scent – a heady mix of cigarettes and aftershave. She flattened her back against the futon, trapping his fingers. He thought everything could be sorted out by making love. But how did his offer work? He'd take her along if she aborted the baby, but if she didn't, he'd leave his child behind in the Soviet Union?

'What would you do if I don't come with you but I have the baby?' She spoke as if she was teasing him, but she knew the answer.

His grip on her shoulders slackened and he shifted on the futon, creating a larger gap between them. It felt as if he'd abandoned her already.

'Will you tell your parents?' she asked.

'No.' He leaned even further back. 'I can't tell them. They are dying to have a grandchild. They'd marry us today.'

She forced out a laugh. 'And you would rather not?'

Roman shrugged. 'What are you talking about, El? We don't know each other well enough to get married.'

'Only enough to fuck.' She pulled away and sat up. She didn't regret what she'd said but it wasn't constructive.

Roman stared at her and she searched his eyes, honey-coloured with brown dots, only a few inches from her own. There was no way to guess his thoughts.

He wrapped his arms around her and pressed her closer despite her resistance. 'Why are you asking me? You are a big girl, El. What do *you* want to do?'

*

The tram rocked and Ella rested her forehead on the frosted glass to clear her mind. Her gaze returned to the script with Natasha Rostova's lines marked in red pencil. She'd planned to study the role during the two-hour trip across the capital to her grandmother Olga's housing estate in Medvedkovo. But instead she kept mulling over her options.

The carriage jerked and her head hit the glass. Behind the fogged-up windows, the domes and minarets of the Exhibition of Achievements of National Economy floated past. She squinted to see the famous fountain. As a child, she used to come here with Olga to play. The fifteen gilded statues, all female, that surrounded it represented the Soviet republics.

Ukraine was her favourite. The giant bronze woman held an armful of wheat to her bust while nursing a child.

Ella stretched her neck to get a glimpse, but her breath fogged the glass and the fountain disappeared from view.

The tram swayed.

If she had an abortion and stayed with Roman, he could still break up with her when his exit permit was granted. He hadn't promised her anything, he'd merely floated the idea of them leaving for Israel and then maybe going to America together. And he was right. Three months wasn't long enough to decide whether you wanted to spend a lifetime with someone. Or maybe it was.

She noticed that she'd pressed the script to her breast like an infant. Ella closed her eyes. She didn't want this baby, but she would love it if she had it. Heat rose up her neck and her arms became heavy, as if she were holding a child. She was Natasha Rostova when she found the meaning of life.

She looked at the script and searched for Natasha's monologue. The lines blurred. How was Tolstoy able to comprehend the soul of a young woman, to identify with her truth? She pictured the novel's finale, with down-to-earth Natasha happily changing nappies.

Ella was startled to realise that she'd imagined Natasha with Raya's face. It was impossible to believe that Podolski would give Raya her role. But Ella would never be the Natasha of the novel's ending. She wouldn't look for happiness in her children or in getting married, but inside herself, in her calling, in what made her different from the others, not the same. The irony was that if she wanted that for her future she'd have to nail this part, to connect with Tolstoy's Natasha and her family ways.

The tram doors opened and a gust of snowy mist chilled the carriage. Ella fastened her coat. Some semblance of insight passed through her like a draught raising the snow dust from the ground. She shoved the script into her handbag. Her grandmother's stop was the next one.

*

Ella sat across from her grandmother in her kitchen, facing the window. The grey sky hung low, pierced by TV antennas from the neighbouring apartment blocks. The taste of freshly baked strudel, straight from her childhood, unnerved her, and her new-found certitude wavered under Olga's loving gaze. She wasn't sure her grandmother would approve of an abortion.

'Is there something wrong, Ellochka? You don't like the strudel?' Olga's eyes were the same chocolate brown as her own.

'I'm in trouble, Baba,' Ella blurted, though she'd planned to start with Roman's offer, however indirect, to follow him to America.

Olga propped her chin on her fist. Her polished nails gleamed. Somehow she always managed to appear well groomed, even at home, baking.

'What did Roman say?' She took Ella's hand. 'You told him you were pregnant, didn't you?'

Ella nodded. 'He wants to emigrate, on a family reunion visa. Or whatever it's called now.'

Olga squeezed her fingers. 'Do you love him?'

That was a question Ella hadn't asked herself, possibly because she didn't know the answer. 'I think I do.' She poked her fork at the strudel.

Behind the glass door that separated the kitchen from the corridor, her grandfather Natan shuffled towards the bathroom.

'Is *Dedushka* feeling better?'

Olga shrugged and got up. When Ella had arrived, Natan had retreated from the kitchen in haste, leaving his 'ladies to their secrets', as he'd put it. Her grandfather was approaching eighty-six, but in the two weeks since she'd last seen him he'd grown older, turning into a withered child. She suddenly became frightened. If something happened to Natan, she wasn't sure how Olga would cope. She couldn't imagine her grandparents living without each other.

'Have you always loved my grandfather?'

Although they'd had their tea already, Olga put the kettle on the stove again. She wore her fire-red house dress, and her back looked unexpectedly stooped. 'I'll tell you a secret. Your heart has to make a decision, not your mind.'

Ella grimaced. It was easy to say, but her heart seemed ill-equipped to make this decision. One minute it screamed, *I want to perform*, and another it cried out, *Don't kill the baby.* What then should she do?

Olga sat back down, her forehead wrinkled. Ella imagined her grandmother as a young woman. She looked beautiful even now with her crown of silver hair that used to be curly and wild. Chestnut like her own. She wished she could just enjoy Olga's company and her baking, but she needed her wisdom.

'Have you ever had an abortion, Baba?' Ella asked as the kettle started to whistle. Shame prickled the back of her neck, but she stared at her grandmother, expecting to be either told off or told the truth.

Olga didn't respond. She looked away as if she wanted to say something, but couldn't bear to do it. Her grandparents never talked about the repressions, and who knows what had happened during the war years. Ella had never asked questions.

She got up to take the kettle off the boil and filled the empty tea glass that sat in front of Olga on the table. She was about to speak when Olga stood abruptly and turned on the tap. Over the running water, Ella could hear the quiet murmur of Natan's radio in the living room.

She stood behind Olga and embraced her, her chin resting on Olga's shoulder. Ella stroked her back, unsure what else she could do to make her grandmother less distraught. Olga turned to face her.

'Ask your heart.' She took both of Ella's hands into her own and Ella felt her grandmother's fingers tremble. 'Think. Is he the one?'

Ella bit her lip. She wished she knew the answer.

4

'And one-two-three, one-two-three.' A tiny weathered woman, the choreographer from the Bolshoi, punctuated her words with her hands.

'Remember, Natasha's first ball is an important scene – it opens the play. All eyes will be on you.'

Ella followed the direction of the choreographer's gaze towards the lofty windows. The rehearsal studio was cold and Ella tugged the sleeves of her black poloneck over her numb fingers.

She curtsied to her dance partner, Oleg Plushkin, the only Communist Party member in her acting class. Five other girls curtsied to their partners at the same time, all of them reflected in the long mirror. The accompanist's hands flew above the yellowish keys of the grand piano and the sweet sounds of a minuet swept the room.

Oleg bowed towards Ella. Then, barely touching her knuckles, he led her around with a scowl that distorted his handsome face. She wondered what it meant. Oleg Plushkin, the academy's well-known informer, usually couldn't wait for the dance class to get up close and personal with any girl he partnered.

She bit her lip to stop her teeth from chattering and imagined Natasha Rostova waltzing about this very room. What would she do if she found herself pregnant? Naive, carefree Natasha. Would she keep the baby?

Raya's eyes found hers in the mirror. Her friend and rival blushed. Ella beamed back but her mouth betrayed her. No one else in the studio was smiling. Oleg dropped her hand and moved on. Her next dance partner was a young man named Denis. He averted his gaze and almost lost his footing.

Ella curtsied. Maybe news had leaked that Podolski had confirmed her for the role of Rostova. That would explain Raya's awkwardness, but why were Oleg and Denis acting so weird?

'What's with everyone today?' she hissed.

Denis widened his eyes but he kept silent while they danced. Ella stepped on his toe and made him wince, her smile fixed in place.

The choreographer watched them. 'Ella, straighten your back, look your partner in the eye. And one-two-three.'

Oleg became her partner again. His expression was stony.

'What's wrong?' She clutched his hand and his bowlike lips twisted. He waited until the choreographer was at the other end of the studio before he let go of her fingers.

It wasn't until the break in rehearsals that she got an answer to Plushkin's discomfort and Raya's flushed cheeks.

A copy of the *Komsomoletz* newspaper was pinned to the noticeboard out in the corridor beside the ballroom, locked behind the glass. Ella stared at her own face on its front page under a banner, *Freedom for* ... She re-read the bold letters of the article title: *Hooligans on the Loose*. In the photograph, her mouth was open as if she was shouting a slogan. She jammed her fist to her heart. A few students that had stopped behind her rushed away. This article made her a traitor.

She stopped herself from imagining the consequences. A traitor would have to be punished, prevented from corrupting others. A feeling of dread came over her. This could spell the end of everything she had dreamed of.

After the recess, Plushkin attempted to blend in with the other actors, his narrow back conveying his desire to avoid her more expressively than his face. He wouldn't want to get involved or appear too friendly. Still they all knew that he reported regularly to the party committee on the minds and souls of his classmates. He could find the best way out of this, if she convinced him to help her.

She managed to grab his sleeve. 'Oleg, I need your advice.' They stood at the doors to the rehearsal studio with acting students pouring past them. 'I was just meeting a friend there. I didn't even know about the rally.'

Oleg lifted one eyebrow. She let him lead her to a nook at the end of the hallway.

'And, the friend's name?' he said.

Ella didn't answer.

He folded his arms. 'Do you understand how you let us all down, mixing with the dissidents? Everyone in the acting department, me, Professor Podolski?'

Behind her back, Ella twisted her wrist. 'I didn't mean it, Oleg.'

As if her pregnancy was not enough to test her commitment, now there was this.

'Help me. I know you can. Tell them at the party bureau this was a mistake. I just happened to be near the synagogue at the wrong time.'

Oleg frowned down at her but he looked less angry, she thought. Being shamed was a low price to pay for his support.

'The party board meeting is at six tonight. Come up with a good excuse for your actions, Ashkenazi.'

*

The academy's Communist Party board met every Wednesday in the assembly hall, but today's special meeting had been called in response to her misconduct. Ella couldn't stop shaking. Void of daytime students, the corridor outside the hall looked different in semi-darkness. The single lamp at the far end made it seem like a stage with only a ghost light on.

The speech she'd been practising in her mind had long stopped making sense. Still, she went over the key points. She had nothing to do with the dissidents. She was meeting a friend at Arkhipov Lane when she got lost in the crowd and was photographed.

'Ashkenazi.' Plushkin had opened the hall door from the inside. Dressed in a suit and tie, he was not a colleague anymore but a Communist Party official. He stepped away to let her pass and shut the door behind her.

Inside the hall, the stage was illuminated and framed by a velvet curtain. On it was a long table covered by a red cloth. The set belonged to some performance about the victory of collectivisation, but what was happening to her was very real.

She walked towards the table and the four men in suits who sat around it. They squinted in her direction. She knew two of them: Colonel Sundukov, the Scientific Communism tutor hated by his students, and the Academy Director, Pyotr Ilyich Hrushev. The other two were strangers — a tall balding man in glasses and a shorter, younger one. The rest of the board members were absent, but whether this was a positive sign, she didn't know.

Oleg nudged her and she climbed onto the stage, feeling as if she'd never stepped on it during her three years at the academy.

The man in glasses seemed to be in charge. 'Sit down, Ashkenazi.'

Plushkin rushed to take his seat, leaving Ella a chair at the head of the table. She sat on the edge of it and clasped her hands.

The tall man in glasses turned to the shorter one. 'Nikita.'

Ella realised she'd met the younger man before. He'd been checking new students' documents at the enrolment. So, he wasn't a party board member but KGB. She pressed her knees together. If the KGB was involved, she could not expect to be spared. The Internal Security police usually acted behind the scenes, letting their foot soldiers, like Plushkin, do their menial work.

Nikita held out a folder. Her personal file, she guessed, and felt a chill rise from her feet to her heart. The man in glasses opened the dossier and perused its contents. She held her breath, her head vacant of all thoughts.

He pulled out the *Komsomoletz* article, which had been enlarged. Even from her side of the table and upside down she could read the placard above her head in the photo: *Freedom for ...*

The man took off his glasses. 'And how does the graduating student of Moscow Theatre Academy, a future actress, become involved in an anti-Soviet demonstration?'

She opened her mouth. The first sentence of her speech was on her tongue like a line from a role she hadn't rehearsed properly. But she didn't manage to speak it.

'Get up,' he yelled.

She stood. Her knees went soft and she had to grip the table for support.

The man turned to the academy director. 'Has this student been implicated in anything objectionable before?'

She glanced at Hrushev. His flabby body shook from his stomach to his cheeks and his fleshy lips moved wordlessly. Ella shivered. If the invincible director was scared, it meant there was something to be scared of. Hopefully they hadn't uncovered her grandfather's brother in Australia. Up to now, she'd managed to hide Leo Ashkenazi's existence from her Komsomol overseers, but nothing could be concealed from the KGB if they wanted to find it.

'No signals, Comrade Surkov.' Hrushev's voice was quiet, but it gave her strength.

Surkov turned to Plushkin. 'What's the matter, Oleg? Your classmate gets mixed up with dissidents and we are the last to find out?'

'I'm sorry, Comrade Surkov.' Plushkin's eyes filled with real tears. 'She disguised her connections.'

Surkov put on his glasses and stared at her, his lenses gleaming. 'Explain. Who did you meet? Who recruited you?'

Ella tried to recall her prepared speech. 'I was there by accident. I didn't know anyone. The photograph—'

Surkov held up his palm. 'Nikita, what do we have on her?'

Nikita whispered something in his ear.

'Hmm. Comrade Smertniy here says you are friendly with the dissident Zacharov. Any comments?'

Ella's lip quivered. She could not deny being Vlad's friend. 'We went to school together.'

Sundukov banged on the table with his fist. 'I demand: expel her. The Soviet actor needs clean hands. They are an example onstage. We don't need friends of dissidents here.'

Plushkin sprang to his feet in support of his mentor. 'What Colonel Sundukov means is that you let down your comrades.'

'Irresponsible!' Sundukov shouted. 'Anti-Soviet.'

Surkov exchanged glances with Nikita. 'That's why we need to ensure this was a one-off incident, not preconceived anti-government activity.' A smile crept across his face. 'You'll write a report, Ashkenazi, with the names of your dissident friends present at this rally to dissociate yourself from our enemies.'

Ella felt as if she might faint. She tried to object. But she caught the director's glare and didn't say a word.

5

The naked trees on the boulevard didn't conceal the illuminated entrance of Pushkin Drama Theatre at night. It stood stately as it had since 1914 when it was still called the Kamerny and led by Tairov. Before many 'enemies of the State' were exiled like he was, jailed or killed.

Ella's steps reverberated off the frost-covered asphalt as she walked towards the foyer doors. Podolski should be inside and he had to help. He couldn't allow the academy's communists to get rid of her. She had done nothing wrong.

She steadied her breath and pushed through the festive crowd of the lucky ones in the queue outside who'd secured tickets to *Uncle Vanya* under Podolski's direction. People parted to let her pass. She must have looked frantic with her tear-stained face and ragged breathing. She gulped a lungful of icy air. She had hoped to open *War and Peace* here at Pushkin Theatre, to act and dance on this very stage.

'Ella?'

She turned around to face a tall man with wavy black hair. His eyes smiled.

'Ilya, hello ...'

He didn't wear a fur hat like everyone else and looked like a foreigner.

Free.

Ella rubbed her cheeks with her woollen mittens to hide her blush. 'I'm in a bit of a rush, sorry. Enjoy the play, it's wonderful.'

He touched her sleeve and his face changed from joyful to concerned. 'What happened, Ella? Are you appearing tonight?'

'No. Just looking for my teacher.'

She stared at his hand on her forearm. The heat spread down her neck and she loosened her scarf. Her own reaction surprised her. They weren't that close. And she wasn't performing – not tonight, and possibly not ever.

'You study under Podolski, don't you?'

Ella didn't remember telling him this, but she must have at some point. She shrugged. Non-committal.

'I'll let you go. Marina is late, as usual.' Ilya laughed, but his eyes searched hers. His eyelashes were long and thick from the wet snow, his gaze gentle.

She was briefly aware of how she must have looked to him, with her face raw from crying. She hoped her mascara hadn't smudged.

'See you soon, Ilya.'

She walked around the corner towards the stage door. Just then, it opened and a group of young actors stepped out. Her classmates should not see her with Podolski after what had transpired at the party bureau meeting. He could not be implicated.

Perhaps it was safer to wait for her teacher at his apartment block, the House on the Embankment. He would go home after the play and she'd have his ear. Together they might find a solution.

Ella waved to Ilya, doubtful he could still see her from his spot at the theatre entrance. She crossed the boulevard and walked away.

*

The courtyard surrounded by the House on the Embankment wasn't lit. Just underneath the giant archway – the only access to the building – an oversized lantern swung in the wind, throwing jagged shadows. From her position by the grand entrance door, Ella could see the archway's entrance. She wouldn't miss Podolski if she kept to her post.

He might not be pleased to find her here. It was one thing to call on him with the rest of her acting class, once a term when he invited them over to tea and asked about their lives. It was a different matter to turn up at his doorstep to beg for a leading role. She would have to tell him the truth – getting to play Natasha could save her from being expelled.

Of course, her esteemed teacher had spent four years in the Gulag as an enemy of the State. That was why she hoped he would help her. Having suffered at the hands of the Soviet regime, he was supposed to be on her side. He would not let them expel her.

She peered across the icy quadrangle. Her feet were so numb she couldn't feel them anymore. She was beginning to regret her decision, when she heard the echo of footsteps under the arch and she pressed her back against the wall.

Under the lantern, a two-headed silhouette emerged – a couple, their arms entwined. Fused into each other, they stumbled towards the opposite doorway. Ella rubbed her eyes. Her body demanded respite and she thought about leaving. Even her eyelashes had become glued together by frost.

'Ella, what are you doing here?' Her teacher's baritone burst into her ears before he appeared, theatrically stepping from the darkness into a circle of light.

'Professor Podolski, sorry.' Her voice echoed under the courtyard's arch.

Podolski edged towards her and held a gloved finger to his lips.

She lowered her voice. 'Only you can help me.'

He turned and hurried back, retracing his steps through the archway towards the street exit. At first, she didn't understand what he wanted her to do. But then she guessed and followed him out of the courtyard, walking slowly, as if they'd gone their separate ways.

She caught up to him on the corner, by a locked-up food store.

'What is it, Ashkenazi?'

She rubbed her hands together. 'They want to expel me. But if you let me play Natasha, then I could sit the exams. They wouldn't dare to kick me out before the end of the course.'

Podolski jutted his chin to indicate the direction they should take, then turned and walked around the corner to the embankment. A gust of wind from Moskva River picked up the fringe of Ella's scarf, throwing it into her face.

'It's not that simple,' he murmured into the fur collar of his coat.

'I'll be the best Natasha in the world. I promise you.'

Podolski pushed his hands deeper into the pockets of his coat and stepped sideways to shield her from the river's chilly mist. 'That's not the matter at all, though unfair to Raya. She is perfectly capable of playing this role as well.' He coughed. 'Why do you think they'll expel you?'

Ella hesitated. They were alone on the dark embankment but she still felt as if she were being watched. 'I was photographed at the dissidents' rally. I didn't even know what they were protesting.'

Podolski looked around. 'And then?' He walked off again; she followed.

'The board told me to write a report. They want me to give them a list of names. I don't know anyone.' *Except Vlad,* she thought, glad Podolski couldn't see her face. 'I just want to act.'

He stopped abruptly by a telephone booth. A car's headlights blinded Ella. Podolski stepped closer, shielding her from the street. 'I have my theatre, Ella. I can't be dismissed. I would let down too many people.'

He stumbled over his words and his hand on her sleeve was shaking.

'Too much time has been lost. Years lost. What I have left, I want to spend in the theatre, instead of retiring to a park bench with a newspaper. Go to the academy director. Ask him to keep you in the course. If you fail, leave the country for good. You're Jewish, aren't you?'

She nodded.

'Go, then. Israel or Canada, anywhere. Apply for a family reunion. The most important thing is to get away from here. We have nothing to do in Russia.'

Her cheeks flushed despite the cold and she felt her throat constrict. 'But you've succeeded.' She had to squeeze out the words. 'You have your own theatre and you are directing. Everyone knows your name.'

He blinked at her, and she thought she saw tears in his eyes. 'You don't want my fate, girl. Go. You have all your life to live yet.'

He turned and walked away. For the first time, she noticed he was limping.

6

The doors to Director Hrushev's office were closed. A desk lamp created a circle of light around Mila Lvovna, his personal assistant, who was hiding behind her typewriter only a few steps away. The central heating failed to warm the wintry waiting room and Ella hunched her shoulders against the chill.

Her legs pressed together and she willed herself to calm down. Hrushev had managed to keep his position for more than thirty years, outlasting Stalin and Brezhnev. To expel her meant to acknowledge his fault – he hadn't been vigilant enough and had overlooked a dissident among his students. Fighting for his own skin, he might defend her.

She peeked over at Mila Lvovna with her 1950s chignon. If only Ella could convince her to champion her cause. But Mila refused to lift her eyes from the typewriter.

Gathering her courage, Ella tiptoed towards her desk.

The secretary's old porcelain-doll face and kitten heels didn't fool anyone in the academy. Mila knew all their names, exam marks and family backgrounds. Indeed, many in the theatre world believed she, rather than Hrushev, was the real head of the famed institution.

Ella leaned in closer. 'Do you think they'll let me stay?'

Mila waved her hands. 'You should be grateful if there are no charges.'

'Charges? What for?'

'What do you mean what for?' Mila whispered hotly. 'For anti-Soviet activity. A KGB general called.'

Ella seized hold of the woman's wrist and stared desperately into her eyes. She couldn't imagine why some KGB general might be interested in her. 'Milochka Lvovna, you have to help me. It was a mistake.'

'I've heard that before. But can you prove it?'

Ella bent over the secretary's desk and the belt of her skirt cut into her waist. She was about to tell Mila about the baby when the phone rang.

'Yes, Director.' Mila Lvovna covered the mouthpiece with her palm. 'He is expecting you.'

*

Hrushev stood by the window, his hands locked behind his back. It was snowing outside.

Ella stared at his fingers and rocked on her heels. To start crying now would be unwise. A call from the KGB spelled trouble, unless it was a giant misunderstanding. She had to believe that herself to persuade the director. Ella recalled how his plump cheeks had quivered with fright at the party board meeting. He hadn't attacked her though.

She took a step towards his desk, a grand affair with carved legs and green leather inlay on the top.

'Ella Gregorievna Ashkenazi.' The director pronounced her surname like it was a foreign dish he'd never tasted but disliked anyway.

She tried to smile, but couldn't manage it. Hrushev indicated the chair facing his desk and squeezed himself into his armchair under the portraits of Marx, Engels and Lenin. Ella sat, and he propped his cheek on his fist.

'What shall we do with you, Ashkenazi?'

So, he'd decided to play the grandfather figure rather than the executioner. She'd heard of Hrushev being a chameleon when it suited him. Maybe he would just lecture her on the actors' morale before letting her go.

'You did something foolish, my dove.' He gazed at her kindly. 'Now, not only is Comrade Surkov interested in your behaviour, but we had another call, sweetie. From above.' He pointed to the ceiling. 'Do you understand, *dorogusha*?'

The only organisations Hrushev could describe as 'above' were the KGB and the Ministry of Culture. Apart from those and the Communist Party supervisor, he had no overseers. Ella's hope, however baseless, disappeared. Why her? Why was she so important?

'See, you are partaking in the rallies, my dove, and we are being questioned by the Committee of Government Security. And for us at the academy it's not pleasant, my dear. We are people of culture, but we are also on the ideological front. We cannot make errors. We have the masses that look up to us.'

Ella couldn't fully absorb what Hrushev was saying and his kindly face became blurry. There'd been a call from the KGB about her – that was clear. Something must have happened in the last week that had made them contact the academy.

'Pyotr Ilyich, I swear this is all a mistake.'

He waved his chubby arms for her to be silent. 'Of course, it's a mistake.' He didn't sound fatherly any longer. 'And we need to correct it. You and I, my dove.' Hrushev left his armchair and approached her from the side. His stomach, in a close-fitted brown jacket, was at her eye level. Wide striped tie, clearly not made in Russia, didn't quite hide it.

'If you, dear, withdraw from the academy voluntarily, our

problems will go away. I won't get any more calls and you will not be under criminal charges.'

'What do you mean?' Ella started to get up. But Hrushev held her shoulder and forced her to stay seated.

His face flushed pink. 'Pick up your student record from Mila Lvovna and go home. Where there is no student, there is no case. Take a holiday or get married, change your family name and after a couple of years we can perhaps enrol you again.'

Blood pulsed in her temples and echoed in her ears. She tried to speak, but no sound came out. Hrushev patted her back, and she searched his expression, hoping to see a glimmer of understanding.

But he stared down at her and smiled, as if he expected her to thank him.

*

The draughty students' toilet stank of disinfectant, but at least it was empty. Ella inspected her face in the mirror above the metal trough sink. She saw a wan girl with dry lips and frightened eyes – a girl who didn't know how long she'd spent in the director's office or in the waiting room after signing some documents.

She took one step towards the exit, but the door banged open and Raya rushed in. Ignoring Ella, she went into one of the cubicles.

'Where have you been?' she asked from behind the partition. 'I called you at home and I called Roman. He hasn't seen you for days and is worried.'

The toilet flushed and Raya came out and stood beside Ella at the sink. Ella dug into her handbag, trying to avoid explanations while Raya washed her hands.

Raya draped her arms around Ella in a loose embrace. They had once been close friends. It would be such a relief to have Raya's ear and ask for advice.

'I'm dying for a pee,' she said instead.

She broke free of Raya's clinch. Inside the cubicle she sat on the toilet and buried her face in her hands to muffle her sobs.

Raya's shoes appeared underneath the stall's door. 'What's wrong, El?' Her voice, so familiar, hurt Ella's ears. Then it dropped to a whisper. 'What did they tell you at the board meeting? I've asked Plushkin, but he went all silent.'

Ella scrunched a wad of toilet paper in her fist and wiped her tears. She felt herself drowning. Raya shifted her weight from foot to foot. Ella inhaled the stench of ammonia and waited. Her so-called friend was about to steal her role anyway.

Then Raya's shoes moved away. 'It's your life, Comrade.' Her voice echoed through the bathroom.

Ella heard the door open and shut before silence fell. She clasped her knees and breathed slowly. How could she live if she wasn't an actress? She remembered Hrushev's vague assurance that he'd let her back into her course after two years had passed. But two years of what?

She sat up and stroked her belly as if it were a kitten. It was possible there was a tiny warm being fitted snugly inside her that she would be able to cuddle. She recalled Roman's arms holding her when they made love and felt the tension ease. Maybe she could have a child, a husband and an acting career in the West.

She couldn't ask her great-uncle in Melbourne to invite her over. No authority would let a single woman travel overseas, unless on a State-sanctioned tour. Besides, they had lost contact. But with Roman, and from abroad, she might try to find them. Leo and Sonya, his wife. Go to Australia instead of America.

Ella adjusted her tight gabardine skirt and straightened her shoulders. She spoke English and method acting was practised everywhere in the world. If Roman accepted the child, she'd love him for that. They had a whole life ahead of them to get to know each other.

She hugged her stomach.

And his parents, he'd said, would be thrilled with a grandchild.

7

A public phone hung on the back wall of the canteen in the academy's basement. Gripping a two-kopeck coin in her fingers, Ella trudged across the room. The canteen stank of yesterday's tea brew and the damp sawdust that covered the marble-tiled floor.

Nura stood behind the counter, dressed in a white uniform jacket stretched over a jumper. She smiled at Ella, showing her gold teeth. 'Want some tea? It's fresh.'

'Later, Nura. Thank you.'

The clock above the door showed that it was past eleven thirty. In half an hour the canteen would be swarming with students. Ella took the telephone receiver off the hook. She leaned against the wall and dialled the number. Roman had to be at work, so they shouldn't discuss the baby. That would be like letting everyone in the academy know her problems.

A woman answered the phone.

'May I speak to Roman Abramov?' Ella asked. She would arrange to see him. Later, she might tell him about the board meeting and what had happened with Hrushev. At least she didn't need to write a report about Vlad's dissident friends any longer.

'Roman isn't at work today,' the woman said, mockingly, Ella thought.

She hung up. So it hadn't been only her who'd been keeping

her troubles under wraps – he had secrets as well. Then again, he might have fallen sick and needed her help. Missing a day at work could often invite trouble.

'Nura, do you have two kopecks? I'll pay you back.'

'What, lost your lover? Them lads are like that. You only look away and they wander off.'

The phone swallowed her coin. She imagined the dim corridor in Roman's communal apartment where he and his parents occupied two separate rooms. Any one of his neighbours could answer the phone, but she hoped it would be him.

'Allo.'

Ella rested her forehead on the tiled canteen wall. The voice belonged to Roman's mother, Lia Issakovna. They had spoken on the phone before, but Ella had never seen her, apart from a picture in the family photo album that Roman had shown her. He always asked her over when his parents were out, or perhaps they left to give them some privacy.

'Lia Issakovna, this is Ella. Roman wasn't at work and I thought …' She hesitated. 'I wanted to find out if he is well.' If Roman was fine but not at home, she might appear to Lia not as her son's girlfriend but as an over-zealous admirer.

Lia's voice was firm. 'He isn't here.'

Ella looked over at Nura who was busy cleaning the counter with a foul-looking rag.

'Do you know where he is?'

'He went to OVIR.'

Ella exhaled. The Office of Visas and Registrations was where people went to apply for an exit permit. Roman had been telling the truth – the Abramovs did plan to emigrate.

The thoughts she'd had in the bathroom stall presented themselves in her mind without warning. She slid down the wall until the telephone cord was fully extended.

'Are you well, Ella?' Lia asked.

Ella let the silence linger. She couldn't think of a way to broach the subject. 'Actually, Lia Issakovna,' she began, and touched her belly for luck.

*

Ella stood behind Roman while he fiddled with the keys. There were five separate rooms in the cavern-like flat. The six or seven other people living there all shared a murky bathroom, toilet and crammed kitchen.

Ella read their names by the doorbell beside the entrance. The last time she'd come here, Roman had smuggled her in unnoticed. It felt like a hundred years ago. Tonight, his parents had invited her for dinner. She stared at Roman's back and hoped he would forgive her for telling his mother about the baby before she'd discussed it with him. It was going to come out sooner or later. Maybe even a proposal wasn't out of the question.

Roman stepped inside and Ella followed. The unlit corridor with its row of closed doors seemed more pungent than usual. It smelled of pickles and fried onions. A door to Ella's right opened and a woman's head, covered in hair curlers, popped out.

'Romochka, is this your girlfriend?' The woman stared unashamedly. But Ella didn't care. It was Lia she needed to impress, not the neighbours.

From the door to her left a middle-aged woman in a burgundy dress with a white lace collar floated out. Lia Issakovna. 'Romochka, you said at six. Your father and I were worried.' She opened the door to her room wider.

Roman stopped on the threshold. 'Too many people on the metro, Mama. There was nowhere to stand on the platform.' He nudged Ella forward. 'Mama, this is Ella. Ella, this is my mother.'

'*Zdravstvuite.*' Ella offered her hand to Lia, but found herself in the older woman's embrace, pressed against her ample breasts. French perfume and sunflower oil.

'Ellochka. Finally. Alexander Borisovich and I so wanted to meet you.'

She let go of her. Behind Lia, an older man who looked like Roman, except taller and balding, gave Ella a half smile. He took her hand and examined her for longer than she felt comfortable with.

Lia stepped aside to let them enter the room. Ella smiled at her. If they didn't accept her and the baby, she might be stuck in Russia. But they had invited her for dinner, so perhaps they wouldn't mind her joining the family.

Alexander helped her out of her coat, and she scanned the room. Near one wall, a table under a white tablecloth was decked with starched napkins and crystal wineglasses. At the far end, a bay window overlooked Leninsky Prospect, an eight-lane thoroughfare.

Lia beamed. 'Romochka, give Ella my slippers.'

Ella watched Alexander draw the curtains. The noise of traffic subsided. She put on Lia's fur-lined slippers and the warmth made her neck muscles uncoil. She inched towards the bookshelves and recognised the familiar compilations – Tolstoy, Pushkin. The same ones they had at her parents' home.

*

Ella sat between Lia and Roman, across the table from Alexander, but she couldn't eat. She picked at the Olivier potato salad and sipped at the chilled riesling.

Lia reached for Ella's almost empty wineglass. 'Maybe you shouldn't drink, darling.' She lowered her voice. 'In your condition.'

Ella cursed herself. If she wanted Roman's parents to like her, she had to behave like a girl from a good Jewish family.

Roman snorted and gulped a mouthful of wine. She saw his jaw clench. 'So, she told you already.'

'Romochka.' Lia admonished her son, but her eyes were on Ella. 'Are you well, darling?'

'Thank you, Lia Issakovna. I'm fine.' Ella glanced at Roman, suddenly wondering if she was making a mistake.

'Roman told us you are an actress.' Lia put a piece of gefilte fish on Ella's plate. 'Try, Ellochka. My mother's recipe.'

Roman's fork paused midway to his mouth. 'She was cast to play Natasha Rostova, Mama. Imagine!'

Ella kicked him under the table and smiled at Lia. Had she rushed to make a decision?

Lia pushed the bowl of potato salad towards her. 'Is that true, Ella? Are you playing Natasha?'

Roman scowled. 'What are you talking about, Mama? Ella has other plans now.'

Ella wanted to kick him again, but she folded and unfolded her napkin instead. Her grandmother's ring sparkled.

'That's a pretty diamond,' Lia said, changing the subject. Her smile looked sincere and Ella grinned back.

'It was my great-great grandmother's.' Ella never took the ring off. The last family relic, it had been given to her on her sixteenth birthday. 'Her Hebrew name was Elka too.'

Roman swished the wine in his glass. 'Ella is having a baby as I'm sure you know. She can't play Rostova anymore.'

Ella turned to Lia, but had nothing to say. They all sat in silence until Lia rose from her seat and started to gather their plates. 'Alexander, help me with the main course in the kitchen.'

Alexander got up. 'You, Roman, behave.' His smile turned crooked, his eyes stern. Perhaps there was something about his son she didn't know.

Roman's parents scurried out of the room and Ella went to stand by the bay window. Her hands trembled as she parted the curtains. If Roman loved her, he would talk to her now while they were alone. Reassure her. 'Roman, I was made to withdraw from my course.' It was the first time she'd said it aloud.

Fresh snowflakes powdered the neighbouring roofs, the ground and the road. She gazed at the world behind the glass where there seemed to be no tribulations, just a sprinkling of light on the snow.

Behind her, Roman remained silent.

She turned and looked at him. Eyes shut, he leaned back in his chair, face tilted towards the ceiling, exposing his neck beneath his tidy beard. She wanted to hug him, but she didn't dare. He seemed to be in a foul mood.

'You shouldn't have told my mother. You knew they were keen for grandchildren.'

Despite him behaving badly tonight, she was sure he cared – he just didn't like to be pushed into a corner, forced to get married. But if he was going to dump her, it was better that he do it tonight, before it was too late. She wondered why, though, he'd brought her home to meet his parents.

'I thought you wouldn't mind if that's what we both want.'

Roman snorted again but didn't argue.

Lia returned from the kitchen carrying a pan holding a roasted duck. She smiled to Ella like they were friends and had a secret to share. Alexander followed with a platter of potatoes. They took their seats again.

'Everyone, the food is getting cold,' Lia said. Ella was the only one still standing.

Roman opened his eyes and she waited for him to speak. He got up and walked towards her. She searched his gaze but failed to read his expression. Then he took hold of her elbow and led her back to the table. Ella slid into her seat next to Lia.

'We are getting married,' Roman announced, and poured more wine into his glass.

Alexander lifted his wineglass in a toast. 'Ellochka, Roman, let's drink to your future, your children.' His face lit up. '*Mazel tov.*'

Roman was silent. Ella clinked her glass with Lia's. 'Thank you, Alexander Borisovich.'

Roman's father wished them happiness. Her future now would be linked to this family forever. They would become her *mishpocha*, as close to her as her grandparents, her brother or even her parents.

Roman gulped at his wine. 'So, it's all sorted then.' He stood up and pushed his chair back to leave the table.

8

Olga
Moscow, USSR
1928

In the crystal bowl underneath the mound of black caviar, the ice had already melted. The champagne fizzled in the sparkling flutes. Inside the red-velvet booth at the Savoy restaurant, the air seemed to be missing.

Olga felt she was sinking. At seventeen, she'd never imagined that places like this existed. Natan had brought her here, the man her parents had arranged for her to marry.

Their candlelit table rocked gently. She watched dancing shadows on the papered walls, sated with warmth, food and music.

She felt Natan shift in his seat. Dressed in a commissar's leather, he gazed at her through his glasses. She knew that his brother Leo had written again from Melbourne, begging them to leave Russia. She'd promised to tell Natan tonight whether she planned to join him.

A girl's hysterical laughter spilled out from the adjacent booth. Olga shuddered. When they'd stepped inside she'd caught a glimpse of a bare-shouldered waif with a man who looked old enough to be her father.

'A fallen woman,' Natan said.

She smiled, wishing she could run away. Only there was nowhere to run. Her family needed this marriage. In the cold hungry Moscow of 1928, life had begun to improve, but not for her family. Her ex-rabbi father, with a sick wife and three of his children still at home, fought for survival. In the Bolsheviks' new Russia, the proletariat had left them two rooms of what had once been their spacious flat, appropriating the rest for the textile factory workers. At least her family hadn't been displaced.

Olga got up.

The gilded mirror above the table reflected her dark curly hair arranged on top of her head, making her look taller and older. Her ears were adorned with her grandmother's pearls – one of the few pieces that had stayed in the family's hands after the Great October Socialist Revolution. Her mother's black satin dress hugged her body.

Natan wasn't the husband she'd dreamed of – he was stocky, short, balding and fourteen years older than her.

She pouted at her reflection.

Natan tried so hard to be a part of the new country, but with his soft Jewish face, he looked better in a tallis and kippah than in a Red Army cap. If she agreed to go to Melbourne, as her parents were urging them to, he would take her away. When they'd settled they could bring her family over.

She grasped the plush curtain that separated their table from the rest of the restaurant. Her betrothed was a fur merchant and her mother's distant cousin. He'd been called expressly from Leningrad to meet Olga. Letters had gone to and from and no one had thought to ask her whether she wanted it or not. Everyone just assumed she would be happy to get married. Natan could feed them all; after seven years of Lenin's New Economic Policy, he had money.

The saxophone solo coming from behind the curtain partition made Olga want to cry. She turned to face the man she was promised to. 'Can we dance, Natan? I know the steps. I don't think Mama would mind.'

Natan nodded and slid the curtain off to the side to reveal the buzzing smoky room with a dance floor. He hadn't said much tonight. Maybe he wasn't that happy to marry her either.

9

Ella
Moscow, USSR
December 1982

Roman's room at night felt like the cabin of a ship sailing towards an unknown future. His sofa bed creaked every time they moved. It was good she'd stayed overnight though. If she'd left after dinner, she might have changed her mind about the marriage and the child. Still, alone in his room, the spark returned and Roman was the same as she'd known him before her pregnancy, funny and sensual.

His breath smelled of wine. 'Sorry, I've been an idiot.'

She stroked his bristly beard and giggled. Every time they made love, she forgave him. When she thought about it, there were a lot of reasons why marrying him might work. He did care about her and could make her happy – if he was in the mood. And he wasn't just a ticket out of the country, but the father of her child. He was a good lover too.

'Rom, let's see my parents tomorrow, ah? I'm too scared to tell them on my own.' She named at last the real reason for her anxiety – her fear of what her parents might say when they found out about her leaving the academy and keeping the baby. Her mother would not be happy. This much she knew.

'You haven't told them?' Roman placed his hands behind his head and stared at the ceiling.

Ella blushed, glad he wouldn't notice in the dark. 'What was I supposed to tell them? I didn't know myself. A baby or no baby, getting married or not.'

'An actress or not an actress.' Roman chuckled. 'In Russia or in America. Have you ever discussed emigration?'

'Everyone does. If they're Jewish, I mean. We have relatives in Australia.' Ella lay on her back next to him and gazed into space. 'My parents are not planning to leave though.'

'Will they let you go?'

Ella shrugged. 'If we get married and I take your name.'

Roman propped himself on his elbow and leaned over her. 'I'll tell you a secret. Like, to my future wife.' He chuckled again. 'I found this fellow. He's a student at Patrice Lumumba University. You know, the one for foreigners? He goes home to Ho Chi Minh City a few times a year and brings back American jeans. Levi's. You know how much they sell for now?'

She yawned, half asleep. 'What jeans?'

'One hundred and eighty roubles.'

'One hundred and eighty? What for?'

'Jeans.' Roman responded grumpily. 'If I buy a pair for a hundred roubles and sell for one-eighty, I can make good money. You have no idea how much emigration will cost.'

She was awake now. What he was talking about had a name – *speculiatzia* – and it was definitely illegal.

'It's dangerous, Rom.' Ella looked him in the eye, unsure how seriously she should take him. Was it just drunk-talk or had he already started acting on his plans?

'You don't understand.' Roman frowned. 'Emigration requires money and those are real dollars falling into my hands. If I buy ten pairs, I can make eight hundred roubles – four times my monthly salary – in one Sunday on the market.'

Excited, he sat up. 'And then I can exchange roubles into dollars and we're flying. We'll travel like kings, not paupers. Or we'll buy some stuff – amber, linen – and sell it in Rome. Have you heard what our migrants do in Ostia? They started a flea market with their *matryoshkas* and caviar and the whole of Rome shops there.'

His shoulder, pressed against hers, was warm and muscular. She touched it with her lips and felt them burn. Of course she'd heard of Soviet migrants earning liras in Ostia and Lido, but she'd never risk her chance at freedom by going to the black market in Russia.

Plus, some of the people that traded in Italy were black-market dealers even before they left Russia. They bought up Soviet watches, black lacquer boxes, cameras and linen tablecloths because they couldn't take their savings out of the USSR. But it didn't make sense for her, Roman or his parents to do that. Besides, they didn't have much savings to worry about.

'Isn't this dangerous?' she asked again.

He sighed. Then he grabbed her forearms and forced her to face him. She felt a low rumble of warning in her heart, but she didn't try to free herself.

'What do you think we're going to live on if I lose my job?' his voice faltered. 'Will you feed us? Guess how long it could take to get an exit permit? I know people who applied more than a year ago and are still waiting. And are unable to work.'

He released her, and she lay down and pulled the blanket over her head. Her romantic mood was gone. But she felt ashamed. Roman was right. If the government fired Roman once they'd applied for emigration, they'd need to fight for survival using whatever means they had. Reselling goods wasn't stealing.

If the only way to make money was to trade American jeans, then she had to support him.

'Be careful Rom,' she murmured.

*

Ella hooked her arm through Roman's and matched her steps to his. The high heels of her best boots tapped the asphalt under the fast melting snow. It felt good to be part of a couple. They strolled along Old Arbat Street towards the sounds of a waltz. The melody soaked the dusk, lit by cast iron streetlamps made to resemble gaslights. The pedestrian thoroughfare had been restored to look like its sepia version – like a photo from Olga's collection.

Ella smiled and looked around her. 'It's like a Hans Christian Andersen fairytale.'

Roman nodded, deep in thought. He didn't like crowds; it was strange that he'd insisted they go for a walk before visiting her parents for dinner. He squeezed her hand.

They pushed through a crowd that had gathered around an old one-legged man. He sat on a crushed cardboard box, his wooden leg pointed towards a tin mug filled with change. The war veteran stretched his squeezebox, as worn as his face, and closed his eyes while he played. Snowflakes fluttered above the man's head and Ella felt strangely moved.

'Do you have any change, Rom?'

He fished out a few copper coins from his jeans pocket. She added two silver ones from her purse and dropped them into the mug.

The old busker stopped playing. From under the flap of his coat he produced a quarter bottle of vodka and raised it in a toast. 'We won the war!' He was missing teeth and his mouth gaped. 'Led by Comrade Stalin.' He gulped down a large mouthful.

Roman laughed. 'God forbid.'

Ella refused to let the moment dampen her spirits. She pointed at the snow-capped trees that edged Old Arbat. 'Aren't those pretty?'

Roman leaned onto her and she closed her eyes for a kiss. His breath warmed her ear. 'You know, I have an idea.' He pulled her away from the crowd towards Vakhtangov Theatre.

Ella took in its lit entrance and marquee. It was impossible to believe she would never act again. She recalled the first performance she'd seen here with Olga and Natan when she was still a young girl: *Turandot*. She'd wanted to climb onto the stage and hug the actress who played the princess.

Roman lifted her chin. 'Where are you? Asleep?'

His eyes shone; his muscles were tense. She stood on tiptoes and caressed his cheek as if he were a child. He grabbed her wrist and kissed the back of her hand near her ring, then he pulled her into a narrow lane beside the theatre. Compared to the liveliness of Old Arbat, the place looked gloomy, as if it belonged in Moscow's outskirts.

She let him lead her and tried to hold on to her feeling of contentment. He must have some surprise for her – maybe a present. Perhaps they were seeing a play. 'What are we doing here?'

He muttered an answer she could not decipher and pushed through a door with a grille. Inside, it was warm – but gloomier still. Roman led her downstairs. Dry timber steps creaked under her feet and she gripped his arm.

'Rom, where are we?'

He shoved a door with his shoulder. They entered a shop of some kind: walls painted white and a few rows of shelves crammed with an assortment of cardboard boxes. Behind a timber counter, a tiny old man sat reading a book. Roman pulled Ella closer to the counter.

'Isaak Zinovievich?' Roman sounded softer and very polite but his hold on her elbow remained firm.

'How can I be of service?' The man stood up, half-hidden

by the counter. He was gnome-like in his short fur-trimmed vest, plaid shirt and wire-rimmed glasses. Ella bet he wore felt boots as well. His eyes were fixed on her, as if he were expecting an introduction.

Roman grabbed her arm and stretched it across the counter. 'Have a look at this ring.'

The diamond flashed on Ella's trembling finger. She winced but didn't retract her hand. The gnome held her palm and took off his glasses. He reached for a loupe and inserted it into his eye socket.

Ella turned her head towards Roman. 'What is this for?' she mouthed.

Roman smiled. 'Just to value it, Ellochka.'

The gnome seized her ring and pulled it from her finger. She heard herself gasp, but neither Roman nor the old man appeared to register it. The man sat down again, his nose touching the stone. Roman exhaled a shaky breath, but Ella didn't take her eyes off the man's practised fingers that clasped her ring.

'I can offer you eight hundred roubles.' He lifted his eyes. 'But I understand if you don't accept. It's worth triple that.' He stood and held out Ella's ring on his palm.

She snatched it back and put it on her finger. 'It's not for sale.' She balled her fist and turned to leave.

Roman took hold of her arm but she shook him off. 'Thank you, Isaak Zinovievich,' he said.

Outside, the snow lay like a quilt lit by moonlight. Ella stomped through it ahead of Roman. She half-turned and saw him lighting a cigarette.

She stopped on the spot. 'It was Olga's. You know that, don't you?'

Roman smirked. 'In a week we can have your ring back plus five hundred roubles – and in two weeks, a thousand.' His cigarette tip flickered and he walked past her. He blew smoke up at the moon.

'You only think of yourself,' he called out, 'but I have us both to think of and the baby.'

10

The landing in front of her parents' apartment remained unchanged from Ella's childhood. Number 124. This was where she'd grown up, the place in which her parents waited for her and Roman now.

The door opened before she could press the bell. Her mother pulled her into the hallway – it was bad luck to kiss over a doorstep – and the aroma of borscht became stronger.

'Come in, come in.'

Ella gave her mother a peck on the cheek and Roman stepped into the flat.

'Give me your coat.' Anna attempted to help her, then turned to Roman, more flustered than usual. 'And you are Roman?'

They were all crowded in a tiny spot between the flat's entrance and the clothes rack on the wall. The glass door to the kitchen was ajar and familiar wafts of garlicky aroma filled the hallway.

'Are the grandparents coming as well?' Hopes that her confession could be delayed flooded Ella's brain.

'No, it's only us tonight.' Anna looked Roman up and down. He took off his boots and stood there in his socks.

'Ella.' Her mother blushed. 'Give Roman some slippers.'

Ella bent to the shoe rack at the entrance and offered Roman a pair of her father's slippers. She couldn't predict her father's reaction to her news about the baby and her and Roman's imminent departure. The scariest part was admitting that she'd been forced to leave the academy.

'Leonid,' Anna shouted. She prodded Ella and Roman into the living room. 'Papa is coming home any minute and Leon is finishing his homework.' She shrugged. 'Or that's what he says he's doing.'

Roman winked at Ella and she touched his hand. At least her situation was no longer irreparable. Then she remembered Olga's ring and the pawnshop, and the warmth dissipated.

From her brother's room came the sound of something crashing. Ella exchanged a glance with her mother, glad to have her distracted.

A moment later, Leon turned up in the living room. He wore a singlet and his hair was messed up.

Anna folded her arms under her breasts and frowned at Leon. Ella hugged her brother's bony shoulders. He tried to wriggle free, but she held him tighter. 'This is my baby brother.'

Roman offered Leon his hand, as if the boy were an adult. 'Roman. And you are Leonid?'

His voice, deep and mature, made her cheeks warm. She met Anna's eyes.

'Do you want me to set the table?' She released Leon and he scurried to the bedroom she used to share with him before she left home.

'Go and wash your hands, both of you,' Anna ordered. She darted out of the living room to the kitchen. 'Oh, my cake!'

*

After everyone's plates had been filled and the wine had been poured, a silence descended upon the table. Leonid chewed with his mouth open. Anna and Gregory sat across from Ella, lit by the lamp above that threw shadows onto the white tablecloth. Ella felt like the party board meeting had never ended and now included her own parents, eager to interrogate her.

She looked at Roman in the hope he would say something to start the conversation, but he kept eating, his head low.

Anna's cutlery clinked on her plate. 'How is the academy?'

Both she and Gregory stared at Ella, and she knew they'd guessed something was wrong. She turned to her future husband. 'Rom, try the *forshmak*.' She offered him the dish, but he shook his head and gulped a mouthful of wine. Ella met her mother's gaze. 'Mum, we have some news. Roman and his family are planning to emigrate.'

Gregory raised his eyebrows and whistled. 'Have you applied already, Roman?'

Roman put his knuckles to his mouth and pretended to still be chewing. Ella nudged his foot under the table. 'We're thinking of getting married too,' she said.

Anna's lips stretched into a taut smile.

Ella covered Roman's hand with hers and continued. 'Mum, Dad, how would you feel if Roman and I got married and I left with his family for America?'

Her father undid the top button of his shirt. He rose to leave the table, but Anna rested her palm on his shoulder. 'Let's make some sense of this, Ella. What about your acting?'

Gregory sat down again. The chair creaked under his weight. 'Let's have a drink.' He filled his glass with white wine – German riesling for the occasion. 'Roman?'

He picked up Roman's glass and Ella saw that her father's hand was shaking. She knew her parents were afraid that if she emigrated, they'd never see her again.

Roman sipped his wine but stopped Gregory from filling Ella's glass. 'Thank you, Gregory Natanovich. That's enough for Ella.'

Her father stopped pouring and frowned. Then he stared at Ella's stomach. There was nothing for him to see. Nonetheless she put her elbows on the table and hunched forward.

'I'm expecting a baby.' The silence returned and she looked at her brother. His mouth was agape.

Anna started to get up, her knuckles white on the table. 'So you decided to emigrate with Roman's family without thinking of your parents or your brother?'

Gregory stood up too and nodded for Roman to follow him. But Ella had had enough. The confusion and pain of the last two weeks had finally caught up with her. She dropped her head onto her arms on the table and let herself cry.

Anna's breath touched her hair and she felt her mother lean over her from behind. The embrace made Ella cry even harder.

Her grandmother Olga had married too early. Now that was her fate too.

11

When the bus finally stopped at Third Road, Ella jumped off without waiting for Roman. He stepped into the snowy grey mud behind her.

'Are you sure it's here? Looks like bloody *Solaris*.'

She recalled the alien planet from Tarkovsky's cult film – a vastness, impossible to comprehend. The prisms of identical buildings lined a nondescript street that ran parallel to the forest. Between high-rises the snow was white. The footpath was a black line.

She took out the scrap of paper Vlad had given her. 'Number sixteen. Should be fifth on the right, if we face the forest.' She giggled and tore the paper in half. 'He said we should keep it secret.'

Roman turned towards the blocks of apartments. His leather-clad back gleamed under the streetlights. 'I don't understand why he told you to come and why it's so hush-hush.'

Ella sighed. 'They'll talk of shortcuts to help people pass emigration.'

She didn't know what to expect from this seminar either, but any information would help, and Vlad had insisted they go. The dinner scene at her parents' still played on her mind. Maybe the seminar would suggest some way out for people whose parents objected to their leaving.

'Who are these gurus?'

'No idea. Why don't you ask them?'

At the entrance to Number 16 she smelled cats and wilted pine needles. The scatter of confetti on the stairs in front of the lift made her think of New Year's Eve. The big night had just passed, but she felt like it hadn't happened yet. It was hard to believe it was 1983; she was two and a half months pregnant and had missed her abortion deadline.

Ella pressed the red plastic button and stared through the wire mesh into the elevator's cavity. Roman's frosty breath and the sound of his tapping foot filled the building's foyer. The lift cage hit the base and they stepped in.

'Ninth floor.' She hoped Vlad would be there as he'd promised.

When they stepped out of the lift, five doors faced the landing. The one they wanted was painted steel grey, the others upholstered in vinyl. As instructed, Ella knocked three times, paused, and knocked once more. The door opened a notch.

'Vlad.' She clamped her mitten over her mouth; she shouldn't have said his name. Beside her, Roman buried his fists in his pockets. 'Sorry,' she whispered. 'Is Galya home?'

The door closed and she heard its chain unfasten. It opened again and a heavily pregnant woman in a headscarf led them into a packed living room. A dozen or so people sat on mismatched chairs with notepads on their knees.

'When you decided to emigrate, you made a decision to fight the Soviet system.' A young man with a black beard spoke under the bright ceiling light. She guessed he was one of the Refuseniks who taught Hebrew and the Jewish way of life.

Ella perched on the balding armrest of a pink velvet chair, leaving Roman to search for a seat. He dawdled, ill at ease, and the speaker eyeballed him.

'From now on your every action will be looked at as a provocation, an attempt to mar the image of a Soviet citizen.'

It seemed a bit overstated and Ella checked Roman's reaction. He sat fidgeting on the edge of a sofa, wedged between the wall and a woman in black. The people around him seemed completely absorbed, like they were studying the Torah – though she'd never been inside a synagogue.

Ella took out a new notepad and pen from her handbag. As far as she was concerned, if she learned one thing that helped her out of Russia, coming here would be worth it.

The man paced back and forth. 'Make sure you fill out all the forms and gather the papers required. If you get rejected, you'll have to wait twelve months before you can apply again. I'll read you the list of the forms.'

She saw Vlad crouched on a low child's stool in the corner. He leaned forward, elbows on knees, eyes fixed on the young man speaking.

'A referral from your place of work. This form has to be signed to make your employers aware that you plan to leave the USSR. That exposes you as a traitor. Those of you who work in science or media, or are doctors or teachers, do not have a chance of keeping your jobs. You will be fired. So do this one last.'

She thought he was being dramatic but she jotted this down anyway. Had Roman told them at work? He seemed to have gone pale, but this might have been the harshness of the naked lightbulb. The man hadn't mentioned engineers.

'The next form to consider is a permit from your parents.' The speaker rubbed his beard. 'Unless they approve, you cannot leave the country.'

'My father is ninety.' The woman next to Roman had turned crimson. 'He wants to stay back with my sister. He calls me a deserter.'

The man stopped pacing. 'If he doesn't sign your permit, your documents won't be accepted.'

The woman became teary. 'He won't let me go. But my children are leaving.'

The speaker nodded. 'You need to ensure your father signs.'

Ella's eyes felt dry and she blinked hard. If her parents didn't consent, she couldn't go. She climbed off her perch and edged close to Vlad, kneeling on the floor beside his denim-clad legs. Vlad was lucky to have a father who brought him blue jeans from abroad, she thought.

'Is that true?' she asked Vlad, not bothering to lower her voice.

'Yes, but you'll be fine if they sign the form. Does your mother know?'

Ella sank down. She told herself she shouldn't panic. Her parents could still be convinced; they knew she was pregnant.

The speaker was pacing again. 'You should learn to be patient. It may take six months to a year before you get a reply and often the answer is "no". In that case you can lodge an appeal, which will take even longer.'

From her place on the floor, Ella glanced over at Roman. He sat with his head in his hands.

The young man spread his arms as if he wanted to embrace everyone. 'If you find yourself fired, get a menial job. A night watchman is good – you can study. Or a cleaner – they finish work early. If you don't work, you could get arrested as a "slacker" as per Articles 37 and 41 in the USSR Constitution: Everyone's right to work.'

He extended his arm towards Vlad. 'We are lucky today to have an expert here on what you should do if you do get arrested.'

Vlad got up to speak.

*

Under the roof of the bus stop it seemed colder than out under the open sky. Ella looked from Vlad to Roman. Since they'd walked out of the seminar, they'd both kept silent. She peered along Third Road, black under the starless sky.

The headlights of an approaching car split the night and she grabbed Roman's hand. 'A taxi.'

Roman eyed Vlad. 'You said there would be a bus.'

The taxi sped by, splashing the footpath with mud. Ella stepped back from the road. 'We should have taken it.'

'Sure,' Roman almost shouted. 'Why don't we splurge? We've just learned it could take us a year until we get a reply and that my job isn't secure.'

Ella checked behind the bus stop in case someone had followed them, but only caught Vlad's eye. He smiled at her, his usual crooked smile. With his back hunched in his overcoat, he looked like a character from one of Gogol's novels.

'I don't believe it's that bad. Lots of people are leaving the country.' Roman's voice quaked and she went to stand by his side.

'But it's all true.' Vlad said. 'That's why I asked you to come, to see what you're up against before you make any decisions.' He was addressing Ella.

'Rubbish.' Roman stomped onto the footpath and patted his pockets. 'All those arrests and expenses. They want to keep us on the leash – these friends of yours – to make sure we go to Israel. Most people are trying for the States or Canada when they get the hell out of Russia.'

Vlad sighed. 'It's up to you whether to believe it or not.'

Roman lit a cigarette, illuminating his red and green mohair scarf. He exhaled smoke at Vlad and turned to Ella. 'You'll have to find some work, and it'd better be soon. In a couple of months there won't be many takers. No one will employ a pregnant woman.'

Ella turned from him and searched for the headlights of a bus.

Roman cackled. 'Come on. That was a joke, okay? I am not *Stepanida Vlasievna*.' He used the dissident slang for Soviet Power.

But Ella didn't feel like laughing. Apart from acting, she didn't have any skills. And there was no bus on Third Road.

Vlad whistled. Ella heard the shuffle of his footsteps and thought he was going to hit Roman, but he jogged past him and around the bus stop, blowing at his fingers. 'You think it's too cold here?' he yelled. 'This is nothing.' He emerged from behind the bus stop and stood beside Ella. 'It is colder in Siberia, Roman.'

12

Ella had landed a miracle – a meeting with an Internal Affairs official who could permit her to apply for emigration without her parents' approval. General Lubov, Ivan Petrovich, could resolve her dilemma with a stroke of his pen.

She lifted her collar to stop snowflakes from melting down her neck between her hat and scarf. The light changed to green and she marched across Dzerzhinsky Square to the grey monolith of Lubyanka, the KGB's headquarters.

It was an odd flaw in the system that anyone with 'Jew' stamped in their birth certificate and their passport had a legal way to escape the USSR. Jews were leaving for Israel in their hundreds to reunite with relatives. Some continued on to the United States and Canada, to Australia and New Zealand, desperate to get away from the omnipresent *Stepanida Vlasievna*.

A red carpet runner bled its way from the entrance to the grand staircase. Ella tried not to let her heels click when she stepped off it.

In the tidy reception area, there were three other people waiting to see the general – lucky or unlucky souls who'd used bribes or connections, or who'd been plucked out of the months' long queue by some unknown power, as she had been, and summoned to Lubyanka.

'Ashkenazi.'

The lieutenant, who'd been sitting by the general's door immersed in his paperwork only a moment ago, clasped her elbow. She felt light-headed as he marched her into the general's quarters.

The room was semi-dark and sparsely furnished. Above the desk that could have seated three people, a portrait of Yuri Andropov hung on the wall. On General Lubov's desk, a bronze bust of Lenin stared at a decanter of water. Burgundy drapes obscured the windows that most likely faced the square. She imagined the snow slush and the blasts of car horns, but the office blocked the entire outside world. Between her and the desk was a chair upholstered in dark leather.

'Sit, Ashkenazi.'

A male voice behind Ella startled her. She turned and saw a sturdy older man in a uniform coming from behind a theatre-like curtain, which, she realised, might not have hidden a window after all. He moved across the carpet without making a sound, his feet clad in smart shoes instead of military boots.

Lubov sat in the armchair behind his desk and opened a numbered folder she hadn't noticed. In it was an enlarged copy of the *Komsomoletz* newspaper article with her photograph and the headline, *Hooligans on the Loose*. Ella gripped the back of the chair.

'Sit.'

She sank into the dark leather and coughed to clear her throat. She really needed a drink. There was an empty glass beside the decanter, and she glanced hopefully from it to the general's ruddy face. She could not read his expression.

'Water?' he offered.

He closed her file and poured her a glass. Ella gulped it down.

'So, what do you want from me, Ashkenazi?' He glanced at her, then turned his attention to his hands. 'Why have you sought an appointment?'

Ella put her water down on the desk. He knew who she was, but he probably didn't know she'd been punished already.

'I am sorry, Comrade General, but I am not here about the article.'

The general inspected his thick fingers and she saw that his nails were missing. Frostbite, she imagined.

He didn't look up. 'I am listening.'

'I wanted to ask permission ...' Her voice wavered. 'My parents—'

'Louder,' the general snapped. He lifted his head but avoided looking at her. 'Why are you here?'

Ella stared at the bust of Lenin. 'My husband, Roman Abramov, and his parents are applying for a family reunion in Israel.' She paused. She and Roman were not yet married, but they would be in a few days. 'I need to be allowed to emigrate with my husband's family. I am expecting a child.' She looked up at General Lubov, who remained silent. 'My father ...' she began.

But the general waved his hand to silence her. He twisted his body to the filing cabinet behind him and pulled out another folder.

'Gregory Ashkenazi.' The frown between his Brezhnev-like eyebrows became deeper. 'I remember.'

Ella's hand flew to her mouth before she could stop it. She could think of no reason why the general would know her father.

Lubov flicked through the documents in the file. 'You know, Ashkenazi, that without your father's permission you cannot leave the country, neither for Is-ray-el nor for Zaire.'

She wondered why he said Zaire. Her lip quivered and she clasped her hands. 'I beg you, Comrade General. My husband will leave alone, but I am pregnant. Why can't we go together?'

The general slammed his fist on the desk. The decanter jingled and Lenin's bust shook. 'Decided to betray your country?'

Ella tried to get up, but her legs wouldn't hold her.

'Go home. There is nothing for Grisha's daughter to do in Israel. You have done enough damage getting mixed up with dissidents.' He nodded towards the files on his desk. 'Listen to your father. If he says no, it means no. It could cost him his job.'

Lubov walked around the desk towards her and, as if obeying a silent order, the office door opened. The lieutenant who'd brought her in grabbed her forearm and yanked her to her feet. He prodded her towards the exit.

Ella wriggled and almost freed herself, but when she looked over her shoulder, the general had disappeared – possibly behind the burgundy curtain and into an antechamber.

She stopped fighting. The lieutenant manoeuvred her into the reception area and shut the general's door. In her head, one thought persisted. General Lubov must have called the academy and had her expelled. Still, it wasn't clear why he had taken an interest. Surely there were others more important than her.

13

Olga
Moscow, USSR
1939

Even before she entered the hospital's headquarters, Olga knew she'd done something wrong. Something so bad she had to be called to the head doctor's office, which she'd only visited a handful of times over her ten-year nursing career.

Olga jammed her fists into the pockets of her white scrubs, her mind running through the list of possible crimes – extra painkillers for the patient in Ward N3, a missed shift when she'd had to collect Grisha from the pioneer camp or another when her mother had a stroke. She touched her grandmother's ring on the chain around her neck and tucked it underneath her nurse's coat.

Inside the office, the light blinded her. Olga blinked. The man in the uniform, who was holding the desk lamp, let the spotlight slide away from her face. The internal police. NKVD.

'Ashkenazi.' The officer's voice broke. 'Tell us about your relatives abroad.'

She blinked harder to bring the darkened room into focus. Obscured by the uniformed man, Pavel Nikitovich – a senior surgeon – pressed himself into the wall by the blacked-out window.

Olga felt her pulse race faster than the typewriter she could hear coming from behind the thin partition. So the secretary was being kept late too, probably to be another witness should they decide to arrest her.

She stared into the light. The NKVD wouldn't know about Leo and Sonya. They'd left twelve years ago.

'I don't have any.' An odd giggle escaped from her lips and she swallowed it in fear.

'Your husband, Natan Ashkenazi, doesn't think so and neither does your brother-in-law in Australia.' The man laughed. He seemed to enjoy his work.

A hand holding an envelope appeared in front of her. The hand was young like the voice and strong with square nails.

Her eyes struck Leo's familiar handwriting, so similar to Natan's. So, he'd written to them again. He'd probably sent them another invite as promised. Though she wasn't sure if they had family reunion provisions in Australia like they did in America.

Olga exhaled, but she didn't let herself show the surge of warmth that washed through her veins.

But it wasn't all good news. A relative abroad could mean a death sentence, if one was accused of spying.

'Leo is dead,' she said. 'Died years ago.' She sobbed unexpectedly. Yet her timing was good, she thought.

They hadn't heard from Natan's brother since 1931 – eight years ago – when he'd last tried to get them out of the USSR. By then, Grisha had been born and they'd had no chance of escape.

The man came out from the shadows and Olga saw that he was very young – twenty at most. He shoved Leo's letter under her nose. 'And what is this? Your husband says he is alive.'

Olga shrugged. 'Sorry, officer, it's a mistake.'

The typewriter stopped. She heard Pavel Nikitovich suppress a sigh in the dark. She rubbed her eyes.

'Sit down, Ashkenazi.' The NKVD officer sounded menacing and she realised she was standing with her hand extended towards the letter.

'Sit and tell us the truth.'

Olga slumped onto the hard timber chair, her legs rubbery.

'When did your brother-in-law die and where?'

She felt resolve coming over her. Natan wouldn't acknowledge Leo's existence. He knew what it meant to have his brother reside in a foreign country, to correspond with an enemy. She had to protect him and her children.

'Leo died in Australia. 1931, I think.' She heard herself say it and begged Leo for forgiveness.

The uniformed boy leaned over her, his pink, never-shaved cheek almost touching her own. 'And how has it happened that the dead person is writing to you? Is he a ghost?'

He stomped around the desk to the window, where Pavel Nikitovich struggled to breathe, weird spurts and whistles battling in his chest.

Asthma, Olga diagnosed. The same disease her daughter was suffering from. Her little four-year-old Faina.

The NKVD officer gulped on his tea and she swallowed. She stood up and straightened her nurse's uniform. She regretted not wearing a hat and gloves as her mother had always done.

'This letter is a provocation.' Her voice built, gathered strength. 'The enemies of our country attempted this lie to lure us into their dirty nets. Thank you, Comrade, for intercepting this letter and stopping the crime from being committed. Someone wants us to believe that Leo had written it. That he isn't dead. To make us trust them.'

She stepped forward and extended her arm for a handshake. Behind the officer's back, Pavel Nikitovich clapped silently, his wheezing quieter. The young man didn't take her hand. He folded the letter and put it back inside its envelope.

Olga felt her fingers freeze as he dropped the envelope back into a cardboard folder. She craved to touch Leo's words.

'That will be all.' The NKVD officer was in a hurry now. To report, probably to his superiors, that they might have bigger fish to fry. 'You may go.'

'Thank you, Comrade. What was your name, I forgot?'

The boy suddenly blushed. He adjusted his leather holster and touched his revolver. He was no older than nineteen, Olga thought.

'Lubov,' he said, 'Ivan. Go now and thank your lucky day. We have too much work without your nonsense.'

14

Ella
Moscow, USSR
January 1983

Ella sat on a frosted bench and wound her scarf around her neck. After the din of Dzerzhinsky Square and the dizzy silence of the general's office, Patriarch's Ponds felt like an enchanted world. The skating rink was closed and only a few dog walkers and women with prams strolled around the boulevard that bordered the pond. From her bench, Ella could make out Vlad's apartment windows overlooking the park, but he was nowhere to be seen.

The snowfall stopped and daylight seeped through the clouds. Under the weak sun, the ice on the pond appeared grey and unreliable. Ella blew on her fingers to warm them. Her head boomed. Without her parents' approval, all her plans of marriage and emigration were futile, but it was too late to retreat.

She slid her hand between the buttons of her winter coat and patted her stomach – hard and flat. For a moment she felt a sharp relief. The baby hadn't happened, it had all been a mistake and she was free to play Rostova.

'Elka.' Vlad's voice broke into her daydream. His arms enfolded her and the familiar whiff of fresh laundry – a testament to Daria, his father's housekeeper – filled her nostrils.

Vlad released her shoulders and sat on the bench next to her. 'What did they say?'

'It's a betrayal of your country,' she said in General Lubov's voice. 'Grisha's daughter should have nothing to do with Is-ray-*el*.' She pronounced Israel incorrectly, with the stress on the last syllable, as the general had done, but Vlad did not laugh. Ella got up. 'Let's walk. I'm freezing.'

He clasped her wrist as she stood up. 'How does he know your father?'

She stared down into his eyes. 'I have no idea. He had the *Komsomoletz* article in the folder. What should I do?'

An urge to light a cigarette and inhale its sweet poison seized her, but neither of them smoked these days.

They walked past a woman with a scruffy dog and Ella became suddenly aware of how they might look to an outside observer. They were behaving like plotters, not friends. Vlad pulled her sleeve towards him and she leaned over. His pale face and his eyes, grey with black dots, moved too close to hers.

'Perhaps you should let Roman apply with his parents ahead of you. If you are married and have his child, they will let you join your husband.'

'I can't take that risk.' She glanced up at the tangled web of poplar branches that obscured the sky. 'I want to leave with them. You think I should give birth alone?' She avoided meeting Vlad's gaze. 'What if Roman doesn't call for me?'

'Then you'll be rid of him.'

'And who's going to feed my child? You?'

Ella laughed without meaning to. Vlad bent down and picked up a thin branch from the ground.

'Roman came up with a scheme to earn money.' She remembered his caution about secrecy, but Vlad was her closest friend. He tossed the branch aside and marched ahead of her. She had to walk faster to keep up.

'He's buying American jeans through a contact and selling them at a market – you know the one near Tula? All speculators trade there.'

Vlad nodded and slowed his pace. 'And what do you think?'

'I'm scared.' Her pulse quickened, but she was relieved to speak the truth. 'It's not legal, is it? But no one gets arrested or there would be no market, right?'

'How many pairs of jeans does he have? If it's only one pair that should be fine.'

He glanced at her. She kept her expression blank yet the tightness in her chest made her slow down. Vlad could be trusted entirely, it was Roman's scheming that gave her grief.

'He's planning to buy a few to earn a lot in one go.'

The scene in the pawnshop popped up in her mind and she touched Olga's ring to make sure it was still on her finger.

A gust of wind rose and Ella shivered despite her headscarf and gloves. Yet she grinned and hooked arms with Vlad. 'This is entirely your fault, you know, inviting me to a protest with your dissident friends.'

The joke wasn't funny. If he hadn't arranged to meet her by the synagogue, none of this would have happened. She would be on stage right now instead of freezing here in the park.

*

Ella smoothed her wedding skirt-suit over her hips. It fitted her well and she cheered up a little. It wasn't a white gown – every girl's dream – but the pearl-grey outfit she'd chosen looked smart. And she did feel like a bride when she held to her breast a bouquet of cream dahlias that Roman had handed her on the registry's threshold.

A crimson and gold sign at the entrance announced that the registry was a 'Palace of Love and Marriages', but she stepped into a foyer that resembled the waiting room of any Soviet organisation. A row of chairs upholstered in dark red vinyl lined the walls. Under a portrait of Lenin, a large vase with artificial flowers graced the corner. Older relatives of brides and grooms took to the chairs – grandmothers in headscarves and men in old-fashioned suits and funny ties.

She watched three couples and their friends either pace the carpeted hall or huddle in groups. The brides dolled up in white dresses wore tulle veils as was expected. She would have it all, Ella thought, just not now. Today she felt lucky just to have kept her light-coloured heels dry when she'd stepped out of the taxi. Snow had melted overnight and sleet covered the pavement.

Her parents were busy preparing the wedding dinner, but at least her witnesses were here. Vlad sat with his face in a book – despite his suit, he looked out of place. Raya hung by his side and avoided Ella's gaze. She'd only agreed to be a witness, Ella figured, to lessen her guilt for getting the leading role by default.

Roman stepped outside, and his parents flanked Ella like guards. She edged closer to the glass exit doors, behind which a few grooms crowded the footpath. They inhaled their last mouthfuls of freedom and hid cigarettes in their fists. Roman joined them. He lit a cigarette and looked at his watch as if he was waiting for someone.

In his gaze, Ella didn't detect the wonder she'd observed in other men looking at their future wives. One of the young women covered her stomach with an enormous bouquet of white chrysanthemums. Ella peered down at her own belly. At almost three months she wasn't yet showing.

Lia caught her staring and smiled. Both she and Roman's father seemed happy. The double doors on the far side of the foyer opened and Mendelssohn's 'Wedding March' thundered. The newlyweds, an older couple, exchanged adoring glances. The wife wiped her tears of joy and Ella felt strangely ashamed, as if she and Roman were deceiving everyone by getting married.

*

Roman got out of bed and she burrowed deeper into the warm spot left by his body. She didn't want to wake up. It was barely morning and their heart-to-heart about money only a day after the wedding stuck in her mind like a splinter. She heard his steps in the dark and the sound of the shower. She breathed in and out in the hope of falling back asleep to avoid a confrontation.

She couldn't pretend any longer when Roman returned and his fingers crept under the blankets. He smelled of his new wool sweater – his mother's handiwork – and freshly washed hair. His lips touched her neck. He held her left hand and toyed with her diamond ring.

'I'll bring it back, El, I promise. It'll just be a week.' She tugged her hand back, but he wouldn't let go. His other hand caressed her body. 'You can come too, if you want.' He kissed her mouth. 'This Sunday the market is on. We'll take a train and stay overnight in a hotel.'

She wrenched her hand free. 'Stop it, Rom.'

He climbed on top of her and held her shoulders down. His beard tickled her neck. 'This is for the baby and us,' he whispered. 'We have to get ready if we plan to leave.'

Her lips opened to his against her will. 'Can't you find money without pawning my ring?' He turned her palm over and kissed her wrist. Her heart beat urgently. 'Whatever it is you're doing feels risky. If something happened to you …' A lump formed in her throat and she didn't finish her sentence.

He kissed her again. Then his lips brushed her eyelids close. 'Don't fight me, sweetheart. You won't regret it.'

He twisted the ring off her finger. She let him take it.

15

Ella stretched across the folded divan her parents used as a bed and examined a chessboard laid out between her and her brother. The scratchy wool rug that covered the divan prickled her bare legs. Leon scrunched up his face in an effort to beat her, yet she felt she'd been beaten already.

She wondered if Roman was scared when he left for the markets with his sports bag full of jeans.

Leon took hold of a white knight. 'Check.' He jumped off the bed and nearly knocked the chessboard over.

Ella lifted her rook, though she knew she had lost.

The telephone rang. Her grip loosened and she almost dropped the piece, but Leon's eyes were fixed on his endgame.

'Checkmate,' he yelled.

Ella reached across her father's armchair and picked up the handset from its cradle. She stretched the telephone cord and turned away from her brother. 'Allo?'

'Why aren't you home?' Roman's voice was tinged with panic. 'I called there a few times.'

She peeked at Leon. 'I told you I'd be at my parents'.'

'The *militzia* – they seized it all. The jeans. Even my bag.'

Ella took a deep breath to clear the fog in her brain. His sports bag was worthless. It even had a side zipper broken. 'Where are you, Roman?'

He might have been lucky. Perhaps the *militzia* just wanted a bribe, but that wasn't how it worked. They would have taken money, but not the jeans, the evidence of the crime.

Roman hiccupped. 'They told me to stay in Tula and see them tomorrow morning. I want to come home.'

'That's disobeying orders.'

'But I didn't sell a bloody thing!'

Now they had nothing – no ring, no money and no American jeans – and Roman might still get arrested. She stopped herself from yelling into the receiver. Even if he hadn't sold anything, he'd committed a crime.

'Rom, tell me what happened.'

He sniffed. 'One asked me the price and I told him, then another came, who asked the same. Then they shoved their IDs in my face and grabbed the jeans. They gave me a receipt, can you imagine? The bastards.'

Ella rubbed her temple. The receipt was bad news – it made everything legal. But maybe they wanted to teach him a lesson and still get a bribe.

'What did they say?' She smiled reassuringly at Leon, who was resetting the chessboard.

'You have to find me a lawyer, El,' Roman said.

Her throat closed. For a moment she couldn't speak. Then she thought of her great-aunt. A chain-smoker and now wheelchair-bound, she was a lawyer and still a force to be reckoned with.

'I could ask Henrietta.'

'Do that.' Roman's breathing shuddered down the line. 'We have to sort this shit out. Maybe I could even get the jeans back.'

And my ring, Ella said silently. She hid her face from Leon. 'Call me when you get your train ticket. I'll meet you at the station.' Her fingers gripped the mouthpiece.

She turned to find Leon standing beside her.

'What happened?'

Ella hugged his bony shoulders. Then she pressed the phone back to her ear. 'Roman?'

She only heard static.

*

Kurskaya railway station swirled around her like a dirty tide. She listened to trains chugging and screeching. *The number five train from Evpatoria will arrive on Platform N2*, a mechanical voice announced. Ella glanced at the clock above the constantly changing timetable. Roman's train must be running late.

After she'd hung up with him, she called her great-aunt. 'Bring him here tonight,' Henrietta had insisted. 'I need to know the details of the scheme he concocted. And you've been a fool to go along with it.'

Someone tugged at her sleeve. Ella glanced down and smiled despite her woes. The black shiny eyes of a barefoot boy looked at her adoringly. His sticky little hand found hers. She crouched in front of him, her handbag tucked under her arm.

'What's your name?'

The boy didn't answer. He sucked a piece of dry rusk and clasped her fingers. His hand felt warm. A skirt, bright and splashed with mud, appeared next to the child. Ella stood.

The boy's mother, or perhaps his sister, grabbed her other hand, the one that clutched her handbag. 'I'll tell your fortune.'

Ella jerked her arm back. 'Thank you. I'm in a hurry.'

The girl wouldn't let go and Ella skimmed the station to check if anyone was watching them. A flock of women, five or six, all in colourful skirts, one holding a baby, whispered a couple of steps away. Her gut lurched. She smiled at the young woman, who held on to her hand and mumbled something about money and love.

'Fire!' Ella yelled.

The women ceased whispering; a few passers-by stopped and stared.

'Fire!' She flushed at the confused glances she received, but her hands came free, the boy wandered off and his mother melted into the crowd. And although she didn't forgive Roman, her anger at him lessened somehow. Those women, Roman, everyone – they all were doing what they thought necessary to survive and to earn a living.

Train number one from Kursk will arrive on Platform N7, the voice from the speakers jolted her back to the matter at hand. That was Roman's train.

*

The squeaky staircase of the old merchant's house at Petrovka Street led them to her great-aunt's flat on the third floor. Henrietta's choice of neighbourhood had been a strange one for a lawyer who had friends in the criminal world. The adjacent address at Petrovka 38 housed Russia's Central Investigation Bureau. Whether that made Henrietta's clients feel safer or more threatened, Ella didn't know.

She knocked on her great-aunt's door, upholstered in black leather, and caught her breath. Roman stood behind her, and she felt the heat of his anger. An impulse arose to say something harsh, but she had to get him onside. Henrietta's cunning might be the only barricade to stop his arrest.

'Rom, try to be charming.' She listened to footsteps approaching and realised they belonged to Masha, a kind and silent Georgian woman who'd been Henrietta's partner since well before Ella's birth. 'And don't be surprised.'

Masha threw the door open and hugged her hard. Ella heard the familiar squeal of Henrietta's wheelchair and smiled despite herself. She'd been spoiled in this home.

Henrietta rolled towards the door. '*Nu, Nu.* Let me see her.'

Ella leaned over to kiss her great-aunt's cheek, which was dry as parchment, while Masha took Roman's coat and ushered him into the entrance hall lined with bookshelves. The apartment smelled of tobacco and coffee that Masha brewed in a Turkish *cezve*.

'Come here, good looking.' Henrietta stared at Roman. 'Let me have a peek. I've heard of you and your antics.'

Ella went red. She should've brought him to visit, but hadn't found the time. 'This is Roman, my husband. My father's aunt, Henrietta.'

Henrietta glared. Her black eyes searched Roman's features. He bent forward to kiss her bird-like hand. She winked at Ella over his head.

'To the kitchen,' she ordered, and made a U-turn. 'Masha, make them coffee. It's not often my grandniece spoils us with her visits, let alone brings us her beau.'

The glass and steel kitchen gleamed, metallic lampshades dangled from the ceiling like props in a foreign movie. Masha stood at the stove making coffee, while Roman perched on a barstool. Henrietta pulled out a pack of her strong filterless cigarettes. She lit one and Roman crinkled his nose but remained silent.

'Tell me everything.' Henrietta manoeuvred her wheelchair closer to him and pushed the footplate into his shins.

Roman waved away the smoke. 'What's there to say?'

On the stool beside him, Ella put her hand on his forearm and prayed he had enough brains to behave with respect and to beg Henrietta for help.

'What did they ask you?' Henrietta squinted at him. 'What did you tell them?'

Roman shifted his legs away from Henrietta's wheelchair.

'I bought those jeans at a good price and there is this market in Tula. You know the one. So I went there. Yesterday.'

Henrietta nodded. The tip of her cigarette glowed.

'I hoped to make us some money,' Roman continued. 'We're planning to leave. Has Ella told you?'

Henrietta drew back on her cigarette and kept her gaze on Roman. Ella looked at Masha's back and then at the tiled floor. She'd never questioned Masha's loyalty, but now she realised she hardly knew anything about the woman, who appeared one day by Henrietta's side and stayed for good.

The last few weeks had passed so fast, and so many things had changed that she'd forgotten of Henrietta's existence until she needed her help. She recalled her mother calling her selfish when she refused to come over and talk babies.

Roman muttered a word under his breath. 'They came straight to me just as I set up to trade and took all the jeans. I tried to argue, but they told me, "Let go of the jeans or come with us."' From his shirt pocket he pulled out a handwritten note and showed it to Henrietta. 'They gave me the receipt.'

Henrietta turned her squeaking chair towards Ella, hunched on her stool next to Roman. 'And where were you when he was at the markets?'

At the stove, Masha stopped making coffee. She peered at Ella over her shoulder, her forehead lined.

'My parents' place.' Ella's cheeks felt hot. She shouldn't have let him go.

'Thank god.' Henrietta exhaled the smoke from the corner of her mouth. 'One less idiot to defend.'

Roman bowed his head and stroked his beard.

Masha served them tiny cups of coffee, black as tar, with transparent slices of lemon. Ella took her coffee and walked with Masha to the stove, from where she observed Henrietta and Roman. She thought of her ring, and the sense of betrayal made her coffee taste even more acrid than it was.

Her great-aunt held her cup beneath her nose and inhaled the scent. 'I'll tell you what you should say, Roman. You must learn this by heart, understand?'

Roman nodded his lowered head.

'You bought those jeans for your friends. How many pairs?' Henrietta raised her eyebrows at Ella. 'Do you have friends?'

'We do.' Ella thought she could ask Vlad and Raya and maybe even Roman's old friend Ilya to testify, if needed. Masha put her arm around Ella.

Henrietta swirled her coffee in the cup. 'The jeans you bought were for your friends, but they didn't suit them. Wrong size, wrong style – sort it out yourself. Just make sure they know the details. They asked you to return their money, *da?*'

Roman nodded again and Henrietta downed her coffee. 'You've been foolish.' Roman winced as if she'd slapped him. 'You went to the market today to sell the jeans in order to give them back their money.' She turned her head to Ella. 'That isn't a crime. The crime is to buy goods with intent to sell for a profit. No intent, no case.'

'Thank you.' Ella went to hug her, but Henrietta wheeled her chair to the side. Roman rubbed his eyes. He probably wasn't convinced but he didn't argue.

Henrietta looked Ella up and down. 'Go with him. Cry. Tell them you're pregnant.'

Ella exchanged a glance with Masha. She wondered how she had guessed. Henrietta put her cup down on the counter.

'Call me from Tula. I need the names of the detectives in charge. They might like presents.'

16

Ella stared at the pale green form.

Detective Suvorova had handed it to her five minutes after they'd entered Tula's *militzia* station and this cell-like office. She hadn't offered that Ella and Roman could take off their coats, and Ella now perspired in hers even with the buttons undone. Henrietta's instructions, so clear to her yesterday in her great-aunt's kitchen, had begun to blur. Ella forgot what size jeans Raya wore and what style Ilya might have asked for. He wouldn't ask for the flared ones, she was sure.

Seated beside her in front of the detective's desk, Roman scribbled on his own pale green form. Ella was meant to be writing her statement too but she looked out the window instead. The day was unusually sunny for February and a fly hit the windowpane with suicidal persistence.

Ella bent down over the desk and wished she could hide from Suvorova's unblinking stare.

She glanced up. The uniformed detective was short and stout, with a beet-red face. Her head attached to her shoulders without the hint of a neck.

Suvorova stepped out from behind her desk. 'Citizen Abramova, do you need some help?'

She stood over Ella, so that her odour of pickled cabbage and leather lingered in the air. Her lips were stretched in a smile.

Ella shook her head and faked a smile back. She had no idea whether the detective would believe their lies and return the jeans, or if she would drop the charges and keep the jeans, or – the worst possibility – lay charges and keep the jeans. It was hard to predict. Still, to have any chance of success their statements had to match.

The detective fixed her eyes on Roman. She walked back behind her desk and Ella noticed dark circles of sweat under her arms.

Red in the face, Roman stopped scribbling. 'I'm almost done.'

Ella finished writing and held out the pale green form to Suvorova while Roman re-read his statement.

'Finished?' The detective snatched Roman's testimony from across the desk. She read it and rocked back and forth in her chair. Ella placed her statement on the edge of the desk, but Suvorova ignored her.

'We'll do it this way,' she said to Roman. She took out a fresh form from her desk drawer. 'You'll write it again. This time – the truth. And I'll let you both go.'

Ella eyed Suvorova and attempted to figure out what she wanted. Roman couldn't change his story now, so what was the point of her game – to catch him out on details?

Suvorova walked behind Roman and read over his shoulder. She brought her mouth close to his ear. 'Why are you lying?' she barked. 'Do you think we are fools?'

Roman flinched and stopped writing. Ella couldn't control her shaking knees. Suvorova wandered back to her desk and glanced at the portrait of Andropov before she sat in her chair.

'Write this,' the detective said. 'You bought those jeans to make money. It was a mistake. You've been under pressure. Your wife is expecting a child. You haven't made any sales and don't have a criminal record.' She leaned forward. 'The crime committed is a minor offence. You'll get probation and won't go to jail. Understand?'

Ella's head throbbed. Beside her, Roman bit his pen and his eyes glazed over. She hoped he wouldn't oblige.

'Would you like water, Citizen Abramova?' Suvorova gestured at a dusty decanter on her desk.

Ella pursed her dry lips. The detective poured herself a glass and drank it.

Roman held out the second form to the detective. He'd barely written a word. 'I bought those jeans for my friends and I didn't make any profit. This whole thing is a mistake.'

Ella blinked at Roman. The detective grabbed Ella's statement and skimmed it.

'You came prepared.' She read from the page: 'The friends who gave Roman the money: Raya Lekhtman, Ilya Bezsmertniy and Vladimir Zacharov.' She glared at Roman. 'I'm going to arrest you today. Destroy your kikes' nest.'

She pressed a button on her desk. A young *militziaman* in an oversized uniform appeared at the door. Suvorova didn't look up from Ella's statement. 'Take him. Lock him up in a cell. I'll do the paperwork.'

Roman's mouth opened, his cheeks, flushed pink only seconds ago, turned white. He stood and crushed his fur hat in his hands. Ella locked onto his eyes and begged him for a sign of what she was supposed to do. She should probably wail and beg Suvorova not to charge her husband, but she didn't move from her chair.

The *militziaman* grabbed Roman's elbow and led him out.

The detective studied Ella's face. 'You sure you don't want that drink?' She dug out a leather-bound volume from the depths of her desk. 'Article 302-bis of the Criminal Code of the Russian Soviet Federal Socialist Republic states that a penalty of up to five years in jail may be imposed.'

'For what?' Ella heard herself ask.

Suvorova scowled at her. 'If you were involved in the purchase, and I think it was your idea, you'll be charged as an accomplice.' Ella watched the detective's hands, stroking the leather of the Criminal Code as if it were a pet. 'But if you cooperate, I will let Roman out today. With your goods worth under a thousand roubles, a judge may consider a non-custodial sentence.'

'What do you want me to do? Lie?'

The officer picked up Ella's completed form with her fingertips. 'If you persist with this nonsense, Roman stays in the lock-up. He'll go to trial and serve a full sentence. You decide.'

Ella felt the floor sway. She put her hand to her brow. 'I don't understand you.'

Suvorova sighed. 'It's hot. You should take off your coat.'

Ella ignored her and sat up straighter. Her blouse was pasted to her back under the jumper and the wire edge of her bra cut into her skin. The detective frowned at her stomach.

'You said you're pregnant. How far?'

'Three and half months.'

Suvorova kneeled at the safe next to her desk and produced Roman's sports bag. She unzipped it and the jeans, packed in transparent plastic, spilled out. They had the value of her grandmother's ring – Olga's ring. A shiver of hatred for Roman passed through Ella.

'Which jeans were meant to be yours?' Suvorova asked. 'What size?'

'Twenty-nine.'

The detective thrust a pair of jeans in their plastic into her hands. 'Have you tried them on?'

'Of course.' Ella inspected the stitching on the jeans. When Roman had offered to show her, she'd refused to look let alone try them on.

'Were they too small?'

'They were all right.'

'Why didn't you keep them, if they were the right size?'

The detective leaned against the desk beside her. Ella lifted the plastic-wrapped jeans to her face and pretended to take a closer look.

'They were too expensive. And I might get wide in the hips.'

The detective folded her arms. 'Try them on.'

Ella dropped the packed jeans into her lap. 'I can't. I have woollen tights on.' She hiked up her skirt to show her thick winter tights and knee-high boots.

'And what size does Roman wear?' Suvorova took back the jeans and returned them to the sports bag. 'Has he tried his pair? When did he buy them?'

Ella's palms were sweaty. 'A month ago.'

'And your friends tried on their jeans and, as you say, they were either the wrong size or style?'

Suvorova crouched and sifted through the jeans in the bag. Ella realised what she was doing – she intended to match the jeans to their purchasers. A tiny hope that Henrietta's ploy might work stirred inside her.

'I told Roman not to take their money, but he didn't listen.'

'This is an amazing case.' The detective packed the plastic-wrapped jeans into the bag. 'You all tried on these jeans, yet the packs look untouched.'

Ella swallowed. 'We resealed them.'

Suvorova tilted her head at Ella and zipped up the sports bag. She rose to her feet. 'So, you are Roman's accomplice. You'll raise your child in a camp.'

Ella blinked hard to keep her tears from falling. Suvorova slumped into the chair under the portrait and drummed her fingers on the Criminal Code. She took a white form out from her desk drawer and started writing.

'You'll give birth in jail,' she said.

Andropov's face above the detective's head twisted and Ella felt herself slide off the chair onto the linoleum floor.

17

She stalled at the open doors of the courtroom in Tula.

Pinned to the timber door panel, a typed note read: 'State v Abramov'. Ella rubbed a tiny crease that had appeared between her eyebrows in the last two weeks since Roman's arrest. If he was sentenced, she too would be jailed, stuck in the USSR with a child and no career. She scolded herself for being too pessimistic. Not all had been lost yet.

With Roman in jail, she'd organised for Raya and Ilya to be coached as witnesses by Henrietta. Vlad had argued he shouldn't be asked to testify with the KGB trailing him, even though Roman's case had nothing to do with politics. Still, Henrietta thought he had a point.

She stepped inside the dusty courtroom that resembled a church hall with its pews. A few older women sat at the front. One of them was knitting a scarf, pulling a dark woollen thread from a grocery bag onto her knees. A group of men, also elderly, sat at the back; some wore sheepskin coats over their shabby suits with medals on the lapels.

Ella perched at the end of the second row and stared at the judge's bench and three high-back chairs. The central one looked like a throne and bore Russia's coat of arms. On one side was a timber barrier, behind which the accused would be placed.

She leaned back on the hard bench and watched the courtroom doors, expecting Ilya and Raya to enter at any moment.

Roman's advocate, Feldman, popped his head in. Ella attempted a nod and a smile. A local lawyer, he'd been chosen by Henrietta and motivated by the fee Roman's mother had paid him. He'd advised Ella that she would be called as the first witness. She knew her lines.

Ilya walked in dressed in a suit jacket. Ella had only ever seen him in his filmmaker's leather one and thought he looked smart. She lifted her hand to wave at him and he replied with a wink, causing her heart to race.

Two KGB men in grey suits that looked like uniforms hurried in after Ilya and the doors of the courtroom closed.

A young man wearing glasses – a court officer of some sort – strode onto the podium. 'All rise for the State Court,' he announced. Ella rose along with everyone else. 'Judge Gusev and the people's jury: Citizens Ivanova and Sidorov.'

From an undersized door behind the bench, Judge Gusev limped to his chair. In his dark brown suit, his chest decorated with medals, he looked like a factory worker. Ella knew the type: an old Bolshevik, World War II veteran and likely Stalin supporter. Gusev was followed by a middle-aged man and a woman wearing a navy skirt-suit with her hair in a bun. The two people's jurors sat either side of the judge.

'The accused: Roman Abramov,' the court officer stated.

The door opened again and two armed *militziamen* led Roman inside. Ella watched her husband trip at the threshold and she felt, for the first time that morning, crushed by the State.

Shuffling onto the stage, Roman kept his eyes down. They'd shaved his head and face and he looked like a withered child. The absence of his beard revealed Roman's prominent nose and weak chin. What she felt was more like anger fused with pity, not love.

Flanked by the *militziamen*, Roman took a seat behind the timber barrier and didn't raise his head.

'The advocate Feldman and the State prosecutor Kukushkin,' the court officer announced.

A gangly man, presumably Kukushkin, entered the courtroom. Alongside him walked Feldman, dressed in a black suit stretched tight over his stomach. Ella realised that everyone else was seated, but she didn't recall being asked to sit. She scanned the courtroom and tears pricked her eyes. Raya had still not shown up or she'd been locked out.

She turned to the front of the court. Feldman was looking at her and she understood that she'd been called as a witness.

*

Once she was on the stand, the courtroom looked larger. She felt everyone's gaze fixed on her. This was a different kind of show though. The ceiling lights shone too brightly and her moist eyes dragged everything out of focus.

'Swear to tell the truth and only the truth,' the court officer said.

'I swear.' In her head, Ella recited the lines Henrietta had given her.

Feldman approached. 'Please state your name, your relationship to the accused, and how you were involved in the purchase or resale of the American jeans.'

She heard the collective intake of breath and loud whispers. Blue jeans – everyone's object of desire – were unattainable except on the black market.

Ella exhaled, said her name and declared she was Roman's wife. She turned to the judge. 'One pair was for me, but I am pregnant. I got wider in the hips.'

Someone in the audience snorted.

In the first pew, the knitting woman glanced up at her with a half-nod. Ella looked back at Judge Gusev, who yawned and covered his mouth. Beside him, Sidorov shifted in his creaky chair.

Kukushkin approached her. 'Where were you when your husband purchased the jeans and how did he purchase them?'

'He bought them at the market in Tula. I wasn't there.'

Kukushkin sighed and Ella felt a jolt in her chest like when she'd given a good performance. The judge measured her with a long look.

'The witness is dismissed.'

She returned to her seat and tried to meet Roman's gaze. He stared, but his eyes were unfocused and she wasn't sure that he saw her. They'd hurt him in the prison, she thought, and felt sick.

The court officer checked his papers. 'Witness Bezsmertniy, Ilya Pavlovich.'

Ella peeked at the closed doors. Raya would be called as a witness next, but Ella knew she wouldn't turn up now.

Tall and slightly stooped, Ilya walked to the stage. His wavy black hair, perhaps too long for a man, sported a few silver strands. She'd met his wife Marina twice now and thought them mismatched.

Feldman clasped his hands behind his back. 'Please tell the court when you met the accused and what you know about him buying the jeans.'

'I've known Roman for years.' Ilya brushed his hair back. His voice sounded smooth and assured. 'We served in the army together. I asked him to buy me a pair when he went to the market last month, and I gave him the money, but the jeans didn't fit.'

Ella saw Ivanova, the female juror, blush and touch her earring. The judge's mouth softened when Ilya mentioned the army. The tension in Ella's neck muscles eased slightly and she prayed to hear Raya's footsteps rush into the courtroom.

But all she heard was Kukushkin, pacing back and forth in front of Ilya. 'Why didn't you take the jeans, if he went to so much trouble to buy and bring them to you?' He smirked at the audience. 'You let your friend down. Not nice.'

Ella's back ached and she sat sideways on the bench without taking her eyes of Ilya. He was addressing the judge.

'Roman tried to pay me back, but as a fellow army man I refused to take his money. I knew he had recently married. I should have taken the jeans.'

'No more questions,' the judge said.

Ilya stepped off the witness stand.

The KGB men in grey suits followed him down the aisle. Both had short haircuts and forgettable faces. There were no sounds in the courtroom apart from the clicking of the men's heels. In front of Ella, a woman crossed herself discreetly.

Ella watched Feldman, who seemed to shrink in his suit.

Judge Gusev looked at Ivanova, who bowed her head and twisted a ring on her finger. He looked at Sidorov, who removed his glasses and began to polish them. The KGB men turned their heads and eyeballed the judge.

'State prosecution.'

*

Roman lowered his head and Ella put her fist on her heart.

'I'm asking the court,' Kukushkin said, 'to sentence Roman Abramov to five years in prison, under Articles 302 and 302-bis of the Criminal Code of the Russian Soviet Federative Socialist Republic for the purchase of goods with intent to resell for profit and an attempt to resell.'

The elderly people in the audience all applauded. Even the woman who'd crossed herself clapped. Ella unclenched her fist. Half-rising, she caught Feldman's eye. What she'd heard was inhumane – their lawyer should have objected. But Feldman covered his mouth and pretended to cough. She promptly sat back down.

Kukushkin's face was blotchy as he approached the judge and jurors. 'Our Soviet trousers were not good enough for Abramov and his kind. These people need American pants. Where did the money come from?' he finished.

'The defence,' the court officer said.

Feldman found a spot above Roman's lowered head. 'Look at this man,' he said. 'Roman Abramov has done the wrong thing. He attempted to sell American jeans for a profit.'

Around her people shuffled and whispered. She wanted to jump and yell that this was outrageous, but remained seated.

'Abramov got lucky,' Feldman continued. 'Our valorous *militzia* stopped him from committing a crime. He didn't sell the jeans and has made no profit.' Feldman looked at Judge Gusev. 'It is his first offence and his wife is expecting. I ask the court for two years.' He wiped his forehead. 'On conditional bail.'

Roman looked up. The colour returned to his cheeks and he started to cry. No one in the courtroom moved. Ella saw the judge whisper to Ivanova and Sidorov. They all nodded in agreement.

Judge Gusev rose to his feet. 'Following Communist Party directions to clear our society of capitalist rot, the court sentences Roman Abramov to two years of labour camp to be served at Tula Arms Plant.'

Again, the elderly people in the courtroom applauded.

The *militziamen* yanked Roman up by his elbows. Ella leaped from her seat and tried to make her way to him. The knitting woman grabbed the hem of her coat.

'Sit down, you idiot,' she whispered, 'or they'll take you as well.'

Ella watched the guards twist Roman's arms into the handcuffs behind his back as he was hauled away.

'He'll be back soon,' the knitter said. 'It's not ten years in Siberia.'

18

Ella planned to pack a few things Roman might need in the camp: sweaters and pants he could wear to work, a woollen hat to replace his fur one in case it got stolen, a scarf and a pair of gloves. But she hadn't moved much since the morning and she hadn't switched on the lights.

In fact, in the few days since the trial, she had done hardly a thing from her list to bring about Roman's early release. She'd just put on her bathrobe and shuffled, unwashed, through the flat she and Roman were meant to share. Or she slept, curled up in a ball on the living room sofa. Or she sat on her bed not touching his clothes.

It wasn't that she missed Roman, but she wished for her life before she'd met him. And now that he was imprisoned, she was punished as well – by many more years in Russia. She kicked the lid of his suitcase closed. Henrietta was right. She'd married a fool and would have to carry her sentence and help him to bear his too, perhaps by moving to Tula. The bedroom grew darker, lit only by the glow of streetlights.

Ella rubbed her eyes with her fists. It was hard to acknowledge that the guilt had been hers as much as it was Roman's. Had she been so naive as to goad him into marriage in a hope that they would grow closer over time, or had her scheming backfired? She didn't stop him when he shared his plans. Her own dream of escape made her complacent. An image of Roman's shaved head and bare face loomed in her mind and made her ashamed of her thoughts.

She sighed and wondered fleetingly about the wives of the Decembrists. They'd exchanged their privileged lives for those of peasants to be near the men they loved. She couldn't imagine sacrificing her life like those women. It wasn't as if Roman had opposed the Tzar or been exiled to Siberia.

Besides, she'd known, in the depths of her soul, that she wasn't in love with Roman. Still, if she harboured hopes of leaving the country one day, she had to be a good wife and fight for his freedom.

The kettle whistled in the kitchen and startled her; she had no memory of putting it on. It was dark now. The snow slush pelted the window. She clicked on the light switch and gazed at the cardboard boxes propped against the bedroom wall. They had never unpacked. Perhaps she could sleep in this room and rent out the other. It would buy her some time and provide money for food. She didn't want to lean on Roman's parents.

The phone buzzed and she waited for it to stop. It was possibly Lia. Her mother-in-law had offered her help but implied that Ella was somehow to blame for Roman's fate. She'd probably spoken to Feldman, who had observed the KGB presence in the courtroom, which was most likely caused by her connection to Vlad. Lia had a point, and it made accepting the Abramovs' help even more problematic.

Ella turned off the gas under the kettle and peered into the empty fridge. The ringing started again. She walked to the sofa where she'd slept the last few nights, avoiding her marital bed, and picked up the receiver.

'We want to come over,' Lia said. 'I packed some tinned food for Roman and I got vodka too. And sausage. You could take it with you when you go to visit the camp. Have you sorted his clothes yet?'

'Not quite.' Ella slid off the sofa to sit on the floor. She leaned onto the armrest and closed her eyes to the snowy night outside and the unlived-in flat, but there was no way to escape her mother-in-law's voice and her instructions.

'Have you eaten? You must look after the baby.'

Ella lifted herself off the floor and stood over the handset.

'We'll bring the food parcel and help you to the train. Make sure you pack the ski pants and gloves.' Lia trailed off and Ella could hear her crying.

'Sorry Lia, I need to go. I'll do it all.'

*

Ella lowered herself onto the mattress and picked up a pair of Roman's old wool-fleece pants. These ones were good. He'd hardly worn them and they were sturdy. She was folding them up when she felt something stiffer than fabric in the lined pocket. An envelope, folded in half, was wedged inside. Ella exhaled and eased it out. It was addressed to her husband at his parents' flat in a neat female hand. She took out the letter and a sentence instantly caught her eye.

When you called me your wife in that hotel, it felt real.

She drew a sharp breath. What did the woman mean by calling herself his 'wife'? Ella turned the page over and searched for a name.

Your Marina, the letter was signed.

She stood and walked to the window. The snow had stopped, but she couldn't see past her own reflection. Ella lifted the letter closer to her face and skimmed it from the top.

It was addressed *My beloved,* and for a moment she entertained a thought that it wasn't directed at Roman. Her glance slid down the page and it tripped on the familiar name

'Romochka' midway down the page. Her hands twisted the paper. The letters blurred.

Tears formed in Ella's eyes and she struggled to make out the words. Perhaps it was something from a time before she'd met Roman. She strode to the bed and picked up the envelope. It was dated December 1982, less than three months ago. So he knew.

Roman had slept with both of them, it seemed, while she was still deciding whether to have the baby. That explained his reluctance to keep the child and to get married, but there was no reason why he had succumbed to her pressure or that of his parents.

She began reading again. *My life with Ilya and your plans to leave Russia are the mistakes that will break us apart. They will destroy us.*

Ella dropped the letter and it floated to the floor. Ilya's wife, she realised. Marina.

She doubled over beside the bed and felt like wailing. Ilya wouldn't have been Roman's witness at the trial if he'd known of the affair. Had it been going on for years? She recalled the photograph on the bookshelf in Roman's old room. It showed him and Ilya with Marina, tall and blonde, between them, holding skis and squinting from the snow and the sun. Then she remembered that they had a child, a boy who lived with Marina's mother.

Straightening up, she laid her palm on her stomach. She wanted to hit something hard, but instead curled up to lie on her side and shut her eyes surrounded by Roman's jumpers and scarves.

*

'Ilya. Sorry to bother you.' Ella was taking deep breaths to steady her voice as her fingers gripped the receiver. The decision to call him had come after she grew tired of crying, but now she almost hung up.

'How are you?' Ilya didn't sound surprised. 'When are you going to Tula? We could help you with food. Marina has some connections.'

Marina. Ella took hold of the telephone cord. The desire to ask Ilya if he knew of his wife's affair was strong, but the shame of her own knowledge kept her silent on the matter. 'I might not need to go.'

'Why? Are you unwell? Is Lia going?'

She opened her mouth and suddenly sobbed, staring at the unpacked boxes.

'Ella?'

She couldn't manage a word.

'Do you want me to come over? I could bring something to eat. Have you had supper?'

He sounded so concerned she wanted to vomit. She released the phone cord.

'Marina went to her mother's and I'm alone.' He cleared his throat.

'I'll cook. Bring some wine,' she said.

It delayed her having to share her news and she questioned the need to share it at all.

'Are you allowed?' he asked.

She held back her sobs.

'I'll get it, don't worry. Give me the address.'

Ella did so, while wishing she hadn't. Sharing would only make it more real, she thought, and began to sob once more.

19

Across the kitchen table, Ilya was saying something. Ella's head was blissfully blank and she watched his lips move, revealing his even white teeth. His bottom lip was fuller than the top one and glimmered slightly under the lights.

Marina's letter, folded in half, fitted snug in the pocket of her cardigan, but Ilya's face and dark eyes had been full of such an earnest desire to help her that she hadn't quite managed to deliver the ugly news.

Now, tipsy after sharing the bottle of Georgian wine he'd brought, she just watched him talk, mesmerised by his fingers that danced in the air between them.

She picked up her wineglass and turned it upside down.

Ilya smiled at her. 'You shouldn't be drinking.'

He eased the glass from her grip. She studied his hands. They were large but fine-boned, more suited to a violinist than a filmmaker. He put the glass down and the fog in her head receded. She rose to her feet and turned on the hot water in the sink to do the washing up. Her back was to Ilya. They'd always flirted a little before Roman's arrest, but now Ella felt awkward.

'I don't want to go to Tula,' she said. 'Let Lia visit her son and bring him his clothes.'

She picked up a plate from the slippery pile in the sink and watched the water splash off its surface. Ilya came and stood next to her. She thrust the wet plate into his hands and he dried it with a tea towel.

'I think he's waiting for you to visit. They'll let you see him.'

Ella stared at her hands submerged in soapy water. She couldn't bear even the thought of facing Roman. Yet while he was locked up in Tula, she couldn't leave Russia and their child inside her would grow.

She handed Ilya another plate to dry. 'Why doesn't your son live with you and Marina?'

'It's better for him to stay with his grandmother – country air, fresh food. I'm often away on location and Marina works full-time.'

Ella turned off the tap. 'Have you been together long?'

'Seven years.'

'Do you love her?'

She felt the colour leave her cheeks. Ilya bowed his head. He passed her the plate and tea towel. She dried her hands and he turned as if he was going to leave.

'I'll make us fresh tea.' She put on the kettle to boil before he had a chance to object.

Ilya sat back down. Ella tore at a foil-packed tea cube and examined the yellow label. Ceylon tea smelled exotic. It'd come from Marina's precious stockpile, she mused as she poured the boiling water into the teapot.

When the tea had brewed, she sat down across the table from him and filled their cups. 'What's your next documentary about?'

'I shouldn't be telling you this, but I leave in two weeks to film the camps.'

Ella blew at her tea. She'd only ever heard of people being sent to the camps to do time, not to work and get paid. A recollection of noble Decembrists' wives whirled again in her mind. Then she wondered what Marina would do with Ilya away and Roman in a labour camp in Tula.

'You've got a permit to shoot there?'

'I signed up to forget what I see.' Ilya rubbed his chin as if to check how well he'd shaved. 'You know, I met this lieutenant. He's in charge of the script and I think he could help us with Roman.'

The word 'us' made her feel queasy, or maybe it was the wine. She leaned forward over the kitchen table and touched the letter in her cardigan pocket.

Ilya's eyes sparkled. 'I can't tell you the details, but the film is about inmates who've been reformed in the camps, a fairytale to brainwash new recruits, or more likely some human rights body. You know, like one was a thief, but studied while serving his time and became a pianist.'

Ella half-smiled at his joke and gazed again at his fingers. Her hand crumpled the letter. Across the table, she could smell his breath, sweet and spicy like Kindzmarauli wine.

He grinned. 'I thought I might extend my research into the labour camp in Tula. What do you think?'

'I have something to tell you.'

Ella averted her gaze. He wanted to help the man who'd slept with his wife. She felt sorry for both of them, but at least Ilya had his job. She had nothing left but her baby.

'You probably heard this from Roman.' She flushed. 'We planned to leave Russia for good. The Abramovs applied and I was about to join them. But with Roman locked up, I can't.'

He finished his tea in one long gulp. 'You could ask Roman to sign a consent for you to proceed as his wife. I'm sure that won't be a problem, if his parents agree. Then you will all have a chance.' He got up. 'Sorry, El, but I have to go.'

She felt heat reach her cheeks. Her lip quivered. 'Please don't go, Ilya. I'll make you a bed on the sofa. You're home alone anyway.' She stood and he fixed her with a strange look. She knew she sounded weird and he might think her drunk but she couldn't help herself. 'I need your advice and it's well after midnight. The metro is probably closed.'

'I need to go. I'll call you tomorrow morning.' He didn't hug her and stepped to bypass her at the kitchen door.

'Ilya. Wait.' She blocked his way. Her heart faltered and she reached into her pocket. She could see in his eyes that she looked mad. But she thrust the letter towards him. 'Read this.'

He leaned against the doorjamb. Ella moved to the side and watched his profile as he started reading the letter. His face collapsed and he slid to the floor. His long legs stretched across the kitchen doorway, his feet almost reached her toes.

She lowered herself to her haunches. 'You didn't know?'

He shook his head and handed the letter back to her. Then he stood up, walked into the unlit living room and lay down on the sofa.

*

In her bedroom, Ella wrestled with her blankets. Ilya's presence next door made her get up and lie down again, take off her bedcovers and turn over the pillows. She jumped from her bed and peered out the window, hoping that might settle her. But the night was moonless and starless, as dense as black theatre curtains. Under her nightdress her skin tingled while her feet and hands felt icy.

She imagined Ilya like he was only an hour ago, with his dancing fingers and flushed cheeks. His wife didn't love him.

Ella tiptoed to the door and pressed her ear to it. Silence. Would it be so terrible if she lay next to Ilya on the sofa and asked him to hold her? Her yearning was so fierce that she couldn't decide whether it was warmth or comfort she sought.

She had never felt this needy before, but maybe it was her hormones that made her so unsettled, or the fear of being left to fight on her own. Ella wondered if it mattered. Sick with worry, she stood on the threshold of her living room.

The sofa creaked. Ilya stirred in the darkness. She felt a sheen of sweat on her neck underneath her hair and took a few steps towards him. He didn't seem to be awake. Ella felt ready to turn and run, but a part of her knew that she wouldn't. There was nothing wrong in wanting some warmth. Besides, what did they owe Roman or Marina now? They both needed consoling.

Ilya slept on his back, half-covered by bed sheets. The blanket she'd given him was bunched up at his feet. Her heartbeat pounded in her throat. She touched his shoulder and he blinked awake.

'I'm freezing,' she said. 'Can I lie next to you?'

For a moment, he didn't respond. Then he shifted onto his side to make space for her and closed his eyes. She shivered again and lay on her back, not touching him at all. He raised his arm from under the covers and draped it over her neck. She kept staring at the ceiling and tried to relax.

'Roman was her first,' Ilya said, 'years ago. I thought it was over.' She turned onto her side to see his face. Ilya's expression was blank and he kept his eyes shut. 'When he left for the army, Marina waited. He returned and just moved on. We were young. Only twenty.'

She sniffed and Ilya bit on his lip. 'Her mother found me,' he went on. 'Roman mentioned my name when he wrote to them from the army. She thought I could change his mind. Marina was heartbroken. I couldn't leave her like that. We started dating and then she fell pregnant with Yan.'

Ella propped herself up on her elbow. She felt his hipbone dig into her side and shifted away. What he'd told her didn't make sense. He'd known that Marina loved Roman and yet he'd got involved with her anyway. But it felt too intimate to ask him about his love life.

'Why did you stay friends?'

'We didn't. For a long while. Then he turned up years later through poker. They barely spoke to each other. I was sure she hated his guts. I didn't know ...' He trailed off. In the darkness, Ella touched his cheek. He gave a half-smile. 'Let's try to sleep, El. We still have a couple of hours.'

She lay on her back again and listened to his breathing.

20

She heard Anna's footsteps pause on the other side of the door. Leon stirred in his sleep. Ella held her breath and stared into the shadows of her childhood bedroom. Her brother's bed, identical to her own, stood an arm's length away.

It was a week after she'd told Ilya, but she hadn't told her mother of Roman's betrayal when she'd snuck into the family home last night. Anna might have tried to convince her to reconcile with her husband.

Leon's blanket slid to the floor, revealing his slender neck and protruding collarbones. Ella bent forward and pulled the covers back up to his chin. She couldn't envisage salvation coming from her family. They believed she'd be better off in the Soviet Union. Perhaps protecting their own livelihood. Both her cheating husband and she, Ella, had been labelled non-loyal, a step away from a traitor or a deserter.

But she had decided. She could not stay Roman's wife. She ignored a pang of conscience when she thought of Ilya. However, nothing had happened between them.

She tiptoed over to the window and peered through the curtains. On this late February morning, the darkness was barely broken by a weak dawn. Ella patted her stomach – a soft swell of flesh still contained under her ribcage. She felt weepy, but that seemed counterproductive if she wanted her father to listen. He needed to let her go. She wanted his blessing even if he wouldn't sign the permission forms.

Outside, it turned grey. She gazed at the courtyard bordered by the high-rises and the snow-encrusted playground. She and Leon had grown up playing there. She pictured a child, her child, sleeping in a pram under the puny trees. Then she drew the curtains shut.

The lock on the entrance door clicked. It interrupted her thoughts but improved her mood. Her mother must have left for work. At least now she had a chance to talk to her father. She slipped out of the bedroom, careful not to wake Leon. Her baby brother's presence would complicate matters.

*

Gregory stood by the open fridge, dressed in his army pants and a white singlet. 'I saw your coat in the hallway.' He smiled and offered his freshly shaved cheek for her to kiss. An omelette sizzled on the stove. Ella's stomach lurched. At four months, she'd thought her days of morning sickness would be over.

'Get yourself some tea.' Gregory covered the pan with a lid. 'Want some omelette?'

She shook her head. Her father's love of food was the subject of family jokes. Having starved during the war, he loved cooking and insisted on turning any meal into an event. He slid the omelette onto his plate and sat down across from her.

Ella poured herself a strong brew from the teapot. 'I need your help, Papa,' she said. 'I need a job.'

Her father dug into his meal. 'What are you thinking of?'

For a moment Ella was tempted to tell the truth: *I want to split from Roman and get out of the country before my baby is born.* But the stench of eggs made her stomach turn again.

'Teaching acting to kids?' Gregory asked.

Ella grimaced. She regretted starting this exchange. Just as well she'd avoided telling her parents about the KGB appearance at Roman's trial.

'Maybe. I'm also thinking of renting out a room.'

Gregory put aside his fork and stopped chewing. 'I'm glad you're having the baby. My mother was not even twenty when she had me in 1929. There were six of them living in two rooms, but that didn't stop her having a career.'

Ella got up and turned to the stove, with her back to her father. Whenever he spoke about the suffering of the previous generations, she always felt like arguing, *Things were different then.* His Uncle Leo had taken off and left for Australia while Natan and Olga stayed behind. But she knew her grandparents had tried to escape. Leo did send for them but it had been too late. Her newly born father's name hadn't been on their exit papers. Then the borders had closed for good. They'd missed their chance.

'You don't understand, Papa. I'm an actress. And I'm only twenty-one. What will I do with a baby here? Alone? No school or pioneers' club will employ me with my husband – a criminal.' *A traitor*, she thought.

Gregory's eyes narrowed. 'But without Roman … Do you still want to leave? Go to America? Who will help you with the child in the West?'

This wasn't how she'd planned her one-on-one with her father to go. Without disclosing Roman's betrayal and the KGB presence at his trial she was unable to explain her urgency to flee. She swallowed the last of her tea. 'I have to go, Papa. I need to get to Pushkinski Theatre to ask for work – in wardrobe or as an usher.'

That at least was the truth, and she felt better for speaking it. Gregory stood up and hugged her. 'Give it some thought. Talk to Olga. Perhaps it's a sign for you to stay put, with us.'

*

Vlad had said the farewell party was only a short walk away from Belorusskaya metro station, one train stop from her parents' place. Ella decided to walk. After a week of mourning her marriage and nursing her hurt, she'd started to feel at peace with herself.

Anticipation of happiness had bubbled inside her since the night she'd opened up to Ilya, and she hummed as she walked through the black icy air, past the locked-up shops.

Provodi – a bittersweet occasion celebrated by people who'd received an exit permit and were leaving the next day – didn't happen all that often, not since the Moscow Olympics. Most applications were now refused and gatherings like the one she'd chanced on took place in secret. On the émigrés last night, friends and wellwishers came to say goodbye, drink vodka and make calls abroad. The next day when their government-owned apartment was vacated, there would be no one to pay the telephone bill, no matter how enormous.

Despite the frost, she felt warm from her brisk walk. The snow, packed at the kerbsides, glimmered under the moonlight. She even took off her gloves and stuffed them into her pockets. Since the trial and Ilya's visit, she hadn't seen anyone except her family. The tiny mound of her stomach – not visible under the sweater and a narrow woollen skirt that wouldn't fasten anymore – made her feel like an adult in charge of her life.

*

The brutalist Stalin-era apartment block stood on a quiet street behind the metro, as Vlad had explained. When they'd spoken, he hadn't asked about the trial, but he knew the verdict. He hadn't offered to visit her either, but she'd been content not having to talk about Roman.

On the building, a banner flapped in the wind proclaiming the victory of communism. She found the entrance lit by a flickering light and the flat's door was left ajar. She entered the smoky hallway, took off her coat and nodded to people she didn't know. No one asked who she was.

The rooms were unfurnished. People stood in groups or wandered around drinking from assorted cups and glasses. She found a pile of coats on the floor in what must have been the children's bedroom. On faded wallpaper she saw a drawing of a little house with a window and a chimney under the circle of the sun. Ella smiled and patted her stomach.

She removed her coat to reveal her favourite angora jumper with batwing sleeves, then looked around for familiar faces. She had no one to call abroad. Leo and Sonya, somewhere in Melbourne, had not been in contact for more than ten years, having been told by her grandparents to stop writing or sending presents.

A moustached man waved to her and she recognised Boris, one of Roman's poker friends. She nodded to him and looked around for his girlfriend Lena, who studied art and spoke the truth.

Boris moved towards her and Lena appeared by his side. 'Sasha's family is going to Milwaukee,' Boris said. 'They found sponsors. But they are still in Ostia.'

Lena raised her cup. 'We will never see them again. It's like they are going to Mars.' She laughed but it wasn't a happy sound.

Someone offered Ella a tea glass with a splash of red wine and she accepted, sipping the cheap drink as she shuffled between the groups, happy to forget her troubles.

'We applied again,' a woman said. 'I heard they stopped giving visas. We waited for over a year.'

Next to her, two men hugged. She saw women and men kiss each other in greetings and goodbyes, some looked happy, others sad.

'My address book is black from crosses. I cross out those who left us behind. And I am a Jew.'

Everyone laughed and Ella looked behind her to locate the joker.

'Ella.'

A man's arms circled her shoulders. Ilya. He stared at her and beamed. They didn't say anything, and stood facing each other until they both realised and started talking at the same time.

'Is Marina here?' she asked.

Ilya shook his head. 'How are you keeping? Do you know the Kogans? They were Refuseniks, you know? You should touch them for luck.'

She giggled. It was likely the hosts' name. The fortunate ones, who would get on the plane at the Sheremetyevo airport tomorrow morning and leave them behind.

'I came to be with people,' she said and he nodded. 'I'll go soon.'

They walked together to the room with the coats and rummaged through the pile, not looking at each other, until Ilya unearthed his worn leather jacket, scarf and knitted beanie. Like a child, she thought. Then he helped her into her coat and they walked out of the flat.

His lips found hers on the landing.

21

Even though she couldn't see well in the dark of her living room, Ella knew it was morning. She shut her eyes and lay awake on the sofa. Ilya lay next to her, still asleep. His hair half-covered his face and she suppressed the desire to brush it off.

The scent of his body made her feel drunk. Ella wished she could lie here forever. The necessity to resolve things with Roman grew less important than the need to be present at this very moment. It was not so much the physical craving, though it did mess with her head, but the feeling of darkness lifting. Somehow, she wasn't alone anymore.

Ilya sighed and turned on his side. Ella longed to stroke his hair, but touching him could tip her again into a freefall.

Safe in the dark, she stretched out her arm and brushed the skin of Ilya's wrist with her fingertips. Electrical currents shot up to her neck. Her lips parted and she ran her tongue over them.

The room seemed suspended in space, full of pearly light, sleepy warmth, and the throbbing of blood in the parts of her body that touched Ilya. For a brief moment she'd dreamed of falling in love, and then only of falling.

'Are you sleeping?' he asked.

She didn't look at him. 'No.'

He swept aside a strand of her hair. 'Did you sleep well?'

Ella heard a smile in his voice. 'I don't want to wake up.' She hoped he wouldn't laugh at the longing in her tone.

'What are you planning to do?'

She turned to him. His eyes were open and he wasn't smiling. Whether he was questioning her plans to see Roman, or asking about them – him and her – she couldn't tell.

'I'll tell him.'

'What will you tell him?'

He placed his hands beneath his head and gazed at the ceiling. She guessed he understood but didn't want Roman to know.

'That I know about him and Marina.' And about tonight, she wanted to add, but didn't dare. 'If they're in love, let them be together. She can visit him in the camp as his wife. I don't care.' That would free up Ella as well, let her behave on a whim, do what she wanted to do.

Ilya pulled up the blanket to cover them both. 'It isn't that simple.'

She pressed her hands to her outer thighs to still herself. He should feel what she felt – she yearned for him, body and soul, but worried he would consider her flighty.

'Roman is locked away in the camp,' Ilya said. 'He needs any help he can get.' His words were moral, but she wanted to shake him. He sounded pained when he continued. 'If they wanted each other, instead of living a lie they could have arranged it. But they chose to cheat.'

She found his fingers and clasped them. 'They betrayed us.'

Her hip touched his and his warmth seeped into her skin. He slid his arm under her shoulders. 'You told me you want to leave Russia.'

She nodded. 'I do want to leave. But not with Roman.' Her face nestled against his chest. His skin felt cool and warm all at once. He drew her closer. His hair was silk on the pillow next to her cheek. Her desire to talk had vanished as had her thoughts of Roman. Ella pressed herself against Ilya's body and felt the rhythm of his heart.

Her own heart thrashed like a bird in a net. He turned his head and brushed her lips with his. Ella longed to melt from his kiss and forget all her troubles. She realised that she'd never loved before and was swaying on the precipice.

But her reverie was shortlived.

Ilya got up from the sofa and walked away. She felt goosebumps on her side where he had lain only a moment ago. She winced, feeling betrayed once again. He stood by the window with his back to her, staring at the drawn curtains.

'Ilya,' she murmured. 'We cannot be like them. Lying and hiding.'

She climbed out from under the blankets. The room's cold air sobered her. In her thin nightdress, she stopped behind Ilya, her eyes fixed on the hollow between his shoulder blades.

'We don't have to lie,' she said. 'I'll tell Roman the truth.' She pressed herself into his back and wrapped her arms around his waist.

He tensed and she panicked that he would just walk away, get dressed and leave. She'd be left alone in her flat facing only her husband's betrayal and his unpacked clothes.

Ilya twisted around. 'It'll only be a week or so. When I come back from the shoot we will tell them.' He brought his face close to hers and gazed into her eyes. His irises were huge. She saw her reflection in them and drew herself up onto her toes, towards his eyes and his lips. She felt cosy and sweet and ashamed, like she'd never felt before.

*

Ilya loved her.

In the night, her room swayed. Ella lay still, wrapped around his body, her burning cheek on his ribs, trying to calm her breathing. Joy flowed through her lungs, uncoiled her muscles and brought a smile to her lips. When he'd returned from his film shoot he'd rushed to her. He hadn't gone home. After the week they'd spent in her flat before he left for location, and his long-distance calls, they were together again, snug in her bed.

She inhaled Ilya's scent. Whether his wife knew of their love, she couldn't be sure, though she'd rather he told Marina the truth. Still, he'd chosen her and she'd certainly chosen him. She stroked her belly and felt something flutter inside her like butterfly wings. Her heart started pumping in a strange ragged rhythm. *The baby*, she thought. Absorbed by her feelings, she had all but forgotten about it. Now it stirred for the first time.

Ella kept still and waited. If Ilya left her because he couldn't accept Roman's child, she would forgive him, but she couldn't fall out of love. She untangled her legs and freed her body from Ilya's, terrified that he'd probably felt it, this proof of new life.

She didn't expect him to like the situation, but she needed to know whether he could live with the fact that she was carrying another man's child and whether he could love her baby.

Ella traced her finger across his ribs. 'Ilya, it moved.'

His eyes gleamed in the dark, reflecting the moonlight that leaked through the curtains. 'What did?'

'The baby.'

She searched Ilya's face. He didn't frown; his lips stayed relaxed. She placed his hand on her stomach. The baby stirred, gentler this time, and her heart thumped again.

'Do you feel it?'

He rolled onto his side and shifted down to press his ear to her belly. His stubble prickled the soft flesh. She ran her fingers through his hair and he looked up at her. If Ilya loved her, he would accept her like this.

'Do you mind it?'

'Shh, let me listen.'

He kissed the slight swell under her ribcage. 'Don't be scared,' he said, and rested his ear against her stomach once more.

She couldn't see his expression. 'You don't feel repelled?' Inside her the baby fluttered again.

He laughed. 'I can hear it now. Like she knows we're speaking about her.'

'Why do you think it's a girl?'

He shrugged and positioned himself beside her again and she pressed her body to his.

'Let's tell them, Ilya,' she said.

He leaned back on the pillow. 'If I tell Marina, she'll leave Yan at her mother's and make sure I can't visit. I don't see him often enough as it is. He's a wonderful boy – you'd like him.'

'What can we do then?'

Ella rested her palm on her stomach. She imagined her child being taken and she sniffed. After Ilya had accepted her baby she couldn't ask him to abandon his son. Still, if nothing changed she'd lose Ilya in time. Marina wouldn't let go unless her affair with Roman became more than that.

Ella got off the bed. 'I can't lie anymore. Lia thinks I've got the flu. She went to see Roman last week. I can't even make myself call the camp.'

In the moonlight, she could see Ilya's profile. She stood there trembling until he lifted the edge of the blanket. 'Come here.'

She crawled back into the bed and curled up next to him. If he wasn't ready to tell Marina, she must do it herself. The thought of Yan crept into her mind and she pushed it aside. She owed Marina nothing, she told herself. Besides, she loved Ilya more and her baby needed a father. The cheat could have Roman if she still wanted him.

'I'll tell him,' she murmured. If she did that, Marina would soon find out.

Ilya stroked her cheek.

'You can move in here with me,' Ella said.

His fingers slid to her neck, then to her collarbone. She melted under his touch, which made slow progress down to her hipbone. His lips brushed against her ear. 'I'm here and so are you. We are together.'

She let herself float, feeling weak and happy about her weakness.

22

If she was going to confront Roman about his cheating and insist on a divorce, it made sense to face him and not to delay her trip to the camp any longer.

After checking into the Hotel Moskva, Ella dropped the bag of tinned foods and warm clothes onto the bedspread. She rubbed her hands together, numb from dragging the overstuffed duffel across Leninsky Square from Tula's train station.

The cupboard-sized room with its peeling walls smelled of stale smoke and bleach. It didn't matter — she wasn't staying the night. The inmates worked in shifts and could be released from the camp for a day or a few hours when claimed by a wife or a mother with proof of a place to stay in the town. Without a hotel receipt, Roman could not get leave, Lia had said. They'd have to talk in the labour camp hall with other inmates and guards all tuning in.

Ella wrapped two bottles of vodka in her shawl. The camp was a short walk away. It supplied labour for Tula's Arms Plant that produced guns and tractors. It had made samovars too in the days of Peter the Great and tanks under Stalin. She trudged past the grey brick walk-ups and a few naked trees alongside a brown stream of melted snow and mud that bubbled down the kerb. Behind the barbed wire, the barracks — built from the same brick as the walk-ups — looked more like dorms than a prison, except they had guards at the gates.

Hugging her bottles of vodka, Ella crossed the street to the camp. Lia had explained that everything went smoothly after a bribe and she was right. Ella's exchange with the guards was brief. The vodka changed hands and she showed them the receipt from her hotel.

Roman signed out. The gates of the camp closed behind him and he buried his fists in his pockets.

'Have you brought food? I'm sick of the garbage they feed us.' He stomped along beside her.

'I left the bag in the hotel. It was too heavy to carry.'

Roman turned to her. 'You look good enough to eat. Fresh and rosy. Why didn't you come last week?'

'I've been sick.'

He took hold of her elbow and pulled her close. 'Must've missed me.'

She shook herself free of his grip. 'My throat. I may still be infectious.'

Roman looked her up and down. 'My mother told me.'

They walked on past an Orthodox church with its windows boarded up and the cross on the onion dome missing. Ella slowed her pace. A group of men, some holding three-litre glass jars, queued at a beer kiosk.

'I wouldn't mind a beer.' Roman licked his lips. Without his beard, his mouth appeared too plump and wet under his prominent nose.

'You're not allowed.'

The white columns that flanked the hotel entrance looked discordant with the red flag on its roof. Taking Roman inside to her room wasn't an option, not with him in this mood, but they could hardly stand on the street to discuss the divorce. She also still wasn't sure of the best way to handle the conversation, whether to be offended to get him to agree, or be his friend and promise her help and support if he went along with her plans.

Ella turned towards a nearby bus stop. There was no one on the bench under its low timber roof. 'Shall we sit for a minute?'

Roman shook his head. 'Too cold. Let's go to your room.'

The baby kicked and Ella stopped walking. 'I have something to tell you,' she said.

Roman stepped over to the bench. 'Look what I have to smoke – this rubbish.' He drew a crumpled pack of cheap unfiltered cigarettes from his pocket. 'Did you get me my Java?'

'Yes, a full carton. And two kilos of sausage.' She leaned on the damp timber wall of the bus stop.

'Roman, I know it all. About you and Marina.' Her anger was gone, but it still hurt when she said it. 'I found her letter.'

Roman lifted his head and squinted.

'If you love Marina, we should get divorced.' There, she'd said it. If he agreed, she could start a new life.

Roman kept his gaze on her face. She'd made her offer of divorce sound noble. Then she thought of Ilya, and rubbed her cheeks with her woollen gloves to cover her blush. Roman tapped out a cigarette from the pack and lit it.

'And what about the child?' he asked.

'I'll raise it myself.' She watched him scowl and suck in smoke. It was the wrong time to tell him about Ilya. That would have to wait. 'Marina could visit you here.'

Roman exhaled smoke. 'She isn't my wife. I won't get released like I would with you.' He spat on the pavement. 'If you move here after the baby is born, I could appeal for relief. They allow some locals who have families here not to live in the barracks, but to check in at roll call at six in the morning and check out at six at night. There are a couple of guys who managed to fix it this way with good behaviour bonds and a few bottles of vodka. You brought some, I hope?'

She nodded and sat down on the bench. 'Roman, I said we're finished.'

He began to pace in front of her. 'You can find a room to rent close by and I'll visit you on weekends.'

A yellow-green tram rocked past the bus stop and halted.

'You must think me a fool. You never loved me. You slept with Marina and you want *me* to make sacrifices?'

Roman fixed her with a glare. 'Marina means nothing to me. And what is so important you can't leave behind?' He was standing over her. 'You don't work and you don't have money to support yourself or the child. What will you do when it's born?'

Ella shrugged. 'I'll rent out the living room and find a job. Maybe cleaning. I have my parents to help and Olga as well.' *And Ilya*, she thought.

'Don't give me this bullshit.' He threw down his cigarette and extended his hand towards her. 'Let's go inside. I'm freezing.'

'I don't love you, Roman.' She almost shouted it.

Roman's shoulders tensed and he withdrew his hand. 'I don't believe you.'

'I love someone else.'

The tram jerked into motion. She leaped off the bench and strode past Roman towards the hotel. He caught her arm and yanked her back.

'Who is he?' He pushed her against the bus shelter, his breath hot with smoke but his eyes cold.

Ella's head hurt. For a moment, she was made of stone. Then the baby moved under her ribs and gave her courage.

'You don't know him.' He wouldn't divorce her if he still had hope.

She tried to move away but Roman gripped her forearms and held her in place. Pushing back her tears, Ella peered over his shoulder but she could only see an empty street and the grey mist of rain.

'What did you think – that you would bury me here and use my flat to pamper your lover?' Roman's face went crimson and he brought it closer to hers. The smell of his breath made her gag.

'You were the ones who cheated,' she said, 'and the flat is my home as well.'

'I won't let you keep my child.' He dug his thumbs under her collarbones. 'I'll sue you for being a slut, unfit to take care of it. Then I'll ask for parole.'

Ella went limp in his grip. The physical pain wasn't as bad as the knowledge that his threat wasn't a bluff.

He pushed her towards the hotel. 'Go and get me my stuff. I'll wait for you here.'

23

The drizzly Moscow evening smelled of scorched metal when the Tula train pulled in at Kurskaya station. Ella paused on the top step of her carriage and searched the platform for Ilya until someone bumped into her from behind.

'Move.' A sturdy woman in a goat down shawl pushed her aside, her suitcase hitting Ella's thigh.

Ella scrambled down the train's ladder-like steps and dropped her duffel onto the asphalt. It was empty of Roman's clothes and the tinned goods she'd delivered to him on her first and, she knew now, last marital visit to Tula. She thought of his threat to fight her for the child and jammed her fists in her coat pockets.

Ilya deserved to know the truth, but he might decide to go to Tula and sort things out with Roman himself, which would only make matters worse.

'Do you think the Americans will start a war?' a man in a rabbit pelt hat asked his companion, a middle-aged woman, her nose and mouth obscured by a fox fur collar, as they plodded past Ella. He had a roll of newspapers tucked into his string bag with a bottle of vodka sticking out.

'Cowards,' the woman said. 'They simply envy us.' She hooked her arm under the man's elbow. A trail of dry salted fish wafted after them and Ella gagged.

The bluish glow from Kurskaya station lit the far end of the platform, leaving the end where she stood in the shadows. All Ella could see was the dense tide of people that shuffled along beside the still puffing train towards the metro entrance.

She stood on tiptoes and stretched her neck. On the train, she'd thought through what she had to tell Ilya when they got home. Roman wouldn't give her a divorce, and if she waited until the baby was born, he'd take her to court. If they wanted to save their love and her child, they should run away. She had a plan.

But right now, the desire to bury her face in Ilya's neck flooded her. She yawned and realised how tired she was and how much she'd lived through today. Maybe she could have a good night's sleep before telling Ilya about her trip.

The crowd thinned and she was no longer being jostled by people, grey-faced after the night on the train.

Ilya appeared by her side smiling. 'Where were you hiding? I passed this carriage two times.'

She walked into his arms. He embraced her and the comforting smell of tobacco and weathered leather brought tears to her eyes.

Ilya took her bag, put his arm around her shoulders and guided them through the crowd. 'Are you well?'

Ella winced. Roman's distorted face swam in front of her eyes, but she looked up at Ilya and attempted a smile. 'All is good.'

He kissed the top of her head. 'Have you told him?'

She couldn't prevent a sniffle and rummaged in her coat pockets for a handkerchief. 'Runny nose.' She hid behind the damp piece of cloth.

From the metro entrance came a blast of humid air and they were carried along towards the turnstiles. Ilya handed her a five-kopeck coin. She dropped it into the slot and prayed he wouldn't persist with his questions. The black rubber claws of the metro gates parted. Behind her, Ilya encircled her belly with his arms and they shuffled through, merged together as one.

On the escalator, she steadied herself and stood one step above him. Her eyes became level with his eyes and her lips with his lips. He smiled and, without saying anything, pressed his mouth to hers. Her heart stopped beating for a second.

A few minutes later, the metro train hissed to a stop at the platform. The doors swished open and Ella and Ilya were propelled deep into the full carriage. She relaxed and clung to him, trying to keep her worries locked inside. They had only a few stops to go before they'd arrive at her flat.

Ilya ran his lips over the crown of her hair. 'You can tell me everything now. What happened? Something bad? I could read it all on your face.'

She bit her lip. 'I'm just tired.'

He searched her eyes for an answer. 'What? He doesn't want a divorce?'

Ella nodded and felt a tear burn her cheek. She hid her face in the lapel of his jacket. The metro train jerked and stopped. Over the speaker, a female voice announced that the next stop was Taganskaya.

'What does he want?' Ilya asked.

She didn't answer. The short version would have been 'my baby', but Roman didn't want her child. He wanted his freedom, as much as she craved hers, but their freedoms were at odds with each other.

Ella twisted to see if anyone was listening. She placed her mouth near Ilya's earlobe. 'He wants me to move to Tula to stay with him.'

Ilya held her tighter. 'Maybe he still loves you.'

His words, almost inaudible over the clatter of the wheels, pierced her like a rusty nail. She pushed back to see his face. He was watching her, his expression pained.

'He loves only himself – not me or Marina. Not even his own child.'

Ilya grimaced when she mentioned his wife and she let her arms fall by her sides. 'He threatened to sue me for custody to get parole.' She couldn't hold back any longer.

His face paled, although it betrayed no surprise. The train stopped and the crowd moved in different directions, pulling them apart.

Ilya reached for her arm and drew her close again. 'Belorusskaya. We're next.'

Ella wanted to wait until they got home before saying more, but she had stopped holding back her tears and they poured freely down her face. The train doors closed again and she pressed her forehead into Ilya's shoulder. 'I thought he was going to hit me.'

*

When they walked into her flat half an hour later, it seemed smaller somehow, and dusty, as if she'd been away for a month, not a day. She took off her coat and bumped into Ilya's arms. His hug held her upright.

'You want us to move?'

She took his hand and led him inside through the darkness. By the window, she stopped and gazed at Ilya's face, lit by the glow of streetlights.

'I want to leave Russia,' she said. 'Start a new life. Be an actress again. Staying here and hiding from Roman is not an option. He can sue me from Tula – file a suit for custody of the baby, he swore. When you get in touch with Marina to see Yan, he'll find us.'

He kissed her. 'But we can't emigrate when we're both married to other people. It'll take us at least a year to get divorced.'

She clutched his hands. 'I think there may be a way for us to leave together. We can apply for a visitor's visa, that would at least get us out of the country. I'll call my great-uncle in Melbourne and ask him to invite us over.'

Ilya stepped back. 'Have you two been in contact?'

'Olga, my grandmother, knows Leo's telephone number. She'll let me have it.' She grinned and made an effort to appear confident.

He released her hands and drew the curtains shut. Then he turned on the lights and sat on the sofa. 'You think we could visit and stay?'

She stood in front of him. 'We have nothing to lose. There are more chances now, while we're both married, then we'll ever have. They might see it as collateral – leaving our spouses behind. You said it yourself – the divorce might take a year and that's if Roman agrees.'

She kneeled before Ilya and took hold of his hands again. 'Please, darling, please. Just let me try. If we get out, we could save Yan too. Marina might let us have him if we are in Australia. She'll want the best for her child. There's no harm in trying.'

He looked her in the eye. 'Not for you, Ella, but your father might lose his job if you start calling abroad from your home number. So could I, if you give Leo my name.'

24

Olga
Kislovodsk, USSR
1941

Ice clumps filled the corners of the industrial-sized refrigerator. The frost spread over its walls, making the hollow cavity appear smaller than it actually was. Olga banged the fridge door closed.

The wall-to-wall shelves held few containers. Overturned. Smashed. There was nothing except broken glass on the long timber counter and the tiled floor. Others had rummaged the sanatorium's kitchen before them; nothing edible was left.

Grisha and Faina stood by the barricaded door, their faces pale, their eyes fixed on her movements.

She squatted to check under the counter inside the baskets where the vegetables were likely kept before the war. Onion skins and some wilted leaves were left behind. Beetroot? Cauliflower?

The stately building shook from the bombs that fell nearby. Painted over, taped and boarded windows with cracked panels jingled, about to lose more glass pieces.

'Let's go, Mama.' Grisha sounded dull, like an old man.

'One more look, darling. It's a long road, we need to find something to eat.'

Olga opened the refrigerator again and reached into the depths of the freezer. A chunk of something hard, covered in slimy ice, was stuck to the back wall. She grabbed it. The ice-brick didn't budge.

'Mummy.' Faina pressed her skinny body into her mother's leg.

Olga crawled on the floor looking for something sharp, but there were just the splintered floorboards ... and a huge meat cleaver stuck between them.

She pulled at the handle using her own weight as a lever and shook it from side to side. The cleaver eased. Olga jerked it out and stumbled to regain her balance. She ran to the freezer and shoved it under the ice-brick to try to release it.

The sanatorium shook again. Weak light that leaked through the shattered windows changed to ash grey. If they wanted to get out of Kislovodsk before nightfall, they had to leave now.

The ice-brick finally came loose. It seemed to be a chunk of butter: whitish-yellow, slippery. A treasure.

Olga looked around again. The canisters that used to contain sunflower oil or lard rolled around empty. A large round tin seemed full but it was sealed. Olga hacked at it with her cleaver and brown powder spilled out onto the counter.

She licked her fingers. Cacao. She felt Faina's warm hand in her own.

'Mummy, I am hungry.'

'I know, my love. Just give me a minute.'

Outside someone screamed and the ceiling vibrated under people's steps. If she wanted to save her children she had to hide the food. But she also had to carry it out, and make it safe to eat. She held her finger to her lips.

The gas stove looked abandoned, but unbelievably it worked. Olga pulled out the matches she kept in her pocket, found a stained enamel pot, and melted the butter brick, stirring the goo with her hand. The whole time, she watched the barricaded kitchen door, ready to pounce, to protect the food and her children.

Olga hacked the tin with the cleaver one more time and the cacao powder flowed freely into the melted butter.

Stir it up. Find the can you could carry inside your rucksack. Now pour.

She moved like a robot, a soldier – quick and silent. When the warm sludge filled the milk can, she found a lid. Then she wrapped the can in one of her two blouses, tied it securely with the sleeves and lowered it into her rucksack. Picked up a spoon, thought a moment, and added another one.

Olga scraped the melted slush off the pot's sides and fed a half-spoonful to Faina, then a half-spoonful to Grisha. She ran a finger around the pot's sides and had a taste herself. Swallowed the taste of home.

The twilight crept in and she nodded to Grisha and Faina to follow her. They edged out of the kitchen through an uneven gap in the wall, the same way they'd climbed in.

The balding Caucasus mountain threw a shadow over the sanatorium – a former mansion – in Kislovodsk where Faina had been convalescing from her asthma before the bombs had reached the town. The gravel path was barely lit by the new moon, the air chilly and fresh. The sky above them – enormous.

The safe way out led through the mountains, away from the bombing, from the German planes she'd seen during the day, towards Pyatigorsk train station. That was their only chance to get back to Moscow, if trains were still running, and if they managed to get there in time.

*

A ray of moonlight lit the mountain path before disappearing behind the clouds. Olga squeezed Faina's hand, thankful for her children's obedient silence. She took one step after another, following people's shadows up the rocky track.

Above her, the mountain grew taller, merging with sky and clouds. In front of them the lighter gap between the two boulders showed the way. That, and the shuffling feet on the gravel of the sparse group of women and children seeking refuge from the bombed town.

Faina stopped. Olga bent down and lifted her up. She whimpered quietly and tucked her face into Olga's neck. They really needed to stop for the night, yet the only way to safety was to walk as far as they could before sunrise, when the Nazi planes would be able to see them from above.

Olga kissed the top of Faina's head and took another few steps to catch up with the group. They'd hardly exchanged a word since she caught up with them in the mountains. The broken chain of twinkling lights in the valley below was the only signpost that united them – to get to the station before the enemy took over the town.

Her arms grew numb and she lowered Faina down. The girl stood there silent, half-asleep, not moving. Grisha whispered something into Faina's ear and she stepped closer to him and took his hand.

Olga prodded inside the rucksack. Her fingers found a spoon, pushed the can's lid aside and dug out a dollop of chocolate butter, still pliable. She stuck the spoon into Faina's mouth, finding her chin in the dark. Her daughter licked it clean, smiling.

A branch snapped and Olga pulled at Faina's sleeve and edged away from the path. Grisha crouched next to her, but it was just another cluster of people, who had followed them up the mountain.

Olga hoped they couldn't smell her food. She didn't move. Her arms hovered over her children until the group passed.

The distant whiff of fire and ash reached her and she guessed that the camp was close.

The women must have decided to take a break up ahead. She wasn't sure she could afford to stop, but she knew she couldn't continue either. Alone in the mountains, they would be less safe than if they stayed with people. The worst the strangers could do was to rob them, not to kill.

The boulders that framed the path got taller, lit by the moon. The path began to descend, or at least it didn't feel like they were climbing anymore. The bushes and the grasses reached out and almost blocked their passage. Olga glimpsed a log fire covered by branches and hunched shadows surrounding it. She would stop for a moment. Grisha needed a break and some food too. She took off the rucksack and rubbed her shoulders.

Her children crouched next to her, a few steps away from the women who were attempting to cook something on the coals. Potatoes. Olga swallowed hard. She quietly pulled the metal water container out of her rucksack. She took one sip and let Grisha and Faina have a few. The water tasted rusty but it was all they had. She hid it back inside her rucksack, trying not to make any noise, then pulled out a spoonful of the chocolate butter, fed it to Grisha and Faina, had some herself. The sweetness spread on her tongue. If they managed to reach the train station before the sunrise, they could probably get to Moscow. Or anywhere. Anywhere away from here. But they would likely have to hide during the day and start walking again after the sun set.

Olga got up and scrambled a few steps away to pee and to check the track. They had to keep moving, if only her children could make it. They probably were safer walking than sleeping.

When she crawled back to them, she saw Grisha and Faina cuddled into each other on the ground in a deep sleep.

25

Ella
Moscow, USSR
March 1983

Ella pushed the empty plate away and sighed. Olga's *blinchiki* had always been her weakness, but today she'd overdone it when she'd accepted seconds. Her wish to please her grandmother combined with her appetite made her feel sluggish and unfocused. At least Olga seemed happy, though. She smiled and put a glass of black tea in front of her. Then she took away the greasy plate and sat down. *Now is the time*, Ella thought.

She stirred her tea and stroked her belly to remind herself why she was asking about her great-uncle. 'Baba, when was the last time you called Leo and Sonya?'

Olga put her hand to her chest. 'Why do you ask, Ellochka?' She retrieved a lace-edged handkerchief from her pocket and dabbed at her eyes. 'I can't even remember. Maybe ten years, maybe more. Not since your father started his army job.'

Ella got up and stood beside her. Calling Melbourne from her grandmother's home had become her backup plan after Vlad, who she'd caught up with a few days earlier, had warned that using the Central Telegraph was 'totally stupid'.

She'd repeated Vlad's warning to Ilya, who suggested they wait until someone else they knew was leaving the country to use their phone. But she couldn't wait for such an occasion, so infrequent these days.

'Do they ever write?' Ella asked now.

Olga lowered her head. 'Nothing. For years. Since Natan asked them to stop.' She picked up a tea towel and turned to the sink.

'Let's call them, Baba.'

Ella attempted a smile. Her grandparents wouldn't be risking much. Vlad thought they were likely on the KGB files already since Leo and Sonya had visited in the late sixties. Besides, they were old and had no jobs to lose.

Unlike my father, she thought. *Especially now under Andropov*, he had argued when Ella had first suggested getting in touch with Leo a few months ago. And she'd responded that surely one call made by his elderly parents would do no harm? He could claim he didn't know. Her stomach turned and she reminded herself that she was doing it for her child.

Olga glanced at her and put the tea towel down. 'I'll go and check on your grandfather. He hasn't been well.'

Ella followed her through the living room, where the sight of Natan's medicine bottles was like guilt trying to overpower her resolve.

In the bedroom, a lamp lit his ashen face. Her grandfather slept on his back, sitting up against pillows piled high. His glasses gleamed on his forehead. The radio murmured in English. Ella smiled to herself as if she'd gotten his blessing. Natan had been listening to the prohibited *Voice of America* when he'd fallen asleep. He would let her call his brother in Melbourne.

Olga pressed a finger to her lips and tiptoed out of the bedroom. Back in the living room, she sat on the couch and patted a spot near her. Ella sat on it, her knees slightly apart, supporting the small bulge of her stomach.

'*Nu?*' Olga prompted.

Ella leaned onto her grandmother, like she used to when she was little, when she and Olga sat side by side on that very couch and read Grimm's fairytales together. Her grandmother felt unexpectedly soft and fragile.

'I want to ask Leo to invite me and Ilya for a visit.'

Olga stroked her hand. 'Maybe you should call them from the Central Telegraph, darling.'

Ella lowered her head on Olga's shoulder. 'It's less risky from here, Baba, for all of us. They check the passports and take down your details at the Telegraph. I've tried.'

Her grandmother stopped stroking her hand.

'You could speak Yiddish to them and I'll speak the Queen's English,' Ella said.

Olga knew it wasn't a joke. After ten years of the language school, Ella was fluent.

'Plus, you don't work or study so you won't get into trouble.' *Like me*, she thought.

'But the phone number I have for Leo must be old.'

Ella threw her arms around her grandmother. 'I have to get out. The sooner the better. If I call Leo now and he asks us over, we may be able to leave before the baby is born.'

She bit the inside of her cheek and imagined what would happen to her and her baby if they stayed in Russia. Roman's threat to sue her for custody felt more than real. She recalled his trial – the dusty courtroom where he'd been sentenced, the KGB men and the frightened judge. She didn't trust the system to handle the fate of her child.

She released her grandmother and peered into her eyes. 'Please, Baba, let me try?'

Olga glanced towards the bedroom. 'What about Natan? We can't upset him. The doctor said to keep him calm.'

'I'll be quick.'

Olga's forehead wrinkled. Ella kissed her cheek and Olga got up with a groan. Ella followed her to the bedroom and watched her kneel at the wardrobe and search among the shoeboxes on the bottom shelf.

Above her grandmother's head, Natan's suit hung beside Olga's blue silk dress. She'd last seen her grandparents dressed up at her wedding dinner only a few months ago. An eternity. She thanked fate for giving her Ilya and bent to help her grandmother onto her feet.

Olga closed the door to the bedroom and handed Ella an old business card with a telephone number. *Leo Ashkenazi*, it read, and something else, but Ella stared at the lucky numbers.

Her fingers felt wooden rotating the dial with Olga hovering beside her. Ella cleared her throat and read Leo's number to a female operator. It should be morning in Melbourne.

The line crackled. She pressed the receiver against her ear and shrugged, giving Olga a half smile. Then the phone rang so loudly that it vibrated. Olga paled, her eyes begging Ella to be quiet and brief. The telephone stopped ringing and, behind the fuzz of static, a male voice spoke. Ella nodded at Olga and the voice mumbled something in English.

'Leo?' Ella yelled, without thinking. Olga's eyes widened and she stared at the closed door to Natan's room. Ella turned away and cupped the receiver with her palm. 'It's me, Ella, from Moscow,' she said in a quiet voice.

The man spoke in English and mentioned Leo's name, but his voice kept falling below the static and Ella couldn't understand him. Olga put a hand on her shoulder and leaned closer. Her face was pallid and the net of tiny wrinkles around her dark eyes seemed even deeper than usual.

Ella stuttered. 'May I speak to Leo or Sonya?' she enunciated in English.

The static cleared. 'They moved out five years ago.'

This statement she understood. Her eyes closed slowly before she opened them again. 'Do you know where they moved to?'

'I think Sydney, but I'm not sure.'

Olga's glance darted from Ella to the closed bedroom door. The crackling resumed and Ella shrugged her grandmother's hand off and jammed her finger in her ear.

'Have you got their address or their telephone number?' she shouted. She signalled for Olga to give her a pen.

From behind the bedroom door, Natan's weak voice called out, 'Olushka, is that Ella?'

Olga shoved a pen into Ella's hand. 'I'm coming, Natan.'

Her brow knitted as she strode into Natan's room and shut the door. Ella sighed and the static on the phone line cleared.

'I misplaced their details,' the man said, 'but I heard Leo died soon after they moved. I don't know for sure. He used to come to my *shule*.'

Ella's vision dimmed. 'And Sonya?'

'I don't know. She must still be in Sydney. I don't have her address.'

Light spilled from the bedroom and Ella saw Olga and Natan on the threshold. Natan wore his striped pyjamas, which he only put on when he was unwell. They seemed too loose on him now. Olga supported him and propped herself up against the doorframe with her other hand.

Static overwhelmed the line and Ella dropped the receiver onto the cradle. She ran over and propped Natan up from the other side.

'Who was on the phone, darling?' he asked.

'No one important.' She brushed his cheek with her lips. 'You look great today, *Dedushka*.'

She avoided Olga's eyes. They couldn't tell Natan about the call, let alone about Leo's death. The Jewish man on the phone wasn't sure and she would now have to find Sonya in Sydney through the synagogue alone – an onerous task without a telephone number or home address. The only person who could help her, once more, was Vlad with his dissident contacts abroad. The KGB followed him, but he still might know the way to locate her Australian relatives.

'I heard your radio,' Ella said to Natan. 'So, what's the *enemies'* news?'

He grinned weakly. She and Olga led him to the bathroom, his body light as a child's.

26

Vlad trailed along beside her with his head bowed, as if he were searching for something under his feet. He hadn't said much since Ella had called him at dawn, he'd just offered to meet at the zoo, where he'd be able to see if he was being followed. Before Roman's trial, she would've called him paranoid, but the image of nondescript men flanking the judge's bench had been etched in her brain.

She pulled out the letter she'd written to Sonya. 'I don't have her address. I thought you could help me find her.'

Vlad's black leather coat glistened with dew. He peeked over his shoulder and Ella did likewise. This section of the Moscow Zoo looked like an abandoned movie set. The ghostly tree trunks either side of the alley failed to hide the animal cages that would be left vacant until late May. Only a few other people moved about the alleys, their inky silhouettes visible from afar.

A woman with a pram passed them. Her eyes, crazy with love, were fixed on her baby. Watching her walk ahead, it was hard for Ella to believe that she would feel what this woman was feeling in less than four months. She returned her eyes to the letter in her hand. 'Listen to what I have written and tell me what you think. It's a draft.'

She paused, expecting him to say something, but Vlad looked at his feet and adjusted his steps to align with hers.

'Dear Sonya,' she read. 'I hope this letter will find you well. Olga and I called you, but we were told you had moved.'

She paused at the memory of Olga's troubled face. Vlad knew the Melbourne man had told her that Leo had died but that she hadn't shared this with her grandparents. Neither had she mentioned to Ilya that Natan's brother, who she'd hoped would ask them to visit, might have died some years ago.

'I hope we could see each other soon,' she continued.

Vlad took the page from her and skimmed it. Ella watched his lips move, as they used to when he read something at school. She always thought it looked like he was praying.

They turned left into another alley as bare as the main one. Vlad halted. 'Are you crazy?' He imitated her voice and read, 'In the last few months I had some problems. I was expelled from my acting course just before graduation.'

He waved the letter at her. 'How do you plan to send this? By pigeon? You can't send stuff like this by mail.'

The volume of his voice surprised her and she surveyed the area around them. The alley ran alongside a black pond with a smattering of sickly ducks. A few timber benches that surrounded the water looked wet from the recently melted snow. On the other side of the pond were naked trees in front of the spikes of the zoo fence; the noise from the road beyond was muffled to a mere rustle.

But there were no people within earshot and she returned her gaze to Vlad. 'I have to explain what happened before asking Sonya to help. I can't say, "Please invite us over, both my beloved and I." It doesn't sound polite, does it? I need her to know we're going to stay.'

Vlad rolled his eyes. 'You are so silly sometimes. This very polite letter will never reach Sonya. It'll just get you into trouble. I bet you also mentioned that Roman was sentenced for reselling goods on the black market?'

Ella felt stupid. 'I said there was a trial and he'd been sent to a camp and now he was threatening to take away my baby to get parole.'

Vlad shrugged and returned to the letter. She touched the trunk of the willow that leaned over the pond. The tree was bare, but the buds were swollen and sticky, hiding green shoots underneath their tightly stretched skin. Ella stroked her belly, but the baby wasn't moving.

Vlad sat on the closest bench and spread the flap of his coat to cover the damp timber. An offer to sit next to him. He clearly understood that she couldn't send the letter without his help.

'If it's difficult for you or unpleasant,' she said, 'you could tell me to back off.' He shrugged and she perched on the bench beside him. 'It's just a draft to get your opinion.'

He turned the page over. 'If you can invite us, we won't be a burden,' he read. 'We both speak English and we'll find work.' He buried his face in his hands.

Ella gazed at the pond and one of the ducks dived in. 'You judge me. You think I shouldn't impose on you.'

Vlad raised his head. 'Why would I judge you? It just feels wrong. Where will you have the baby? And who will pay for it? Sonya?'

She'd thought of that too, but those were problems she could deal with when they arose. He put the letter on her lap and she covered it with her palm. She'd forgotten her gloves and her fingers had turned red from the sudden March frost.

Ella stood and stuffed the page into her pocket. 'What do you suggest? Having my baby here, for Roman?'

'Give me that letter.' Vlad got up. 'The problem with you, Elka, is that you don't listen and then refuse to take responsibility for your actions.' He adjusted her scarf. 'I'm trying to be realistic. You're an actress. What would you do in the West?'

She shoved his hand away. 'There, I plan to act. Here, they won't employ me without a theatre degree.'

'And in Sydney? Acting in English?' Vlad started to walk away. 'Let's go somewhere warm. We could freeze to death out here.'

'I'll study.' She addressed his back. 'I'll find a job!'

He peered over his shoulder with pity carved on his face. 'With the baby?'

She scrunched up the letter. He was right, but she couldn't stay in Moscow and wait for the birth of her child with Roman's threats looming. While she did something – called Melbourne, wrote to Sonya, waited for her to answer – she at least had a chance. The Australian man mentioned his *shule*, the congregation Leo had belonged to. Maybe Sonya was still a member in Sydney.

Vlad wandered back and put his arm around her. 'Let's go eat dumplings,' he said, as if they hadn't argued. 'Roman probably won't win if he sues you over the baby.'

On the street corner, she and Vlad turned left and set out towards Barrikadnaya metro station. They headed for a bistro-type joint called Pelmeni, which used to be their after-school haunt. The place had always made her feel safe. She pushed the door open, letting out a miasma of steam.

An old woman, familiar from their schooldays, sat in the corner. She nursed a glass of hot tea and waited for someone to buy her a meal. Ella sat at a formica-topped table and waited for Vlad to get the food, her stomach rumbling.

Vlad brought over a tray with two plates of steaming dumplings and two glasses of milky coffee. Ella met his eyes and he took one of the plates to the woman in the corner. Ella watched her spread a handkerchief over her knees and wait for Vlad to sit at his table before she started eating – silently, neatly, as if she were at a formal dinner.

The old woman might have once been landed gentry, Ella thought, like Natasha Rostova. Or maybe she offered a glimpse of Ella's own future: destitute and stuck in Russia for life. The baby stirred inside her; it must have been hungry. She bit into a dumpling and felt queasy.

Across from her, Vlad stopped chewing.

'Something wrong?' Ella asked.

She swallowed and Vlad studied her face.

'I have an acquaintance – his name is Jack and he writes for *The Times*. He may agree to post your letter when he's abroad.' He bit into another dumpling. 'Have you told Ilya?'

'What do you want me to tell him? Leo is dead and Sonya has moved without a forwarding address?'

'You can't keep it secret. If Ilya is named, he needs to know. It's risky.'

She watched Vlad take a sip from his glass. Her own coffee was barely warm and overly sweet from condensed milk. 'I don't believe that Leo is dead. When Sonya replies, I'll tell Ilya the truth. It may not even work out with the letter. You said so yourself.'

Melted butter had started to congeal at the edges of their plate, on which two dumplings remained.

'I'll call you when I've spoken to Jack, if he agrees to meet you. But you should tell Ilya.' Vlad speared a dumpling with the fork, put it in his mouth and seemed to swallow it whole.

27

Ella sank the ladle into the borscht and peeked at Ilya. She filled up a bowl and placed it on the kitchen table in front of him, adding a spoonful of sour cream. Then she sat and rested her cheek on her hand, like a dutiful wife feeding a husband after a hard day at work. Only the way things were progressing, it would be a while before she could call Ilya her husband. They never spoke of Marina and she hadn't told him about writing to Sonya. Vlad had come good though and had arranged for her to meet Jack and pass on her letter.

Ilya gulped down the first few spoonfuls. 'Like my mother's, only better. You're not eating?'

'I'm not hungry.' Her belly was full and not only with a child. Since her letter had left her possession, she couldn't stop eating, impatient for news and anxious about keeping her secret. 'I ate dinner before you came home. Twice.'

She grinned at Ilya. It didn't help that he was absent at work from morning till night, leaving her with nothing to do but cook his dinners, which made her peckish. Shifting in her chair, she felt how tight her top was over her almost six-month-pregnant belly. She couldn't bring herself to ask Ilya for money to buy something loose though, not until she'd told him about Leo, Sonya, the letter and Jack. He wouldn't be angry at her for her deception if Sonya asked them to come and stay.

She put her palm flat on her stomach but the baby was still. She switched her attention back to Ilya, who was immersed in his borscht. 'Tired?'

He nodded, hunched over his bowl. If she weren't feeling guilty, she would have loved to preserve this moment – her and Ilya together with no one else to consider, not Marina, not Roman, not even Ilya's poor son Yan. There was only her, her child and this man, without whom she couldn't imagine her life.

The buzz of the doorbell spoiled the moment. Ilya moved to get up.

'I'll get it,' she said.

He looked at his watch and shrugged. Her footsteps slowed when she approached the door.

'It's me, Elka.' Through the timber, Vlad's voice sounded dull. 'Open up.'

She unlocked the door and stepped aside as he stumbled into the hallway. She moved to switch on the light, but Vlad held her hand to stop her. He peeked out through the open entrance door onto the landing before pulling it shut and fastening the deadbolt. She wanted to hug his slumped shoulders but she also wished him gone.

'Who is it?' Ilya called from the kitchen.

'It's Vlad,' she shouted back. She watched Vlad's clumsy fingers fight with the buttons of his coat. 'Ilya is eating. He works far too much. The borscht is still hot, if you want some.'

But Vlad didn't seem to hear her. He counted under his breath and stared at her stomach with eyes that glinted crazier than usual. 'How far along are you?'

Drugs, she thought, but immediately threw away the idea. She was sure he hadn't touched the stuff for years, and he couldn't work as a nurse and swallow pills. They wouldn't let him. He'd also promised his father.

'I'm due in July. In about three months. Why are you asking?'

She pried Vlad's coat from his clenched fists and hung it up, feeling a tug in her stomach when she lifted her arms.

'What are you two whispering about?' Ilya called. 'I might finish this borscht by myself.'

Vlad's head jerked as if he'd heard a strange sound. 'You must run,' he mumbled.

Her belly tightened. 'What's wrong?'

She nudged him towards the living room, away from the kitchen and Ilya, but he resisted. Ella stepped closer and took hold of his elbow.

Vlad bowed his head. 'Jack was arrested.'

On each of the ten days since she'd passed her letter to Jack by the pond at the zoo, she'd fought with her conscience. Still she'd failed to muster the courage to tell Ilya the truth. Jack had promised to post it when he was abroad and she had been waiting for Sonya's reply.

Her heart sped and she started to sweat. She recalled Jack's gloved fingers taking the letter from her. His piercing blue eyes. He'd told her to take care. It seemed that he hadn't followed his own advice.

Ella stole a glance towards the kitchen. She couldn't allow Ilya to find out about Jack's arrest before she had a chance to explain herself.

'When?' she whispered.

Vlad rubbed his eyes. 'A week ago. We didn't know – I thought he went back to the States.'

'My letter?'

She'd pictured it being sorted in a mailroom in Sydney and lived in hope of receiving Sonya's goodwill. Now she imagined her letter on the desk of some KGB bureaucrat who was arranging her fate. She remembered all too well her attempt to sway General Lubov in his office at Lubyanka. She'd prefer not to meet him again, but she might have to if Jack had been caught with her letter on him.

She searched Vlad's face for a clue. By now she knew that his paranoia was warranted. If he was scared, she should be scared too.

'You think I'm in trouble?' She lowered her voice, ignoring the pinch in her heart.

'Depends on what the instructions from the top are — nail the dissidents or chuck them out of the country. It still would be safer to get out in case they want to question you.' Vlad paused. 'Or maybe they'll lock us up in loony wards like they did under Brezhnev.'

Vlad's two-month stint in a psychiatric hospital had caused his expulsion from medical school. If it hadn't been for his famous father, he would likely still be locked up.

He tugged his coat off the hook and struggled to put it on. 'Tell Ilya you need to take a break. Go somewhere south, to the Black Sea. You can hide there among the holidaymakers. Trust me on this — you don't want to be questioned.'

Ella's mouth dried. To tell Ilya the truth at this point, when she'd tried it her way and failed so miserably, would be like signalling defeat. But to run to the Black Sea, to hide there until the birth of her child, she needed his support.

She could, of course, pretend that nothing had happened. Make new plans. Hope the trouble would go away. She might have nothing to fear — Jack might have destroyed her letter before his arrest.

Ilya threw the kitchen door open and strode towards them with a smile on his face. 'Enough of your secrets. Get him in here.' Vlad was trying and failing to button up his coat. 'Where are you going? You've only just arrived.'

Vlad rushed to open the door, but Ilya hooked his neck with his arm. 'Stop it, you. If you came here, you stay for dinner.' He turned to Ella. 'Why are you letting him leave? Did something happen?'

Vlad hunched more and Ella's lips twisted into a tiny smile. 'Let him be, my love.'

But Ilya had already pulled Vlad's coat off. 'You have to try Ella's borscht. It will brighten your world.'

*

After serving Vlad his borscht, Ella watched him devour it and prayed he would leave without revealing her secret.

Ilya sat at the kitchen table next to Vlad. He hadn't asked any questions after making him stay. The silence was interrupted only by the water drops that hit the sink. Ella met his gaze over Vlad's bent head and he winked at her. She shouldn't keep her letter to Sonya and Jack's arrest from him. This whole affair concerned Ilya as much as it did her.

Vlad put down his spoon and stared at the window. Ilya's eyes shifted from Vlad to Ella.

'Vlad thinks we should go away for a while,' she said.

Ilya lifted his brow. Vlad took his bowl to the sink and watched her.

'I wrote to Sonya through Leo's synagogue.'

Ilya turned to face her. 'When?'

'About two weeks ago.'

He glanced at Vlad sidelong. 'You arranged it?'

'Jack's a journalist who helps us sometimes. He agreed to post it abroad.' The colour left Vlad's face. 'I mean, he used to help us.'

Ella looked from one man to the other. Ilya's fingers tap-danced on his knee. 'What happened?'

She opened her mouth, but no words came out.

'We don't know where Jack is,' said Vlad. 'We think he's been arrested. And he might have had the letter on him,' he added. 'You need to get out – the sooner, the better.'

Ilya snickered. 'Look at you two – great conspirators. Where do you suggest we hide?'

Vlad's face turned ashen. 'You should disappear. Go away for a couple of weeks, a month. Let the dust settle.'

Ella noticed that he kept fastening and unfastening the top button of his shirt.

'Ilya,' she said quietly. It was for her child – he knew that.

'I can't go now and miss the premiere of my *Baikal* documentary, but that's beside the point.' He gripped the edge of the kitchen table. 'Tell me what you wrote that has him so upset.'

She looked up at Ilya and didn't utter a word. It was not only the contents of the letter. The fact that it might have been found on Jack with other dissidents' papers made it even worse.

'Go on a trip to the Black Sea,' Vlad said.

Ilya didn't react.

Vlad opened the kitchen door and a draught cooled Ella's cheeks. He stopped at the threshold. 'You don't want to be questioned.' He attempted a fake laugh and pointed at Ella. 'Though for you, Ilya, it might be even scarier. They could ask how you, a married man with a child, got involved with this woman.'

28

Dawn slipped into the bedroom with the sound of rain. Ella lay wide awake. To hide by the sea among the holidaying crowd felt like a wise option for now. Ilya's eyes were closed, but his eyelids quivered. She hadn't got far pleading with him after Vlad's hasty exit. The last thing Ilya muttered before falling asleep was, 'There are always dramas when your friend is involved.'

She stared at the wall clock but couldn't make out the time. If he left for work unconvinced, a whole day would be wasted. She sat up and listened to the low rumble of thunder. 'It's warm there in spring. The Black Sea.'

Ilya stirred beside her. 'Ella, it's early. Can't we talk later?'

Lightning cracked in the distance. 'I'm scared, Ilusha. What if they come to arrest me for meeting a foreign journalist? Maybe they've been watching us.'

Ilya sat up beside her. 'I can't go before the premiere.'

His documentary was scheduled to premiere the next week and took up all his attention. He shifted to the side of the bed and she grabbed his hand to stop him from getting up. He had to hear her out. If Jack had her letter on him when he was arrested, they might be in trouble.

'Could you just take me there and come back before opening night?'

She released his hand and he walked to the window, peering out at the storm. 'I wish you'd spoken to me before you wrote to Sonya.'

There wasn't much she could say. He knew she had risked their freedom when she passed her letter to Jack, though it could have been a ticket to a new life for her baby and for both of them too.

Over his shoulder, Ilya watched her, not smiling. 'You have your mother here and Olga. Moscow doctors. It doesn't make sense to leave.'

She stood behind him by the window. The neighbours' radio boomed the Soviet Union's anthem, marking 7 am. Ella shut her eyes and took a deep breath. 'I wanted the best for us.'

Ilya sighed and turned to face her. 'I have to go.' He kissed the top of her head. 'There is a meeting at nine at Dom Kino. We were put up for an award by the Film Guild.'

She patted her belly, hard as a volley ball. 'When is the premiere exactly? Maybe we could leave Moscow after the screening, if it's not too late by then.'

'You shouldn't worry so much. After all, what's your crime? Asking your Australian relatives to invite you over?'

Ella felt like shaking him. He didn't know, of course, that she'd written of being expelled and of Roman's antics. But meeting a foreign journalist and passing him an envelope might have been a crime in itself – she could be arrested for spying.

The telephone in the living room rang. Neither her mother nor Olga called so early. She sprinted past Ilya and lunged at the handset – something might have happened to Natan.

'Abramova? Ella Gregorievna?' The male voice on the line was unfamiliar. She exhaled, her knees wobbly. It wasn't about her grandfather, she hoped.

'Yes.'

The caller cleared his throat. 'Allow me to introduce myself. Nikolai Ivanovich Seriy. I am from the Committee of Government Security. KGB,' he said. 'We would like to ask you a couple of questions. Informally.'

The baby moved inside her, reminding Ella to breathe.

'I'm busy right now,' she said. 'Could you please call tomorrow?' Maybe she and Ilya still had time to leave if they took a night train to Crimea.

Seriy sighed. 'Would an appointment on the third of May suit you? In two weeks.'

She looked at Ilya, who hadn't moved. *KGB*, she mouthed. He glanced at his watch and didn't seem to register it. Her fingers gripped the receiver. 'A later date would be better,' she said to Seriy. Sweat gathered on her top lip. 'I am expecting, you see. I might need to go to hospital. What is this all about?'

Seriy hesitated. 'We would like to question you in regards to Jack Cullen.'

She glanced pleadingly at Ilya and he sat down, wrapping an arm around her. 'Sorry, Nikolai Ivanovich, but why do we need to meet in person? I might be able to answer your questions over the phone. It's difficult in my condition to take public transport.'

Ella thought she heard Seriy chuckle. 'One more request, Citizen Abramova. Do not discuss this conversation with your friends or family. We would like to keep it confidential. It's better this way, don't you agree? And please, do not leave the city prior to our meeting. The third of May, 10 am.'

29

Prokofiev's Sonata No. 7 floated to the ceiling of the Dom Kino movie theatre. The credits of Ilya's documentary rolled down over the blue expanse of Lake Baikal, which filled the screen.

'*Baikal*,' a voice boomed from the stage. 'The Grand Prize nominee for best documentary.'

The audience burst into applause. The lights came up and Ella saw Moscow's filmmaking crowd clapping – young women in miniskirts and over-made-up older ones in maxis next to bearded men in leather jackets. She jumped from her seat, forgetting about her belly. Her heart swelled with pride for her beloved. Next week's meeting with Seriy, which loomed over her like a storm cloud, receded momentarily.

'The winner of this prestigious award will be announced in Warsaw.' The speaker hiccupped with excitement. '*Baikal*'s director, Ilya Bezsmertniy, and his crew will be heading there in May, carrying with them our hopes for the Grand Prize.'

Warsaw, Ella thought. The name of Poland's capital sounded sweeter than Prokofiev's sonata. Already an idea pierced through her consciousness, not fully formed but heady, as if drug-induced – Poland was a socialist country, but it bordered Czechoslovakia, which bordered Austria.

The crowd started towards the open doors and Ella allowed herself to be pulled along. She stuck out her elbows to protect her stomach as she moved towards the exit. In the foyer, she jammed her back against the wall and stood on tiptoes to search for Ilya among the throng. She had to find him and tell him her crazy idea before he was swept away to party with his crew. But the details of her brainwave remained hazy. They could defect – jump on a train to Bratislava then head to Vienna. Or hide in Warsaw until his film crew returned to Moscow.

She spotted Gleb, Ilya's cameraman, shaking men's hands and accepting kisses from women. 'Gleb,' she shouted. He waved at her and raised his glass. 'Have you seen Ilya?'

Even yelling, she was barely audible above the commotion. She edged forward, but the stream of people swept Gleb away and she lost sight of him.

She scanned the foyer again and saw no sign of Ilya. She pardoned her way through the pack and approached the steps that led to the courtyard upstairs. Perhaps Ilya had gone for a smoke. If he found a way to take her to Warsaw with him and his crew, they could be in Vienna before the end of May. And if he agreed to defect, she could promise Seriy the earth at her impending appointment. Or even skip the meeting altogether. Bribe the polyclinic for a medical certificate and tell Seriy she was sick.

The enclosed courtyard swarmed with people. Would a bribe work to get them to Poland, she wondered. Ilya had told her of the bottles of French cognac it'd cost him to lock in his locations. Armed with a bottle of Camus or Napoleon and perhaps a box of Havana cigars, he could ask his studio manager to include Ella in the film crew travel papers.

The smokers let her pass to the club's gates, where the bored guard pretended to watch over Bolshaya Gruzinskaya Street. The gates were half shut, and through the cast iron spikes she saw a lone man walking a dog in the distance.

She found a quiet corner behind a potted tree and tried to think her plan through. Crazy as her idea seemed, Ilya should like it more than Vlad's insistence they hide by the sea. He would have to be careful though. They couldn't risk him causing suspicion at work.

A bearded man with a pipe caught her eye and smiled. 'Are you looking for me, babe?'

'No, Bublick, she's my girl.' Ilya cut in, appearing by her side.

Ella grinned at Ilya and tugged him out through the gates onto the unlit street. A car sped by. Its headlights briefly illuminated the dog-walker across the road, then the footpath returned to darkness.

'I loved your film.' She ruffled his hair. 'Did you know about the prize?'

Ilya stroked her cheek. 'I sort of guessed,' he said.

Ella felt the baby kick. She tried to fight back an urge to blurt everything out. 'What about me joining you in Poland? We may try to stay longer.'

Ilya's face fogged with thought, as if he were trying to make a decision. Then he nodded.

Blood pumped in her ears and she raised her voice above its surge. 'Do you think we can do it?'

He frowned and checked over his shoulder. Ella's face felt hot. She should have let him enjoy the night of his triumph, but now she had to keep going. 'We can take a train to the border. Then maybe walk. Then take another train to Vienna. Or someone could drive us. We could hire a car.'

Her voice had grown loud, and Ilya embraced her. His warm breath smelled of wine and tickled her ear. 'I thought of it too,' he whispered. 'But how can I take you along? You're not one of the crew.'

The dog-walker passed them and gave Ella a sharp glance. His dog was a German Shepherd without a leash. She shivered, recalling the endless TV movies where Nazis used those dogs to hunt partisans and Jews hiding from slaughter in Belorussian forests. Suddenly her plan to walk across the border, seven months pregnant, seemed insane. And they couldn't hire a car. She leaned into Ilya.

'Do you know Gleb, my cameraman?' he said into her hair. 'He's not coming with us. His mother is ill.'

Ilya pulled back, and Ella felt a glow of hope being lit again in her soul. He took her face in his hands. 'Listen, if Gleb stays, one place would be vacant, but we'd need the studio's agreement to fill his spot.'

He let go of her, and they both glanced at the bulge of her stomach under the tight black dress.

30

The breeze, oddly warm for May, burst through the open window of her father's old Volga. It tousled Ella's hair and wiped the pieces off Leon's chessboard, balanced precariously on his knee. She leaned onto Ilya so her brother could search under the car seat for his chess pieces.

In the driver's seat, Gregory had his eyes focused on the road. Anna laughed next to him and turned to face Leon, her cheeks flushed. 'So, Kasparov, who had the game? I told you to wait till we get to the dacha.'

'Leave him be, Anna,' her father said.

With her foot, Ella prodded her handbag under her mother's seat. Zipped in its pocket was a letter from the film studio confirming her status as a researcher with Ilya's crew. Who he had to bribe and what it had cost, she didn't dare ask. Ilya seemed to be on the same seventh level of heaven as she was, at least about their departure in a few days' time. There were loads of things to take care of before then though, and she'd skipped her appointment with Seriy at the KGB.

Ilya shifted uncomfortably in his seat. Helping her parents to clean their dacha, outside of Moscow and abandoned during the winter, should give her a chance to say goodbye, even against Ilya's wishes. She clenched her jaw and faced the window.

Towards them, on the opposite side of *Okruzhnaya* – Moscow Ring Road – a procession of tanks rolled on its way, most likely to Red Square for the ninth of May – Victory Day Parade. Gregory and Leon both turned their heads to follow the lethal floats. She saw Anna grab her father's knee to return his attention to the stretch of bitumen ahead. The clucking of steel tanks' treads against the gritty surface muffled the whooshing of tyres. A farewell from the State, Ella thought.

*

On the country road the car rocked her back and forth. Pots and pans were wrapped in blankets and placed on top of cardboard boxes that filled every centimetre of the Volga's vast boot. They clanked each time the car hit a pothole.

'Mama, can I borrow your suitcase?' Ella asked.

Anna sat half-turned with her elbow over the top of her seat. She patted Ella's knee. 'Of course, *zaika*, take it. Only it's quite large for a short trip. It's five days, isn't it, Ilya?'

'Yes.'

Ilya glanced at Ella sideways. She blushed. Asking for her mother's suitcase was thoughtless. She couldn't return it. 'There'll be official events and some sightseeing.'

Anna frowned at Ella's stomach. 'Is it kicking you hard?'

Ella realised she was caressing the taut round ball of her belly under the new summer dress her mother had sewn. 'No, today it's been quiet.' The feel of the starched cotton made her blush again. 'Thanks for the dress, Mama.'

Leon tore his eyes from the chessboard, which he'd reset. 'I chose the fabric. She wanted pink.'

Anna laughed. 'Mama, not she.'

Ella laid her hand on her brother's skinny arm. It was difficult to fathom that she would never see him grow, become an adult.

'Thank you, *bratishka*.' She kissed his hair, chestnut and wavy like her own, only wilder. Her baby's curls might hopefully turn out the same, rather than reddish like Roman's.

She checked on Ilya. He looked out the window at the forests that edged the road. Her father was quiet too, his neck tendons tense; perhaps he was considering all the chores they had to complete in one day at the dacha.

Anna smiled at her. 'When the baby's born, I'll take a month off. We'll stay in the country, eat strawberries from the patch and walk to the lake with the pram.'

Ella tried to smile back, but her lips felt thick and rubbery like after a dentist's injection. She'd never have guessed her mother would be willing to take time off to spend with her and the baby. Anna loved her job at the academic magazine and her crazy scientist authors. Plus, Leon still needed her attention.

Gregory adjusted his rear-view mirror. 'We haven't had little ones at our dacha since you and Leon grew up.'

This year only her grandparents and Leon would stay at the dacha, Ella realised. She would not be in Russia to join them. Her fingers trembled on her knee, and Ilya took her hand in both of his. Only now did she fully grasp that she might not see her family again. If her father lost his job because of her defection, she probably wouldn't even know.

Anna rolled up her window. 'Close your window, Gregory. You'll freeze the baby.'

'Don't close it, Papa,' Leon whined. 'It stinks of petrol.'

'Think of your sister,' Anna said.

Gregory rolled up his window, and Ella felt she might faint. The idea of spending a day with her parents without letting them know of her departure seemed impossible to bear. But to tell them the truth would mean spoiling the last day they could enjoy together. She rested her head on Ilya's shoulder.

'I heard Warsaw has been rebuilt after the war,' Anna said. 'You'll have to take photos.'

Gregory glanced at Ella again in his mirror. 'It's a shame you won't go to Lodz. Natan was born there. Did you tell him you're going to Poland?'

Ella shook her head. 'No, it may disturb him.'

She felt a chill. Every time Poland was mentioned, Natan talked of his sisters who'd stayed in Lodz when he and Leo ran away to Petrograd after the Revolution. Stalin's rule and the Nazis had made sure that none of his family survived, except him and his brother. Now Leo was dead and Natan didn't know. And she hadn't told Olga she was accompanying Ilya on his trip to Warsaw.

Beside her, Ilya gazed at the black and green fields. He was almost certainly thinking about his son, judging from the pained expression on his face. She wondered if he had the same ache in his chest as she did.

He gave Ella a melancholy smile. 'Maybe we could stop for a break? Ella looks a bit tired.'

Anna turned solemnly to her. 'Perhaps you shouldn't go to Poland, risking your health and the baby?' She took hold of Ella's hand and squeezed her fingers. 'Don't go, sweetheart. Stay with us until Ilya comes back.'

Ella lowered her eyes to hide tears pressing at them. Gregory stopped the car at a clearing beside a timber table with benches. 'Everyone out. Toilets – boys to the left, girls to the right.'

Ella grimaced in the direction of Ilya, hoping he wouldn't leave her with her mother. But he'd already followed Gregory and Leon towards the clearing.

31

The four-berth train compartment didn't feel spacious anymore. Or clean. Ilya's film crew – two men and two women – had taken over the lower berths. And now that they had finished their meal, the table was strewn with chicken bones, eggshells and an almost empty bottle of vodka.

Ilya ignored them. Squashed into the window seat across the table from Ella, he stared out at the afternoon. She traced his gaze and saw fields and forests stretched along the railway lines beneath the falling sun. She focused her attention on the newspaper underneath the food scraps, dated 14 May 1983. Her last day in the USSR. The Moscow to Warsaw train would cross the Polish border in Brest early the next morning.

Ilya's raucous mates had just finished singing. Ella leaned over the table to catch his eye, ignoring the edge that cut into her swollen belly. He looked far too relaxed. They both knew there was likely an informer in the group, someone reporting back to the KGB, so they had to be careful not to raise suspicion.

'Let's go to the restaurant, guys,' Ella said. 'Get some champagne.'

Dmitri, the soundman, raised his empty glass. 'Let's finish here first. Pour, Ilya. Don't be mean.'

Ilya smiled and picked up the vodka bottle. Dmitri grabbed the montage-queen Nina's knee and she laughed. Both Nina and Dmitri were married, but not to each other.

Beside her, Tonya, the assistant director, began to bellow a famous folk couplet: 'We shall drink and we shall party—'

Before she could sing the next obscene line, Alex, the second cameraman, punched her in the shoulder. 'Let's drink to us, guys. And to Gleb – the best cameraman in the country.'

He inverted his glass and drops of vodka trickled onto the chicken bones on the table. Ella turned sideways, her belly almost on Tonya's lap. 'There's more alcohol in the restaurant.'

Tonya nudged her and laughed. It wasn't a kind laugh, Ella thought. Bitter. They probably hated her being here.

Ilya got up. 'Shall we go, comrades? We deserve it.'

'I want champagne. And a pregnant woman's wish is law.' Ella hoped her acting skills weren't lost completely. She'd certainly lied plenty in the last few months. At least now it was for a good cause.

Alex rolled a cigarette and glanced at Ella's stomach. 'Let's go, Ilya. Hell with them. We can smoke there.'

'Dmitri, Nina.' Ilya used his best director's voice. 'Champagne's on me. For all your hard work and to Poland.'

Ella tensed. Was Ilya drunk to propose this toast, or too carefree to consider the allusion?

'I think I'll change,' she said. 'It's still a restaurant, isn't it, Nina? My suitcase is underneath where you're sitting.'

Ilya pulled the door open and stepped into the passageway. 'You go, guys. We know where to find you.'

She waited until the others were out of sight before she squeezed his hand. 'I'll stay back – they don't want me anyway – but you should be careful, darling.'

Ilya rubbed the crease between his eyebrows. 'I can't leave them there. It will look suspicious if I don't celebrate with my crew. I won't be long,' he said. 'I'll tell them you're tired.'

She nodded. 'I feel like we forgot something. And if they're so sticky now, how are we going to lose them in Warsaw?'

He embraced her. 'Put everything essential into my rucksack and I'll carry it around with me, until we get a chance. But don't pack our passports until we cross the border.'

Ella edged closer and felt reassured. 'Go.' She pushed him away. 'Just watch it, please.'

32

In their compartment, the dusk outside the window had thickened to near blackness. Only a string of yellow lights along the railway line adorned the night sky. Ella pressed her forehead into the glass. This was it. Freedom. Soon they would arrive in Brest, the last stop before Warsaw.

She sat on her berth, propped a pillow behind her back and peeled off her heels. The last hours of her Soviet life were rushing past like the station signs, unreadable in the dark, one long platform after another, swept by wind and void of people.

It surprised her to discover that she didn't feel happy. She loathed the country she was born into. But she hadn't told her parents she was leaving for good when they saw her off at Belorusskaya station. She sensed her mother knew, her eyes dull with pain. Ella wished she'd said goodbye. Yet she couldn't tell them the truth in case her defection plans failed. She wasn't sure how she and Ilya would cross the border. Or reach Vienna.

The upper berth hung above her like a casket lid. She imagined herself buried alive in this compartment, her body cold and stiff, transported towards the border and offloaded there when the train reached its destination. She heard steps and voices behind the locked door. The train rocked and the baby seemed strangely still.

Ella reached for the window and yanked it open a crack. The breeze chilled her face. The baby stirred and she sat back on her berth, breathless from the magnitude of what they'd embarked upon and the finality of its consequences.

*

Ella opened her eyes to the pitch black of the compartment, as she'd done every few minutes over the last hour. Her back ached, and she arched her body on the thin mattress. A swell of nausea rose to her throat but she willed it down. Her teeth clattered and her abdomen felt bloated. She rolled onto her side to face Ilya, who slept across from her on the other lower berth — only an arm's length away.

Ella burrowed her head in the pillow and breathed through her nose. But the urge to vomit only got stronger. She turned towards Ilya. His skin looked pallid and there were shadows under his eyes. He breathed evenly. She couldn't wake him. The last thing she wanted was to cause a commotion before the train reached the border.

The next stop — the last one before Brest and the *militzia* checkpoint at the border — would be in Minsk, the capital of Belorussia. If she could pull herself together, she could wake Ilya and they would get off at the station for a sip of night air. She swung her feet to the rocking floor and draped the blanket over her back. Her stomach contracted and she doubled over, not taking her eyes off Ilya's face. It wasn't the baby, she told herself, but she'd only had one glass of champagne, and there were no offensive smells to cause her sickness.

A hot sour mass arrived in her throat. She jammed her fist against her mouth and swallowed. Careful not to make a sound, she dragged the compartment door open. The barely lit passage felt like a tunnel. Light spilled out from underneath the neighbouring door where Ilya's colleagues were supposed to be asleep. Inside, a male voice spoke.

Holding her stomach, Ella scurried to the end of the passage. The toilet door gaped open, but the substantial rear of the uniformed train conductor, who was washing the floors, blocked the entrance.

The smell of chlorine hit Ella's nose. Cold sweat ran along her spine, and she could taste bile. She pushed past the uniformed woman, slammed the door and leaned over the steel bowl. Hot fluid burst from her mouth, burning her nostrils. Her knees buckled, and she kneeled on the damp floor beside the conductor's bucket and mop.

After a moment, her head cleared. It had to be the chicken or hard-boiled eggs she'd shared with the crew earlier in the evening. Ella flushed but tried not to inhale. The sour taste lingered and she splashed a handful of stale water onto her face.

The conductor knocked on the door. 'When are you due?'

'Two months.'

She pushed the door open and came face to face with a rosy-cheeked Russian countrywoman. 'It's starting,' the conductor said. 'We have to get you off the train, doll. In Minsk. They have some good hospitals there.' She sounded sincere.

With her eyes, Ella measured the conductor's hips. The woman had obviously given birth more than once, but that didn't make her an obstetrician.

'Champagne. I drank too much. Or it was yesterday's chicken.' Ella paused to weigh her words. 'I'll pay you for the inconvenience. I'll go get money now. Just don't tell my friends and don't send for help at the station.'

The woman's gaze seemed to palpate Ella's stomach. Then she gave a nod and backed against the passage wall. 'Do you want tea? With lemon? It cures … hangovers.'

Down the aisle, Ella saw a head pop out from the crew's compartment – Dmitri. She suppressed a shudder. 'Tea would be great,' she said. 'Bring it to my compartment and I'll pay you then.'

She strode past the conductor towards Ilya's soundman, who smiled at her. 'Insomnia?'

'Nothing a hot tea can't cure.' She laughed and reached for her compartment's doorhandle.

'When did you say you're due?' Dmitri asked.

Another cramp twisted Ella's guts, and she hid her wince. 'Eight weeks.'

She stepped inside and pulled the door closed behind her, leaving only a crack to see in the shadows. The cramp moved lower in her belly and she felt like she'd swallowed a rock. Her stomach rumbled and another bout of nausea hit. She breathed in and out and thought of the spring air on Minsk train platform – the free air in Warsaw, when they crossed the border, only a few hours from now. But if her sickness persisted, she wondered if she should even step out at the next station. She couldn't risk any of Ilya's crew reporting her condition.

She fumbled for Ilya's wallet and her wedding band, which she'd put back on to look properly married, clinked against the vodka bottle.

Ilya shifted on his mattress. 'What's going on, El?'

She pressed a finger to her lips and pointed at the wall between their compartment and his crew's. 'I ordered some tea.'

Ella took out a fifty-rouble note from his wallet. Twelve days of any teacher's or doctor's earnings. How much was enough to stop the conductor from talking? A wave of dizziness washed over her, and she realised that the train had lost speed. They must have reached the outskirts of Minsk.

Ilya propped himself up. 'You look a bit pale.'

'All is fine, my love. Sleep.'

She smiled at Ilya's tired face. The baby stirred and another cramp, stronger than the first ones, seized her stomach. She groaned and covered her mouth, pretending to stifle a yawn. Ilya's forehead wrinkled. He reached out and lifted the blind. Lit by the pre-dawn glow, rows of workers barracks swam past in slow motion.

'I'll go and pay,' Ella said, turning her back to him. 'She's taking forever.'

She slid the door open and stuck her head out into the passage. Pain radiated from her belly, and she doubled over on the threshold. An animal fear hit her under the ribcage, and she recalled the conductor's words about Minsk hospitals. She stumbled out.

Ilya's arms circled her from behind. 'Elka, are you not well?'

In the compartment next door, a female voice spoke. Tonya. The train slowed more. Through the windows, Ella saw that the barracks had given way to five-storey housing estates from the Khrushchev era, identical to the ones on Moscow's fringes. They were in the city now.

She twisted free of Ilya's embrace and breathed through her nose to ease the pain. She couldn't let him see. This was a false alarm anyway, caused by her nerves. 'I'll get the tea.'

A couple of strides down the aisle, she almost bumped into the conductor. The woman carried a pewter tray with a single glass of black tea in a matching glass-holder. 'Here you are.'

The voices in the crew's compartment became louder, and someone turned the doorhandle. Ella stuffed the fifty-rouble note, fifty times the price of the tea, into the woman's jacket and grabbed the tray.

The conductor smiled. 'Be careful, girl.'

Ella rushed back inside and slammed the door with her foot. Ilya stared at her, a glint of understanding in his eyes.

Then someone banged the flimsy wall. 'Guys, we're in Minsk,' Alex yelled. 'Let's go for a stroll.'

33

The night air at Minsk central station smelled of linden trees in bloom. Ella clambered down the steps onto the platform. Black tea with lemon had worked wonders and cured her upset stomach. The pains in her belly had vanished, leaving her light-headed but otherwise fine. Reaching Brest no longer felt impossible, just the next stop on their way to Warsaw. Four hours to go.

She leaned against the warm wall of their train carriage. Not far off, Ilya and Dmitri wandered along the platform towards a few women who were selling boiled potatoes and pickles.

The conductor peered at her. 'Feeling better?'

Ella shrugged. 'Food poisoning.'

The woman raised an eyebrow. Then Dmitri materialised in front of them with a soaked-through newspaper funnel full of apples. 'Want one? They're pickled.'

The vinegary aroma tickled Ella's nostrils. Inside her everything trembled, but she kept her face blank. She accepted his offer of an apple.

'How're you feeling?' he asked.

She sank her teeth into the salty-sweet apple pulp. 'All good, thank you, Dmitri. Yourself?'

He scowled and tilted his head. She strolled down the platform to join Ilya. Her pain had subsided, and the spicy taste of fruit cheered her up. She took Ilya's hand. More than anything else she dreaded letting him down. He loved her even though she was pregnant with Roman's child. And he was leaving behind his own son, maybe forever. She owed Ilya their chance at freedom.

'Five minutes to departure,' the conductor called out.

Ella kissed Ilya's cheek. The fresh air had revived her. Her future with Ilya and the baby in faraway Australia gleamed on the horizon.

*

After the freedom of the open space, it felt like there wasn't much air in the compartment. Ella stretched out and prepared to wait for the *militzia* checkpoint in Brest, which would be their last ordeal on Soviet ground before they could defect in Warsaw. A socialist country, Poland was not a part of the great Russian empire any longer.

The train rumbled and pulled away from the platform. In only four hours, after they'd passed the checkpoint, their carriage would be transferred to narrower gauge tracks, the same width as the rest of Europe. And as soon as they crossed into Poland, she and Ilya would need to be ready to take their chance and escape.

Ilya switched off the lights and lay down on his berth. 'All good?'

'Fine.' Ella grinned in the dark. She counted her breaths, exhausted from the previous ordeal, but too excited to fall asleep. Then a spasm seized her stomach and made her lose count. Pain stabbed her like a thug with a blade. She curled into herself. Every part of her body ached. Her lower back cramped.

She bit her lip until she tasted blood. *Ellochka, hold on*, she told herself, like Olga used to say to her when she was a child.

Four hours. The pain would pass. She scrambled from her berth to the door, grinding her teeth.

Ilya sat up. 'Where're you going?'

'Bathroom.' She shut the door before he had a chance to follow her.

Out in the passage, she waited for another spasm to pass. This time she had no doubt about what was causing her pain. Yet she couldn't tell Ilya. If her contractions stopped and she had a pain-free window, they could pass the checkpoint in Brest. But if Ilya thought she was in labour, he'd insist they get off the train.

Ella scurried down the aisle towards the service compartment. The idea to ask for help didn't feel so crazy. She had no choice but to trust the woman. With her childbearing hips, the conductor surely knew what could be done to slow her labour. She'd heard of women doing this forever. Camomile to relax the muscles. To stop the contractions. In this job, the conductor was likely used to nursing all kinds of casualties.

If she gave birth in Poland, they could still try to defect. They might even have a better chance for refugee status when they got to Vienna. But she wasn't sure how to explain this to the conductor. The baby. It was still under term. She had to stop it coming.

What if my baby dies?

She rapped on the service compartment door.

'What happened? Can't I snooze for an hour?' The woman's hair was in curlers, and she was struggling to drag her uniform jacket over her camisole.

'Sorry.' Ella barged past her into the cramped single-berth space. 'I need your help.'

'Sit.' The woman's face softened, and she patted the homemade quilt that covered the berth. 'What do you want me to do? I have to telegraph ahead for an ambulance.'

'Please don't.' Ella sank onto the berth and hugged her stomach. 'You have to help me. The baby shouldn't be born now. It's too early. It could be a false alarm, too – I heard it happens.'

The woman grimaced. 'Are you crazy? You need to get off in Brest at the checkpoint and admit yourself to the hospital. You don't want to have the baby abroad.'

Ella stared at the floor. 'I'm not due until July. Isn't there something we can do to stop it?' She crushed the woman's calloused hand. 'The border *militzia* won't look at us too closely at the checkpoint. We're a film crew. We've been nominated for an award in Poland.'

The conductor withdrew her hand. Gently. She rummaged in a tin with a red cross on it. 'Until your water breaks, you are safe.' She spoke over her shoulder. 'It hasn't broken yet, has it?'

'No.' Pain crashed over Ella like a wave. It contracted all her muscles. She lay on her side and brought her knees to her belly. But the moment she felt she couldn't bear it any longer, the pain released her. Ella straightened her legs and watched the conductor prepare a mixture. Then the next spasm twisted her again into a foetal position.

'Drink this.' The conductor offered her a tumbler of dark brown liquid that stank of herbs. 'Don't make faces. It's valerian root. You need to calm down.'

The pain eased a little, and Ella drank the concoction. She chased it down with cool water from another tumbler that the woman handed to her.

'Now, let's talk.'

Ella sat up and winced.

The conductor frowned. 'If you make a face like that in front of *militziamen*, you won't get to cross the border.'

Ella nodded. But it wasn't clear to her whether the conductor was fully on her side. She had no reason to help her either.

Ella unclasped her watch – a gift from Anna for her twentieth birthday – and pressed it into the woman's hand.

The conductor pushed it back. 'Put that back on. You might need it. Do you have someone in Poland?' Ella shook her head and the conductor sighed. 'Your mama?'

The woman's worry lines reminded Ella of her mother. She needed to reassure her, to get her goodwill. 'We have a hotel in Warsaw and there'll be a doctor at the film festival,' she lied.

The conductor kneeled in the corner, her back to Ella. Was she praying? An agnostic Jewess, Ella couldn't rely on a Russian God. 'Tell me what to do. Only not something dangerous for the baby. And how can I pay you?'

Her pain grew duller before it subsided altogether.

'Well.' The woman eased herself onto the berth beside Ella. She held two vials in her hand. 'If I help you but if it doesn't work and you end up in a hospital, you must forget about me. Don't tell the doctors what you took.'

Ella started to shake. 'But the baby is premature.'

The conductor examined her face. 'That's why I'm helping you, girl. To stop your baby from being born too early. Why else?'

A painful contraction saved Ella from having to reply. It wasn't as strong as the previous ones. But it made her groan and doubled her over. It lasted longer too, leaving her without air in her lungs.

'Look here.' The conductor held up the vials. 'These are herbal solutions. They won't hurt the baby. One is a painkiller. Strong.'

She paused and listened to a noise outside. Ella prayed Dmitri and the others were asleep. She wondered if it was Ilya, looking for her. The carriage fell silent and the woman put her lips to Ella's ear.

'The larger one is a sleeping potion. Drink it when you get back to your compartment. It'll stop the pain and make you sleep. Warn your fellow not to wake you in Brest. Tell him to show the customs officer your passport and put fifty roubles in it.'

Ella nodded her agreement. She felt another contraction, a weaker one, as if she'd been hit with a wooden sword rather than stabbed with a knife. The valerian root was clearly working. She bent to the woman's hand to kiss it.

The conductor jerked her hand back and nudged her towards the door. 'Stop this nonsense.' She checked her watch, which was cheaper than Ella's. 'We'll be there at five thirty.'

'Thank you.'

The conductor prodded her out. 'Now go to sleep. I need some rest too.'

In the shadowy passage, Ella clutched the vials. Her belly felt tight. Pain gathered in her lower back. She pulled out the cork and lifted the pain-relieving vial to her lips.

She stumbled towards her compartment. Maybe she should tell Ilya about the vials. But he wouldn't agree to risking her or the baby's health. He would demand they get off the train and go to a hospital.

It would be her secret, she decided.

Ella pulled out the cork of the sleeping potion and inhaled the acidic scent. What if it hurt her baby? She shook her head. The woman had clearly tried to help her. She raised the vial towards her lips.

Before she could take a sip, the carriage jolted and she tripped on the carpet runner. She fell to one knee still clasping the vial. Inside her, something tore. Lukewarm liquid rushed down her bare legs under her dress. Her fingers trembled as she reached out to touch the damp spot that spread fast on the carpet.

34

Her baby girl's tiny mouth latched on to her swollen nipple, and a combination of love and pain made Ella close her eyes. She pressed the swaddled baby to her breast. Three weeks had passed since her waters broke on the train, ruining their chances of crossing the border. Her world had shrunk to feedings and sleep. For the first ten days of her life, her daughter had been too weak to latch and had to be fed from a dropper. Now Ella felt bliss descend on her with every pull of the baby's mouth.

The nurse grunted approvingly. 'See. She suckles. I told you – be patient.'

Ella smiled and watched her push a three-tiered trolley, with babies wrapped in washed-out blankets, through the maternity ward. In two rows of beds, sixteen women breastfed their babies, expressed their milk or slept, even with the early June sun bright on their faces.

Ella smoothed out the wrinkles on her daughter's forehead with her fingertip. She and Ilya had named her Lilly, after his mother, Lilya. A desire to see him flooded her. Made her press her baby closer to her heart. Lilly sucked greedily. Although Ilya wasn't allowed further than the lobby of the *Roddom*, Birthing Hospital Number 1, the nurses conveyed a note from him to Ella every morning and from Ella to him every afternoon.

The night before, she'd written to ask whether they should stay in Brest or return to Moscow. She'd give a year of her life to find herself at home with Ilya and her baby girl. To forget about this ward. If Ilya adopted Lilly, they could leave Russia as a family, even if they had to start the emigration process anew. She'd asked him about this too and was only staying awake to receive his reply.

She detached Lilly from her right breast and helped her latch on to the left. Her love for this snuffling creature was larger than her own self, more intense than her desire for Ilya. The moment the baby had been placed on her belly, just after the birth, and she felt the baby's weight and her warmth, the horror of the labour had transformed somehow into a pure love for this helpless being who needed her to survive.

The nurse who'd taken her note to Ilya continued to wander the ward. Ella knew he'd say yes to adopting Lilly, but they had to get Roman's consent. For that alone she needed to return to Moscow, however terrifying the prospect of facing Roman again. This time though, she'd get Ilya to accompany her to Tula.

Lilly had fallen asleep at her breast, and something shrank inside Ella. She wondered if a return to Moscow would put them at risk, exposing Ilya and her parents to whatever awaited her from Captain Seriy or his KGB colleagues. Her non-attendance at his office at the appointed time would surely have consequences. She'd be summoned again. She'd have to explain her letter to Sonya in Sydney and her meeting with Jack. Worse still, they might detain her as his recruit.

Ella turned to her side and placed Lilly on the pillow next to her face. She gazed at her baby in wonder, admiring her rose-petal lips and high forehead, furrowed in sleep.

Maybe it was better to hole up in Brest. To rent a room in the suburbs and wait out the storm, as Vlad had begged her to do after Jack's arrest. But then Ilya would have to return to Moscow alone. That would postpone Lilly's adoption, and it was hard to predict to what lengths Roman would go to get his freedom. He might start court proceedings to take custody of her child even from his labour camp.

To wake the baby, Ella tickled her nose as the nurse had advised. Lilly's mouth seized her nipple again. But after two or three energetic sucks, she grew drowsy. Ella yawned and touched Lilly's cheek. Silky. She bent to kiss the crown of her head. It was perfumed by the sweetest aroma in the world – breastfed baby.

'Let me take her. You'll squash her sleeping.'

The nurse's voice jolted Ella into consciousness. She'd fallen asleep with Lilly wheezing at the crook of her arm.

The elderly nurse snatched Lilly away and laid her on the top tier of her trolley. 'Sleep while you can.'

She pushed the trolley towards the ward door, and Ella lowered her legs off the bed. She shoved her arms into the sleeves of her hospital gown and hobbled after the nurse to the corridor. 'Has somebody brought today's letters already?'

She kept her eyes on Lilly's face, memorising the details. Her daughter's name was handwritten on the rubber tags attached to her wrist and to her tiny ankle, but Ella's fear of losing her baby in the hospital's unending walkways felt as real as her fear of going back to Moscow.

'I'll go check, if you'd like.' The nurse patted her pocket. 'Some fellows are still hanging around in the lobby. Nothing else to do. What's yours look like?'

Ella found a crumpled rouble note in her gown's pocket and gave it to the nurse. 'Black hair. Leather jacket.'

*

The daylight behind the ward's window was fading, but the elderly nurse hadn't returned with a note from Ilya. Ella lay on her back and stared at the ceiling. She listened to the sounds of the other mothers and their infants. A different nurse, wearing a white doctor's coat over her street clothes, arrived at her bed. She flicked her eyes at the door and pretended to adjust Ella's pillow.

'Abramova, you owe me a rouble.' She held her hand out for money. 'I brought you a parcel.'

Ella found a rouble, folded in four, among the few Ilya had sent her last time. The nurse placed a string bag with oranges on the bedside table and vanished. Ella grabbed the bag and tipped the fruit onto her blanket. A note from Ilya tumbled out.

My love, she read. *Of course, I want to adopt Lilly and I hope Roman agrees. After all, he wouldn't want to take care of the baby. He seems too preoccupied with other things. I called Marina but her mother told me that she is in Tula, with Roman.*

Careful not to push the oranges onto the floor, Ella slid under her blanket. She felt shivery whenever she thought of Roman. Fear or hate – she wasn't sure. The words of Ilya's note blurred under the dull ceiling lights. She brought the note closer to her eyes and stroked Ilya's handwriting to calm herself.

Ellochka, I'm sorry, but it looks like it's safer for you to stay in Brest. Your doctor promised to discharge you as soon as Lilly's weight reaches two and half kilograms. They told me she is only two hundred grams short of it.

Ella thought of Lilly's warmth at her chest, and her milk leaked. She read on.

I spoke to your mother. They had a call from Captain Seriy asking after your whereabouts. And Vlad is gone. He just disappeared. His father doesn't know where he may be or what happened to him.

Her milk might turn sour. The last paragraph made her twist in pain. She wasn't due to feed Lilly for another hour, but her engorged breasts burned. Hiding in Brest wasn't an option, away from Ilya and without her family's support. But if Vlad had been arrested, she wasn't sure going back to Moscow would be safe either.

35

Ella parked Lilly's pram in the shadow of the giant oak on the slope above the murky waters of the Moskva River. Ilya stretched out on the grass next to the pram. Krasnaya Presnya Park, her never-changing childhood hangout, only a few minutes' walk from her parents' home, felt unfamiliar now.

Discharged from Brest's maternity hospital, she'd returned to Moscow only to feel displaced in her own city. It was as if with her daughter's arrival, almost nothing remained of her old self. A new woman had emerged, one who thought endlessly of the baby's feedings and nappies. This preoccupation brought with it a weird sense of calm. And although nobody knew where Vlad was, with him out of the picture, maybe the KGB would just leave her alone.

Her parents hadn't questioned Ella's one-month stay in hospital or expressed any suspicion about the failed trip to Poland. Everyone doted on Lilly and pretended that no plans had ever been disrupted.

Plans. That was what connected her old self to the new Ella, along with a desire to escape the USSR and start afresh with Ilya and Lilly. The day after their arrival in Moscow, Olga had kissed the baby's forehead and told her that word had got to Sonya and she was happy to have them. The man on the phone in Melbourne had contacted some people through the synagogue. But to get to Australia, she still needed to divorce Roman and convince him to let Ilya adopt Lilly.

Ella peeked under the pram's hood at her sleeping daughter. The oak canopy shielded them from the afternoon sun. It offered relief from the heatwave that melted the streets of Moscow and made Ella's adjustment to being back home even harder. Lilly's clenched fists flanked her rosy face. Love pierced Ella's heart once again like a rapier leaving a sharp sweet pain.

Lilly was hers. She had no intention of sharing her with Roman. He'd never wanted her child to be born, and Ilya adopting her would only formalise what had already happened. They were a family.

'Let's go see him on Sunday.' She lay down and rested her head on Ilya's chest. 'Get the divorce and adoption papers sorted out.'

He shifted. 'We can't go together and rub it in his face.' The dappled sunlight changed his expression from loving to sad and almost distant. 'He won't sign anything if he sees what he's lost.'

Ella felt grass blades needling her legs, bare under her summer dress. 'I don't want to go alone.'

She sat up and stared into the river. An old memory of its frozen surface cracking beneath her feet popped into her mind. 'I almost drowned here when I was ten or eleven.' Despite the heat, she shivered and rubbed her arms.

Ella turned from the river back to Ilya. 'You know what Roman wants. He figured if I move to Tula, he'll be allowed to rent a room and only report at the barracks twice a day for the roll call. He'll never grant me a divorce.'

'You want *me* to go?' Ilya picked at the grass. 'If Marina visits him, that means she might be pleased to have him to herself.'

'But how do you feel about seeing them together?' She brought her lips to his cheek and brushed them against his skin. They hadn't talked much about his life with Marina. Ella refused to pry and he didn't volunteer anything. He visited Yan at Marina's mother's house when Marina wasn't around.

Ilya closed his eyes, probably hiding from her gaze. And her questions. 'She must have never stopped loving him. I was just blind. I imagined myself her rescuer when he ditched her. We stayed together because of Yan, I think. Everything else died out a long time ago. Or has never been there at all.' He sat up and cleared the dry leaves from his jeans. 'If she's there with Roman, he might sign the papers. I'll take them to him. Then you can get divorced without ever seeing him.'

She stroked his face. 'You have to shave more often,' she said, 'but I still love you.'

*

Raya sat across from her at the kitchen table in a black strapless top that revealed suntanned shoulders, her elbows brushing Ella's old ironing blanket.

Ella licked her finger and touched the iron before placing it down on one of Lilly's nappies, which she'd just brought inside from the balcony line. She left the glass door open and the scorching July breeze caressed her flushed cheeks.

'And so I stayed in Brest for almost five weeks until Lilly started feeding and put on some weight,' she said.

Raya's face was attentive. Ella felt grateful that Lilly was sleeping and she could spend some time talking to another adult, even if she was her rival and now an actress at the Moscow Theatre for Young People.

'I can't wait to hold Lilly,' Raya gushed. 'And Roman. You surely keep in touch? He'll be released soon, won't he? Your mother-in-law called. She said they are collecting good witness statements, like how he helped kids in the neighbourhood or any other such deeds.'

Ella wondered what Raya knew about Roman, apart from what Lia had told her. He had coached Leon in chess but she wouldn't imagine he'd helped others.

'He came to the Pioneers' Palace, where I worked, to talk to the young pioneers about his engineering job, so Lia thought I might write a statement,' Raya said.

Ella folded another nappy on top of the warm stack, eyeing the never-ending basket of dry laundry. 'What are you working on?' She wiped her brow and straightened, now wishing Raya would leave and feeling ashamed that she couldn't be happy for her. Something about her former friend felt like she enjoyed rubbing her news into Ella's face.

'A Soviet play. You won't know it, but mine is a great role. A girl with a limp who wants to become a cosmonaut, like the one in Soyuz,' Raya enthused.

She leaped up from her seat and pulled the iron out of Ella's grip. 'Let's have a *ciggaretta* on the balcony. You are allowed one, surely?'

Ella play-acted denial but followed Raya outside into the oven-heat of Moscow's summer. The whiff of ash from the burning forests grew stronger than the scent of her own body, her breasts unpleasantly heavy under the chintz dress, sweat gathering under them. She lifted her arms and let her hair out, combing it with her fingers. She leaned forward, grabbed the balcony's railing and stretched.

Moscow floated like a mirage, losing its contours in the afternoon's blaze.

Raya's cigarette made her want one too, but she held herself in check remembering Lilly's greedy mouth on her breast. Wincing from pain and pleasure.

Raya stood with her back to Ella, facing the streets below, her cigarette squeezed between her manicured fingers like an extension of her well-deserved professional life. Acting – being free.

She would be free too, Ella thought, when she finally got her divorce sorted out. 'Have you heard any more about Podolski?'

Raya lifted her shoulders. 'No one knows. Some think he left for Israel. Others say he's in a mental asylum. His apartment is empty and the phone doesn't answer. He's just gone.'

Ella's eyes teared at the thought of what had happened to her old teacher and she looked up at the sky. Discoloured, it didn't let the sun's rays through.

'I need to finish ironing before Lilly wakes up.'

She stepped back across the threshold, her bare soles touching the cool kitchen linoleum. Raya followed her inside and Ella turned to admire her yellow culottes.

'Did you make them yourself?' She pinched the muslin-like fabric of Raya's skirt-pants that reached her mid-calf. 'Beautiful colour.'

'It's a Burda magazine pattern. Mum sent me the fabric from Minsk.' Raya was lucky she knew how to sew.

Ella moistened the tip of her finger to check the iron again. 'What do you think about the Samantha Smith story? The American girl. Do you think it's true?'

Raya smiled. 'It was published in *Pravda*, wasn't it? Must be true then.' They both laughed.

While *Pravda* meant the Truth, no one really believed the State's main newspaper, at least none of their actor friends did. *It could be different in the provinces*, Ella thought. A tiny whimper from the bedroom made her put the iron down, the dry spot on her dress where the nipple touched it getting wet.

'Lilly.'

Raya got up, but Ella gestured for her to keep seated. 'Give us a few minutes. You wouldn't want to try the nappy change, would you?'

She snorted. 'Samantha Smith – the Goodwill Ambassador. I think the girl is real, but her letter – I am not sure. How did it reach Andropov? Does he read all letters from children all over the world – the former KGB chief? The Butcher of Budapest? And of course, he only thinks of peace, not war, like other Russian tzars before him.'

'Maybe Samantha's parents are Russian spies,' Raya said, 'And it was a clever way to bring them back home to the USSR?'

They both giggled, and Ella felt better, not quite forgetting Roman in Tula, but for a moment feeling that all might turn out well.

*

At dawn, the buzz in her ears woke her. Still not fully awake, Ella rolled out of bed and dashed to the living room. She stood naked in the semi-darkness, hoping the phone ringing hadn't woken Ilya or Lilly. 'Allo?'

'Missed me?' Roman sounded strange.

'Am I supposed to? Why are you calling at this hour?'

'I'm celebrating.' He laughed. 'Marina checked us into a hotel overnight and gave me the news about my baby daughter.'

Ella wiped her palm on her bare hip. She wished she was dressed for this call.

'When are you coming? The camp's advocate told me I have rights.' He snorted. 'Maybe I can look after my baby while *you* work.'

Ella's skin felt prickly with heat. His intentions were clear. 'What about Marina? Is she celebrating with you?'

She felt Ilya's presence before she saw him. He stood in the doorway, his silhouette making her lose her train of thought. She managed a tiny smile at him...

'Don't make this a joke.' Roman's voice sounded instantly sober. 'I sweat here in muck at this fucking plant and you take it easy in Moscow with your lover.'

Ilya stepped forward. She glanced at him, at his strong arms, ready to protect her. 'You didn't answer my question.'

'What's my daughter's name?' Roman asked. 'I thought Raquel, like my grandmother.'

'You never even wanted this child.'

'No, doll.' Roman laughed loudly, as if he had an audience. 'You are confused. When you come to Tula and bring my daughter, we'll rent a room. I might get my sentence reduced. And then I'll return home, where you're having a grand time now.' He hiccupped. 'How is Ilya, by the way? Is he treating you well?'

Ilya touched her arm and shook his head. But the words tumbled out of her anyway.

'You never loved me,' she shouted. 'You were vile after you found out I was pregnant, long before your arrest.'

'Bullshit!' He was yelling too. 'My parents wanted a grandchild. We applied for emigration together.' He breathed heavily down the phone line. Then his voice dropped to a hiss. 'Don't play games with me, El. I have connections in Moscow. If you don't come to see me, they'll visit your toy boy. Maybe he won't be—'

Ella slammed the phone down. She pressed her face into Ilya's chest and felt unable to cry. Were Roman's threats real? She didn't know.

36

Olga
Saratov, USSR
1943

The chirping of the movie projector blended with the moans of the wounded. Olga's eyelids felt heavy but she continued to squint at the makeshift screen, an outstretched infirmary bedsheet, set up in the canteen of War Hospital Number 2.

The scraping of crutches, squeaking of rusty bedsprings and rustle of the oaks outside made for an unlikely symphony. She yearned for her life with Natan and children in pre-war Moscow, though tonight it felt less real than the patriotic movie they were obliged to watch.

Natan's last letter from the front – rushed and black from censor's ink – was dated March 1942, more than a year ago. Their regiment had moved and she wondered if she would ever see her husband again. Olga touched the breast pocket of her nurse's uniform and stared ahead.

Convalescing soldiers sat squeezed between junior nurses on the benches. In the front row, Lieutenant Lubov's blond head blocked the screen. Olga's two children were tucked next to him on either side. The boy who had interrogated her four years ago had turned into a fully-fledged NKVD officer. Handsome and dangerous. His arm, bandaged from the elbow down to his fingertips, hovered above her son's narrow back, her daughter's curls spilled over his other arm. She watched him fumble inside his pocket and hand Faina something tiny, probably a sweet or a sliver of rock sugar, before he pulled out a pack of his Kazbek cigarettes.

Olga's heart pounded. She didn't feel safe or peaceful when Lieutenant Lubov was present. He was her patient and ten years younger. He desired her, but they were not equals.

Lubov turned his head and she felt his icy blue eyes on her breasts. If she said no, would he make her disappear?

The other nurses envied her. There were no young men left behind the front lines and an NKVD officer could provide protection, or lipstick and a pair of stockings. Or he could make her kids orphans. Her choice.

She hadn't asked for his attention, but Lubov wouldn't take no for an answer. Ever since she'd saved his life he'd been in love with her. His wounds had healed and his frostbitten fingers had not been amputated. He did not die from gangrene as the head surgeon had feared.

Olga recalled Lubov's baby-pink cheek, freshly shaven, and too close to her own. She simply couldn't submit. If she did, Natan wouldn't return from the front. It would be like she had buried him.

As the movie drew to a close, Olga rose from her seat. She grabbed her medication trolley and stepped into the corridor, readying herself for a round of injections and dressings, catheters and soiled sheets. It wasn't her shift and she had younger nurses to take care of this, but she couldn't face going back to her room. Not with Lubov on the prowl.

She heard his steps behind her. The lieutenant's breath scorched her neck, but she bent her head to the trolley and picked up a syringe.

'The soldiers are waiting.'

His bandaged arm weighed down her shoulders. 'Come now.'

Olga dropped the syringe and flinched when it clipped the kidney-shaped metal tray.

'But the children?' She still hadn't turned to look at him, but his heat assaulted her. Her knees jammed into the trolley. 'I can't.'

The scent of male sweat plugged her nostrils. She recoiled. He pressed into her, their bodies locked in embrace. His boyish urge seeped from his body into hers.

'Come later when the kids are asleep.' It didn't sound like a plea, more like an order.

'Nurse, nurse!'

A call from the ward gave her strength and she tore away from the man and the temptation.

37

Ella
Moscow, USSR
July 1983

Ella switched off the morning radio and faced her nappy-clad baby. This year's most popular song, 'A Million Scarlet Roses', dissolved into the scorching breeze that puffed through the balcony door, bringing no relief from July's heatwave. She hummed the catchy tune as Lilly cooed happily, secured in her bouncer.

Ella kneeled on the floor and made another attempt to feed her daughter. Lilly's plump pinkish body was too warm to the touch. Ella spooned milky liquid between her rosebud lips, and Lilly scrunched her face and spat it out.

'Silly girl.' Ella stroked her cheek and then wandered towards the open window.

Limp tulle curtains drooped on either side. Fires continued to burn at Moscow's fringes and the smell of smoke hung in the air as if the flat was placed beside a giant woodstove. She wished she could be at the dacha with Olga and Leon, but she stayed put, waiting for Ilya's return from the film shoot.

Ella checked the courtyard, an obsessive habit she'd developed since Vlad had vanished. There was no life outside, neither kids nor grandmothers, and the sun burned the empty square and the street beyond it. The thought of leaving her building terrified her. She couldn't even go to the local shops in daylight in case the KGB waited for her around the corner. Maybe in the evening, when it was cooler, she could take Lilly for a walk.

The doorbell tinkled, as if it'd been rung by mistake. It was likely a neighbour, she figured. The KGB would knock harder or kick the door in. But she wouldn't open the door to a stranger anyway. She kneeled again and rocked Lilly's bouncer, soothed by her daughter's delight.

There was a knock on the door. Gentle. 'Ella, it's Lia. Please open up.'

It'd been a few months since she'd seen Roman's parents, and she wondered what they wanted. She stared through the peephole. Her in-laws seemed to have shrunk in size. Lia wore a measured smile. Rigid beside her, Alexander stood like a guard. He held a floral bouquet wrapped in cellophane.

'We came to see our granddaughter,' Lia said.

They had a right to see Lilly, Ella reasoned. She unlocked the door and stepped aside to let them in. Alexander shoved the flowers into her hands and pursed his lips at her bare legs. Ella tugged at her denim cut-offs and led Roman's parents into the living room.

'Oh, she's so lovely,' Lia cooed, squatting in front of Lilly. She pulled out a parcel from her shopping bag. 'A pretty dress for a pretty girl.' She held up a pink dress that looked far too large.

Alexander sat stiffly on the sofa. He didn't take his gaze from Lilly, who blew bubbles.

Lia noticed the half-full baby bottle. 'What are you feeding her, Ella?'

'Milky drink. I've just made it.'

Lia's lips became a red line. 'She's only six weeks old. You should be breastfeeding.'

'I am.' Ella walked over to the balcony and pulled at the tulle curtains. 'I breastfeed twice a day. Morning and night. And Lilly is almost two months. She was born on the fifteenth of May.'

Roman's parents exchanged glances. Alexander nodded at Lia.

'We'd like Roman to see her,' Lia said. 'He wants to spend time with his daughter.'

'He may want to take care of her,' Alexander added.

Lia's speech seemed rehearsed and Alexander's words sounded like a threat. So that was why they'd come – as emissaries for Roman.

Ella closed the window. Her eyes fell on the street corner and an image of Vlad being shoved into a black car materialised out of the scorching air.

'Roman's in Tula,' she said.

'Well, we are here, in Moscow.' Lia tickled Lilly's neck under her chin. The baby puffed out her cheeks. 'We could certainly help. She is our only grandchild – aren't you, darling?'

Ella's head ached. She picked Lilly up and moved her away from Lia. She yearned to get her in-laws out before they got settled. 'I was planning to do some shopping. I need to buy milk.'

Lia stood and inspected the room. Her eyes were deep-set, like Roman's. 'We hope you're a good mother, Ella.'

Alexander got up too, and Lia took his hand. 'You are not the best wife, you know?'

Ella lifted her chin. 'And your son is not the best husband.'

Alexander turned to go.

Ella led her in-laws to the front door. In the end, it didn't matter what they thought of her. Alexander stepped onto the landing, and Ella waited for her mother-in-law to cross the threshold.

'OVIR called us,' Lia said. 'They're about to process our emigration papers.' She paused and stood face to face with Ella. 'We want you and Lilly to join us. You get Roman an early release and we leave as a family.'

*

Ella eased the pram off the porch of her apartment block and glanced both ways. The courtyard and the street looked deserted. She'd decided to run to the corner store and back, get milk and bread.

It had cooled overnight and Lilly had slept through. The sun hadn't yet started bearing down on the cracked asphalt, and the air still tasted fresh. A row of dusty poplars provided some shade as she stepped onto the footpath alongside the motorway.

She pushed the pram and walked fast. Lilly wasn't asleep, her little face was pinched, shadowed by the pram's hood. Ella hoped she wouldn't start crying in the few minutes it took to reach the corner store. She broke into an easy jog.

A sleek black Volga dropped speed and cruised along beside the kerb. Ella slowed to a stroll. The car outpaced her for a moment. Then it came to a halt. Ella's pulse quickened and she realised she was panting. She spun around and strode back towards her block of flats.

The car door opened behind her and she sprinted. Footsteps pounded after her on the pavement. She had no doubt to whom those footsteps belonged, even before a hand grabbed her elbow. She tried to shake it off.

'Ella Gregorievna, please.' The man was almost pleading. 'You don't want to hurt your baby.'

His fingers tightened their grip and all strength seeped out of her at once. Ella looked at Lilly and looked around. A few people rushed by, some distance away. She saw a woman with a pram nearby and tried to get her attention but the woman turned away. Two cars drove past. The man was right – they wouldn't harm her or Lilly. If that was their intention, they would have turned up at night.

'It won't take long,' he said. 'Only a few questions.'

Ella finally checked his face. Nondescript. He didn't meet her eyes, but his grip eased. She pushed the pram towards the car's back door and picked Lilly up. Then she stepped into the Volga's air-conditioned trap and let the man deal with the pram.

The car smelled of leather upholstery and cologne. She held Lilly tighter. Her baby's face strained and Ella kissed her forehead. Lilly whimpered, and before Ella knew it, the car had sped out of town towards the Moscow Ring Road.

*

General Lubov's office felt like a space capsule, existing outside of time and place. The cacophony of traffic from Dzerzhinsky Square and the hazy July air were left outside, together with the sunlight. Ella coughed, expecting an echo to bounce off the wood-panelled walls. But no echo came.

She reclasped her hands. They hadn't stopped twitching since the black Volga dropped Lilly off at the family's dacha. The driver had handed the baby to Olga, who looked frightened, while Ella had to wait in the car.

Lubov, dressed in a suit rather than his KGB uniform, stood beside his mahogany desk and towered over her.

'I am pleased you're here, Ashkenazi,' he said. He seemed to relish the sound of her surname. But it wasn't clear why he'd summoned her.

'I expected you to visit us sooner.' The general walked over the thick carpet and sat behind his vast desk. 'I don't have much time.'

Ella eyed the glass of black tea and the bronze bust of Lenin in front of Lubov. Lenin's bald head gleamed. Her eyes flitted to an older-style folder, and she felt sick with the idea that it spelled out whatever he wanted from her.

The general opened the file. 'Your friend Vladimir Zacharov has signed a confession, listing his foreign connections and his local ones.'

He checked that Ella understood and she managed a nod. She had to stop herself from bolting to the door and banging her fists on it, pleading for freedom. If Vlad had revealed any names, she didn't have a hope, even if she'd never helped his dissident group.

She sank into her seat.

Lubov looked at a note in the folder. 'I'll give you the address and the names. You could add a couple of details.' He paused. 'We can help you,' he said. 'Isn't that why you're here? So we can help each other?'

She met his gaze. The prospect of being arrested had been on her mind since Vlad's disappearance. Lubov stared at her with his icy-blue eyes as if he were trying to remember what else he wanted to say.

Breaking eye contact, Ella examined her white knuckles. Her hands were flaky from washing nappies, her eyelids itchy from lack of sleep. She could not second-guess the general or figure out what made him tick. He wouldn't have brought her here if he didn't have plans for her. What he was asking for wasn't that bad. She could warn those people.

He rose from his chair with the note in his hand. 'What was it you wanted ... to emigrate with your husband?'

Ella exhaled, yet she still couldn't speak. She recalled Lia's offer for her and Lilly to be added to the Abramovs' emigration papers. If she asked Lubov now, he would likely help her. Roman was serving a sentence in a labour camp, sure, but she might be able to get her exit permit through his parents and take off with Lilly. She thought about how that would work for Ilya. She'd have to beg Lubov.

The general stepped closer. 'Think of your child. You don't want to join your friend here, do you?' He handed her the note, which had an address and a few names written in purple ink.

'Thank you, Comrade General.'

It was all she could think to say. She got to her feet and took the note from him, and she noticed that her hands had stopped shaking.

'You have one week to confirm those names,' Lubov said.

38

The sun was going down. Ella's pulse raced as she ran towards the lake near the dacha. Steam rose from the earth. She pushed through the juvenile forest, ignoring the leaves that slapped her bare arms. She wanted to throw herself in the water, to feel it run down her face, rid herself of the rotten taste in her mouth. A *kukushka* screamed in the trees. Ella stopped and wiped a spider web off her cheek. They had to accept Lubov's offer, whatever Ilya might think of it when he returned from his shoot. There was no other way out. They had to be clever about it.

She peeled off her sleeveless top and touched the lake with her toe. A ripple spread over its glassy surface. The ride in the black Volga felt like a fever dream. And the dacha smelled of valerian drops, even though her grandfather had been away in hospital for the last two weeks. Not having visited him there only added to her guilt.

But she'd held Lilly and it fortified her. She was able to smile at Olga and tell her that all was good. That she had nothing to do with Vlad's cause or his dissident friends. Olga didn't seem convinced, but she'd stopped prying.

The fading sun's rays hit the lake and made Ella squint. She dived into the dark water. Vlad wouldn't have revealed the names, she thought, he wouldn't cave in so quickly. So the general's list was likely a ploy. He wanted to use her to confirm his suspicions. But she must not do Lubov's bidding, and she had to warn Vlad's friends first.

Ella swam fast to avoid the whirlpools. She couldn't let Vlad rot inside. But his lauded father wouldn't let that happen either. Boris Zacharov – the writer – was too well connected for even Lubov to tackle. She stood on her tiptoes in the lake, her head above water. If she got Vlad's father's support, Lubov might leave her alone. She would stop being useful to him if she wasn't discreet. Though if she confirmed the names he knew already, she would at least appear of use, and he would be more inclined to assist her.

The lakebed shifted beneath her and the current dragged her away towards a whirlpool. A willow branch hung low over the water, and she grabbed it to swing herself back onto her feet.

*

A train horn sounded in the distance. Ella bent over Lilly's cot and watched her frown in her sleep and then relax. She straightened up. The country train should have dropped Ilya off at Saltikovka station. In a few minutes, he'd arrive at the dacha. Then she would hug her beloved and forget about her worries, if only for a moment.

The house was quiet. She walked towards the door, careful on the squeaky floorboards. Olga had locked herself in her bedroom after Ella's return from the lake. She hadn't asked any more questions about her meeting with Lubov. In fact, she'd hardly spoken a word.

She rehearsed what she'd say to Ilya. Lubov's offer that she join the Abramovs was their only chance of escape. He had to accept it.

The bang of the front gate filled her veins with warm honey. She fumbled with the lock. Ilya might not agree with her. Instead, he might blame her for yielding to Lubov. She threw the door open to fall into his arms in the cool night air.

She clutched his duffel bag, pulled him inside and started kissing his face. A week apart felt like months.

'Wait, Ella, wait.' He crouched to his bag and lifted out a huge oval-shaped melon. It had come all the way from Uzbekistan and she'd never seen anything like it in Moscow shops. Its scent made her mouth water.

Ilya looked up. 'I popped in at home before coming here. There was mail.'

His lips were set in a line. He stood and passed her a white postcard. She skimmed it. It was a court subpoena. The room seemed to lurch. She buried her face against Ilya's jacket and he stroked her hair.

'It's Roman,' she said. 'He wants to take Lilly.'

The typed lines on the card refused to stay still. *Krasnaya Presnya district court for Citizen Abramova. In regards to a custody application.* She swallowed a sob.

Ilya held her. 'It's only a summons, El. We'll take Lilly with us, so they see she's fine. He can't prove you're a bad mother. You're not.'

Ella heard her own voice as if from afar. 'I won't let him take her.'

*

She sat on the dacha's porch and looked back through the kitchen window. Olga's silhouette moved around. Ella rested her head on Ilya's shoulder. The darkness covered them with its flimsy blanket, and the red dot of his cigarette burned a hole in it. He put his arm around her and she nestled in closer.

'I saw General Lubov today.' She lifted her head and tried to make out his expression. But she could only see the pale oval of his face. 'Are you angry?'

He smoked his cigarette. 'Did you go there?'

'No, they picked me up from the flat.' Ella laid her head on his chest again and listened to his heartbeat. 'We have nothing to lose and we need his help.'

Ilya's body stiffened. 'Are you crazy, El? Why would he help us? He's the KGB, remember, not an angel.'

She faked a smile. 'You don't understand, my love. Lubov could set us free and he isn't asking for much.'

Ilya didn't ask what Lubov wanted and she didn't tell him. She kissed him on the lips, willing him to submit, to let her into his heart. She needed him to love her. He kissed her back.

'I think we can make it work,' she whispered.

He snuffed out his cigarette in the grass and rose to his feet. 'Let's go inside,' he said.

*

The brightly lit court corridor started to warp around her. Lilly had been whining on and off for the last hour. Ilya surrendered the child to her and sat on a hard plastic chair next to a dying pot plant. Ella rocked her daughter and paced the nook outside the duty solicitor's office. She eyed the posters depicting happy families that decorated the walls. The subpoena had thrust her out of her new life, however unsettled it was, into her old one with Roman. Proving herself a good mother while failing to soothe a crying baby seemed an impossible task.

A beet-faced woman in a pink crimplene dress rushed past, her hands full of string bags. 'Come in.'

She unlocked the office and Ella carried Lilly into the windowless space. The woman dumped her shopping beside an overstuffed filing cabinet. Folders lay in piles on the floor and on the visitor's chair. A ceiling fan struggled to fight the heat. Lilly whimpered and contorted her tightly wrapped body. Ella had to move quickly so as not to drop her. The solicitor sat at her desk and frowned.

'Sorry, she's probably hungry.' Ella looked at the oversized clock on the wall that neared eleven. 'It said nine thirty in the summons. I thought we got the date wrong.'

She pressed Lilly to her breast and held out the court's notice. They'd woken up before dawn to be at the Moscow courthouse by 9 am. The woman waved for her to sit and grabbed the stack of files from the chair.

'Abramova, Ella Gregorievna?' She looked past Ella into the corridor. 'Is he one of your lovers?'

Ella peeked over her shoulder. Ilya stood by the office door. Before she could answer though, the solicitor called out, 'Please, close it.'

Ilya shut the door between them. Ella turned back towards the desk. The woman flicked through her file.

'We've received an application from your husband to transfer the role of guardian to him and his parents.' She turned the page; the gold rings on her fingers made them look like sausages. 'Abramov informed the family court of your dissident friends. He reported you living with another man in the flat, which he as your husband has a permanent share.'

The solicitor sighed. Lilly squealed, and Ella realised she'd stopped rocking her daughter. She started again. Roman was obviously talking about Ilya and Vlad. Yet she had no idea how he'd found out about Vlad's visits before his arrest. She opened her mouth to explain but the woman held up a hand to stop her.

She looked at Lilly, who wriggled in Ella's arms. 'There is also a letter from the grandparents, promising support in bringing up his daughter.'

Lilly let out another loud wail. Ella cradled her and swayed side to side. The solicitor's torrent of words washed over her.

'Lia and Alexander Abramov have also provided the court with a witness report and a character reference.' The solicitor read on and her cheeks paled. 'You stole another woman's husband?' she whispered.

'Not exactly,' Ella replied.

The colour returned to the woman's face. 'We have to check the child's circumstances. You'll have to supply a signed affidavit before the court hears your case.'

Ella nodded.

'Do you have a source of income, Citizen Abramova, to support yourself and your child? What's your occupation?'

'I'm an actress.'

The solicitor looked her up and down. 'So I see.' She made a note. 'We'll send you another notice with a hearing date in a week or so. Make sure you have a proof of income and employment.'

She closed the file. 'Your lover, he looks thin. Is he ill? And he's married. Does he have his own children to support?'

39

Ella touched the bubble glass of the bus stop and recalled the time she'd waited here with Roman and Vlad. It'd snowed that night in Chertanovo. The white dust had covered the sleeping suburb with a magic veil before turning into mud. Tonight, nothing moved amid the scorched mirage of Brezhnev-era architecture. The heat seemed to have melted the buildings together, merging them into a single formidable block.

She tried to remember which way to go and took a few steps. It felt like she was moving in the right direction. What Lubov planned for her to do with the list of names wasn't clear, but she'd made up her mind. She'd instruct Vlad's friends to lay low, tell them not to bring in any newcomers.

On the street corner she recognised a grey metal telephone booth and felt reassured that she was in the right place.

Ella rushed past it and entered a courtyard with a muddy sandpit and a square of wilted grass. Beside a sickly tree, she waited and counted to ten to make sure no one had followed her from the bus stop.

If she walked away, didn't warn anyone, didn't name anyone as a dissident, these people might get arrested anyway. There would be no more Hebrew classes or Torah study, and no more legal help. Ella wiped her palms on her dress. She couldn't imagine Vlad giving his friends up though. Lubov's note might be a fake. Or a test.

Sweat trickled down between her shoulder blades. She went through the entrance doors of the apartment block and stepped into the lift, which stank of urine and had scuff marks on its linoleum floor.

On the ninth floor she walked to the door at the end of the hallway. It wasn't upholstered like the four other doors and a mezuzah, signalling a Jewish home, winked at her from the doorframe. They must have chosen not to hide. She pressed the bell, and a wave of shame washed over her. Her fingers stroked the mezuzah and her lips moved, asking forgiveness.

The door opened a crack. A young woman appeared, her hair covered by a headscarf, a baby at her breast. A toddler hid behind her long skirt.

Ella lowered her gaze. She thought of Lilly at the dacha with Olga and felt sick. 'I am Vlad's friend. I came here last winter.' She wished she'd rehearsed what to say. 'I wanted to tell you' – her face grew hotter – 'you can't run any more classes.' She raised her eyes and met the woman's glare. *They know*, she mouthed and stretched out her hand with Lubov's note squashed between her fingers.

The woman glanced at the note. 'You've got the wrong address,' she said and slammed the door.

*

Ella didn't recall catching a bus out of Chertanovo or boarding the train to Revolution Square after her visit to Vlad's friends. She closed her eyes and knew that they were here with her. That the KGB had been following her around since Vlad had disappeared. She saw them on the train, mirrored in shop windows, loitering among trees in the park. She could feel their presence behind her now, standing on the platform.

A blast of warm air from the metro tunnel dried her damp temples and she opened her eyes. Blood-coloured granite surrounded her. Steel chandeliers hung low, lights reflected on the polished marble floors. Statues of bronze workers and farmers, pilots and aviators lined the metro station on both sides.

She peered over her shoulder. There was no one there, except a giant bronze soldier crouched nearby. The statue's gun pointed down, but that didn't make it look less threatening. The barrel shone, rubbed by too many hands.

The yellow and blue train arrived. Its doors slid open with a dull rubber thump. People spilled out onto the platform while others started to board.

'The next stop is Sverdlov Square,' a female voice announced over the loudspeaker.

Ella realised she wasn't far from Lubyanka, the KGB's headquarters. She retreated to a marble-topped bench and sat, leaning her back against the granite wall. If they arrested her now, no one would know where she'd gone.

A man sat next to her and her heart began pounding. Without raising her eyes, she slid to the edge of the bench and waited. He'd come to take her away, she thought.

'Doors closing,' the loudspeaker said.

She jumped up and darted into the crowd, let the human river absorb her in its current. The stream carried her onto the escalator and spewed her into the metro hall, breathless and confused.

A man in a grey suit turned to her without a smile. 'Do you have the time, please?' His eyes measured her. Their colour matched his suit. He was probably one of them.

Ella stood frozen, unable to reply.

He frowned at her watch and wandered off. She felt like she was spinning in a fog. A statue stared at her from across the hall. Ribbons streamed from the sailor's cap like bronze snakes and coiled on his shoulders.

Ella thought of her baby and felt the fog recede. She would return to the dacha. Take care of Lilly. What she had done wouldn't harm the Refuseniks, it might actually save them.

40

Inside Lubov's office, Ella rocked Lilly's pram and waited for the general to appear. The young soldier who'd brought her in guarded the door. This time she had come prepared. She pictured herself through the guard's eyes – young mother in need of assistance. Modest, but pretty. She dressed the part too in a knee-length skirt and blouse. Almost no make-up, just a touch of mascara and shine on her lips.

Ella smiled at Lilly, who stared back, dour-faced, but at least she was calm this morning. The decision to bring her baby along hadn't come lightly, but the hope that it might soften Lubov's heart and make him an easier target bolstered her.

She had done her best. She'd met the Orthodox Jewish woman at the address Lubov had given her, yet Ella couldn't confirm any names. They'd never been introduced. But she suspected Lubov knew this anyway and just wanted to test her.

'Ella Gregorievna. Welcome.' Lubov adjusted the curtain he came through. She hated to think of the secrets those drapes concealed. The rooms. And the victims.

For a moment she felt her facade of an innocent young woman asking for help shatter, and she saw herself for what she was here, inside Lubov's world at Lubyanka – prey that had walked into a trap, seduced by the promise of freedom.

Her hand gripped the pram handle. She stood to greet him, but looked instead at Lilly, aware of using her child as a prop.

Lilly puffed her cheeks, her face content, trusting Ella with her future.

Lubov spoke. 'Please, take a seat. I don't have much time, but would you like some tea?' Before she could respond, he nodded to the guard by the door, who promptly left the room.

'So?' He squeezed into the armchair behind his desk. 'Any luck?'

She shook her head. 'I went there, but they didn't let me in. It was the same woman though, as the last time.'

The general's gaze became sharper. 'When was the last time?'

Ella almost slapped her forehead. She had no reason to offer him any new information. Yet at least this way it appeared she'd sincerely tried to assist him but had failed.

'December. Or maybe early January. I don't remember.'

'And what was the purpose of your visit there?' Lubov got up from his seat.

Ella bent to the pram and picked Lilly up. Her baby's warmth steadied her and she met the general's eyes over her daughter's head. His face looked like a mask carved from hardwood, dry and weathered by time. He stared at her and ignored Lilly.

'Had Vladimir Zacharov accompanied you on that night?'

She wrinkled her brow pretending to think. There was no point lying about it. If she and Roman hadn't met Vlad there, she wouldn't know the place. She shrugged and stayed silent.

'Did he speak there or did someone else? How many people were present?' Lubov returned to his desk and pulled out a notepad from the drawer. 'I'd like you to write a report. List everything you witnessed and name everyone.' He looked at her. 'Everyone you know by name. Or describe them.'

Ella lowered Lilly back into her pram, giving herself a moment to decide what to do next.

'Comrade General, you promised to add me and my

daughter to my husband's emigration documents. I would be really grateful if you could help me with that.'

Lubov laughed. 'Ashkenazi,' he said and wiped his eyes with a handkerchief. Ella wasn't sure whether he was being sincere. 'We'll see about it, if you cooperate. Nothing is impossible. And what does your father think about you emigrating?'

Ella closed her eyes for a few seconds. It wasn't clear what the general wanted to hear. 'My father cannot sign the permission form without losing his job,' she said. Surely he knew that. He could help her with this, as well as with Ilya's permit.

Lubov rocked on his heels. He suddenly looked his part – the KGB general. Even his well-tailored suit looked like a *militzia* uniform.

'We could sort this out,' he said. 'You stay with us for a couple of days. We'll take your daughter back to the dacha and you help us with Zacharov junior's case. You could also write a report on meeting Boris Zacharov, and tell us how the renowned author offered you funds to support his dissident son. Didn't he?'

Ella rubbed her temple, trying to stop the room from toppling over. 'I didn't see Vlad's father,' she said, but could hardly hear her own voice.

Lilly gazed at her and curled her lips, her face turning darker. She whimpered. Ella moved the pram back and forth. Yet nothing could save her any longer from Lubov's silent waiting. The trap she'd walked into had closed.

*

Ella felt weary as she approached the dacha. She had hardly slept for the last few nights, blaming herself for Vlad's awful fate one minute, and deciding that Lubov had played her the next. The report he had forced her to sign was a lie. Vlad hadn't confessed. She didn't betray him.

The aroma of wild mushrooms fried in sunflower oil reached Ella before she opened the crooked timber gate. She lifted the pram onto the porch and entered the kitchen, grateful to find it empty. Olga was probably resting after cooking supper.

A spasm in her stomach reminded Ella that she'd forgotten to eat. She'd called Lia from Saltikovka train station hoping to hear the good news while also feeling ashamed at wanting to hear it. The Abramovs had got their permit and she and Lilly had been added. Lubov had held up his end of the bargain. Even if Lia was reluctant to leave without Roman, Ella could still escape and if she played her cards right, Ilya could too.

And now she had to tell Olga — not about the horror of her deal with Lubov or the report she'd signed confirming Vlad's sins — but that she was leaving Russia. Worse still, when Ilya arrived at the dacha later this evening, he might be angry with her. She had to convince them that if she broke out, it could open an escape route for those she loved.

Except for the crackling of logs in the stove, the house was silent. Even Lilly had fallen quiet, tired from the long summer's day. Her bath and feed could wait, Ella thought. She buried her face into her daughter's neck and carried her to the cot in the bedroom they shared.

Ella sat and took off her sandals. 'Baba, where are you?' she called.

Olga entered the bedroom with her finger pressed to her lips. 'Your grandfather is sleeping.' Natan had spent the summer in and out of hospital, coming to the dacha when her parents brought him with more food supplies.

Ella hugged Olga as a twitch of guilt stirred in her. She might never see her grandparents again. Or her little brother.

'I spoke to Lia. They've got their exit permit.'

She couldn't see Olga's face, with her head resting on her grandmother's shoulder, but Olga tensed. 'For you as well?'

Ella withdrew from her embrace. She would never divulge the cost of her pass. 'Sorry, Baba. I'm starving.'

She dashed to the kitchen, and Olga trailed her. 'What about Ilya?'

'I'll tell him when he comes home tonight.'

She tried to sound casual as she grabbed a slice of fried potato from the pan on the stove. If Ilya adopted Lilly, as they had planned, he would have no problem joining them, even if she left earlier with her in-laws. She stuffed the question of properly divorcing Roman and getting his consent for the adoption into the darkest recess of her mind. They'd deal with that later as long as Ilya trusted her.

She glanced at Olga, hoping for a smile or a nod, but her grandmother's face looked grim. The weather changed abruptly and a cool wind howled outside, turning their cosy house into a prison cell.

Ella sighed. 'Lilly needs a bath.'

She retreated to the bedroom. Olga followed and stood at the doorway.

'I've never told you this, darling, but Natan got arrested after the war. In 1948. I knew if I did nothing, he'd vanish like many others. People were taken every day, but no one came back.'

Ella peeled off her shorts, listening to Olga's story.

'The only person I knew who could help us was Ivan. He had the power. But I couldn't ask him.'

Olga sat next to her on the mattress. She stopped talking, but her silence hung heavier than her words. Then Ella leaped up. Ivan was General Lubov. He'd clearly played a more sinister role in her family's past than she'd imagined. She wondered what he had asked of Olga.

'So, what did you do?'

Her grandmother looked fragile in her fire-red housecoat, her eyes closed. 'Don't trust him, my love. He is an evil man.'

41

Olga
Moscow, USSR
1948

The snow in December was the lightest since the war had ended. It didn't stick in wet clumps to Olga's felt boots and it didn't melt into a slush under her galoshes. It whirled its airy flakes around and turned bleak, war-ravaged Moscow into a crystal castle.

Olga stamped her feet at the portico of the nineteenth-century tenement house at Chistye Prudy to knock off the merry snowflakes. She inhaled a mouthful of frosty air. If only she didn't need to carry her sack of food rations up three flights of stairs to her and Natan's flat on the third floor, she'd probably feel happier.

Being alone with Natan didn't come easy after the wartime separation. Five years apart. The shame of her almost-betrayal hadn't dissolved, despite Natan's attempts to revive their love. It felt better when the children were around, but Grisha had been conscripted the previous year and Faina spent most of her time with girlfriends at the pond's skating rink.

Her brother hadn't come back from the war.

She grabbed the handrail of the unlit stairway. Upstairs, a door banged. The forceful steps of multiple people thundered onto the landing above her head. She flattened herself against the wall.

Olga knew who they were, those stomping down the staircase – the NKVD footmen, the People's Commissariat for Internal Affairs, the secret police. She wriggled into the niche that separated two flats – once the servants' entrance, locked and not in use. The footsteps echoed nearer. The tang of exclusive tobacco, familiar from the war, seized her throat.

The men marched past her hiding place and across the landing. Four of them. But only three were NKVD. Wedged between two guards in fur-lined leather coats, with their holsters out for everyone to see, walked Natan, his head bowed.

Olga swallowed. She eyed the third man, an officer, who followed a step or two behind. His face looked familiar. Lubov.

She nearly stepped out from her hole in the wall to stop him from taking away her husband. But her shoulder blades seemed fused to the damp render.

Neither Natan nor Lubov had seen her. Only the other two, with the well-fed faces of non-frontline soldiers, had. But they didn't slow down. Olga's legs wouldn't move. The sack of food cut into her palm.

Lubov stopped.

Olga bit the inside of her lip. The dim stairwell warped around her. All thoughts vanished.

When the guards' steps had faded, she eased her shoulders from the wall. A puddle of melted snow spread under her rubber galoshes. She dropped the sack. She had to find Lubov, rush to the NKVD headquarters and beg him to free Natan. Maybe it wasn't too late to catch up with them if she ran. She sprinted down the stairs after her husband, leaving their monthly supply of food rations outside a strangers' door.

42

Ella
Moscow, USSR
August 1983

The late evening train should have unloaded its passengers by now. Ella leaned on the fence outside the gate and listened for the train horn, for Ilya's footsteps on the gravel. She would need to come clean – she couldn't keep lying. The moon hung low like a streetlight. A dog barked in the distance. She ran.

The unsealed country road was empty and only the trees, silhouetted against the moonlit sky, accompanied her from the dacha to the station. Then a shadow crossed her path and Ilya was standing in front of her.

'What are you up to?' His whisper sounded coarse, like he'd lost his voice. His eyes would not meet hers.

'I'll explain, Ilusha.'

'What the hell have you done? This arrived at the flat.'

He held up a page, an official-looking note, and began to pull her by the wrist towards the dacha. She strode alongside him, flushed and puffing but reluctant to resist his force.

'Ilya, stop, for goodness sake. Let me see it. I didn't have time to tell you.'

Without breaking stride, he passed her the letter. It stated what she already knew – her exit permit was ready to collect from OVIR.

'So, you've planned everything? You'll pack Lilly and go.' Ilya released her hand and marched off so fast she had to jog after him.

Near the dacha, he slowed down. Ella searched his face for a trace of understanding. She loved this face, the thick eyebrows and high forehead, the eyes usually so caring and warm. Now Ilya's brows were knitted and his eyes gloomy.

'Aren't you happy we can all escape?' she asked.

'We? How am I going to get out to be with you and Lilly? You think the KGB will grant me a visa?'

'Yes.'

'Why? Have you signed something?'

She nodded, so slightly that he couldn't possibly see it in the dark. What if Ilya was right and there would be no exit visa for them all?

Ilya sighed and continued on his way to the dacha. Ella stared at his back.

'Just let me sort this out, Ilusha. I promise you,' she said and began jogging after him again.

*

A threadbare linen sheet separated their bodies and Ella inhaled Ilya's familiar scent. He hadn't spoken to her all evening. Now all she could hear was Lilly's soft breathing and the buzz of mosquitos. She desperately wanted to tell Ilya the truth, to break into his silence. She draped herself against his back and felt him stir.

'I have to get Lilly out of Russia,' she whispered. 'I've always dreamed of being the grandmother, the matriarch who relocated her family to another country. It sounds silly, doesn't it? But I've carried it inside me forever, since I was a girl. I thought I could change my destiny and my family's too. Do you think I'm just a romantic fool?'

She stopped short of confessing the rest – Lubov's offer to help her if she signed the report confirming Vlad's betrayal to distance herself from him and his dissident friends. Ella tucked her head into her favourite place, above Ilya's collarbone. His body was still tense. There she floated between dream and reality hoping he would forgive her.

Ilya enveloped her in his arms. She moulded her body against his and clawed at his back, his damp skin. Her guilt made her grip harder. It was not the gentle love of their first days together. She heard their bodies slap at each other as if from a distance and muffled her moans, afraid to wake Lilly or Leon. She scuffed her knee on the plaster wall and welcomed the pain. The night encased them, humid and dark. It prevented her from seeing Ilya's face, but in the slippery heat, she sensed his body as an extension of hers.

Ella shifted onto her belly and her chin rubbed on the canvas of the mattress. Her tears mixed with saliva. It felt like saying goodbye. She didn't let the thought possess her and instead turned over to hold him. She wanted to wrap herself inside his skin, to become one with him. She didn't want herself without Ilya. She was his and he was hers, at least for now. Ella swore not to leave him behind and to tell him the truth.

She let a dreamless sleep descend on her and resolved to tell him in the morning. Her last thought before the blackness came was about Ilya being Lilly's father. He'd be the only father Lilly knew. She promised this to herself and felt blissful.

*

Ella's toes touched the rusty bed frame and she turned seeking out Ilya's warmth. But a cold spot where his body had lain shocked her into full consciousness. She opened her eyes and sat up. Outside, a crow cawed. She'd missed Ilya getting up. He hadn't planned on leaving and she hoped they'd spend the day together as a family. She'd resolved to discuss their future and admit to her failings. She would be honest with him, and from now on, she'd let him in on her plans for their escape.

Ella checked under the bed. Ilya's boots were gone, so were his jeans and his shirt, the one he'd worn last night. She couldn't see a note.

She dashed into the kitchen, where Olga stood in her long white nightgown, her silver hair plaited. She held Lilly in her arms. 'Our little one needs feeding. You were asleep and Ilya seemed upset when he rushed out.'

Lilly let out a wail. Ella took her daughter and held the tightly wrapped bundle to her breast, though they both knew she had no milk. 'Shh, my sweetie, let me find your bottle.'

She stomped back to the bedroom, keeping Lilly hugged to her chest. She knew what had made Ilya leave. But hadn't he forgiven her?

43

Olga
Moscow, USSR
January 1949

Snow had begun to fall as Olga stepped onto the footpath that encircled the frozen surface of Chistye Prudy pond. In the dusk, twinkling red and yellow lights were strung around the skating rink like a necklace. A rasping waltz poured out from pre-war loudspeakers. Couples glided by, their skates clanking on the ice. Racing skaters blew past on their long blades, but even they could not shatter the snowball fairytale of 1949 Moscow.

She knew not to trust it. People had started to disappear again like in 1937 and newspaper headlines screamed that 'rootless cosmopolitans' were enemies of the Soviet State. Jews like her and Natan.

She peeled off a mitten and upturned her palm. The spinning snow slowed her heartbeat. But the snowflakes melted and turned into teardrops on her skin. To seek help from Lubov after she'd shunned him for years made her feel sullied, but her husband's arrest had left her no other options.

Olga walked to the rink's entrance and eyed the clock above the pavilion. She remembered its huge yellowing face peering down on her childhood at Chistye Prudy. A hand touched the back of her neck, and Olga shuddered. She'd waited fifteen minutes for Lubov to turn up.

'Shall we sit on the bench, Citizen Ashkenazi?'

She nodded and smiled at Lubov. It'd been three years since he'd written to her from Berlin and six since she'd last seen him. In that time, his ruddy face had become wider and harder. In front of her now stood not a boy in love, but a man who'd fought the war as an officer of the State's secret police, the NKVD.

She hooked her arm through his. The waltz hissed above them, crying about love from a 'spoils of war' record. The officers who'd seen Berlin fall hadn't come back to Russia empty-handed, and the flea markets of post-war Moscow were awash with German goods: fur coats and bicycles, gramophones and silverware and, of course, records.

They wandered under a street lamp and Lubov winced. He pulled her into an alley and sat her down, out of public view, on a bench under a naked tree mottled with fresh snow. His black leather coat shone like snakeskin. She sat in obedience and prepared to beg.

'Why did you call?' He peered at her body under her mother's karakul coat with his sharp eyes. Olga didn't hope for kindness, but she wasn't expecting hostility either. She wasn't sure what tone to adopt.

'You know why, Ivan.'

She brushed the snow off his fur collar in an attempt to flirt. It felt morbid, knowing the crimes he'd likely committed as a member of an internal security unit. It was called the MGB now, but its function hadn't changed – to control, arrest and murder fellow citizens if they had or were reported to have anti-Soviet sentiments. The alley looked empty and black as an abyss.

'Save Natan,' she whispered close to Lubov's cheek. 'He is almost sixty. He'll perish in the camps with your comrades.' Natan was fifty-three but the war had aged him.

Lubov chuckled and put his arm around her. 'You haven't changed at all, Olushka. Just become more beautiful. What's the need of an old husband?'

He stared at her. There was no love in his eyes. There was lust and hurt. But she also sensed curiosity and a lazy thirst for power – a desire to use and break a living toy.

'You've changed, Vanya,' she said. 'You've become strange and cruel.' She made a mock angry face, aiming for something playful, and glanced at Lubov sidelong. She considered touching his wrist but didn't dare.

A young couple strolled past, entwined. The girl's shiny hair covered the back of her unbuttoned coat in a long platinum wave, and the bright stars of her eyes rested on the boy's face. Olga felt a prick of envy before she caught Lubov's gaze on the girl's hips. Then her heart joined her stomach. She had no hold over this man, she realised, and grabbed his sleeve.

'Help me, Ivan, for old time's sake.'

Lubov's eyes remained fixed on the young woman's rear. 'I'll get your ancient one back – don't fret. But you owe me.'

He turned to her and his gaze settled on her neck. She let go of his arm, and he sprang to his feet.

'We shall meet again, Ashkenazi, and have a chat like colleagues.'

Stomping the earth with his boots, he strode towards the far end of the alley, where the carefree couple had stopped to kiss only seconds ago.

44

Ella
Moscow, USSR
August 1983

'Samara – booth number five.'

Ella watched a female operator at the Moscow Central Telegraph direct a pasty girl into an open telephone booth, one of twelve separated by tinted-glass partitions.

She shifted forward on the wall-to-wall timber bench crammed with people like her, queueing to make interstate phone calls.

Ilya hadn't forgiven her. He hadn't returned to the dacha last night and he wasn't waiting for her at their Moscow flat when she'd arrived there at dawn. So she trudged to OVIR to collect her exit permit. Only this was in vain as well. Without Roman's permission to take Lilly out of the country, her visa couldn't be issued. She had a week to supply the document. How she would manage this, she wasn't quite sure.

A clock ticked inside her ribcage.

Ilya was in Novokuznetsk with his son – and Marina and her mother – the film studio manager told her when she called him in tears.

Ella looked over at the crowded post office hall, the largest and busiest in Russia. Massive floor scales groaned under the weight of cardboard and plywood boxes and pillowcases packed with foodstuff and goods. People swarmed about, keen to collect provisions from relatives scattered throughout the vast land, or to send some of Moscow's luxuries to their families across the empire.

'Novokuznetsk, booth number three.'

The operator's voice startled her. Ella hurried towards the third booth. In number four, a young man covered the receiver with his palm. 'Mum, I told you already. I cannot come home this year. I don't have money.'

Ella took in his haircut, new Wrangler jeans and leather jacket and felt sorry for his *mama*. The woman didn't stand a chance of seeing her son anytime soon. She thought of Ilya's son and picked up the phone, praying she wouldn't have to speak to Marina.

'Hello?' Ilya's voice was brittle.

'Ilya, I found you.' She pressed her face into the receiver. 'The studio told me where you were.'

The stares of those waiting to use the phones crawled up her spine. She could hear people talking all around her.

'Are you well? How is Lilly?'

Her heart lurched at his words – urgent, caring, real. The man she loved. She needed him so much to be next to her, to join her and her daughter. There must be a way to get him out of this cursed country. She would need to call Lubov. But the general might want more from her than she was prepared to give.

'Ilya, my exit permit will expire soon. I have only a week.' Ella let out a sob.

'Did you know this when you were getting it?' He never spoke to her in this tone.

'Oh Ilya, I couldn't imagine it happening this way. I thought we had time. Please, my love, come back to Moscow.' She raised her voice. 'Please, Ilya.'

'Novokuznetsk, your time is finished,' the operator called out.

'One minute, please,' Ella called out, then opened her mouth to ask about Yan, but the phone line was dead.

She slammed the handset down. Whether he was coming back or not she had to return to the dacha.

*

In the twilight, the dacha seemed deserted. The usual heartwarming aromas of Olga's cooking failed to greet her in the kitchen. The woodstove was cold.

'Baba?'

Her whisper was louder than she'd intended with Lilly probably asleep in the bedroom. She nudged the door open. The curtains were shut and in the semi-darkness she saw that her daughter's cot stood empty. Lilly's pram was gone too. Olga and Leon must have taken Lilly out for a walk by the lake.

'Baba,' she called out.

'Ellochka? Is that you?' Olga's voice sounded frail.

Ella rushed along the corridor to her grandmother's room. But Lilly wasn't there either. Olga lay on her bed with a compress on her brow. Leon was perched on the chair next to her, his chin buried in his skinny knees. The scene looked like Repin's painting of a funeral, and Ella's breathing grew ragged again. 'Baba, where is Lilly?'

Leon lifted his pinched face. He jumped up and darted past her. She heard the front door slam and held herself in check so as not to scream. 'Where is she?'

'Roman's parents.' Her grandmother's whisper was faint. 'Roman's parents took …'

'Lilly?' Ella staggered back. 'Why did they take her? Where to?'

'They came today, before noon.'

Ella fought to grasp the meaning of Olga's words. She lowered herself onto the edge of the bed. This was her fault. What had possessed her to leave Lilly behind when she went looking for Ilya?

Tears ran down her face. 'Why did you let them take her?' she wailed.

Olga tried to lift herself up, but she fell back down into the pillows. Ella put her palms on Olga's shoulders.

'Lie down, Baba, lie down.'

'They said they'd take Lilly for a stroll in her pram. Lia started to cry, and I thought, there's no harm in them going for air. They're her grandparents.'

Ella stared at the cracked render on the wall. Her in-laws had no right to take her daughter.

'They must have gone back to Moscow.' Olga's eyes teared. 'Sorry, Ellochka. I didn't take care of her. I went to the station with Leon to call them but no one answered. Maybe you could go there? They'll give Lilly back to you, I am sure.'

Ella couldn't allow herself to fall apart and she couldn't bring herself to stay angry at Olga. Her grandmother blamed herself already. What good would it do to make her feel worse? She wiped her cheeks and kissed Olga's forehead.

'I'll go, Baba. I'll go to Moscow now.'

'Where is Ilya?'

Ella's lungs tightened. 'He went to visit his son.'

It was impossible to comprehend why Roman's parents had taken Lilly. Perhaps to blackmail her into staying in Russia. Had someone at OVIR called the Abramovs? Or perhaps Olga had let it slip to Lia about Ella's plans to leave the country.

Ella's exit visa was waiting for her at OVIR, but without Lilly nothing mattered. She had to go and get her daughter back.

45

In the glowing early morning light, Ella faced the door of the Abramovs' communal apartment. She pressed her cheek to its worn upholstery and felt closer to her daughter. They couldn't keep her. Lilly was hers. But Lia would never let her in.

The names above the doorbell caught her eye – four rings were meant for Lia's elderly neighbour, Tatiana Markovna. If she managed to get inside, only the flimsy internal door would separate her from her in-laws' quarters.

She rang the bell and waited. She heard the sound of shuffling footsteps and blood thumped in her temples. The steps moved closer. Then they stopped.

'Who is it?' The shaky voice seemed about to fade away.

'It's Ella, Tatiana Markovna, Roman's wife.'

'Roman's wife?'

'I forgot how many rings for the Abramovs.' Her hand stroked the door's surface, cracked with age. 'I need to see Lia. Could you let me in? Please.'

The squealing of chains and locks sounded like aging machinery, its joints affected by rust. Ella shoved the door open before Lia's neighbour could change her mind. The old woman stood, almost cowering in the wallpapered corner. She glanced towards Lia's door and held her twig-like finger to her lips. Then she padded towards her own room.

The gloomy corridor smelled of Ella's previous life. A strip of light underneath the common bathroom door accompanied the hum of running water. The low-hanging laundry line stretched from the front entrance to the end of the hallway sunk in shadows. Between a discoloured bra and an oversized plaid shirt hung a pink baby's wrap. All the doors were closed.

Ella wiped her palms on her jeans and switched her handbag onto the other shoulder. This break-in hadn't been planned, but she had to do it. *Knock. Grab Lilly. Run.* She unlocked the entrance door behind her, preparing her escape route.

There were voices in the communal kitchen. Ella counted her breaths to calm down and tapped at the Abramovs' door. It opened a crack, as if Roman's mother had been waiting behind it. Lia wore a bright dressing-gown printed with birds and dragons. She squinted at her and attempted to slam the door.

Ella put her foot against it to keep it ajar. 'I came to take Lilly home.'

She peered over Lia's shoulder into the room but could only see the fridge in the corner by the window. She couldn't see or hear her daughter.

Ella leaned all her weight against the door, but Lia pushed back. Their eyes locked. Lia's black pupils looked dogged. She allowed the door to give a little. Then she stepped out into the corridor and shoved Ella backwards. She shut the door behind her and spread her arms across it.

'I can't let you in.'

Ella made a tiny step towards Lia and began to sob. She wanted to shake her mother-in-law, grab her shoulders and shake her so Lia's head would hit the door she'd put between her and her baby.

'You cannot stop me from getting my child,' she shouted, so the neighbours would know what was happening.

She lurched towards Lia, sobbing uncontrollably now. She reached past her and grabbed at the doorhandle. Lia swatted her hand away.

'I want Lilly back.' Her tears ran down between her useless breasts and onto her belly. 'Please, Lia, you are a mother yourself.'

'Ella, listen to me.' Lia was crying too. 'Lilly is safe. She is with us. Calm down.'

Ella reached for the door again. But someone's fingers squeezed her forearm. A male hand. Roman's father stood beside her.

'If you don't leave now, I'll call the *militzia*.' Alexander let go of her arm and joined Lia in front of their door. 'We won't let you take our granddaughter away. Roman has rights too. You should wait until he's released.' His hands shook. He pulled out his handkerchief and wiped his glasses.

Ella couldn't fight both of them, but she couldn't leave without Lilly. A tide of anger threatened to swallow her. 'She is my daughter!'

'A child needs both parents,' Lia said.

'He didn't want the baby!' Ella yelled. 'He doesn't care for Lilly.'

Lia became teary again. 'If you emigrate, we won't see her – you know this, Ella – and neither will Roman. You cannot deny the child her father and grandparents.'

'But what can I do?' Ella's sobs rocked her body. 'I have an exit permit. I need Lilly with me.'

Lia grabbed her forearms. 'What do you mean, Ella?' Her spit landed on Ella's cheek. 'We told you we are not going anywhere without Roman. You used our exit permit to try and take our granddaughter from us. We won't let you get away with this.'

A whimper from behind the door cut through the scuffle. Ella threw herself forward, elbowing the older people out of her way. But the door wouldn't budge.

Lia stumbled. 'Alexander. Call the *militzia*. Now.'

He hesitated, and Ella dropped to her knees and grabbed Lia's ankles. 'Lia. Please.'

Lia clutched her chest with one hand and the door with the other. Her face collapsed, but she nodded at Alexander. He ran to the telephone that hung on the wall by the entrance door and began to dial.

*

Ella smelled the *militziamen* boots before she saw them. The revolting black gunk the guards used to polish them. Seated on the floor by the Abramovs' door, she banged the back of her head against the plywood membrane that separated her from her child. Her jaw would not unclench. Lia stood over her, leaning against the doorframe. Alexander stood next to his wife and fidgeted with his glasses.

Ella looked up. At the end of the corridor, Lia's neighbours surrounded two men in grey *militzia* uniforms. Ella stretched her legs out, anchored her palms on the floor and prepared to fight.

The young militziaman with a broad peasant's face stepped between her and Lia. 'Citizen Abramova, please follow me.'

He beckoned for Ella to stand and she scrambled to her feet.

'Sergeant, they stole my daughter.'

The *militziaman* held out his hand. 'Your passport, please.'

'She is a traitor,' an old man in long johns yelled from his doorway.

The sergeant's face reddened. Ella glared at his shiny buttons and brown leather shoulder holster. 'I need my daughter. Please. They're not letting me see her.'

The *militziaman* clasped Ella's elbow with two steely fingers and led her towards the communal kitchen. She saw Alexander rush into the Abramovs' room and shut the door, leaving Lia to guard it from the outside. At the flat's entrance an older *militziaman* questioned the neighbours.

The kitchen looked larger than Ella remembered, with two stoves, five cooking tables, and a sink where a few grimy pots soaked. The sergeant nudged her to sit on a stool by one of the tables.

'Passport,' he repeated.

'I am leaving the country, Officer.' Ella pulled out the receipt for her confiscated internal passport from OVIR. The voice of the OVIR lieutenant still boomed in her head: *On departure for permanent residence one stops being a citizen of the USSR.*

The *militziaman* inspected the stamped form and the blood drained from his country boy's face. 'Emigrating to Israel?' He looked towards the corridor, where she could hear the older *militziaman* talking to Lia.

She reached for her receipt. 'I have an exit permit for my daughter too.' That was a lie, but she hoped that in a matter of days it would be the truth.

'Petrov,' the sergeant called out. 'I have her document. She has an exit permit.'

'Officer.' Ella stood, but the guard pushed her back onto the stool.

'Sit down, Citizen Abramova, before I arrest you for perverting the course of justice.' The boy in uniform smirked and the colour returned to his face. Then the older *militziaman*, Petrov, joined them in the kitchen.

'Show me.'

He examined Ella's receipt and again she attempted to stand. This time Petrov placed his hefty palm on her shoulder and held her in place. 'Do you have permission from your husband to take his daughter?'

'I have an exit visa for both of us.' Ella steadied her voice. She thought of General Lubov and wondered if naming him would help or make matters worse. The *militzia* and the KGB despised each other.

Petrov's oily face gloated above her, his eyes full of hatred. To the *militziamen*, she could only be a defector. An enemy. Mentioning the KGB general would not change it.

'Follow me, please.'

With her receipt in his meaty fist, Petrov marched out of the kitchen and into the corridor. Ella followed. The sergeant walked behind her. She looked around, not quite understanding what was about to happen. The neighbours glued themselves to the walls, absorbing every word, every gesture, probably to retell the story in years to come.

She observed Lia guarding her door. A baby's wail from behind it tore at her insides. Ella darted towards her mother-in-law and saw Lia's body brace for impact. But the sergeant grabbed her from behind.

'Citizen Abramova!' Petrov yelled in her ear. 'Leave immediately or you'll be arrested.'

He stood aside and pointed his chin towards the exit. The sergeant twisted Ella's arm behind her back and prodded her forward. 'Walk.'

Ella tried to drag her feet. She tried to fall. But the ache in her shoulder made her obey the command. The sergeant marched her down the corridor to the exit. Petrov followed, and the front door closed with a thud behind all three of them. The sergeant yanked her arm, making her cry in pain. He released her, and Ella's head spun.

Petrov exhaled vodka fumes in her face. 'If I see you here again, you'll emigrate to the Gulag instead of Israel.' He handed her the OVIR document. She noticed his reluctance, but he wouldn't dare withhold an official form.

The sergeant chuckled. 'Get your husband to sign the permission. He may be happy to be rid of you both.'

She stared at the tiled floor of the landing, all her strength gone. But she didn't feel defeated, only dead tired.

'Go now and don't come back.' Petrov gave her a little push down the stairs.

Ella stumbled, refusing to accept this was real. She was walking away from her daughter, forbidden to return.

46

Henrietta had earned her fame as Moscow's best defence lawyer, loved by criminals and feared by prosecutors. Surely her great-aunt, with all her connections, could figure out a way to snatch Lilly back from Roman's parents and turn this nightmare around. Ella had to make it happen. Tomorrow or the day after.

She ran up the stairs to her great-aunt's apartment and knocked with her fist. From behind the door she heard footsteps, then the clank of chains and locks. Masha opened the door and hugged her.

The stink of filter-less cigarettes wafted over the tang of coffee and medicine. Henrietta, dressed in her house robe, sat in her wheelchair in the middle of the living room.

'You haven't spoiled us with your attention lately, have you?' Her acerbic laugh made Ella sweat. She leaned over to kiss Henrietta's papery cheek and hoped she would be forgiven.

'Lilly ...' she began to explain her absence, but Henrietta broke into a coughing fit and swatted her words away.

'Don't waste time on apologies,' she said after she'd recovered. 'Masha, make us some coffee, love.'

Ella perched on a stool next to her great-aunt. Henrietta lit another of her putrid *papiroses* and inhaled the bittersweet smoke. An urge to please her great-aunt made Ella's head swoon. 'Can I have one too, please?'

'Help yourself.' Henrietta waved her bird-like claw in front of her piercing eyes. Ella fumbled with the matches and lit up. '*Nu,*' Henrietta said.

'Aunty, I'm leaving Russia for good.' Smoke burned her throat and she suppressed a cough. 'Flying to Vienna. I don't have tickets yet, but my visa is ready on Thursday. I cannot delay leaving.'

Henrietta listened, and her eyelids drooped as if she were in a trance.

Ella looked at the ceiling to stop her tears from spilling. 'They stole Lilly away from me.'

Henrietta lifted her head and Ella cringed under her stare. Masha brought them mud-like coffee in tiny eggshell cups and sat next to Ella. She held her hand. Ella's mouth filled with bile, and she jammed her half-smoked cigarette into the full ashtray on Henrietta's lap. Masha got up to empty the ashtray.

'For God's sake, Masha, sit down a minute.' Henrietta straightened, and Masha sat back down. The old criminal lawyer's trance-like expression had been replaced by one of intense concentration. 'Who took her?'

'Roman's parents. They're not letting me have Lilly.' Ella jumped from her stool and paced the room. She felt like screaming. Her hesitation to come clean to her great-aunt made her swallow her scream. 'And I can't take her out of the country without Roman's permission. He hasn't even set eyes on her!'

'No histrionics, Ellochka.' Henrietta waved her claw. 'You're not at your theatre school. I know someone who can do the job.'

'You do?' Ella stopped pacing and kneeled in front of Henrietta's wheelchair.

Henrietta winked at Masha, her co-conspirator. 'He'll get Lilly back from your in-laws. Is she included in your exit documents?'

Ella's breathing quickened. 'I haven't got my visa yet.' She kissed Henrietta's hand, but didn't dare to meet her eyes. 'OVIR has demanded that I get permission from Roman.'

'They need your husband's approval, we'll get them his approval. I'll handle the signature. But first things first.' She jerked her bony hand out of Ella's grip and began to laugh. 'Masha, remember that bastard who killed his wife, and how he went crazy when he saw a letter from her?' Henrietta's boasting didn't end with her forgery skills.

Her laugh morphed into another coughing fit. Masha dashed to the kitchen and returned with a glass of water. Ella held her great-aunt's wrist while she drank it. She stroked the translucent skin and hoped the cough would subside. Whoever Henrietta's contact was, she needed to trust them.

*

The square around Taganskaya metro bubbled with people, swept up and down the stairs, in and out of the station's pneumatic doors. They were oblivious to Ella's mission – to find Mark Davidovich and convince him to rescue her baby. Henrietta had told her to mention her name and ask for a favour.

The linden trees shimmered gold in the late afternoon, lit by the low sun, and the white moon floated just visible in the transparent sky.

Ella made a fist. There was no point meandering any longer. Mark's locksmith kiosk, an inconspicuous metal shed painted scruffy green, stood right in front of her.

There was no signage and no one at the poky window, but she could detect movement inside. Ella stepped closer. The window reflected her tense face. 'Is Mark Davidovich there?'

She shrank back and waited. A middle-aged man in thick glasses, dressed in dark blue overalls, leaned onto the counter. He measured Ella with his magnified eyes. 'How can I help you?'

His gentle voice and educated accent didn't match the image Ella had in her mind of a hardened criminal. But then, he probably wasn't one anymore.

She had to say something. 'Henrietta sent me. She said you'd help.'

The change in the man's demeanour shocked her. His sharp glance sized her up and apparently reached a verdict. At once, she had no doubt that he was capable of committing a crime.

'Come in, girl.' He opened the side door, his eyes skimming the busy square while he remained in shadow.

Ella entered the dusty shed and the metal door shut them in. It was so dark she could barely see, but she didn't feel scared. He wouldn't hurt her – she'd been sent by his lawyer.

Mark Davidovich switched on the radio and a tune from *The Nutcracker* filled the stuffy lair. He pushed a rickety stool towards her.

'If it wasn't for Henrietta, I'd still be chopping wood in the Gulag, if I was alive.' His low voice sounded harsh as a corroded blade. 'Now, tell me …'

Ella sat, and a chill ran up her legs. She had to be straight with him.

'I need you to kidnap my daughter. Her father—'

'Don't bother with explanations,' Mark Davidovich interjected.

The dense air shifted, and he stood close enough for Ella to touch.

'Lilly is with my in-laws in their communal apartment at Leninsky Prospect.' Her voice wavered between confident and helpless. 'It's urgent,' she added.

He grunted. 'Urgent, you say? That's a big ask, girl.'

Ella turned her head and gasped. There was a woman, young, about her age, sitting motionless in the corner in the dark, not making a sound. Only the whites of her eyes betrayed that she was not a mannequin.

'How do you know Henry anyway?' Mark asked.

'I'm her niece.' Ella slid off her stool and stood tall. 'Can you help me or not?'

He snickered, and the girl in the corner shifted. 'I can go there,' she said.

Ella forced herself to stay still. Whoever the girl was didn't concern her. Mark looked at the young woman for a long while. Then he shuffled about in the kiosk.

'Write down the address and the names.' He handed Ella a sheet of paper and a pencil. 'You'll have to be there, waiting outside, when I tell you. Leave your number too. I don't want your brat on my hands if I can help it.'

47

Ella sat on the edge of the bed, where Henrietta's books and magazines were strewn. Today they would attempt to write Roman's permission letter for Lilly to leave the USSR.

She held Henrietta's hand, icy-cold. Her aunt's eyes remained closed, and her face on the pile of pillows looked papery, more so than it had on Ella's last visit only two days ago. Beside her, Masha exhaled. Ella could sense her desire to kick the intruder out and let her beloved rest.

'I'm not sleeping, Masha. Stop hovering.' Henrietta's voice sounded stronger than Ella had expected. With some effort, Henrietta propped herself up. 'So, what are we cooking? Masha, bring me some paper and pens. Do you have any samples of Roman's handwriting? His signature? Anything?'

Ella pulled out her marriage certificate and a 1975 photograph of Roman and Ilya before either of them knew her. Roman had written a date on the back. What possessed her to bring the photo she didn't know, but somehow it felt right.

She looked at Ilya's face – she might be risking her daughter's life for him.

Masha placed a tray on the bed in front of Henrietta and turned away, but Henrietta reached for her hand. 'Relax, love. It'll take an hour, at most. I'll rest after that.'

Masha smiled and the tension eased somehow. Still, an hour spent here would leave Ella with less time to collect her exit permit from OVIR and visit Vlad's father, before kidnapping her own child. Zacharov senior would know what she should do in Vienna to help his son.

Henrietta coughed and her body shook. 'You didn't tell me how it went with Mark Davidovich. Is it all set?'

Ella wanted to ask what crime had put this man in jail, but it was none of her business, as long as Henrietta had faith in his abilities. She couldn't suppress a shudder when she imagined a criminal holding her baby. 'You trust him, don't you?'

Henrietta nodded. 'He'll do what he promised. Call Lia to meet you outside to say goodbye.'

Ella's eyes stung, but she kept herself in check. It was her mother-in-law's fault that Lilly would be put in danger. Lia had left her with no other options. 'What if she refuses?'

'She won't. The woman has a heart.' Her great-aunt chuckled. 'Cheer up, girl. Roman Abramov is about to start writing his statement.'

*

Ella's mood had improved. She felt light-headed at the thought of snuggling together with Lilly on her way to freedom. They would fly to Vienna. Ilya could follow them. She would beg Lubov for his exit permit.

The corridor of OVIR was lined with steel doors and rows of vinyl chairs. Ella consulted the frayed receipt in her hand. A door swung open and Lieutenant Solntzev, a large man, snug in his uniform, stepped out. Ella leaped to her feet.

'Captain Solntzev?' She raised his rank in a hope of being received without delay.

The officer had a blank expression on his puffy face, and Ella noticed bristles sticking out of his nostrils. She stretched out her hand with the receipt and saw his face morph from almost human to machine-like.

Solntzev straightened and looked above her head. 'Come in.' He turned on his heel like a toy soldier.

She followed him, the reddish fold of his neck visible above the not-so-white of his collar. Ella felt these details were important, as though she was already telling her story to her grandchildren – the day she got her exit visa. Only a few chosen ones had the privilege of transcending the Soviet borders. She was about to become one of them now.

She saw the document on Solntzev's desk the moment she stepped over the threshold – a pristine, olive-coloured card with a few typed lines. Unable to take her eyes off it, Ella moved closer. She yearned to touch her visa, to grab it and run. But she had to make sure that Lilly's name was included.

She clasped the proof of her daughter's existence: Lilly's birth certificate and the forged letter with Roman's permission to take his child out of the USSR.

Solntzev sat behind his desk. 'Take a seat.' He sounded almost polite.

She lowered herself onto the chair without losing sight of her visa.

'So, Citizen Abramova, ready to leave us behind?' His voice had a strange intonation. Irony, threat or envy? She couldn't tell.

'I brought my daughter's birth certificate as you requested. She is included, isn't she?' Ella thrust Lilly's birth certificate in his direction.

Solntzev examined the document. 'Do you have permission from Roman Abramov to take his daughter?'

Her hands itched as she put the forged letter on the desk. He looked at it briefly, then slammed a giant stamp down on the new card, leaving it marked with a purple bruise. A visa stamp, she guessed. An actual exit visa. Her ticket to freedom – so sought after – finally before her.

'You have to leave the USSR in forty-eight hours.' His tone was mechanical and precise with no emotion.

'Your exit visa expires at …' He paused and checked his watch. 'At 10.20 am on Friday.'

*

Ella staggered out of OVIR and onto the worn cement steps. The white-hot sun burst from behind a cloud and momentarily blinded her. She clutched her exit permit, which still smelled of fresh ink.

Her legs felt wobbly. She sat on a step, sweeping off a few cigarette butts. Tears blocked her nose and her throat. She had one day to rescue her daughter, one day to say goodbye to Olga, Natan and her parents. To Leon. And to Ilya, she thought, unless she called Lubov now. The sun dived behind another cloud and a shadow fell upon her.

Then a mad thought sprouted in her mind and brought her to her feet. Ilya could have arrived already and was waiting for her at home.

There were forty-seven hours and forty minutes left.

48

Vlad's address at Patriarch's Ponds was etched in her mind from her school years, when she and her closest friend had skipped classes together. Indulged by Daria, his father's housekeeper, they had hidden in his cavernous flat.

One of the few Moscow apartment mansions, it appeared in front of Ella lit by streetlights. Only celestials like Vlad's father, Boris Danilovich Zacharov, resided here. His novels had survived the Great Terror, as had he, miraculously staying alive in the Gulag. To ask for his advice – she'd only met the literary giant a few times – felt like seeking help from a god. But she needed guidance on how to help free his son when she got to Vienna or later on, to Australia. She thought briefly about confessing that she'd signed the report to escape arrest and pay for her freedom, but then thought again.

Her visit to Zacharov's household didn't seem timely. By now though, the Aeroflot office was shut for the night, and tomorrow she'd have to secure her flight, farewell her parents, pack up a few things and witness her daughter's abduction by Henrietta's *zek*. She hadn't told Zacharov senior any of this over the phone, yet she'd conveyed her urgency. He'd asked her to come round.

She had called Lia too, begging and crying until her mother-in-law promised to step outside to let her see Lilly 'one last time'. Lia's tone was icy, but it hardly mattered. If only Ilya would come back to Moscow, she would whisper her plans in his ear. He could meet them in Vienna. General Lubov had promised her.

A familiar middle-aged woman with a down shawl on her shoulders sat by the lift.

'Zacharov? Third floor. You have to sign in.' The concierge didn't greet Ella, but her eyes seemed to narrow in recognition.

Ella signed in. She rushed up the marble staircase to a grand vestibule where Daria waited at the entrance to Zacharov's residence. She hugged Ella and her face fell. Her body felt weightless in Ella's arms.

'Any news from my *boychik*?' Daria asked.

Something caught in Ella's throat. She had nothing to offer this woman. Daria had fed her sweets when she was a schoolgirl. She'd blocked her ears when they listened to *Voice of America*.

Ella backed off. 'I hope Boris Danilovich knows more.'

Daria dabbed her eyes with a handkerchief and nudged Ella inside. 'Vladechka is in Moscow,' Daria said. 'They take food parcels. But no letters.'

Ella looked her in the eye. 'I'm leaving for good, Daria. I'll get him out, I promise.'

The museum-like living room was lit by floor lamps and light glinted off gilded frames. Next to the glass-enclosed bookcases stood the crooked figure of the renowned writer.

'Ellochka.' Boris Danilovich took her fingers in his trembling hand and his eyes glistened. 'Have you heard from Vlad?'

She looked down at the intricate parquet motif and let go of his hand. It took all her strength not to cry alongside him.

Vlad had been arrested before, but this time they didn't know what the charge was or how to fight for his release. Should they alert the West that he'd been jailed as a dissident or that the KGB had cooked up a criminal case?

Vlad's imprisonment was her fault, at least partially, but from outside of the USSR she could try to correct that.

'Boris Danilovich, I'm leaving Russia. I need your help.'

'Sit down, Ellochka. Are you hungry?' he asked, Daria hovering behind him.

'Thank you, Boris Danilovich, but I can't stay. I want to help Vlad, yet I've never been abroad. What do I do in Vienna? Do I go to a newspaper? Is *Radio Svoboda* in Vienna?'

She kept talking to avoid his questions, afraid he would feel her shame. 'Will they believe me? Could you write a protest letter that I can post? Or should I take it to them myself? Or call radio stations? Which one shall I talk to?'

Ella fell silent, and Vlad's father lowered himself into his armchair.

'It would be wonderful to have some tea.' Daria covered his knees with a plaid blanket and he watched her leave the room. 'Ellochka, I'll tell you what newspapers, but write it in your own words. I cannot get involved. Do you need money?'

Boris Danilovich pulled out a roll of American dollars bound by a rubber band from the pocket of his velour house jacket. 'Take it, Ella, for Vlad.' He beckoned her to come closer and slid the money into her knapsack.

*

Her parents' apartment door swung open, Anna's skinny hands clinging onto it. Her mother's eyes were puffy, her face drawn. It looked like a plaster mask in the morning light. Anna slid to the floor.

Ella kneeled next to her and hugged her shoulders. 'What's wrong, Mama?'

She'd never seen Anna upset like this and prayed nothing awful had happened to her father or Leon. The need to say goodbye while keeping her troubles to herself had already killed any joy she could muster in her last days in the Soviet Union.

'Mama, *nu*, Mama?' Deep in her gut, a dread stirred. She didn't want to explain anything, least of all Lia's kidnapping of her baby. Whatever Anna had uncovered, Ella would call it a lie. 'Tell me. What's going on? It can't be that bad.'

Her mother turned her face away. 'Lilly,' she sobbed.

Ella felt as if a rock had shattered her breastbone. What did her mother know about Lilly? Henrietta wouldn't have betrayed her and neither would Masha. And while Olga stayed at the dacha, it was unlikely she'd spoken to Anna.

'Lilly's fine. She's with Roman's parents.'

Anna attempted to get up, and Ella helped her to her feet. She wished her father would come home soon. She guided Anna towards the living room and sat on the sofa.

Anna took a sharp breath to suppress a sob. 'You're leaving your baby behind, Lia told me.'

Ella stiffened. There was nothing she could do to reassure her mother. She couldn't explain – she had to keep going.

Anna snuggled next to her on the sofa. She put her arm around Ella's neck and clasped her fingers. 'Please don't leave her, my love.'

Ella rested her head on Anna's shoulder. 'You've got it all wrong, Mama. I'll pick Lilly up tonight.'

She hoped that was the truth. But she pictured Mark Davidovich and the faceless girl spiriting Lilly away, and the fear made her shiver.

'You don't have to go, my love. You can't.' Anna held her hand and rubbed it. 'I would have never abandoned you.'

There was no point arguing, Ella thought, and the situation could become worse when her father got home. 'Mama, I told you, don't worry. I won't leave without Lilly. I'm going to get her. I promise.'

Anna wiped her tears. 'Then why did Lia say you're leaving Russia alone? Where's Ilya?'

'He's on his way back from Novokuznetsk.' At least she hoped he was. She got up. 'I must run, Mama. I'm sorry. I need to get home.'

She took a step towards the door and Anna followed her. 'Promise you'll come back with Lilly,' said Anna. 'You need to see your father. I can't believe you're doing it.'

Ella embraced her. Inside her soul were ashes, all burned out, but she had to keep going. Whatever her mother felt at the moment was secondary to the risk of her missing Ilya. Or worse. She pictured herself hugging Lilly in farewell and then watching her parents-in-law take her baby back inside. This was an unthinkable outcome. She banished it from her mind.

49

The balmy August day and her final one in her homeland lurked behind the open window. Ella listened out for any sign of Ilya's return, but she heard nothing. In less than four hours she'd meet Mark Davidovich and collect her daughter from him.

She'd already made a successful trip to Aeroflot Central. Now she clutched a plastic sleeve with her ticket and the exit visa for herself and Lilly. Ella unzipped her knapsack and hid her priceless possessions in its internal pocket next to the roll of dollars Vlad's father had given her. The notion of passing customs with hard currency in her bag terrified her, but she couldn't leave it behind. The money would help her fight for Vlad.

She didn't need to pack much, just a few clothes and some of Lilly's things. As refugees they'd be housed and fed while being processed in Austria. In Ostia and Ladispoli, the recent émigrés waited to be granted entry to other countries. The stories of the lucky ones who'd departed the Soviet lands became a blueprint, retold by the friends and relatives they left behind.

The clock on the wall showed 4 pm. What time was it in Vienna? It seemed foolish trying to guess what she would do there, let alone in faraway Sydney. She'd have doubted the latter city existed if it wasn't for Sonya and its famed Opera

House. At least the country treasured the arts. She would act again there, she believed.

Right now Ella felt like an actress in a ghastly play. Whatever she attempted to do seemed somehow false.

She opened a dresser and her baby's scent hit her in the face. She packed Lilly's pacifier, bottles and cloth nappies. Then she found herself sitting on the bed with Lilly's wraps on her lap. Indecision about what was important and what wasn't paralysed her. Her half-packed bag lay on the floor and the flat looked abandoned. Water dripped in the bathroom, otherwise, the silence suffocated her.

She listened again for Ilya's arrival. But the door didn't squeak and his footsteps didn't pad down the corridor. He hadn't come back.

After a time, the telephone rang and she picked it up. 'Ilya?'

'No, it's me,' Olga said. 'Have you got Lilly?'

Ella slumped. She had to remind herself where she'd left things with her grandmother: Olga had been feeling frail, and Ella had gone to get Lilly back from Roman's parents. That seemed like weeks ago, although it'd only been days. But with no time to spare and no news of Lilly, Ella hadn't tried to reach her at the dacha.

'She's still with Lia, but I'm picking her up in an hour or two.' She twirled the phone's cord around her finger. 'Our flight is tomorrow morning. Are you back home?'

'We are. Your father came to get us today, me and Leon. Natan is in the hospital.' Ella wondered why Anna hadn't told her that. The line crackled with static. 'Ellochka, I may not see you again.'

'I know.' Ella's reply was flat. She didn't recognise her own voice.

'Should I come to the airport tomorrow? Are your parents taking you and Lilly?'

She was doing the right thing, but Ella pictured her family crying at the airport. 'No need, Baba.'

'Ilya isn't with you?'

Olga's question turned something upside down in her chest. Suddenly, she sobbed with her mouth open like in her childhood, making loud snorting sounds, and she rocked like an elderly Jew deep in prayer.

'Sorry, Baba,' she managed to say. 'I have to go and pick Lilly up.'

'Leo and Sonya did come back to visit us, my love, though it took them far too long. Almost forty years.' Olga fell silent, and Ella listened to her gasping through the static. 'Call me from the airport, darling, and kiss Lillechka.'

50

Ella fixed her eyes on the entrance to Roman's parents' apartment block. A single light bulb shone above the front door and an empty vodka bottle sparkled near the kerb. The bottle lay in a puddle halfway between the porch and an oak tree, from where Ella would witness the abduction of her daughter by Mark Davidovich.

The glint of the bottle disturbed her. She felt an urge to creep from her hiding place and shove it out of the way. But she didn't. She couldn't risk being seen. Instead, she pressed herself deeper into the shadows, her duffel bag at her feet. She leaned against the tree and the damp bark of the oak trunk imprinted its pattern on her cheek. The desire to wake up on the other side, ready to collect Lilly from the agreed place by the zoo, made her weary. She wanted to close her eyes and fall asleep.

Any minute now, Lia would come out with her daughter. A passing car drowned the hum of television sets that spilled from the open windows. A girl with a pram walked past the entrance. Ella hoped Mark Davidovich wouldn't hurt anyone. She prayed that he wouldn't have to.

More windows lit up. The door to the apartment block banged open and shut. Her attention was slipping. The reflection of light on the vodka bottle mesmerised her.

Then the door opened again. Ella's focus returned but her shivers worsened. Her mother-in-law pushed Lilly's pram out under the porch light. She lowered the pram down the steps onto the footpath, from the light into the shadows. There was a man with her. His broad shoulders made Ella drop her arms and let go of the tree trunk.

Ilya.

She wedged her knuckles into her mouth to muffle a scream. He'd probably called her while she was at OVIR or consoling her mother, but she could not comprehend why he'd gone to the Abramovs without finding her first. He must have believed he could persuade Lia to let him bring Lilly home. And what had Lia told him about Ella's intentions to leave? He wouldn't believe it.

Ilya stood on the footpath next to Lia. He held the pram's handle. Thoughts of how to warn him about the kidnapping turned her mind into a hive. She wanted to rush forward and alert him but her limbs were heavy. There was no way to explain her plan to Ilya. Worse, she couldn't interfere without jeopardising the abduction. If Mark Davidovich backed off, her daughter would remain with Lia – and she would be forced to stay in Russia.

Ella's muscles tightened and the young woman she'd noticed earlier walked in front of her mother-in-law. The woman's pram almost collided with Lia's. She stopped beside Ilya for a few seconds and blocked Ella's view. Lia said something to her in a friendly voice, but Ella couldn't make out the words.

Her body relaxed. The stranger and Lia were probably talking babies. Ilya remained silent. Ella willed the woman to go.

Then the woman spoke and it made Ella's head spin. She'd heard that voice before, in the locksmith's kiosk.

A shadow approached, and Ella saw a man join the group on the footpath. He put his arm around the young woman and whispered in her ear. Immediately she stepped sideways, closer to the road.

Ella felt she might faint. She inched towards the vodka bottle, ready to jump out and protect Lilly if she had to interfere. She could not predict Ilya's actions or those of the kidnappers. Would Mark Davidovich abort his attempt to abduct Lilly? Or would he pause to regroup?

The man wrenched the pram's handle free of Ilya's grip. He pushed it towards the girl from the kiosk. Ella heard a shriek. It didn't sound human. Ilya launched himself forward. The girl snatched the swaddled baby from Lia's pram, abandoning her own. Ilya grabbed Mark Davidovich – by now she knew it was him – and wrestled him to the ground. But Mark rolled over and swung something shiny at her beloved. His fist connected with Ilya's head. The men's shadows danced in front of her.

Ella watched on in horror at the clump of yelling people in front of the building. Their voices grew louder and sharper. She thought she recognised Lia's wail.

A silhouette on the ground had melted into the asphalt and lost its contours. Shards of glass shimmered near its head. Someone screamed, echoed by the people in the windows.

Dazed, Ella noticed a black car parked at the kerb only a few metres away. It reversed loudly, its revving overpowering the voices, and disappeared around the corner. She hadn't seen Mark Davidovich get in, but he must have. In any case, the girl had escaped with Lilly. They had her daughter. Soon they'd be speeding along Leninsky Prospect towards the zoo, where she was meant to meet them.

The cluster of people on the footpath had grown larger. In the distance, an ambulance siren sounded. Ella crawled out of the shadows, wanting to see more but dreading what she might see. The broken man on the asphalt could not be Ilya. It couldn't be.

Her eyes zoomed in on his leather jacket. Her entire being went numb. If Ilya died because of her scheming, she would never forgive herself.

She ran and kneeled beside her beloved. She touched his forehead with her fingertips, afraid to hurt him. His skin was warm and clammy, and her fingers turned wet. Crimson. Ilya's eyes were closed. He looked asleep; a trickle of blood was beginning to dry on his temple. She lowered her face to his. Ilya's lips parted and she swallowed his breath together with her own. He was alive.

Still crouching by his side, she found her parents-in-law in the crowd. Alexander had joined Lia, his arms around his sobbing wife. Lilly. Ella had forgotten to pretend. Roman's parents must not guess that she was behind what had just taken place.

'Where's my baby?' she wailed. 'What have you done with my child? Where's Lilly?'

She didn't need to put it on. Her grief halved her. She replayed the scene in her mind. Mark's girl had grabbed Lilly from the pram, pressed her into her chest and run. It dawned on Ella that she didn't know who this girl was or why she'd got involved. Maybe she wanted Lilly for herself.

Alexander whispered in his wife's ear and avoided looking at Ella. Lia babbled like a child, her head in her hands. 'I'm so sorry, Ella. So sorry.'

Lilly's pram was empty. Ella glanced inside the other one, just to confirm her suspicion that it was a prop. She bent over Lilly's pram and inhaled her baby's scent. Her sobbing became more intense. She buried her face in the abandoned blanket and hugged the hollow space.

The sound of duelling sirens, probably from a *militzia* car and an ambulance, hushed the crowd. Ella kneeled and took Ilya's hand. She wanted to lie next to her love and let herself be. But she also wanted to run, to jump into a taxi and rush to Mark Davidovich to get her baby back.

Blue and red lights pulsated in the distance. The ambulance arrived, and the sound of the *militzia*'s siren grew louder. Lia's fingers covered her puffy face. Yet Ella felt her mother-in-law's gaze follow her every movement.

Another woman helped Ella to her feet. If she stayed with Ilya, Lia and the law would suspect she knew where Lilly had been taken. If she ran, they'd judge her as one of the kidnappers. Ella watched two medics lift Ilya onto a gurney and load him into the ambulance. She'd see him in the hospital, she decided, but she had to find Lilly first.

Her duffel lay on the ground under the oak tree where she'd dropped it. She hadn't planned to return to her flat but to go straight to the airport with Lilly, take cover among the people, wait for her flight in the morning. It took her seconds to duck into the shadows and retrieve the bag.

'Which hospital, please?' she asked the ambulance driver.

He squeezed behind the wheel; the other medic stayed in the back with Ilya. A *militzia* car stopped behind the ambulance and two officers stepped out.

Ella glanced at them and backed off. She met the driver's eyes and he nodded. He must have guessed she was trying to avoid the *militzia* but didn't look surprised.

'Krasnaya Presnya – Filatov Hospital,' he announced, as if giving orders to himself.

Ella faded into the crowd, away from the *militziamen*. They wouldn't chase her. They had other witnesses to question. But once they spoke to Lia, she knew they'd catch up with her soon enough.

51

The pale halos of street lamps undid the starless night, and the branches of linden trees reached through the spikes atop the towering fence of the Moscow Zoo. Ella's arms ached. She couldn't believe she might get to hold her daughter in a few moments.

There appeared to be no one waiting for her by the locked gates. No one waited for her in the flanges of the zoo entrance. Then again, she didn't expect Mark Davidovich to stand in full view of the street. He'd probably watch her from a distance, from a parked car, to make sure she'd come alone.

She leaned against a soaring column underneath the zoo's portico. The cars sped by along Krasnaya Presnya. Wet asphalt reflected the headlights.

The traffic lights changed a few times from red to green. But Mark didn't turn up with Lilly, and neither did his girl-helper. Perhaps they were parked somewhere in an unlit spot. Or they weren't coming. Ella walked around the corner to the side lane. There were only a few cars parked there: an older style Moskvitch and several Zhigulis.

She passed a sleek black Volga with tinted windscreen and sensed movement inside. The car's windows reflected only her drawn face. Most of the new Volgas belonged to the authorities or the state's enforcement agencies, but Mark Davidovich had been picked up from outside Lia's apartment block in a shiny dark-coloured one.

Ella stood under a streetlight, so he could see her and approach. She shut her eyes and imagined the girl hopping out of the car with Lilly in her arms. It looked so convincing, like in a movie, and she didn't want it to end.

A few blocks away, her parents waited for her and Lilly in their flat and a few blocks the other way was the hospital where the ambulance had taken Ilya. His face had been so pallid as he lay on the ground. Ella yearned to rush to the hospital, but first she had to get her daughter.

She opened her eyes and traced her steps back to the illuminated street corner. She followed the arc of the zoo fence like a caged beast. Her legs started to give, buckling under her weight, and she fought blacking out.

The criminals wouldn't want to keep Lilly, she was sure. If they hadn't turned up, it simply meant they wanted something else. Was it money? Maybe the dollars Vlad's father had given her could get her baby back. He'd meant for that cash to save his child, but she could replace it later.

She could jump on a metro train and go back to the locksmith's kiosk where all of this had started. Mark Davidovich might be waiting there. Or, given how terribly wrong the kidnapping had gone, he might have taken Lilly to Henrietta's place.

*

Under the blinding lights of Taganskaya metro, its polished marble floors resembled an ice skating rink. Ella ran towards the escalators and almost slipped.

She bolted up the moving stairs and imagined Lilly's warmth next to her breast; she could almost touch her baby's downy hair. Her steps echoed the thumping of blood in her temples. She whimpered with hope and burst through the rotating doors onto the deserted street.

In the gloom, the black square behind Taganskaya metro seemed unfamiliar. The dense bulk of the theatre squatted across the road. Its doors, usually thrown wide open for a show, were blocked for the night.

Ella circled the station. It was as if Mark's shed had vanished from the earth. She passed an ice-cream kiosk and a newsagency. Tomorrow's headlines would announce more lies about the rotting West and the success of the Soviet space program, but she wouldn't be here to read them. She'd be on the plane to Vienna. Mark Davidovich had no reason to keep her daughter. Then his den reared up in front of her, locked and solid, with no flicker of light escaping from within. She knocked on the rusty door.

She placed her mouth to the keyhole. 'Mark Davidovich. It's me, Ella. Please open.'

Inside the kiosk, something seemed to stir, and Ella's heart filled with hope. 'I have the money.' Her lips brushed against the door and she tasted metal. But now nothing moved. 'Please, give me my baby,' she begged.

She wanted to howl into the night, but was scared to make a sound. She covered her mouth and wept.

*

'Is she here? Do you have her?' Ella ran up the creaky stairs to Henrietta's apartment.

Masha gripped her shoulders and almost hurt her. 'Ellochka, what's wrong?' Ella opened her mouth to say something, then Masha moved aside to let her through.

Henrietta sat in her bed surrounded by pillows, a lit cigarette between her crooked fingers. Lilly was not there.

Ella's heartbeat stopped. She collapsed into her great-aunt's empty wheelchair. 'Where is she?'

Henrietta snuffed out her cigarette in the ashtray. 'What happened?' She lowered her yellowish feet to the floor and bent to look for her slippers. 'Masha, run her a bath and find her something else to wear.'

Ella noticed her jeans, caked with dirt, her grubby hands and muddy top. Masha left the room, and she recalled kneeling in the mud over Ilya's body. 'Has Mark Davidovich called you?'

Henrietta shook her head. 'Tell me what happened, Ellochka.'

'There was a fight.' Ella peeled off her blouse. Masha returned and offered her a shawl, which she wrapped around her shoulders.

'You have to tell me the full details.' Henrietta's voice sharpened. With Masha's help, she moved herself into her wheelchair. 'Was Mark there?'

'I think so. I don't know.' Ella gulped. 'He sent this girl – I saw her in his kiosk – to kidnap Lilly. It must have been her. I'm not sure now.'

Masha perched on the bed. 'The bath is ready.'

Ella stood up. 'Mark's girl grabbed Lilly and they all screamed. Ilya was there. I don't know how he knew. He didn't know it was arranged.' She gasped for air again. 'Someone hit him with a bottle. His head …' She rubbed her eyes with her knuckles; the shawl slipped off her shoulders.

'Sit,' Henrietta ordered. 'I'll try to locate Mark. They should have come here. He knows the address.'

'Is Lilly safe?' Ella choked on her words.

'Stop it, Ella. We'll find her.' Henrietta's voice didn't waiver. 'Where is Ilya? Have you talked to the *militzia*?'

'He's at Filatov Hospital. An ambulance took him. He was unconscious.'

Ella stumbled to the lofty window that faced Petrovka Street. The night outside lay foggy, pierced only by the shafts of light from passing cars.

When she turned, Masha was kneeling in front of an icon in the corner. A candle flickered above her head and threw a shadow across the face of the Virgin.

Henrietta watched Masha with soft eyes. 'Go and wash, Ella. Get changed too. I'll send Masha to you when she's done. I have to make some calls.'

52

Gregory's old Volga powered through the city. Her father gripped the wheel and stared ahead. His back accused her. Beside him, Henrietta sank into the seat, dwarfed by his bulk. She led their search for the kidnappers in Moscow's criminal haunts. Mark Davidovich had fallen into the cracks of the communist metropolis and unless they found him and Lilly, Ella would rot here, in this godforsaken motherland of theirs.

Ella rolled down the rear passenger window. The night's breeze diffused the tension in the car. It felt like the city had been deserted and they were the only people left. She let the wind cool her face. The road looked velvety under the streetlights, yellow and white, like eggs cracked onto a cold pan.

Gregory slowed the car and turned to Henrietta. '*Nu?* Where is it? What's the street name?' He rubbed his eyes. She had never heard him speak like this to his aunt.

'Calm down, Grisha. Don't push me. There should be a restaurant called Kalinka on the ground floor.'

Gregory swore under his breath and pressed the accelerator. Ella rested her palm on her father's shoulder. 'Papa, slow down, please. Let Henrietta show you where to go.'

'I told you to call the *militzia* an hour ago. We cannot drive around Moscow hunting these low lifes. They would know what to do.'

Ella tensed. She remembered the *militziaman*'s fist jammed into her backbone, her arm twisted.

'They're bandits, Papa. They despise the people they're supposed to serve. They are boys from the collective farms, drunk on power.'

Henrietta turned around and took her hand. 'We shouldn't involve the *militzia*, Grisha. You know it yourself. We can't risk Lilly's life.'

Ella felt acid tearing at her throat. Gregory slammed on the brakes.

'There are some restaurants here, but they're closed. Do you want to check it out?' He looked tired and old, she noticed, though he was almost the same age her grandfather was when he got arrested.

She opened the car door and faced the neon Kalinka sign on the grey brick walk-up. The restaurant's chairs were stacked upside down on top of the tables. No one seemed to be inside.

Fighting the wind, she stumbled back to the Volga. Behind the car window, Henrietta's face looked like a death mask. Ella climbed in and sank into the weathered seats.

'Let's try another place,' Henrietta said.

Her father glanced at her in the rear-view mirror and turned on the engine. 'It's not even midnight. We'll find her, I promise.'

*

At one in the morning, with Henrietta hunched in the back next to Ella, Gregory drove the car up the hill to Moscow University, with the capital, its lights extinguished for the night, below them. It felt as if darkness had descended not only on her but the whole universe.

'You cannot leave the country, Ella.' Gregory's gaze followed the bend of the road. 'You can't go without Lilly. It doesn't make sense. Anyway, where do you think you're going?'

She let the silence linger. Gregory slowed the car to a crawl. In the mirror, his eyes were red-rimmed and dull.

He hit the brakes. 'What's this blasted obsession with emigration? I don't understand.' Her father turned to glare at her. 'You haven't even asked your mother or myself what we think of your decision. Just went ahead and got yourself an exit permit. Didn't it occur to you that you could hurt us all? And to deny us our grandchild – what's wrong with you?'

Ella held in her tears. She had no strength to argue that this was for all of them, for Lilly and Leon too.

Gregory rubbed his cheek. His ashy stubble had grown more visible in the last hour. 'Tell her, Henrietta. Why are you encouraging her?'

Henrietta's eyes were shut and she slumped against Ella, her face pinched.

Ella sat up straight. 'Are you not feeling well, aunty?'

Henrietta opened her eyes, unusually bright and youthful in her lined face. 'Let her go, Grisha. If she can get out of here, she should. When you and Anna are ready, you'll join her, or Leon will.'

'Are you mad?'

Gregory threw the car door open and climbed out into the quiet night. The chilly air soothed Ella's itchy eyes.

Henrietta spoke from the back of the car. 'Do you remember how my David died?'

Her father sat back sideways in the driver's seat, his feet on the ground.

'My husband wasn't killed in a battle during the Soviet–Finnish war.' Henrietta's voice sounded like that of a young woman, Ella thought, the age she was when David had perished in Karelia. They'd just married. 'He wasn't murdered by Finns in 1939, he was slaughtered in the Gulag after we'd signed the Moscow Peace Treaty. Did you forget that, Grisha, or maybe you were never told?'

He bowed his head.

Ella, hearing the story for the first time, clasped her great-aunt's bony fingers.

'That's what the country we live in does – it kills its sons and daughters if they don't fit.' Henrietta squeezed Ella's hand back. 'My David didn't fit and neither does Ella. Let her go.'

Gregory shut the door and started the engine. 'Where do we head to next?' he asked gently.

'Take me home. I need to call in some favours.' Henrietta leaned into Ella. 'We will find her, doll. You'll see your baby before dawn.'

Ella squeezed Henrietta's fingers to warm them. 'Could you take me to the hospital, Papa?'

53

Ella ran along the endless hospital corridors with her muddy duffel bag and struggled into a doctor's coat she'd procured from a nurse for a crumpled rouble. Blinding fluorescent light flooded the walkways and the stench of ammonia filled her nostrils as she rushed past unlit wards.

The thought that Ilya had been injured because of her actions tortured her. She prayed he was awake. As long as she could explain herself, they had a chance. She and Ilya loved each other and only that mattered.

One hallway she entered looked like a warzone: half a dozen patients in portable beds with various contraptions awaited admission to one of the heaving wards.

A lump lodged itself in her throat. Ilya lay motionless in one of the beds, the colour drained from his face. But he was alive. His chest rose and fell under a coarse blanket and his eyelids twitched in his sleep. A gauze bandage was wrapped around his forehead, and only a russet spot that spread underneath spoiled its pristine whiteness.

Ella noticed a young man in a grey suit loitering a few steps away. He held a writing pad, but he was no journalist. Not at two in the morning. And his plain face seemed familiar.

She touched Ilya's hand and imagined her hope spreading above them like a *chuppah*. She felt guilty for thinking of a wedding canopy. She grazed Ilya's wrist with her mouth. His pulse beat weakly under her lips. If only he'd come back to Moscow a few hours earlier, this whole nightmare wouldn't have happened. What had caused his delay? Nothing made sense and now Lilly was missing.

Tears that she'd thought had all been used up poured out of her. She rested her head on the bleached white hospital sheet and gently stroked the stubble on Ilya's cheek, terrified of inflicting more pain.

He opened his eyes and winced under the lights. She leaned over his face.

'My love,' she said. Joy broke through her grief, as pure and sweet as this man who she'd met too late but hoped to spend the rest of her life with.

Ilya stared at her, hard, unblinking. Unknowing. As if he couldn't recall her. His dry lips parted, but no sound escaped. He closed his eyes and turned to face the wall. She'd thought nothing could hurt her more than what she'd already suffered. But now it did.

She put her mouth to his ear. 'Ilusha, please listen,' she said. 'I'll explain.'

The suited man came closer and she could feel his presence behind her. He was KGB.

Ella took Ilya's hand. 'Lilly is missing, my love. Please talk to me. We might never see each other again if you don't. I need to tell you what happened.' She glanced over her shoulder. The KGB man was clearly listening. 'I'll find Lilly, I promise. It's not my fault.'

She heard herself blubbering nonsensical, stupid words that she hoped would make him listen, but underneath the hospital blanket Ilya's back was rigid.

The man smirked. He stood over her and inspected Ilya's body. His face was typical – Slavic, wide with pale eyes, clean-shaven. A murderer, a jailor. But Ella knew where she'd seen him before. He was in Lubov's office when she'd been forced to betray Vlad. Lubov's adjutant.

She let go of Ilya's hand and bent to kiss his cheek. He flinched, his face contorted with hatred, final, like a curtain fall. He didn't want to see her and he couldn't bear her touch. Ella's heart broke in that moment.

'Citizen Abramova.' The KGB man motioned for her to follow and Ella trailed after him to the lifts. Writing pad in hand, he pressed the down button. 'I have a few questions.'

The lift arrived and she stepped in and pushed the button for the ground floor.

'Where are you going, Abramova?' The KGB officer shoved her to the back of the lift. He leaned in and placed his hand next to her face. 'We haven't even started.'

Ella refused to yield to her fear. If he was going to arrest her, he wouldn't do it in front of patients and nurses. He'd wait to get her alone outside the hospital. She stepped sideways and asked, 'What did you say to Ilya?'

The man leered at her breasts. Then he raised his eyes to meet hers. 'Why, Abramova, only the truth, of course – that you organised the kidnapping and know where your daughter is.'

'That's a lie.'

The lift doors opened and she barged past him. His footsteps trailed her through the brightly lit foyer.

She stopped and stared into the man's eyes. 'Why would I steal my own daughter?'

He brought his face close to hers again. 'So, Citizen Abramova, you insist you don't know who attacked Ilya Bezsmertniy and kidnapped your daughter Lilly?'

'It was dark,' she said. 'I didn't see any faces. I heard screams and glass being smashed. It's disgusting you think I know more.'

She glanced at the wall clock that ticked towards 2.30 in the morning. It was possible that Henrietta had found Lilly. The KGB officer scribbled in his writing pad so furiously that he almost tore the page. She wondered what he'd written.

'Where exactly were you in relation to the kidnappers? Why didn't you hold on to your daughter?'

Ella bit her lip. She remembered the kidnapping in flashes, as if the lights were flickering in her head.

'I was a few metres away when the fight started.' If he was going to arrest her, she decided, she couldn't avoid it. 'I have to go. I need to be searching for my child rather than standing here talking to you.'

The KGB man stopped writing. He fixed her with a loaded stare. She felt her knees wobble. But she turned and walked to the exit, and she didn't hear his footsteps behind her.

54

Ella pressed the button for the elevator. She couldn't believe she'd made it home. Clearly, Lubov's man didn't have instructions to arrest her. They would come for her in the morning though, she knew it. It didn't matter. She'd be gone before dawn. And after Ilya's rejection, the only thing she wanted was to find Lilly.

Ella pressed the elevator button again, but it didn't come. The lift's cage looked abandoned. She'd have to walk up. Almost glad for the effort, she climbed the stairs, switching her duffel bag from hand to hand.

The image of her flat on the sixth floor and the telephone next to the sofa floated in her mind like a mirage. She'd call Henrietta. Neither she nor Masha would be asleep despite it being three in the morning. Maybe Henrietta had found her baby, or perhaps her father had. He could have taken Lilly home, to Anna.

Ella sprinted up the remaining flights of stairs. She passed the fourth floor, the fifth. Her floor, the sixth, was pitch black. Someone must have smashed the ceiling lights on the landing again. Ella swore under her breath. She kneeled beside her duffel bag and groped for her keys.

Shadows shifted. A man's hand yanked her to her feet. 'Don't scream.'

Ella choked on her fury. She'd hoped never to hear this voice again. 'What the hell are you doing here, Roman? I thought you were in Tula.' They must have let him out on day release.

Her vision adjusted to the darkness and she saw his unshaven chin.

Roman snickered. His eyes inspected her breasts, her waist, the curve of her hips, as if he were taking an inventory of goods.

'A long time not to visit your husband.' His voice shook with emotion, she couldn't tell which one. 'Where's my daughter?' He ripped the duffel bag out of her grip and shoved her towards the door of her flat. 'Open it. We need to talk. You'll tell me what you're up to.'

Ella fiddled with the lock. She couldn't run. He had her exit visa and her ticket. She'd zipped those precious documents into the inside pocket of her knapsack before she'd stuffed it into the duffel bag. The American dollars too.

Roman snatched the keys from her clumsy fingers and unlocked the door. He manhandled her inside, threw her bag onto the floor and kicked the door shut.

The look on his face made her back up. She didn't remember this man at all. He was a stranger. But she refused to avert her gaze. 'I need to make a telephone call.'

'Did you pay someone to kidnap her?' Roman sounded on edge.

She tried to step around him but he blocked her path.

'While I rot in Tula, you want to frolic in Europe? And take my daughter away? My parents told me everything.'

His breath reeked of sausage as he moved closer. Ella kept backing up until she'd flattened herself against the wall. He stroked her throat. His fingers found her windpipe and started to squeeze – at first almost tenderly, then with enough force to stop her breathing. She struggled against his arms but he wouldn't let her go. She couldn't escape. Behind her eyelids something exploded and she changed tactic. She relaxed her muscles, became floppy, and virtually hung from his grip like a rag doll.

Roman shifted his hand to her chin and jerked it upwards. The back of her head hit the wall. It made a hollow sound. She didn't feel pain or fear but the same rage she felt upon hearing his voice.

She gathered strength to speak calmly. 'Let me go, Roman. Let's talk as humans.'

His eyes were half-closed, glinting. 'Yes, let's talk – behind closed doors, so to speak.' Without loosening his hold, Roman turned the key to lock the front door, pressing himself against her.

Ella swallowed. She'd done shameful things – to Vlad, to Ilya, to her family, even to Lilly. But if she could only find her baby, she would make things right.

'I have to call about Lilly.' She could barely move her tongue to form words.

His fingers on her neck squeezed, and then released to let her slide down the wall onto the floor.

*

Red and green circles swirled behind her eyelids. Air seeped into her lungs and she imagined herself running up the stairs covered in sticky sweat. She buried her face in her knees. The swirling slowed down. The circles became yellow, then white.

Squinting, she peeked into the shadows. The lights were on and she could hear Roman's footsteps in the kitchen. She heard water stream into the sink and the rustle of matches. He was putting on the kettle. She had a few minutes until it whistled, which would mask any noise she had to make. Then the bathroom door creaked and Roman's belt buckle jingled.

Ella lifted her head. Her bag lay nearby where he'd tossed it. She crawled towards her priceless possessions.

Roman sighed, and his piss spattered the toilet bowl. She picked up her bag. The whistle of the kettle shattered the silence and Ella dashed for the door, fumbling with the lock. For a moment it wouldn't budge, then the cheap ply shifted and she slipped out of the flat in one swift movement.

Clutching her bag, she stepped inside the elevator and pressed the button for the ground floor. She heard the toilet flush in her flat, then the lift rattled and began to descend. Her throat felt scorched and she could hear blood roaring in her ears. The elevator touched the ground and she bolted out, leaving its door open. It'd take Roman some time to catch up.

The starless night absorbed her as she kept to the shadows. Her progress was silent, her steps muffled by the fallen leaves and wet patches of grass on the narrow turf strip that surrounded her apartment block. She rounded a corner and faced an identical building. Thunder sounded. Ella looked to the sky in wonder as raindrops slid down her face and she held her hand out to catch them. Lightning fractured the sky and revealed a shortcut that wound its way through the turf to the bus stop.

The rain felt like a blessing. Ella rushed forward. Water splattered under her feet and soaked into her rubber-soled sandshoes. She paused at the bus stop. There was no bus on the horizon and no cars on the road either. She burst into a nearby phone booth and wiped her face with both hands. Her hair formed a wet helmet around her head. The jacket Masha had insisted she wear retained little warmth. She crouched beside her bag and pulled out her documents and the American dollars. They were safer on her, inside the inner pocket of her jacket.

She leaned against the wall, holding the weighty receiver to her ear and praying for Henrietta to pick up the phone, to say that Lilly had been found.

'Allo... Ellochka, where are you?'

Ella gulped. She'd hoped to hear her great-aunt's voice, not Masha's. Her father and Henrietta must not have returned from their search yet.

'Is there any news? Did they find Lilly?'

'Mark Davidovich called,' said Masha. 'He says Lilly is fine, but he wants money. Lots.'

Ella stared through the misted glass at the blackness outside. Her stomach clenched in a knot. Her little baby, her *devochka*. They wouldn't harm her.

She fingered the wad of dollars in her jacket's inner pocket; they were not hers to spend. Vlad's father had begged her to fight for his son, but she had her daughter to save.

'Did he leave a number to call?' she said. 'I have money.'

'He wants a thousand dollars. He said he'll find you. Are you home?'

'Masha, listen, if Mark calls, tell him to meet me at the airport. Sheremetyevo.' The rain eased and tapped lightly on the roof. 'Tell my mother too, in case he contacts her first.' Ella stood up. 'International airport. Under the main departure board.'

'But what if he doesn't call? He said he'll find you.'

Ella opened the door of the booth with her foot to let in some air. A new black Volga cruised past the bus stop. It was the same one she'd seen near the zoo, she realised. She recalled the feeling of being observed through the window. It had to be Mark's car.

He'd brought her baby to her.

55

The rain had stopped and so did Mark's car. Ella dropped the receiver, leaving it to sway on its steel cord, and rushed out. She thought of Roman prowling around and sprinted through the puddles to get to her baby.

But the man who stepped out wasn't Mark Davidovich. He was a different kind of criminal – stocky, in a brown leather jacket and a kepi hat that covered his eyes. He had to be the driver.

Ella halted. 'I've brought the money. Where's my daughter?'

The man opened the passenger door and General Lubov looked out at her.

This couldn't be happening. She backed away and turned to run. Lubov's man stopped her by grabbing the handle of her duffel bag. She dug her heels in and tried to wrench it free. At least her ticket and exit visa were secured in her jacket's inner pocket.

'Ella Gregorievna, could we offer you a lift?' Lubov said.

Ella stood there. Silent. He wouldn't know of Mark's ransom demands.

Lubov smiled. 'Sheremetyevo. That's where you're going, isn't it?'

She pulled again at her bag but the driver's grip was like a vice. She rubbed her throat, tender from Roman's fingers. She couldn't fight them, and a lift to the airport seemed like the only way to get to her daughter on time.

*

Rebuilt for the Moscow Olympics, the airport came into view like an alien spacecraft. It appeared larger than life, like nothing she'd ever seen. She'd come here before to say goodbye to her friends leaving Russia for good, but never at daybreak.

The car whizzed into the almost empty parking lot. Lubov's driver opened the door for him. The general signalled for Ella to follow and she obeyed. She couldn't run now, not with Lilly so close and within reach.

The airport seemed too sparse, too cold, full of odd-looking people. Some turned to look, making her aware of her damp jeans and matted hair. She squinted at the sparkling lights and mustered a smile. Don't let an enemy see inside you, she recalled Olga saying.

All the while Lubov watched her. He stood a couple of steps away – an elderly uncle seeing off his niece. Only the uncle happened to be a KGB general and the niece wouldn't be going anywhere without her daughter.

Mark wasn't standing underneath the constantly shifting departure board and neither was his girl-helper. But maybe they hadn't arrived yet. The clock above the board showed that it was almost 7 am – three and half hours before her flight to Vienna. The desire to hold her baby made her weak. The exhaustion and horror of the night before kicked in too.

'May I call my parents?'

Lubov stroked his chin. His ruddy face broke into a smile. 'Of course you can.'

He and the driver followed her to the row of phones on the wall, each one encased in an open plastic hemisphere. She stood at one; the driver stood at the one beside her.

Her mother answered on the first ring. 'Where are you?'

Anna often made her feel guilty, but now she had the right.

'Come home now. I can't believe you trusted this man with your child. I promised to pay him when he brings Lilly here.'

Red fog floated before Ella's eyes. 'I'm at the airport, Mama.' She wavered. Surely she'd misheard. 'Didn't Masha call you?'

Anna gasped. 'He took the address. We borrowed money!' She was yelling now. 'He called us, you hear? He said you didn't answer.'

Ella slammed the phone down. Her message to Lilly's kidnappers hadn't got to her mother. She remembered the receiver swaying on its steel cord inside the telephone booth. Maybe Masha couldn't make the call because Ella hadn't hung up. But if she jumped in a taxi and rushed to her parents now, there was still a chance of escaping with Lilly.

She met Lubov's eyes. His face was blank. He didn't resemble a kindly uncle any longer. Then she remembered how Ilya had rejected her at the hospital. He would forgive her if she stayed. Her freedom was not hers alone. She had to get to her daughter.

Ella walked towards her captor. Would he stop her if she ran to the exit? The driver was behind her and there were plenty of *militziamen* around to help corner her. But she had to try.

'General, I need to collect my daughter from my parents.' It took her all her strength to control her face. Maybe he'd see reason. If he wanted her gone, perhaps she could change her flight for later today.

Lubov's expression didn't alter. 'And your permit? You may not get to use it.'

She shrugged, not quite believing how it had all come to an end. Without Lilly, she didn't want to escape.

Ella measured the distance to the airport exit sign. Beyond it lay the country she hated, the life she didn't want to live. Yet if she dashed towards the sliding doors, there would be no return. Lubov would make sure of it. This was her one chance.

The loudspeakers announced: *Aeroflot flight thirty-five to Paris, proceed to gate number eight.*

She edged towards the clear sky outside and Lubov took hold of her elbow. 'Let's have some tea.'

He led her towards the coffee shop and pointed to an orange plastic stool. His driver sat nearby and picked up a newspaper from the neighbouring table.

The general ordered black tea. Ella gulped her scalding drink without tasting it. She peeked at Lubov and met his hard, unblinking stare.

'You have Olga's face.' There was both hatred and wistfulness in his voice.

'General, I have to stay, to be with my daughter. But if our exit visa is extended, I'll emigrate with my partner and Lilly.'

He brought his tea-glass to his lips as if he hadn't heard her. She had to make a decision. Sprinting to the exit seemed impossible. But she decided to gamble and got up from her stool. She took a step away from the table towards the pastries laid out inside the glass counter.

Another announcement boomed through the speakers: *Aeroflot flight number two to Vienna open for check-in.*

Lubov got up. 'That's yours. Shall we go?'

Ella burst into a run, but the driver blocked her way. She slammed into his body and punched at his chest with her fist. It felt like she was striking a wall. The KGB man held her in a bear hug, her face squashed into his chest. She thrashed about, her feet not quite reaching the floor. The driver squeezed her and the last remnants of strength left her body. This was the end of her life as she knew it.

56

Olga
Moscow, USSR
1960

The painting was a sombre portrait of a miner at the end of his working shift. Olga wondered if she'd chosen the right place to talk to her husband, crowded and surrounded by the Soviet-themed art at the Manezh Exhibition Hall. She had delayed her confession for too long.

On the other wall, the paintings looked more informal and she breathed out with relief. There were only so many portraits of soldiers, workers and farmers one could endure. She hooked her arm with Natan's.

'Which one is your favourite?'

The still life with apples on a windowsill brought back the memories of pre-war Moscow and their summers in the country. Now, the children were adults with lives and homes of their own, and there was more time for themselves, yet they seemed to work longer hours.

Her heart skipped a beat. 'There is something I need to tell you.'

'I like the one with the flowers.'

She followed Natan's eyes. A bunch of peonies with water drops on the petals, as real as though they were just freshly cut.

Olga smiled. Social realism didn't bother her when it produced paintings like that.

They paused in front of another work of an onion, a bowl of boiled potatoes, half a loaf of black bread with a slice cut off. The artist had managed to make a statement without going to the barricades. She needed to follow suit, to stop obeying orders. Stalin was dead and the times had changed.

She touched Natan's ear with her lips. 'Remember in 1948 ...'

He stopped. They never really spoke of his arrest and the prompt release, or her role in it. She had not mentioned Lubov.

Around them, the hall teemed with people. Everyone seemed to gather here at the central Moscow Exhibition Hall to look at the art that depicted life as it was portrayed on television and radio, in films and newspapers – happy and heroic. Factory workers thrilled with the results of their production. Collective farmers rejoicing in the cornfields. Women gathering flowers and twisting them into garlands, men playing *garmonikas*. All lies. Their own life was a lie.

They shuffled to the next painting, a part of the throng with no one paying them any attention. Or so most of them thought. Olga had noticed a few nondescript men with army type-haircuts leaning against the walls, observing people.

She decided again that today was the day for her disclosure. She hadn't heard from Lubov for almost seven years, since Stalin's death, but a few days ago he'd sent her a signal. She hadn't gone.

'I had to sign some papers then,' she breathed close to Natan's cheek, 'to help them with information. He had a flat. I went there monthly. I'm sorry, Natan. I had to do it, I didn't have a choice.'

He squeezed her elbow

A woman in an ostrich hat caught Olga's attention at the far end of the hall, where the sculptures were exhibited. She clasped Natan's hand. 'Let's see what's there.'

He raised his eyebrows but followed anyway, past the birch trees landscape with a row of electric towers on the horizon. Past the canvas of new Khrushchev-style walk-ups where everyone was promised a flat of their own instead of a room in the communal domain.

'Olushka.'

Olga lost her footing and bent to check her heel. She would recognise that voice anywhere.

A man in a suit and a tie waved to them from across the hall.

Lubov.

It was as if he knew she was about to confess to Natan, to break their poisonous bond. He looked older than she remembered. His blue eyes, now shot with red, were fixed on her face.

'Natan, this is Ivan Lubov. He was my patient during the war.' She pressed Natan's forearm, begging him not to ask questions.

She fretted about the coincidence of it, of Lubov being here on the same day as her among thousands of people who had come to the 'Soviet Russia' exhibition over the last four months. And then she wondered if anyone at work had known they were coming today. Had she told anyone?

Only now did she register that the men dressed like Lubov everywhere, younger than him, but still cut from the same cloth.

'Olushka, you haven't changed at all.' Lubov stood close, his hand extended towards Natan in greeting. 'Your wife saved my life, did she tell you? We're good friends, but we lost contact.'

Natan nodded. Not smiling.

'How are the children?' Lubov turned to Olga and she froze, even though he didn't have any power over her these days.

'They are adults.'

'I've got two of my own,' he offered like a peace branch. 'I thought you'd come here one day. You always liked art. In Saratov …' He trailed off, his words hanging heavy in the air.

She felt Natan's fingers tense on her wrist.

'And are you still at the hospital?' Lubov continued.

He knew where she was. The note to meet him had been placed in her nurse coat's pocket inside the locker. Nothing really changed with The Thaw, she thought. They allowed people to let out steam, to show their true colours, to make it easier to arrest or recruit them.

Natan tugged at her sleeve, feeling perhaps her despair. 'Will you excuse us, Ivan, we still haven't seen the other side.'

'Enjoy.' Lubov lay his palm on her shoulder. 'I am sure we'll meet again soon, Comrade Ashkenazi, won't we?' He chuckled before blending into the crowd.

The vast hall with its soaring ceiling wasn't spacious enough to share with Lubov and his KGB thugs. Olga needed fresh air.

57

Ella
Moscow, USSR
August 1983

The glass partitions and shiny steel trimmings played tricks with Ella's vision. Across the customs counter, a woman in uniform was asking her something, but Ella just stared at her own reflection behind the female officer. Beyond that, she saw Lubov's dark silhouette blocking the escape route.

'Your passport?' the woman asked again. Ella placed the documents into her manicured hand. The customs officer examined her exit visa. 'Are you travelling alone?'

The woman's dark blue uniform stretched tight over her belly. She was pregnant, Ella realised. Bitterness filled her mouth and settled on her swollen tongue. 'My husband will join me shortly with our daughter.'

Ella didn't know where the words had come from, but she would've killed for them to be true. She could not comprehend how she'd finished up here, at the border of the USSR without Lilly and Ilya.

The customs officer handed Ella her boarding pass. Lubov hadn't left his post beyond the partition. He probably intended to escort her all the way to the departure gates.

'May I use a bathroom, please?'

The woman nodded and stepped out from behind the counter. She led her into a bathroom in the corner – a white-tiled sanctuary, brightly lit and quiet. The officer stopped by the flimsy cubicle door.

Ella locked herself in and sat on the toilet seat in her jeans. She hugged her knees, rocking back and forth. It was clear that Lubov wanted her on that plane to Vienna. What wasn't clear was why.

By taking this chance to get out, wouldn't she open a path for her loved ones? Not only for her daughter and Ilya, but also for her brother and her parents? She could change her family's fortunes, like many had done before her, fleeing from pogroms and revolutions. Like Sonya and Leo, who ran in 1928. And she could free Vlad.

She could save them all. But the thought of leaving alone, even temporarily, made her stifle a sob.

A knock on the door startled her. She flushed the toilet and marched out of the cubicle. The customs officer leaned against the wall. Ella glanced at the mirror and flinched. Her face was ashen, her lips cracked and her hair tangled. Suddenly thirsty, she drank straight from the tap.

The woman touched her shoulder. She stared at the ground and muttered, 'Make sure your husband has your daughter's name in his permit, like you do. Otherwise he won't be able to take her abroad.'

*

Lubov hooked his arm under her elbow and led her towards the departure gates. She let him guide her. She felt like a pawn. Powerless. Ignorant even of what the game was.

The general walked her to a section separated from the main departure lounge by another glass wall. The automatic doors opened and closed behind them. The space was unoccupied except for a few KGB-looking businessmen with attaché cases and a woman in a power skirt-suit in the far corner.

'Sit.' Lubov dropped her into an armchair in front of a round table. He sat in an identical one opposite her.

'If you are a good girl' – Lubov leaned towards her, his elbows on his knees – 'I could be of assistance.'

She cast her eyes down.

'I could bring them to you,' he said.

She glanced up. Blood drummed in her temples. But she'd learned that any favour he did her would have to be repaid and repaid.

Lubov studied her face. 'Both your daughter and the man, if you behave.' He spoke quietly.

She leaned forward and asked, 'Why would you do that for me?'

His face broke out into a wide smile. 'You stay in Vienna. And I'll make sure Ilya gets his permit and visa, all the paperwork, providing his health improves. He could join you in Austria with *his* baby daughter.'

'And what do you want me to do?'

Aeroflot flight number two to Vienna boarding at gate five.

She didn't even stir at the announcement. They would hold the plane until she boarded. There was no point pretending, even to herself. She had lost.

'Not much. Not much at all, Ashkenazi.' He used Olga's family name. Ella's maiden name. 'I need someone I trust, there in Vienna.'

Ella covered her face, but she couldn't unhear his words.

'Just stay where everyone is,' he continued. 'Talk to people. Listen to their stories. Be friendly. Refugees are put in the hostels. You are one of them. Jewish. Your family has been delayed. You wait for them to arrive and you listen. I need one of you to tell me the truth, to report.'

She stared at the lines on the general's forehead. He wanted her to spy on her own people and he had no doubt that she would do it.

'From Vienna, some go to Israel, others to Rome.' Lubov sat back. He spoke slower, as though in a trance. He must have planned this when she'd first asked for his help. 'They wait for their American visas. Or Canadian ones. You speak English. You could help them, and us.'

He sighed. 'Or you go alone. Forget about your daughter and the man. I'm not convinced that your Australian relatives would accept it though. But it's truly your choice.'

Ella got to her feet. 'My plane is about to take off.' She eyed his face – the burst blood vessels, enlarged pores. He was evil, but he was human too. She had no choice but to get on the plane. 'I'm not doing it,' she whispered. Not sure he'd heard her, she said in a firmer tone, 'I'm not doing it.'

Lubov chuckled and remained seated. 'Olga was like that too. Strong. Independent. You don't have to decide yet. Think about it on your flight. It'll give you something to do.'

He stood and touched her back. She flinched and walked to the security gate, towards her terrible freedom.

58

Ella's knees buckled on the gangway and she let Lubov's driver drag her onto the plane. He eased her into her seat. She was the first one to board. The flight attendant, smartly suited in a navy jacket and tight skirt, helped him cram Ella's bag into an overhead compartment. The driver whispered in the attendant's ear. She nodded and fastened Ella's seatbelt for her.

The plane began to fill with voices and bodies, and the KGB man feigned a smile. 'Don't worry, dear, I'm only a few seats away.' He put his lips near her cheek as if he was kissing her in farewell. 'Behave.'

Then the lights went off. Or had the sunlight stopped blazing through the plane's windows? Gravity pressed Ella into her seat. She couldn't hear a thing. The plane rocked and there seemed to be not enough air to breathe. She felt she was drowning, and she decided to let herself sink.

*

She smelled smoke and opened her eyes. Next to her, in the aisle seat, a portly man in a checked jacket dragged on a cigarette.

'Would you like something to drink?' the flight attendant asked.

The man pushed Ella's elbow off the armrest between them and stretched out his legs. 'Rum and Coke, please,' he said in a German accent. 'On the rocks.'

'I'll have the same.' Ella stared into the surprised blue eyes of the flight attendant, the one who'd helped Lubov's driver lock her into her seat. She was probably one of them too – a KGB informer, like Lubov wanted her to become.

Ella gulped her drink while the man next to her was still nursing his. She'd ask for another, and then another. She could do whatever she wanted and no one would care.

The second drink tasted even better than the first. 'May I have a cigarette?' she asked her neighbour.

The man offered her a pack of slim brown cigarettes. She took one and he lit it for her. The menthol smoke soothed her throat. She realised that her encounter with Roman, which seemed to have happened so long ago, was only recent, and the pain lingered. She laughed and heard a touch of mania in it. Her head started to fill pleasantly with fog.

Her neighbour suppressed a smile and extended his hand. 'Herr Schmidt. Hans.'

'Ella.' She didn't mention her Jewish surname, just in case. She thought of what was going to happen if she tried to ditch the KGB. Would she ever see her daughter again? It was just as likely she'd find herself 'disappeared'. Locked up in a mental institution somewhere in the depths of her motherland. Was Russia still her motherland, she wondered. She belonged to no land now, no country. She was stateless. A refugee.

In need of a bathroom, she climbed past Hans's plump knees. Her head grew foggier. 'Excuse me.'

He raised her empty glass. 'Would you like another one?'

She made no reply and staggered towards the end of the aisle. The floor swayed. She couldn't feel her legs. The red lights above the toilets twinkled.

The flight attendant touched her shoulder and Ella realised she was sitting on the floor.

'I'll bring you some water. Would you like me to take you back to your seat?'

Ella shook her head. 'Toilet.'

The woman smiled. 'Let me help you.'

She hoisted her up. Perhaps she wasn't the KGB, Ella thought, and she was actually offering help. She leaned onto the young woman's bosom.

'Is he still on board?' she whispered.

'Who, sweetheart?'

'The driver.'

The flight attendant grimaced and guided her into the bathroom. 'Let's wash your face.'

Ella stumbled and clutched the sink. She tried to shove the woman out, but the flight attendant squeezed into the cubicle with Ella and shut the door.

'I'm Maria.' She was maybe a couple of years older than Ella. 'I want to help you.'

'I need to get off.' Ella refused to cry. 'To get back to my daughter.'

'You can't get off, darling.' Maria averted her gaze. 'It's a plane. Is someone meeting you in Vienna?'

Ella whimpered. She couldn't trust the woman; she couldn't trust anyone. Her legs gave in. Maria held her up and rocked her. Ella felt one of her nails pinch into her arm. Or was it the prick of a needle? She couldn't be sure.

'Shh. Don't cry,' Maria said. 'Let's take you back. Get some sleep and it will all be over.'

Ella pushed her away. The plane lurched. Sleeping seemed like a good idea.

59

Ella
Vienna, Austria
August 1983

Chez Greta's used to be a whorehouse. A Latvian girl only a few years younger than Ella had whispered this to her from the bottom bunk before they both fell asleep. A brothel. The girl had giggled as she toyed with the local knowledge, and Ella grinned in response. But when dawn crept in through the lacy curtains of the bedroom she shared with three others, she remembered the girl's words and didn't feel like smiling.

The women who used to live in this house sold their bodies and Ella was about to sell her soul. She was expected to report on this girl too. Her name was Katya and she was seventeen. But the KGB couldn't be watching her here, Ella thought, and stretched out on her back.

Her arrival in Austria had not gone as she'd hoped it might. After the plane landed, she was escorted to the VIP lounge, where Comrade Stepanov of the Soviet Embassy greeted her. Now she knew the knives were out. Stepanov had promised to look after her family if anything happened to her. And she was right where they wanted her – among Jewish migrants awaiting their visas.

The sickly sweet whiff of baking invaded her consciousness. She swallowed and imagined a kitchen and breakfast room downstairs. Chez Greta didn't belong to her past, but neither did it resemble the future she wanted for herself and her daughter.

The previous night when Stepanov's chauffeur had dropped her off, exhausted, the house had resembled a gingerbread cottage with its pink windows all lit up. Sleepy and peaceful. Nothing like a brothel or the refugee transit hostel it'd been converted into. By the time she'd reached the stuffy upstairs room furnished with a baldachin bed and bunks, she could have fallen asleep on the floor.

The KGB did have long arms but it still wasn't clear why Lubov needed her. Ella wouldn't be the first they'd recruited. Perhaps his ideas had expanded beyond turning her into a spy. Maybe this situation was linked to Vlad and his group somehow.

In the daylight, the bedroom looked tacky and worn. Katya moaned in her sleep and Ella sat up on her bunk. She could make out the sleeping shapes of a mother and daughter from Kiev in the four-poster bed by the opposite wall.

Following Lubov's orders, she was supposed to find out all that she could. Who'd helped them get a family reunion invite from Israel? Did they have relatives in America to assist with entry visas? She would have to question them about their lives before their departure from the Soviet Union and inform on them and the people they'd left behind. It was as if Lubov was certain she'd break. He had broken her before, after Vlad's arrest, when they forced her to sign a report in exchange for her freedom. Spying on refugees would be just a start, a way to smear her, to trap her forever.

On the floor, her duffel bag looked like the remnants of her muddled life. She kneeled in front of it and tipped its meagre contents onto the faded carpet. The hint of home leaked out. Something soft caught her fingers and pinched her heart. She pulled a baby's wrap from the pile and held it to her lips.

Her favourite black dress hadn't creased much. She dived into its silky darkness and smoothed it over her hips. The thought of Ilya's kisses on her neck the last time she'd worn it to the Bolshoi Theatre made her sob. The room had no mirrors, but her lipstick and brush felt like weapons in her hands.

Down the corridor in the shared bathroom, Ella sat on the tiled bench attached to the wall. It was anyone's guess how long she had in Vienna before she was transferred to the next transit point in Italy. In the meantime, the KGB would expect her reports. Unless she refused to hear a word. Avoided talking to people.

Someone opened the bathroom door and she jumped up. An elderly woman entered, wearing the sort of floral house dress that Olga vowed she would never own.

'Are you well, *devonka*?' *Devonka*. Girl-child, the woman called her, in a soft Ukrainian drawl. She was probably someone's grandmother.

'Where're you from?' the woman asked and began to undress.

Ella watched, mesmerised. It was as if she was back in a bathhouse anywhere in the vastness of Russia. She had to get out, away from this woman, but felt unable to do so.

'Moscow.' She took off her dress and stepped behind the tiled partition into the shower recess, hoping the conversation would die. Surely this woman had no information of value to Stepanov or Lubov.

'We're from Kharkiv,' the Ukrainian woman said. 'My daughter and son-in-law and the girls. We're lucky to leave all together.'

Ella hummed and lathered her skin with handfuls of liquid soap. Maybe it was shampoo. No one at home would use it to wash their body. It seemed far too expensive.

The water drilled into the crown of her head. She didn't want to give up, but the desire to melt into oblivion overcame her. Her body went from numb and cold to stinging from the almost unbearable heat. No punishment for her betrayal seemed strong enough though. No volume of tears would bring her closer to her baby and Ilya unless she submitted to Lubov.

'My oldest son is in the army.' The woman spoke over Ella's humming. She just wouldn't stop. 'We were scared they wouldn't let us out because of him. They usually don't. But he got married and took his wife's name. Now he is Ivanov and can pretend to be Russian, not a Jew like us.' She sounded bitter.

Ella rinsed the foam from her body and spat out the acidic residue that gathered in her mouth. Stepanov could use this information against the family. Find Ivanov, confirm that he's Jewish, make sure he'll never see his family again. Maybe send him to Afghanistan. They did this to Jewish conscripts to make them *neviezdnie* – ineligible for emigration.

She turned off the taps. Two little girls burst into the bathroom, laughing. A young woman with a full laundry basket followed them in.

'Mama, wash Roza's hair and Rita's too, if she lets you.' She looked at Ella. 'You're so pretty. Where're you from?'

Ella imagined her mother with Lilly in her arms and flinched. She should beg for a telephone call to her parents. That might work in Austria.

Ella pulled the dress over her wet hair and scurried out of the bathroom. She couldn't bear to watch them, or to listen ... or to invent her own story.

Back in the bedroom, she dried her curls then tiptoed into the unlit corridor before the others got up. While she was by herself, she hated them all for being together. And that was before she opened her mouth to inform on anyone. Now silence enveloped her. If she couldn't contact the press, let them know of Vlad's imprisonment and her own terrible story, she had no hope at all. Without Lubov, she didn't have any means for a reunion with Lilly, not for some time.

60

The reception hall downstairs had seen better days. Its velvet burgundy curtains looked faded and dusty in the morning light. So did the woman who stood in the lofty room's centre, surrounded by ten or so tables covered by tablecloths that used to be white.

'Madame Bettina,' the hostess said. 'And you?'

'Ella. Nice to meet you. Do you need any help?' She hoped her English sounded friendly and polite.

The madam gestured to her assistant, a skinny boy in a white cotton jacket, who was setting up the buffet-style counter with a coffee urn and trays of pastries. The heavenly scent hit Ella's nostrils, and her mouth filled with saliva.

Then she heard voices shouting in Russian outside the hall's entrance. A group of male refugees of various ages walked in. Their eyes studied her with a mixture of curiosity and suspicion. She wondered whether they'd been locked in Chez Greta's – men and women – families separated to fit more people in. She managed a smile and grabbed a plate from Madame Bettina. Three unfamiliar baked goods were on it – a piece of baguette, a bun and another pastry she thought might be a croissant.

She filled her cup with coffee and added milk under Madame Bettina's watchful gaze. The woman clearly intended to make a profit from her humanitarian efforts. *Gesheft ist Gesheft,* as her other grandmother Chava used to say in Yiddish. 'Business is business.'

Soon Ella's cup was empty, and a boy stopped by her table to speak to her. He was about her age, with curly black hair and shiny eyes. Like a curious crow. 'Hello, I'm Misha. We're from Odessa.'

'Sorry.'

She got to her feet and strode away. She didn't want to find out anything about Misha or his family. Stepanov would be asking for her first report soon and she hoped to have nothing to say. If he and Lubov doubted her though, her days in Vienna would be numbered. She might be moved along to the next transit stop, in Ostia or Ladispoli in Italy, where people who waited for American or Canadian visas were transported.

If she told someone of her Australian relatives willing to take her in, she'd be transferred tomorrow. But she couldn't imagine what would happen to Lilly and Ilya, or to Vlad, if she was gone. With her baby and her beloved held hostage, she didn't have the luxury of behaving morally.

Still, she rushed out of the breakfast hall, out of the gingerbread brothel, and yanked at the wrought-iron gate in the front yard. It was locked. She shook the metal bars and they rattled, but didn't give. The fence felt solid and damp from the morning dew. It glistened under the pastel-blue Austrian sky.

She recalled Madame Bettina saying there would be a bus to take them to various embassies after they'd filled in their forms. She had to find a way to bring her daughter and Ilya to Vienna, not send herself to Italy. Meanwhile, for better or worse, she was trapped inside Chez Greta's.

*

She pushed open the stained glass door and entered the breakfast hall. While she'd been outside, her fellow travellers had queued to talk to a man and a woman from the JOINT and HIAS, as the signs on the tables informed her. The refugee agencies had sent their people to help émigrés plan their next move.

Ella wondered how the young man and the girl, who were now answering the questions of the queueing refugees, had got inside Chez Greta's while she was in the courtyard. There must be another entrance.

She needed to stay in Austria, despite Stepanov and Lubov. But also because of them. Remaining in Vienna was her only chance of fighting for her family to join her and for Vlad to be freed. She thought of the cost – informing on those around her – and shrank into herself.

Ella queued for the young woman from the JOINT.

'Zelda Katz.' The girl beamed and pointed to a curved Viennese chair in front of her table. Without the tablecloth it looked even shabbier. 'Are you alone?'

The question, asked in Russian, hurt something deep inside her. Ella's vision blurred. If she closed her eyes, she could imagine Ilya sitting next to her, his warm hand on her shaky fingers.

Zelda offered her a tissue. 'Are you going to Israel?'

Ella shook her head. Her Jewishness seemed to have been squeezed out of her by her Soviet existence. A reunion with her Australian relatives in Sydney was her dream destination for now.

She wished she could tell this slim, fair-skinned girl her story, but she couldn't. There were people around them. The woman from Kiev, from the baldachin bed in her room, was standing right behind her, leaning on her chair and waiting to speak to Zelda.

'I need to stay in Vienna to ask for asylum. Political asylum. Is that possible?'

The girl raised her eyebrows. Even her wild springy hair stood to attention. Stateless refugees mostly wanted to get somewhere fast, Ella knew, if not to the promised land then to the New World. Only a few attempted to stay in Europe. Usually, these were mixed families who were worried they wouldn't be accepted elsewhere.

Zelda gave her a form and told her to fill it in, she'd talk to her later. Ella sat in the corner next to the window and set out to argue her case. The chance to tell the truth made her head spin. She wondered if she could risk it. Despite her doubts, she found herself writing about General Lubov and how he'd forced her to confirm Vlad's supposed crimes. She wrote about the KGB's threats to her and her family. And how she had refused to incriminate Zacharov senior.

Then she paused. She didn't know who Zelda was connected to and what she would do with her statement. They could take her out of Chez Greta's and resettle her anywhere. To get away from General Lubov felt more than enticing, but it wouldn't bring Lilly to her. Or Ilya. Or free Vlad.

Ella lifted her head and saw clusters of people, all absorbed in themselves, in their own lives. Her envy was hard to swallow. She walked to the table where Zelda stood, getting ready to leave but still surrounded by new immigrants.

'Can I talk to you privately?' She lowered her voice and spoke in English even though she'd heard Zelda speak Russian and Yiddish to the others.

Zelda pointed towards the kitchen with her chin. 'Just let me finish.' She packed the forms and brochures into her briefcase and picked up her knapsack. The young man from HIAS, Joshua, was sighing and looking at his watch.

Madame Bettina lingered nearby, a set of keys hanging like a necklace. She led Zelda and Joshua through the kitchen to the back door and Ella trudged after them. They were about to leave. She'd lost her chance to tell the truth. The disappointment was like a glass shard in her chest.

Near the exit, Zelda slowed. 'Thank you, Madame Bettina. A few words with this girl and I'll lock it on the way out.'

Joshua left, closing the door behind him. Madame Bettina retreated to the kitchen's entrance. She kept an eye on her charges and her ear likely on Ella.

Ella edged closer to Zelda. 'Could you help me get asylum? I'm in danger, but so is my daughter in Moscow, if I talk.'

Zelda leaned in, a smile glued to her lips, her eyes fixed on the pension's owner. 'Have you filled in your forms?' She touched Ella's fingers.

Ella withdrew her hand. 'No.' She couldn't risk it. If Zelda got her statement, Lubov might find out that she'd asked for asylum. 'If I'm resettled, I may never see my daughter again.'

She couldn't cry anymore. Her eyes held the girl's gaze and wouldn't let go. She didn't want to become an informer, but she had to conceal the truth while she fought for her freedom.

61

Ella curled into a ball on her bunk and pulled the blanket over her head to muffle the voices of the other women in the room. She had penned the truth but she couldn't share it with anyone. The affidavit she'd written for Zelda, hidden under her pillow, could be used to trap her.

If Zelda knew the facts, she might not help her, unless Ella spoke to her first. And if the KGB learned she'd disclosed the story of Vlad's imprisonment and had sought asylum, they could harm her baby or Ilya to silence her. The words on her statement were buried explosives. While they were concealed she could survive, but if they were uncovered, there'd be no salvation. She recalled Zelda's touch on her hand.

'I know how to get out.' Katya's words made Ella's ears prick up. 'You can buy the key from Bettina. I did! Where do you think I got this new dress? I went to that place in the old town where they give you free clothes. And here I am.'

Ella peeked from underneath the blanket at the room.

Katya admired herself in a hand-held mirror. The woman from Kiev spread the contents of her suitcase on the double bed. 'When we get to Italy we need to prove we have relatives in America.'

She sorted and repacked her treasures: *matryoshkas* and linen tablecloths, miniature black lacquer boxes and painted wooden spoons. The usual bits and pieces that people brought with them from their Soviet motherland to sell at the markets – to top up their allowance. Some got stuck in Italy for months, unable to find a sponsor. But she was more interested in Katya's gossip.

'So, you gave money to Bettina?' the daughter from Kiev, Yanna, asked in a soft drawl. 'Does it cost much?'

Katya laughed. 'She even lets us call home. But you have to call "collect". And she watches you. You think she's a spy?'

Ella sat up. It made sense that the madame was an informer – why else would Stepanov steer Ella to Chez Greta's?

Katya twirled, kissed herself in the mirror and burst into song.

Yanna scowled at the younger girl. 'They ask for proof you're Jewish in Rome. What proof do I have? They snapped up our passports in Kiev when we got the exit permits. I had "Jewess" written on the front page. Same as you, I suppose.'

Heat spread from Ella's neck to her face. They had lived their lives in the Soviet Union with their Jewish 'nationality' recorded everywhere – on class rolls, in their passports, every time they filled in a form for a job or study. Finally, they'd got to leave it behind, and now they needed to provide evidence they were Jews. *Just look at us, for god's sake.* Ashkenazi, Kogan and Rabinovich – who would want to live in Russia or Ukraine with those surnames?

'Some men got themselves circumcised in Rome, I heard. To prove they're Jewish. Now they walk like this.' Yanna ambled around the room with her legs wide apart. The others laughed, albeit without cheer.

Ella felt ill. She placed a pillow over her head and shut her eyes. They were stateless now, with their ethnicity and religion questioned in the West.

But she did crave to call home, to hear her mother's voice and to ask about her baby. She rolled off the bunk and smiled at Katya. 'How much does she charge for a phone call?'

Madame Bettina's office under the stairwell must have once been the servants' quarters or a broom closet. Through the bars of the poky window, Ella glimpsed the afternoon sky. A beige handset graced an antique-looking desk. The rest of the space was crammed full of boxes and shelves.

The former brothel-owner placed herself firmly by the door that she kept ajar, perhaps so she could observe Ella as well as the foyer.

'Dial the number and say "collect".' Bettina's scarlet mouth moved without affecting the rest of her face. She spoke English as if it was German, pronouncing every syllable.

Ella shut her eyes to block off Madame Bettina and her pension. She envisioned her mother in the squat corridor of the parents' flat, where the telephone rested next to the bookcase. The image was so clear that the aroma of borscht wafted from the kitchen and Lilly's baby-powder scent hung in the air. Ella's heart pounded at her ribs like a trapped bird. She said 'collect' and listened to the ringing phone.

'*Da.*' Her father's voice crackled down the line.

'Papa?'

'Ellochka, where are you?'

'Vienna. How is Lilly?' Her nose twitched and she watched Madame Bettina watching her.

'Lilly is good. Asleep.' Gregory cleared his throat. Ella could hear that something was wrong. 'Do you want to talk to your mother?' he asked.

'I only have a minute. How's Ilya?'

Her father hesitated. 'He's being discharged tomorrow. Don't worry. He is a good man and he loves you, he told us. What about you, *dochka*?'

So, it wasn't Ilya that her father was worried about. Relief flooded her and washed over her guilt. 'Papa, I can hear something's not right. Is it mother? Olga?'

Gregory sighed. Bettina tapped her wristwatch.

'What happened? Tell me.'

He sighed again, as if deciding what to disclose. 'General Lubov.'

Madame Bettina stepped towards her and pointed at the telephone cradle.

'Papa? I need to finish this call.'

'He came to see us.' Her father started to say something, but Madame Bettina grabbed the receiver and slammed it onto the cradle.

'*Danke schoen*,' the madam said. 'You owe me five schillings.'

*

Later, Ella pressed herself against the wall outside Madame Bettina's office and listened. The shouting in the reception hall became louder. Chairs scraped the tiled floor and a man's voice spoke in accented English. He switched to German and some older voices chimed in – those who spoke Yiddish, the few of them who'd survived.

It sounded to her like most of the pension's residents had gathered to listen to a lecture and wait for dinner. It might be a good time to slip out if she wanted to find Zelda at the refugee agency before it got dark. She'd seen the address on the flyer. Judengasse. Jewish Street.

She couldn't wait to bribe Bettina to be let out tomorrow. The truth of Vlad's detention and her own involvement in it would need to be told. She wanted the JOINT and Zelda to help her stay in Vienna. She needed them on her side to escape Lubov's clutches.

The dusk filled the cramped reception hall with gloom. Madame Bettina was clearly saving on electricity. Ella squeezed behind the chairs that were pulled together to seat the old and the frail. In front, a man in a yarmulke spoke candidly of Israel, the country that wanted them all, and pointed to a slideshow. A couple of elderly women, setting up tables for dinner, looked preoccupied.

Ella slipped into the kitchen, which was bright and noisy. No one asked her why she was there. The cook and her helper cut and mixed and stirred. A woman in an apron stacked plates and cups onto trays, and a massive saucepan simmered on the gas stove. The aroma of meat stew made Ella feel sleepy. She'd missed dinner last night and hadn't had a hot meal in days.

The back door gaped open, probably to let some air in. The cool autumn draught beckoned. Ella stalled. It shouldn't be that easy. She edged closer, ready to retreat if questioned, but the kitchen staff paid her no attention. She peeked outside and saw the corner of the building, a tree and a street lamp. It was beautiful, foreign — a still from some film. Bertolucci.

She slipped out; the image of her mother with Lilly in her arms floated before her like a beacon. The dusk had turned lavender and the street, quaint and quiet, now looked like a backlot after the crew had departed. She took a step and then another and another.

The fresh damp air — the free air — licked her face. Ella knew she needed to rush, but she strolled along and let this new world absorb her. Nothing around her resembled the Soviet capital. The pastel-tinted buildings with their unique windows and gable roofs were unlike the ones in Moscow, which were grey and uniform outside the city centre. Ahead of her, a shop or a cafe spilled its neon light onto the sidewalk. Ella hurried towards it.

A shiny foreign car turned onto the street and stopped a few metres ahead of her. Ella eyed it sidelong. She hurried to get past it. Over her shoulder, she saw the car door open. A man stepped out. He wore a light-coloured trench coat, like a local, but something in his posture told her he wasn't. She sped up, suddenly sweaty. Then she heard footsteps behind her and ran. She could see the cafe getting closer.

From behind, the man grabbed her. He jammed her face into his coat sleeve and held his hand over her mouth. She bit into his leather glove. She kicked out. But then she felt something wet and sharp-smelling over her face and a smooth blackness enveloped her.

62

Dark space surrounded her. Her tears soaked the silky bedcover she held under her chin. She was sticky with sweat, and sore. Lying on her side in the foetal position on the princely bed, she still had her shoes on.

She had no memory of getting into this room that smelled like a museum, but whoever had brought her here knew who she was.

She swung her legs off the bed. Her feet touched the carpet. She stretched out her arms before her and stepped away from the bed, careful not to trip or bump into something.

Her fingertips brushed a thick velour curtain. She pushed it aside and found herself high above a boulevard, looking out over the treetops that lined it. A car's headlights sliced through the night and faded away.

She turned her back to the window and surveyed the room. Beside an ornamental floor lamp, a chair with curved legs was tucked under an old-fashioned writing desk. In the moonlight, the bedcover and curtains gleamed the colour of blood, and above the four-poster bed hung a painting of St Stephen's Cathedral that she'd seen on postcards.

She was probably still in Vienna, in some central hotel. But she'd never seen a suite of this kind, and she could not comprehend why she'd been brought here. Maybe Zelda had told someone about her seeking asylum. Or perhaps Madame

Bettina's phone had been tapped. That might have triggered Lubov to change his plans – even pushed him to get rid of her.

She tugged at the window, but it had been bolted shut. The door wouldn't budge either, locked from the outside. The eerie stillness behind it confirmed the late hour. She didn't know how long she'd been unconscious. They must have drugged her.

She switched on the lights in the bathroom and stared at her wild hair, her drawn face and sick eyes in the mirror. No one knew of her plans when she'd fled from Chez Greta's. She wished she'd told Katya more. The statement she'd written for Zelda and left under her pillow could end up in the wrong hands.

Ella ran the hot water to fill the bath. She wouldn't give them the pleasure of breaking her, nor would she wait to be slain to prevent her from talking to the media. They had less power here. She'd just plug the bathtub and let the room flood. Have the hotel staff rush in to unlock the door and question her. They probably knew more than she did about how she'd finished up in this suite, who'd lugged her inside and paid for it. Steam filled the bathroom and she stumbled back to the bed.

On the desk by the window she spotted a leather-bound folder and a telephone. A sepia photograph showed the Hotel Grand Imperial, a palatial building overlooking a boulevard named Ringstrasse. If she didn't fight back, this would be her last address before she disappeared.

Ella lifted the mouthpiece and listened. What she heard was the click of the door being unlocked.

Stepanov walked in.

*

Stepanov clasped her forearm and led her down the carpeted hallway to the lift, then to a suite three times the size of the previous one. Brocade drapes hung over the lofty windows near a grand writing bureau. She spied a leather settee with two armchairs either side and an oversized television set with a box next to it that was shaped like an attaché case. Ella guessed it to be a video cassette recorder.

She heard the hum of air-conditioning, but the suite felt overheated and it stank of rot, perhaps from the arrangements of lilies in the oriental floor vases. The room lacked any personal touches. She turned to assess Stepanov's expression, but he'd vanished without making a sound.

One of the curtains that likely masked the entrance to an adjacent bedroom shifted and she saw the sombre face of General Lubov. She watched him closely. He wore a grey civilian suit, the unofficial KGB uniform.

'Ashkenazi. I hadn't expected to see you so soon.' There were no more fake smiles. 'Take a seat.' Lubov lowered himself into an armchair and pointed to another, less than a metre away. She remained standing.

'Would you like something to drink?' He stretched his legs. His polished shoes caught the light. 'I saw your daughter last night.'

The words hit like a punch. She stumbled and leaned on the armchair next to the general. He wouldn't harm her baby if he wanted her to obey. While Lubov needed something from her, her child was safe.

'Don't want to talk?' He lifted himself out of his armchair and walked to the TV and the bar cabinet underneath it. His back to Ella, he poured an amber liquid into a square glass. 'I could bring her to Vienna.'

Pain tightened her airways. She wanted to say, *Yes, do it, bring Lilly to me.* She folded her arms over her chest and bent forward. The general strolled across the room and stopped by the window. He inhaled from the glass.

'You can smell a good whisky.' He took a sip. 'Would you like to try?'

She straightened and controlled her quivering mouth. 'What do you want from me?'

'Ella, why so rude? We could be friends. You know I loved your grandmother.'

She closed her eyes to block out his face. Was he wistful? Full of revenge? She couldn't imagine Olga next to this man, but she knew he was telling the truth. Perhaps he would help her with Lilly if she agreed to conform.

'What do you want?' she repeated.

'Not much at all, my sweet.' Lubov returned to his seat and pulled the other armchair closer to his own. Then he patted it with his meaty palm. 'Sit.'

Ella let herself drop into the armchair. Her knees almost touched Lubov's and she twisted her body sideways. He edged forward, his face so close she could see his bloodshot eyes. She could hear his wheezing too and she averted her gaze. It reminded her – he was human.

Lubov cleared his throat. 'You will have to talk to the press.'

She crossed her ankles. The hems of her jeans were frayed over her scuffed shoes. Her confession to Zelda must have found its way to the media and forced Lubov into negotiations. She felt like a chess player, only she had no idea what Lubov's ultimate game plan was.

She stared into his steel-grey eyes. 'I want my daughter and Ilya.'

Lubov laughed. 'She wants ...!' He clapped his knee and kept laughing.

'And I want Vlad to be released.' Ella held her gaze on his thick eyebrows.

Lubov's laugh faded and he strolled back to the bar. He poured himself another drink and switched on the TV. It seemed like a trick to distract her. Then he fiddled with the video recorder and the screen came alive.

On it appeared a leafless park and black tree trunks lining an alley. Ella saw the spiky fence of Moscow Zoo. A woman walked into the frame and she realised it was her. She watched the on-screen Ella open an umbrella. The camera shifted to a tall man – Jack.

Ella squinted to see. She focused on a close-up of herself passing Jack some papers, an envelope. It was the letter she'd written to Sonya. The exchange had been recorded, but she couldn't understand the purpose of it. It could be judged as a crime in the USSR – meeting a foreign journalist – but they were in Vienna.

She glanced at Lubov. He observed her with an odd grin on his face. 'So, what do you say?'

Ella stood on unsteady legs and forced herself to face him. 'I gave a letter to a friend. Is that a crime?'

As if that was a cue, there was a knock at the door. The general walked towards it. 'Let me introduce your friend again, Frau Ashkenazi.'

He threw the door open and moved aside. Jack stepped in. Ella blinked. She'd only met this man once and he'd looked different then – younger and more American. Her heart somersaulted.

'Please meet my colleague and your mentor, Jack Cullen. But you two already know each other.' Lubov swigged the rest of his drink and turned to Jack. 'Explain to her what needs to be done.'

He left the room before Ella mustered her breath to speak. Not that she knew what to say. She couldn't bear to look at Jack. He was KGB and Vlad had trusted him. Lubov must have had him get involved with the dissidents to learn their plans, to thwart them.

Jack sighed and glanced at Ella. 'So, Comrade, where shall we start? You really don't have much choice. No refugee agency or media outlet will touch you if they think you work for us.'

Ella let her shoulders slump. Only now did she fully comprehend the meaning of the tape. They'd filmed it to compromise her, to have her appear to be an informer, to make her cooperate. They'd play the tape to the media if she didn't do what they wanted. But the media might not believe it, and Lubov would have to out Jack as a KGB agent. In his jeans and pullover he didn't look like one of them, yet he clearly was.

Jack wandered from the window to the settee. 'You could live in Europe or Australia with your man and your daughter. Or be exposed for who you are – a traitor – and never see your family again.'

He poured himself a drink. 'Would you like some cognac?' His gentle murmur scared her. They were the only people in this dark cave of a room. He could easily kill her if she didn't oblige. She had no documents and was stateless. Hate rose inside her.

Ella marched towards the door. 'Take me back to my room.'

'Not yet.' Jack stepped between her and the exit. 'I just want to be clear before seeing you off. Will you talk to the press for us?'

Her pulse quickened. 'Tell the general I refuse.' She reached past Jack and turned the doorhandle, but it was locked.

'Your daughter is still there,' Jack whispered in her ear. 'Think about her. Your family may not be safe if you don't behave.'

She leaned on the doorframe to stop herself from falling onto her knees.

Jack opened the door and spoke a little louder. 'Something else for you to consider. Your friend Vlad has informed on you, as you did on him.' He snickered. 'Apparently, you're part of his group, which leaves you with us, Comrade. I would take this offer if I were you. It's a good one. You won't regret it.'

He put his arm around her to prop her up and led her to the lift. 'We shall see you later this morning. Be ready to work.'

63

The hotel room was still humid after her failed attempt to flood it. Ella sat at the desk by the window. She couldn't allow herself to collapse, but she yearned for the freshly made bed.

Pre-dawn light seeped through the glass. She had only a few hours to accept or refuse the general's offer – to save or risk her loved ones' lives. A few hours until Jack returned with Lubov's orders, which would pay for the reunion with her daughter and Ilya.

Ella thought of her grandmother and how she'd stood up to Lubov. She imagined the war hospital in Saratov where Olga had served as head nurse, and the wounded young Lubov – the NKVD officer feared by everyone. She had her life and her children to lose, and Lubov had wanted her love in exchange for protection. What would Olga advise her to do?

Ella heard clattering in the hallway. It was far too early; she needed more time. Either she obeyed and did Lubov's bidding or Lilly … Ella couldn't finish her thought. They were capable of anything – a car accident, poisoning, disappearance. It was impossible to say 'no'.

She had to act smarter. Lubov wouldn't be able to silence her when she met with the press. She could refuse his deal until her loved ones were safe in Vienna. Olga would approve of such a plan.

The knock on the door startled her. The handle turned, and Jack stood in the doorway.

'The general asked you to join him for breakfast,' Jack said in English.

Ella stood up. If she planned to state her conditions to meet the press, this would be as good a time as any.

*

The hotel's grand staircase gleamed with its pearly marble and polished brass trimmings. Jack walked next to her in his faded blue jeans. He belonged in this world. She wondered why he'd chosen to work for Lubov and where he'd come from with his fluent Russian and American English.

The restaurant dazzled. Arched windows let the daylight in, reflecting off the crystal champagne flutes and silver-plated cutlery.

Ella's head spun and she wavered. She felt guilty for being here surrounded by this opulence when Lilly and Ilya were still in the USSR and Vlad imprisoned. The aroma of freshly baked goods made her stomach grumble. She picked up a dessert plate and lifted a meringue-topped pastry from the closest tray.

'Ella Gregorievna.' The general's voice came from behind her. 'You must be hungry.'

Jack nudged her towards a table where Stepanov and Lubov sat side by side.

'Frau Ashkenazi, honour us with your presence.' Lubov's lips glistened and Ella lowered her gaze. A few people glanced in their direction. At least she wouldn't get harmed here. Her stomach shrank and she no longer felt hungry.

Lubov eyed the lone pastry she'd chosen from the buffet. 'Would you like to order something to drink?'

'I'll have coffee.'

Stepanov leaned towards her. 'You should try this pâté. Or salmon. It hasn't been frozen.' He tucked into the smoked salmon piled high on his plate.

Lubov touched his lips with a crisp white napkin. 'I have an offer to make and it's a generous one.'

The waiter poured her a coffee. She sipped it and let the hot liquid thaw her insides. Dazed, she picked up the pastry from her plate and bit into its sweet almond core. It was easy to fall, so easy.

'You'll talk at the press conference. A few journalists and a couple of TV channels. Informal. Here at the hotel.'

The general's words came from far away, from a world in which everyone ate breakfast in places like this. But she knew that behind the glitz, there was torture and blood. The KGB worked in contrasts.

'They'll ask you questions. You must give the right answers. Jack will help you.'

Jack grinned. 'You'll say you made your story up to get your family out. Zacharov's group doesn't exist. Your friend Vlad is in prison for trading in hard currency,' he said.

She almost laughed out loud. They had counted on scaring her into silence, but now she was certain that Zelda had contacted the media, otherwise they wouldn't be so insistent on her cooperation. At least the KGB's use for her had become clearer. If she belonged to a dissident group the West had supported, and she declared it didn't exist, then the motherland won, and so did Lubov and Jack. Vlad's claims of persecution would be perceived as hot air.

'Trading currency is a criminal offence – a domestic matter.' The general's hands clenched into fists.

Ella thought of Zacharov senior's dollars, hidden in the inner pocket of her jacket upstairs. Her cheeks flushed and she almost spilled her coffee. Stepanov stopped chewing and watched her. His dead eyes noted her reaction. Jack glanced at her too. Out of those two, Jack was the one to fear.

Lubov's fist opened and he picked up a shell with something slimy in it. 'Try this. It's delicious.' He squeezed lemon juice onto the oily creature and licked his lips. 'Have some.'

Ella felt as helpless as the wobbly grey mass he held under her nose. It smelled like the ocean. She glared at him above the shell.

'And when will you bring Lilly here?' Ella asked. 'And Ilya?'

The general shrugged and looked wounded. 'If you do your job well with the press, I'll bring them to Vienna. We will help you settle. You can choose the country. But if you don't …' He tilted his head back and sucked in the sea-smelling creature.

Stepanov got up and wandered off. Jack lingered over his plate. It all felt rehearsed. But they were toying with her life and the lives of her loved ones. She probably didn't have much bargaining power, although they wouldn't be feeding her here, if they didn't need to secure her cooperation.

'I want Ilya in Vienna before I meet any media.' She imagined Lilly's weight in her arms and her resolve grew. 'I'll not say a word without seeing my daughter and Ilya first.'

'Well, Ella, that's all fine but have you considered the alternative?' said Lubov. 'If you don't talk to the press, Ilya will get arrested as your accomplice. You're a part of Vlad Zacharov's group, aren't you? And that would be it, my sweet. You'll never see him or Lilly again. Is that what you want?'

Ella got up. 'I'll do what you say once I see them both in Vienna.'

Lubov yawned. 'Take her back to her room, Jack. We'll rehearse later.'

64

'The press conference is tomorrow. You have to practise your answers.' The general's tone had changed from relaxed to commanding. He stretched out on the sofa in front of the wide-open balcony doors, an unlit cigar in his fingers. His suite was filled with sun and fresh air.

Lubov tapped the seat next to him, but Ella remained standing.

'Jack, ask her a couple of questions – in English. Let's see what we are dealing with.'

The seduction was over; the planning stage of the conspiracy had begun.

'Frau Ashkenazi, how did you end up in Vienna? Did you arrive as a Jewish refugee?' Jack spoke with a German accent and handed her a glass to replicate a microphone. 'Speak.'

Ella hesitated. She thought of Anna and Leon, of her father. There was no way of predicting what Lubov's revenge might be if she didn't deliver. Still, she knew she'd tell the truth to the media, given the chance. But right now, she should pretend and repeat what Jack told her to say. In any case, it was true – she had entered Austria as a refugee.

'Yes, you did.' Jack paced the room. 'You came to Austria using the excuse of Jewish repatriation.' He closed the balcony doors to mute the street noise. Then he changed his accent to an American one and asked, 'Where's your family? Are you here alone?'

She pondered the question and thought of Olga's last call. She couldn't protect them all, yet to keep lying was not an option anymore.

Jack cleared his throat. 'My daughter and my spouse are here in Vienna.' He glanced at Lubov. 'Is that true?'

The general nodded. 'Isn't that what you wanted, Ella?'

She clutched the back of his sofa, her knees weak. Lubov would bring her baby here. And Ilya. But he might also lie about that to make her comply.

Jack pinned her with his stare. 'Why did you ask for asylum?'

Lubov joined Jack in eyeing her. 'Do tell us, Ella. What was your agenda?'

She dropped herself into the closest armchair and glared at Lubov. If she was allowed to talk, she'd tell the truth. But emptying her heart in front of Lubov and Jack would be madness. They were her enemies. Whatever she said in this room would be used against her. Still, she had to prepare what to say to the press beyond her statement.

'Tell them you lied,' Jack said. 'To get your family here. You made up a story to join your lover. You could not emigrate together because he's not Jewish and is married. And so are you.'

'Ilya isn't Jewish, is he?' he asked in Russian, and winked at the general.

Ella leaped from her seat. She felt like hitting him. But Jack motioned for her to sit.

'So you invented the persecution to get your gentile lover out of the USSR. He could bring you your daughter, who you've left behind to give him leverage to emigrate as her father. Wasn't that the case?'

Jack turned to Lubov and grinned. 'What a clever plot, whoever came up with it.'

Silence fell and the weather outside changed. Clouds shrouded the sky and the suite darkened. Ella let her muscles relax. She felt like a boxer given a moment in the corner. Her heartbeat slowed down and she tried to control her breathing. She wiped her palms on her knees.

'Tell us of your work with Zacharov's dissident group,' Jack said.

'I don't understand your question,' he replied, imitating her Russian accent.

Then he asked, 'What could you say about Vladimir Zacharov's arrest? Weren't you his associate?'

Immediately he responded, 'My friend got arrested for trading in hard currency.'

He switched to Russian. 'Didn't he, Ella?'

'He is serving his sentence. I've never heard of Zacharov's group,' Jack said in English, imitating her voice.

Both Jack and the general laughed. Ella felt goosebumps along her arms. She hadn't realised Lubov spoke English. A hush settled over the room. Jack poured himself a whisky and gulped it.

Lubov's face grew sombre. 'You can repeat what he said' – he stood and walked to the bar underneath the TV set – 'or never see your daughter again.'

*

With its towering columns, inlaid marble floors and elaborate chandeliers, the Grand Imperial's atrium resembled the Hermitage in Leningrad. Jack pulled Ella to sit beside him on a golden velvet divan. He selected a newspaper from a side table and ordered something in German from a waiter. Ella wondered why he'd brought her to the hotel's lobby. The press conference wasn't until tomorrow. But Jack had drawn her from her bed, half-awake, and escorted her here.

Not letting hope stir in her soul, Ella checked his face. It was blank, buried behind his paper. She watched an oversized brass-framed door rotate at snail's pace. The street beyond was lit with neon and every time the door spun, she glimpsed a car that let out a passenger or the doorman in his livery signalling for a bellboy to carry luggage inside.

Then Stepanov entered the lobby pushing a pram she recognised. She scrambled to her feet. Jack yanked her down and put his arm around her in an embrace she couldn't escape. She struggled, but had to give in and found herself jammed against him.

Ella gazed at the entrance, mesmerised. Ilya stalled, as dazzled likely with the atrium's lavishness as she had been. Her whole being, her soul and her body, longed to melt in his arms. But her eyes flitted back to the pram. Stepanov had paused by the concierge.

She searched out Ilya's face and prayed he'd notice her, but he was preoccupied with the pram, adjusting Lilly's pink blanket. She couldn't bear it – her daughter being so close. She lurched to get up again and Jack held her tighter.

'One wrong move,' he breathed into her hair.

Ilya tried to take over the pram, but Stepanov shouldered him aside. They walked to the lifts, both clasping the pram's handle, her beloved in his worn leather jacket.

She opened her mouth to yell. Jack held his palm over her lips. Ilya stepped inside the elevator and scanned the lobby. Ella beamed at him – and for a fleeting moment before the lift doors closed, Ilya's eyes found hers.

She couldn't be certain he'd actually seen her from the distance and over the crowd. But she'd caught a spark of recognition in his eyes, a hint of joy beneath the fury of being held captive. With Ilya and Lilly in Vienna, she couldn't wait for the press conference, so she could tell the truth to the world.

*

Even before she woke up Ella knew that her privacy had been invaded. She felt a presence in her hotel room, not far from the bed where she'd lain sleepless for hours, only falling into a deep slumber just before dawn. She opened one eye and realised the night was over and a man was watching her sleep.

The general coughed. His bulk occupied the stool by the desk, against the pale light that leaked from beneath the closed curtains. 'Good morning, Ella.'

She squeezed her eyes shut again. But then she remembered that Lilly and Ilya were in Vienna, in this hotel, and she sat up in bed. Maybe she could talk Lubov into letting her hold her baby for the briefest moment before she fronted the media.

'I have to see my daughter,' she said.

The general shrugged. 'If you recite what you practised, you can see your child tomorrow.'

Lubov got up and paced. Something was bothering him.

'Is something wrong?'

He stopped, his eyes rheumatic and bloodshot. 'Do you think she ever forgave me?'

Ella stared at him. She wasn't sure what he was talking about.

His face sagged. 'When your grandfather was taken, I made Olga pay for his freedom.'

Ella felt herself shrink. Crumple.

Lubov scowled at her and seemed to recover. 'If you don't deliver, we'll make sure you pay too. You know this, don't you? I won't harm your child, but your man is another matter. You do understand?'

He stepped closer to where she sat on the bed. Ella grew taller. She'd find a way to protect Ilya, or at least give him the best chance of not being hurt. But if they put her in front of the media, she'd tell the truth.

'Lilly,' she said. 'I need to see her, just for a minute.'

'Like your grandmother. She would also rather injure herself than serve her country.' Lubov shook his head. 'Why are you people so restless? You got yourself tangled up with dissidents. You could have studied and worked like everyone else. Your country fought for you during the war. You are all so ungrateful.'

Ella didn't know what he really wanted.

'Get yourself fixed up.' He turned to the exit. 'And don't think you can play us for fools, Ashkenazi.'

He stepped out and locked the door behind him.

65

Everything inside Ella quivered. The portable stage on which she stood facing the press looked out of place in the wood-panelled conference hall full of smartly dressed people. Cameras flashed and the projector-like lamps of TV channels singed her skin. Stepanov lurked behind her, pretending to act as her lawyer.

A young man in the front row thrust his microphone towards her. 'Frau Ashkenazi, were you a dissident in the USSR?'

Ella thought for a moment and looked over towards the exit. Behind the journalists she could just make out the bulky shape of General Lubov.

'I'm not a dissident,' she said. Wasn't that the truth? If not, it was close to it.

'But your friends are?' The question came from the middle of the hall.

The double doors at the rear were guarded by a man in livery, his hand on the brass handle. Next to him she saw Jack, his face obscured by shadow.

Ella opened her mouth to reply, not really sure what to say. The honest answer would be that most of them were not dissidents, only because they were afraid of being persecuted. She'd planned to tell the media this, planned to tell them the whole truth. But she couldn't do it with Ilya and her baby prisoners.

Under her feet the stage felt unsteady, like a raft sailing into a sea of lies.

'I don't know any dissidents.' Her face flushed and she pictured Vlad in his black leather coat hunched next to her on the park bench when he read her letter to Sonya. She'd betrayed him again.

'But how did you manage to escape?'

Ella peered in the direction of a female reporter behind the camera flashes to her right. Lubov wouldn't be pleased with the word 'escape', but that didn't bother her. She searched the room for her daughter or Ilya. Her eyes swam and she could only see Jack's mauve shirt behind General Lubov's imposing stature.

Stepanov's fingers dug into her spine. 'I applied on repatriation grounds.'

A woman at the front squinted through her glasses. 'Are you going to Israel?'

'Not now.' She could hardly hear her voice over the murmurs of the press. She couldn't explain that being Jewish in Russia had nothing to do with religion. Born Jewish, they had no choice – 'Jew' was a stamp in their passport; it meant discrimination at school and at work, it didn't mean prayers and candles on Shabbat.

'You're seeking asylum,' an angry female voice said from the back of the hall. 'Were you punished for staging a dissident protest?'

She tried to remember what Lubov and Jack had instructed her to say. 'I withdrew from the Moscow Theatre Academy to apply for emigration.'

'When did you last see your dissident friend, Vladimir Zacharov?' a male voice demanded from the front row. 'Is he in prison? What's his crime?'

She met Lubov's glare. Stepanov placed his palm on her shoulder, as if to comfort her.

'Vlad was arrested in June.' Ella paused. 'He is serving his sentence.'

'Is he a dissident? What was he accused of?' a journalist asked.

She remembered Jack's coaching. 'He was accused of trading hard currency.'

A buzz went round the room. This clearly wasn't the answer the journalists had expected.

'And you? Were you a member of Zacharov's group? Wasn't that the reason for his arrest – the group's demand that the USSR follow the Helsinki Accords and allow freedom of speech?'

Stepanov's fingers slid down to her upper arm and gripped it. If she obeyed Lubov's orders, they'd be free to leave Vienna and could forget what happened. Move to Australia. Raise Lilly in a free country. But if she chose to be honest, she might lose it all.

'I haven't heard of that group,' she found herself saying. That was a lie she couldn't undo.

A sound broke through to her consciousness, a whimper she recognised with an ache in her womb. Lilly's cry. It wasn't loud. But she heard it as if it was the only sound in the noisy room. She searched for her baby. One of Lubov's men must be holding her.

'Frau Ashkenazi,' a voice called out. 'Where is your family? Did you leave them behind?'

Ella broke free of Stepanov's grip and took a step towards the edge of the stage. She gazed above the journalists' heads. 'My daughter is here.'

She pointed at Jack, next to General Lubov. He held a swaddled baby in his arms. Lilly. He must have picked her up from the pram. Her child was pressed to the chest of the double-faced brute.

It was time to act. Time for the truth to come out.

'The man holding my child is a KGB agent.' Ella jumped off the stage before Stepanov could stop her. 'They are keeping my baby hostage.'

The crowd parted. People turned to look as Jack made a dash for the door, still cradling Lilly. But now another man, probably a journalist, blocked his exit.

Ella pushed and clawed her way through the pack, her eyes fixed on the stranger stopping Jack's escape. Reporters thrust microphones into her face, photographers snapped photos, but she could not let them slow her down.

'Where is your daughter?'

'Do you need help?'

She felt a grip on her forearm, shoves at her shoulders and back, bodies blocking her progress. Then she found herself in the stranger's arms, but he didn't have Lilly.

'Lilly,' she yelled as panic seized her. Spotlights found her as if she was onstage in a theatre. The media circle tightened around her and the stranger.

'Is he your lover?'

Ella twisted to face the man. He looked familiar, like her father, only younger. She stared at him.

'I am Yaakov,' he said, 'Sonya's son. From Melbourne.'

'Look this way!' a woman shouted.

'Frau Ashkenazi, one more, please.'

Ella fought to locate Jack or Lubov but couldn't spot them in the crowd. She scrabbled past the people next to her and saw Yaakov pushing his way towards the exit.

'Help me to get my daughter,' she shouted into journalists' faces. Fear turned her into a panting animal fighting for her cub. She craned her neck and saw Jack with the pram, trying to shove his way past the man in livery, who guarded the entrance.

'Lilly!' she screamed.

Jack managed to knock the doorman off his feet before Ella and Yaakov reached him. Yaakov launched himself at Jack, but Jack spun and pushed the pram back into the crowded hall. Yaakov caught the pram and wheeled it towards her. Ella bent to her baby and time stopped.

Lilly sucked her dummy, her little face flushed from the drama. Ella picked up her daughter, the warm precious bundle, and held her to her pounding chest. The weight and heat of Lilly's swaddled body flooded her senses. Cameras kept flashing.

Ella heard a commotion behind her and turned to look at the stage. Then the lights went off and a film started rolling, projected onto a screen above the makeshift podium.

66

In the darkness the hall lost its dimensions. On the screen, Ella handed over an envelope to a lanky man in the alleyway of the Moscow Zoo. Jack. The crowd jeered.

She clutched Lilly closer to her chest and dived into the mob, her elbows out to shield her child, her eyes fixed on the screen.

'Please let me through. Watch the baby.'

'So, you work for the KGB too?' someone yelled.

She had to convince them to hear her out. Let her tell her story. Not the one unfolding in the video, but the real one.

Lilly's gentle wheezing at her breast gave her strength.

As she drew closer to the stage, a new portion of the video was playing. She watched herself in the Grand Imperial's lobby being embraced by Jack as if they were lovers. So they'd filmed her with him in the USSR and in Vienna to prove her a traitor. Another scene played. This one showed her at Chez Greta's.

She neared the screen and tried to speak, but her voice was drowned out in the racket. The journalists shouted out questions. If they wanted her to answer them, they would have to quieten down and move aside.

Ella stopped. She used her best actor's voice, like Professor Podolski had taught her at the Moscow Theatre Academy. Loud and clear above the din of the press.

'The video you're watching was produced by the KGB to discredit Vlad and me. The man on this tape tried to silence me.'

People hushed. The rays of the film projector stopped Ella from seeing past it, but she felt the crowd part and a path to the stage open up. It was her last chance to be heard. Ella felt someone's hands grab her elbows and lift her and Lilly. More hands pushed them up onto the podium and, with her daugher cradled in one arm, she reached for the microphone. She could sense the film projected onto their bodies but it didn't stop her.

Stepanov's steel fingers clasped her wrist. 'Frau Ashkenazi is unwell. She and the baby need rest.'

Ella steadied herself, wrapped Lilly tighter into her body with her arms, and head-butted Stepanov's face. Something cracked and she hoped it was his nose. She thought she heard Ilya's voice cheering her on. Stepanov stomped on her foot and she yelped, but then he backed off, perhaps afraid to be captured in action by a photographer. He didn't leave though. She could sense him waiting in the shadows.

'I want to tell you the truth.' Her voice caught in her throat, and she steadied it. 'The USSR signed the Helsinki Accords, but it doesn't follow them. There is no freedom of conscience, speech or religion in the Soviet Union,' she shouted.

The room gasped. In the silence, she continued. 'My friend, Vlad Zacharov, was detained by the KGB. He and his group fight for human rights. He is one of hundreds jailed for their beliefs. You can help me save them. Demand freedom for political prisoners in the USSR.'

There were no sounds apart from the hum of the video projector. Even the flashes of cameras had stopped. The journalists didn't trust her. The film that played on a loop exposed her as a traitor. Was Ilya listening to her somewhere in the crowd? Had he managed to escape Lubov's clutches?

She thought about what else to say and remembered her grandfather's hand stroking his *tallis* – his prayer shawl – which he'd kept hidden at the back of his wardrobe. She pictured Vlad's friends, lit by a *militzia* truck's headlights, chanting *Freedom! Freedom!* in front of Moscow's only synagogue. Afterwards, they'd run with Vlad through the streets to avoid being arrested.

'Vlad's case is one of many. The KGB under the Communist Party General Secretary – and its former boss – Yuri Andropov, controls the country. They have eyes and ears everywhere. Dissidents like Zacharov who dare to speak out are imprisoned, locked in mental asylums, suffer mysterious accidents and die.'

Ella fell silent and everyone seemed to exhale in unison. Then a booming male voice called out, 'How did you get to Vienna?'

If she told them of her betrayal, they would tear her to pieces. To have the journalists believe her though, to be able to live with herself, she needed to tell the whole truth.

'I was arrested as Vlad Zacharov's accomplice. And I was forced …' The words sliced her open. 'I was forced to sign a report that confirmed his so-called crimes.' Her arms stiffened around Lilly and her resolve weakened for a second, but there was no holding back. 'I was offered an exit permit from the USSR, in exchange for betraying my friend. And I did it.'

The journalists circled the stage like hungry wolves. She had misled them and now they were angry.

Ella transferred Lilly into the crook of her other arm and wiped the sweat off her brow. 'They showed me Vlad's confession and threatened to lock me up if I didn't cooperate. I'd just given birth to my baby.'

She scanned the crowd for Ilya. If he was here, he'd learn of her treason, but she needed him to know the truth as much as she wanted to tell it, even though it would risk losing his love.

'The KGB sought to recruit me. They flew me to Vienna without my daughter. I was planted at the refugee hostel with instructions to inform on my fellow migrants. But I refused.'

The mob came alive. Everyone shouted questions at once, voices coming from all directions.

'Why should we trust you?'

'Tell us the facts!'

She felt Lilly stir in her arms and whimper. Her time was up. Her baby started wailing.

'Dissidents like Vlad are rotting in jails and labour camps, or being turned into zombies in psychiatric wards.' Ella thought of Podolski. 'Don't let those brave souls perish without a trace.'

The ceiling lights flickered. She rocked Lilly in her arms and wondered whether General Lubov had heard her speech, if it would be dangerous to get off the stage. Then her fear receded. They wouldn't dare touch her or Lilly – at least not right now.

The lights turned brighter and she saw the puzzled expressions of the journalists after hearing her out. But she couldn't see Jack or Stepanov or General Lubov, who'd likely left long ago. And she could not find Ilya. Her legs wobbled and she kneeled on the stage. She rested her head on her daughter's pink blanket and closed her eyes.

Listening to Lilly's heartbeat, Ella stopped hearing the crowd around her. It was like only two creatures on the planet existed: herself and her daughter. Then a sharp pain entered her consciousness. Ilya. Her beloved. Would he ever forgive her? Was he even safe?

And then through the waves of human chatter, Ilya's voice reached her. 'Please, let me pass. This is my wife and my daughter.' She didn't believe she was hearing it.

She felt Ilya's arms, strong and familiar, wrap around her and hold them both. Ella let herself soak up the strength before she looked up at her beloved. Happiness flooded though her. At last, they were together.

67

Curled next to Ilya on the four-poster bed, with Lilly fast asleep between them, Ella dissolved into her lover's arms and her daughter's milky sweetness. Ilya, thankfully unhurt, had forgiven her. She still remembered the relief she'd felt when he found her and Lilly on the stage, but she couldn't recall much of what followed, as Ilya described it – the hotel manager who'd escorted them to the attic room and suggested they stay until they got help, or Yaakov offering to pay for it.

Ella wished she could lie here forever – fall asleep and wake up by the ocean on the other side of the world.

Soon, she thought.

The telephone on the bedside table rang, and Ella waited a few long seconds before picking it up. Ilya squeezed her shoulder.

'Frau Ashkenazi?' the voice purred. 'There's a gentleman here to see you.'

Her fingers clutched the handset. 'Please, ask him to come upstairs.'

Ella shut her eyes to absorb the peace of this room. The horrors of Lilly's kidnapping and her forced departure were in the past, painful memories that made her and Ilya's love for each other stronger, she hoped.

She willed herself to stay calm, but her muscles twitched as she listened for the ding of the elevator and footsteps in the hallway.

The knock on the door was faint. Ella waited for Ilya to greet the visitor. A male voice said something in Russian from the hallway before she registered Ilya's smile. She slid off the bed to join him at the threshold.

Yaakov towered a head above her, out in the corridor. He extended his hand and she took it, then she hugged him and started to cry, burying her face in his shoulder. He let her cry until she finally collapsed into giggles. She'd never seen her Australian relative before until he'd burst into her life at the press conference.

'Did Olga send you?' she asked.

He smiled and nodded. 'Sonya too. The Melbourne *shule* placed an ad, I think, in the *Jewish Times*. After you called.' Yaakov pressed a finger to his lips.

Ella followed his gaze across the room. Lilly's tiny shape was barely visible in the middle of the queen-sized bed. She shouldn't talk to Yaakov in the corridor and she couldn't invite him inside without waking her baby.

'You look like your great grandmother,' he whispered. 'Same features. You must have been named after her. Elka.'

She grinned and reached for his arm. 'Let's talk in the lobby. I have so many questions.'

Ilya kissed the top of her head. She stepped out and he shut the door behind her. She stood with Yaakov in the brightly lit hallway surrounded by the hotel's splendour.

Yaakov took her hand again. 'You are tired, darling. We can talk in the morning.' He embraced her. 'I just came to say thank you. I had to find out more about my parents' country.'

She felt her cheeks warming, but it was more from joy than shame. She liked Yaakov's face. He reminded her of Natan, her grandfather, except taller. He was part of her lost family. Olga must have begged Sonya for help.

Her uncle's eyes shone. 'I brought the papers to confirm we're related. You can come to Sydney. Lilly would love it.'

Ella trudged after Yaakov along the corridor towards the lift.

Yaakov looked at her. 'What's wrong, Ella? It will only take a few days to clear Ilya's status. He is stateless like you. A refugee.'

Ella watched the elevator's cage slide down to the floor below. She heard the lift come to a stop and remembered Vlad hugging her goodbye before her and Ilya's failed defection attempt to Warsaw. His upturned face. Counting stars, no doubt.

She could not run away while her friend remained captive. 'I need time, Yaakov, to sort things out. I couldn't possibly leave Vienna now.'

He bowed his head. 'Tell me what you plan to do. I'll try to help.' He attempted a smile. 'Sonya won't let me come home without you and Lilly.'

Ella caught their reflection in the hallway mirror. She saw her uncle beside her – a slightly stooped man who shared the same almond-shaped eyes, although hers were brown like Olga's and his were green.

'I need to stay for my friend while he's in jail.'

He nodded. 'I heard you telling the journalists. But what can you do?'

Ella squared her shoulders. 'I'll go to every newspaper, every radio station, appeal to the Austrian government.' She met his eyes and didn't flinch. 'Will you tell Sonya the truth about me?'

Yaakov shook his head. 'It's not my truth to tell. You can do it yourself when you come to Sydney.'

She hugged herself to gather strength. 'I haven't told Ilya yet that I want us to stay in Vienna until Vlad's release. I haven't had time.'

'I am sorry.' Yaakov's arms encircled her. 'I shouldn't have come tonight, but I couldn't wait. We'll see each other tomorrow.'

He released her, and she felt numb. She had to sort out the mess she'd left behind in Russia.

*

Ilya's heart was beating under her cheek, but its pace slowed and the thuds grew quieter. She didn't want to talk. Just let this night be. Lose herself in the cushioned shelter of the hotel bedroom. Inhale the mixed scent of their bodies and Lilly's sweet baby warmth.

'Yaakov wants us to leave Vienna with him.' Ilya held her tight, and she spoke into the shallow above his collarbone. 'I have to stay. The Soviets might ignore all the noise of the foreign press, and I need to see Vlad get out of jail.'

She lifted her head, strained to see his expression. They were safe in this haven, but for how long she didn't know.

'If I leave Europe, they might bury this story as if nothing happened. I have to be around to keep up the momentum. While the media is on it, there are greater odds that the KGB will let Vlad walk free.'

Ella paused. She could hear her own heartbeat, a car passing by and Ilya's watch, ticking on his wrist. If only they could just vanish, accept Yaakov's offer and go to Australia, that unknown sunny country. She couldn't do it though, not yet, not with Vlad still locked up.

'I'll try to reach his father, tell him of the press conference. Maybe he can influence people in Russia, if he knows Vlad has support.'

The silence felt like black wax. Ella's throat contracted. What if Ilya insisted they leave? She couldn't let him down once more. They were bound together.

Ella felt his lips touch her eyelids. Ilya blew at the damp strands of her hair that fell onto her forehead.

'Don't worry,' he said. 'I'm actually relieved. Everything has happened too fast. The visa. The flight. I didn't have a chance to see Yan. He doesn't even know I've left.'

Ilya's hand found hers, the hand of her soulmate. She felt his pain in her bones and cursed herself. She had asked after his son, but hadn't probed further when he'd told her that Marina was taking care of Yan. Marina and Roman.

She wasn't sure Roman was capable of love.

Ella hid her face in Ilya's neck. 'Do you want me to call them? I'll beg her to let Yan join us. She might agree. What do you think, my love?'

He stroked her hair. 'She'll need some time to get used to the idea. We'll stay in Vienna for as long as it takes. Let's just move out of here. We don't want the KGB to keep tracking us.'

*

The next day their attic room seemed gloomy, despite the light that spilled through the porthole window. Ella's bag on the floor had been zipped closed. Lilly had fallen asleep in her pram.

Ella sat on the bed and waited for Ilya to join her. They held hands.

'We have to know what's true,' she said. Lilly opened her eyes and Ella's heart surged.

She put her hand on the telephone by the bed. Snippets of prepared speech dissolved in her mind. She hadn't spoken to Zacharov senior since she'd taken his money. Her face flushed when she dialled his number and held the receiver against her ear. Then the line crackled.

'Boris Danilovich, it's Ella.' She paused for only a fraction of a second. 'I am in Vienna. There was a press conference with major newspapers and TV networks. I spoke about Vlad.'

Ella heard the older man cough and her guts twisted. She hoped she wasn't making matters worse with her phone call.

'Please forgive me. I had no choice. They threatened to arrest me if I didn't sign the report confirming Vlad's dissident actions.' There was no escape from her guilt; she had to face it. 'I have no excuse.'

'I don't understand you, Ella.'

His voice reminded her of Vlad's. Ella searched for the words to reach out to the famous writer who'd been so strong and powerful until his son's arrest.

'I think they might let Vlad go.' She caught Ilya's glance and remembered to breathe. 'Have you heard anything?'

Zacharov senior coughed again as if he was about to cry and Ella held back her own tears. 'I'll stay in Vienna and keep in touch until Vlad is out. I won't disappear again, I promise.'

There was silence. She imagined Vlad's father sitting alone at an empty table in his museum-like dining room.

'My son is here with me,' he said and let out a single sob.

Epilogue

Bondi Beach, Australia
1984

The sky and the ocean framed Ella's view of her baby daughter. Wherever she turned from where she sat on the windswept sand of Bondi Beach, blue sky and the darker grey-blue of the water met her eyes. She leaned back into Ilya's warmth, his hands on her shoulders, his body propping her up.

In front of them, silhouetted against the sea and the sky, Lilly tried to get up on her feet. She fell back again and giggled. Her smiling face was shaded by a hat.

The June sun rationed its rays like a miser, saving its heat for summer, but Ella lifted her face to the light in bliss. Winter in Sydney had become her favourite season. From where they sat by the shore, she couldn't see other people, and it felt like they were the only ones left in the world.

Lilly swayed, her legs planted firmly in the sand, her arms outspread to balance her small frame.

Ella got onto her knees and reached towards her baby. 'Come to Mama, my love. Come here.'

The sun blinded her for a moment. Ilya laughed. The ocean waves crashed in the background and a lifeguard's whistle blew.

Lilly took her first step.

Acknowledgements

For bringing *The Girl From Moscow* to life, I owe my gratitude to many wonderful people.

To my agent, Catherine Drayton – thank you for believing in me and in my novel.

To Kathy Hassett and the amazing team at Pantera Press, for selecting my manuscript for publication and for Kathy's incredible support throughout the editing process. To LinLi Wan, Dianne Blacklock and Bronwyn Sweeney for their insightful input that brought my novel into focus – I really appreciate it.

To the Australian Society of Authors – for shortlisting my unpublished manuscript for the ASA/HQ Commercial Fiction Prize in 2022. It was a welcome surprise; despite having to withdraw from the competition before the winner was selected, thank you for choosing my work from a few hundred others.

I am immensely grateful to Heather Morris, author of *The Tattooist of Auschwitz* and *Sisters Under the Rising Sun* for her invaluable help and encouragement. You inspired me.

Much appreciation for the magical touch of Lauren Draper, Kajal Narayan and Katy McEwen for marketing, publicity and rights. For the beautiful book cover design – Christa Moffit – I love it. To Kelly Morton of Looking Glass Creative for her vital assistance with social media and my JuliaLevitinaAuthor.com website, I am so thankful.

To Kathryn Heyman, for having me take a fresh look at my completed manuscript to make it tighter and clearer. Thank you for your mentorship.

To The Writers' Studio: Roland Fishman, Kathleen Allen and Zahid Gamieldien, a fellow writer and my very first editor, for their belief in my writing – thank you.

To Natalie Kestecher, for suggesting some years ago that I should keep writing, and for acquiring my short story for ABC Radio National's *The Night Air* program.

To my dear friends, Nora Goodridge and Janna Madorsky – for listening patiently as we walked and talked.

But most of all, to my family, for the inspiration and for being there for me. I am blessed with my partner, Walt Secord, who read every word, every line, of the manuscript many times over, and has always supported me in my desire to write with his reassurance, unbridled criticism and praise.

The Girl From Moscow is a work of fiction, but the USSR and Moscow of the 1980s are not. Three generations of my father's family lived in Moscow, while almost all of my mother's relatives were murdered in Ukraine in the Holocaust. This novel is inspired by my own and my contemporaries' lived experiences; however, the names and characters are the product of my imagination.

I feel incredibly grateful to be able to tell this story. It is for my family: Isaak, Jacob, Noah, Ellie, Dorin, Stan and Walt. My life is so much richer with you in it. I am grateful that we are sharing this journey.

And to my grandmother, Olga, who I loved dearly ... Always.

'This is the book of the year!'
Tess Woods